JANE ARCHER

SILKEN SPURS

PINNACLE BOOKS
WINDSOR PUBLISHING CORP.

PINNACLE BOOKS are published by

Windsor Publishing Corp.
475 Park Avenue South
New York, NY 10016

Pinnacle and the P logo are trademarks of Windsor Publishing Corp.

First Printing: October, 1993

Printed in the United States of America

Again, for Dean,
Speedy, R.C., and T.C.C.

"If we revert to history, we shall find that the women who have distinguished themselves have neither been the most beautiful nor the most gentle of their sex."

Mary Wollstonecraft
Vindication of the Rights of Woman, 1792

Table of Contents

Part One
Mask of Silk and Sin

One

As the train pulled out of the station at Las Cruces, New Mexico, smoke from its engine obscured the town. Thor Clarke-Jarmon looked away from the window, not caring. The town hadn't much to recommend it anyway, not when compared with fascinating cities such as New Orleans or New York City.

He brushed dust off the sleeve of his fine gray suit. October was warmer than he had anticipated on this trip to Tucson, but he had no intention of loosening his tie or the collar of his shirt. After all he was a Clarke-Jarmon, the single male heir to a distinguished family. He had an image to maintain even in the rugged West.

He smoothed his blond mustache. He'd grown it after graduation from college the previous summer of 1888. He thought it gave him a distinguished look and added years to his age, which at twenty-one he needed to compete with more experienced men.

Not that he was inexperienced. He thought of the women who had graced his bed for many

11

years. But he couldn't focus on any one face. Blue, green, gray, brown eyes melded together just as blond, brown, black, red hair blended to become one, and bodies tall, short, slim, plump, from young to mature became one vague shape. No single woman stood out in his mind. Or in his heart.

That suited him fine. He had no intention of getting saddled with the responsibility of a wife and children at his age. Eventually he'd have to make sure the family name continued, but when that time came he would pick a Southern lady of impeccable heritage, easy temperament, and lush body to fit his needs.

He thought of soft breasts with rosy tips swinging over his face as he reclined on a bed of satin sheets. He could smell the scent of magnolias on a soft breeze, the scent of musk mixed with French perfume of the woman herself. He imagined pushing long fingers into her dark hair to pull her face close. He anticipated the kiss, her lips parting to expose a pink tongue. He hardened, and smiled at the pleasure of his secret fantasy.

The hard sole of a boot crushed the hand he rested on the seat of the cushion next to him. The pain broke his concentration. Angrily he looked up into the barrel of a Colt .45.

"Your money, mister." Husky and low, the voice challenged anyone to disobey.

"Or my life?" Thor smirked. "A runt like you'd have a hard time carrying out that threat." He thought of his six-foot-three-inch frame of hardened muscle. His size alone scared off most predators. They'd called him the Viking in college and with damn good reason.

The boot on his foot lifted and dug the rowel of its fancy silver spur across the back of his hand before returning to the floor. Furious at the insult and the pain, he jerked upward. And heard the gun cocked.

He hesitated. Could this fool be serious? His icy blue gaze met that of brown eyes, so hard as if to be flint. The outlaw *was* serious. He sat back down, for the moment outgunned by the great equalizer of the West and a determination he seldom saw in a person twice the size of this bandit.

About five feet tall, maybe two or three inches over, the bandit wore a black silk handkerchief to cover the nose and mouth. A black cowboy hat pulled low concealed the head. A black shirt, black trousers, black leather vest, and black cowboy boots completed the outlaw's costume. Thor thought a fashionable designer couldn't have done better.

"Your money!" The bandit's fancy spurs jingled as a booted foot moved in agitation.

Disgusted, Thor glanced back down the train to see if help were coming his way. That's when he realized he should be flattered. They were being held up by the notorious Wild Child Gang. All the outlaws were children, but just as deadly as full-grown people with the guns they had trained on the passengers.

He handed over his money, fascinated by the diminutive outlaw in black. He'd read in Western

13

newspapers about the merry chase the Wild Child Gang was leading local law officers. It seemed the children were smart, well planned, quick, and never made the same mistake twice. Who the hell was their leader?

"Your watch."

"What?" Thor decided the bandit's voice was too low for a child's range so the clever wretch probably disguised it.

"Hand over your—"

"I heard you! This is a priceless family heirloom." He could have sworn the outlaw grinned beneath the mask. Never should he have revealed that fact. At least the bandit couldn't see the Norwegian medallion he wore around his neck. It was his only legacy from his great-grandfather and he'd have fought before giving it up.

"The watch!" The outlaw's hard gaze never wavered.

Thor handed over the watch, noticing the bandit wore black leather gloves though it was a warm day. The newspapers had been right. Smart. Crafty. Ruthless. Who'd have thought it of children?

As the bandit uncocked the pistol and turned from him, the thought of revenge ran swift and sweet through his heart. Given half a chance, he'd have his money and watch back, then turn the brat over his knee and swat the rounded bottom.

Narrowing his eyes, he knew what Deidre, his soft-hearted sister, would have to say about that. And it wouldn't be anything good. In fact, he wouldn't be on this train at the mercy of wild

14

children if he hadn't agreed to meet the family in Tucson for the dedication of the Flora McCuskar Institute for unwed mothers and orphaned children. The place was the idea of Hunter, the half-Apache Deidre had let steal her heart, and the man's Spanish Grandee father.

Children! He'd had enough of them and he hadn't even reached his destination.

He would have plenty to say on the subject of discipline and control when he got to Tucson. He and his sister had been raised with a light hand and a firm voice by his parents. But what did his mother, an orphan and the celebrated heiress Alexandra Clarke, know about *wild* children? And his father, the dashing Captain Jake Jarmon from a Louisiana plantation, thought anything shorter than him should be cosseted. Well, about any damn thing was shorter than his father. And he'd never met the Wild Child Gang.

He looked over the compact body of the outlaw. He itched to spank no matter what his family might think. Maybe pain would knock some sense into these bandits. Again, maybe not. Success had a way of making a person thickheaded.

Still watching the outlaw, Thor felt the train slow. Were they getting help? Had the Wild Child Gang finally miscalculated? He heard the door at the front of the train bang open. He glanced backward. Armed men stood in the open area, guns drawn, wind whipping around them. The train slowed further. Thor felt the sweet surge of vengeance sweep through him.

15

But only for a moment.

The outlaw leader turned to him, pointed the pistol at his chest, then gestured for him to stand.

What now? He didn't move. He'd be damned if he would take any more orders from a child.

"Up!" The bandit kicked him, then motioned again.

He stood up, regretting every move he made. But there was no denying the determination of this outlaw. Once he stepped into the aisle, the bandit grabbed his arm and rammed the barrel of the .45 against his side. He didn't move. Life was too good to have a hole blown in him.

Watching the men in the doorway, he knew they didn't dare advance now that he'd been taken hostage. Instead they tried to talk the Wild Child Gang into throwing down their weapons in surrender.

It didn't do a damn bit of good. Thor glanced down at the black hat of the outlaw and felt the heat of the small body near him. He responded in a way that surprised him. He'd never been concerned about children before. Why should he suddenly be worried this one might be hurt? He forced the feeling away, reminding himself that these brats all needed a thorough spanking and nothing less.

The outlaw leader motioned and the other two bandits sprang into action. Obviously well trained, they pocketed their haul, gave quick bows to the armed men, then ran down the aisle to the back door. The train slowed almost to a stop as they stepped outside.

Thor felt a tug on his arm, but he was going no place. When the outlaw pushed the muzzle of the .45 against his side, he rethought his position. He didn't want to leave the relative safety of the train. He wanted to struggle, to twist around and overpower the bandit, but an innocent passenger might get shot by mistake. He couldn't take a chance on others being hurt, or himself for that matter. He had no choice but to go.

He walked slowly toward the door leading outside. When he reached it, he hesitated to glance behind. Everyone watched. He should have been glad the authorities would know to send help if he didn't escape soon. Instead, he felt like a damn fool to be kidnapped by somebody a foot shorter than him. It was downright embarrassing and infuriating. He felt the gun prod his side and he stepped outside onto the platform.

Now was his chance. He looked down the length of the train. Outlaws jumped from the cars, rolled, then ran toward a rock outcropping where somebody held horses. They were experts, all right. Maybe he should have felt fear, but all he could feel was fury.

He turned to confront the outlaw, take the pistol away, and punish, but instead he was pushed over the side. He rolled, cursing as he inhaled dust. When he came to a stop, he jumped to his feet. Fists clenched, he was ready to pummel the outlaw to a pulp. Spanking wasn't bad enough anymore.

But he was outmaneuvered again. The leader already stood with the Colt .45 trained on him.

He cursed, glanced back at the train, saw no help, and realized they still wouldn't endanger him. He looked around, his mind whirling to find some means of escape. The bandits had already mounted horses. He was impressed, despite himself, at their organization. He cursed even harder when the leader motioned him to a horse.

Glancing back at the train, he feinted a movement away from the leader, then turned back to catch the bandit off guard. He was kicked in the knee hard enough to bring him to a kneeling position. While he gritted his teeth, fighting the pain so he could get up, the leader motioned to the outlaw holding the horses.

The child ran over, grabbed one of Thor's wrists, jerked his hand behind his back, then went for the other. Furious, he blocked the pain from his mind and pulled back, knowing they could do nothing against his superior strength.

He heard the .45 cock as the outlaw leader pushed the muzzle of the pistol against his temple. He froze. How much more indignity could he take before life ceased to be worth it? He grimaced as his hands were tied behind his back with a piece of rawhide. Life was too precious to give up yet.

"Get up!" The outlaw leader stepped back, but held the pistol steadily pointed at Thor's heart.

He stood, giving the leader the coldest, meanest blue stare he could manage. "You won't get away with this."

"Get on the horse."

"I'm not that stupid." Two of the outlaws rode double, leaving an extra horse for him. They obviously left nothing to chance. The one who had tied him had already mounted. He pushed down his anger, trying to think straight. "Look, I'll ride with you till your gang is out of sight of the train, then I'll circle back. Nobody'll be the wiser."

"No games. No deals. Mount and be quick about it or you're a dead man." The look in the bandit's brown eyes backed up the words, along with the .45.

"I'm a dead man if I go with you."

"Your choice." The outlaw's gaze didn't waver.

"They saw you on the train. They know you're part of the Wild Child Gang. If you take me, you'll be caught for sure."

"Scared, rich man?" The leader's voice held scorn. "Worried you'll ruin your fine suit?"

"No. I can buy another." Thor fought to keep his voice level.

"Get!"

Suddenly nothing seemed sweeter to him than punishing this arrogant outlaw. But he'd have to live to accomplish it. He walked over to one of the horses. He'd get away later, or the railroad would send somebody after him, or his family would get worried and find him. Somehow he'd get free, then he'd deal with these pint-sized villains. He stopped beside the horse, realizing he needed help to mount. He cursed again.

"Quick! I'll help."

Putting a foot in the stirrup, he felt the outlaw leader's hand on his leg, giving him a boost upward into the saddle. While he sat still, the leader picked up the reins of his horse, pistol still aimed at him, then moved to the other horse. Another bandit rode close, weapon drawn and covered him while the leader mounted.

The outlaws took off fast. The leader led Thor's horse. He glanced back at the train. He hoped to see a party riding after them, but he didn't figure there'd been any horses on the train. Instead, men with drawn guns stood outside. They opened fire as the bandits rode away. Thor cursed again. If they weren't careful, the fools were going to hit him. He hoped they didn't have rifles. Fortunately, pistols would do little good at this range.

He lay low over the horse's neck, gripping hard with his knees so he didn't lose his balance. The scent of dust and sage and horse were strong. The gunfire didn't last long as they rode out of sight of the train, headed north away from Las Cruces and into the desert. He didn't curse anymore. Now he needed all his strength to stay alive.

He thought back to his fantasy of satin sheets and willing women. That vision as well as his day had been ruined, along with his gray suit, his trip to Tucson, and his mood. By the time he reached the Flora McCuskar Institute for *vicious* children he'd be ready to burn the place down. But that'd be after he singlehandedly put the Wild Child Gang behind bars. And punished the leader till his own hand hurt.

That was for later. For now he had to concentrate on staying in the saddle on the back of a galloping horse with only his own expertise to hold him in place. The late afternoon sun was hot and bright against the left side of his face. He'd left his hat behind on the train, along with all the other comforts of a fashionable man.

As they rode hard, his thoughts twisted back to the Bar J Ranch in South Texas. He'd learned to ride there, to rope, to track, hunt, shoot, but he'd left that all behind when he went to college. He'd become an educated gentleman, used to the luxuries of life. And he'd never planned to eat dust again. He'd leave that to his father and the ranch hands. The Jarmon Plantation north of New Orleans was where he'd set his sights long ago.

Cursing, he focused on the black-clad outlaw leading him across the desert toward what could only be the Rio Grande River. He'd ridden across it from South Texas into Mexico many a time, but he hadn't thought much about it here in New Mexico. Now he did. The bandits were fools if they planned to follow it north. Staying near water was the obvious choice and any lawman worth his badge would know it.

When they reached the wide river, they continued north, hardly slowing their pace. He decided maybe they'd gotten overconfident and if so it was to his advantage. The water rippled blue and gold in the sunlight. The land around was dusty and dry, with purple mountains rising to cut into the blue sky to the north and west.

He inhaled deeply, having forgotten the clean, astringent scent of the desert. The wide open spaces, the grand beauty of the area made him remember how a man could feel free and wild and abandoned out here. He contrasted that with the lush green beauty, the gray moss, the magnolia trees, the satins and silks and perfumes of the best brothels in New Orleans. The women there knew just how to please a man.

How could the wild West compare with the sumptuous South? He'd made his choice long ago and he had no intention of being seduced by thoughts of a West where a man was free to be wild with nobody to stay his hand, or his lusts, or his freedom.

He shook his head. What the hell was he thinking about? He'd been kidnapped by wild children. He was being forced through the heat and the dust to who-knew-where. And he was thinking of the beauty and majesty of the land, the wonders of the West. Obviously, he'd had too much sun.

As the river narrowed, piñon trees, scrub oak, and cactus formed a thicket along it. The leader headed into the growth, pulling Thor's horse behind. The other bandits fell back into single file.

Again, Thor cursed. He wasn't dressed for riding through brush and his suit was torn and tugged as they rode onward, following the curve of the river. Not long after, the leader headed into the river and the others followed. Thor glanced south, hoping to see a sheriff's posse riding after them, or even some of the men from the train. Nobody chased them.

They headed up the river. He realized they would lose anyone who trailed them here, for not even dogs could follow a scent lost in water. Smart. He knew children grew up fast in the West, but these were as smart as most adults he'd known. After a while, the leader turned west and crossed into the desert again.

Thor glanced into the distance. If they kept going west, they'd reach a section of foothills that might make a damn good hideout. Somewhere in the hills would have to be water, food, and shelter for the outlaws. It was possible. He looked back again. Still he saw no dust that might indicate riders following them. If he didn't miss his guess, he'd have to fight his own way out of this mess.

They rode onward, the sun slowly sinking until rays of red and orange and magenta filled the western sky. At one time Thor might have appreciated the beauty of the approaching night, but for now he was too disgusted and angry with his situation to enjoy anything.

As the last of the sun illuminated the land, they reached the foothills. Again the leader took charge and led the others single file into the hills, the horses surefooted as they picked their way around cactus, rocks, and piñon trees. Not long after, the river and desert disappeared from sight as they moved deeper into the hills.

When they turned into a box canyon, Thor was

not surprised. As they rode down into it, he noticed buffalo grass and trees to shelter the area. They stopped by a bubbling spring. He nodded in approval. Food and water for the horses. Shelter and safety for the outlaws. Somebody had done well, real well, but how had they known about this place? Indians would know about it. Prospectors, maybe. Even ranchers. But bandits?

The leader dropped the reins of Thor's horse, got down, then walked back to him. "Get down."

He looked around. The other outlaws were already off their horses and removing saddles and bridles, making quick work out of the job, even if the saddles were too heavy and big for them. He was impressed despite himself. They knew what they were doing.

But if they hoped to see him fall on his face when he dismounted, they were in for a surprise. Where horses were concerned, he knew a lot of tricks. Maintaining his balance, he swung his right leg over the saddle horn, lifted his left foot out of the stirrup, then slid to the ground.

The leader simply looked at him with cool brown eyes, then gestured to the shade near the small pool of water. He wanted a drink bad, but he figured the horses would get water first. A basic law of the West was to take care of your mount before yourself or there might not be a second chance for anything.

Sitting down in the shade, he watched them

work. He stretched out his long legs. It'd been a while since he had ridden so far or so long and his body would complain tomorrow. Already he was a little stiff and sore. But he didn't much care.

He was grateful they hadn't blindfolded him. Now he had a general idea of how to get out of the foothills and back to the desert. But he'd need a horse to get very far. He observed how they hobbled the horses, knowing he'd be stealing one the first chance he got.

Soon darkness enclosed the camp and he watched the leader make a campfire. When a cheery fire crackled, a pot of stew or something was put on to heat. He realized he was hungry and hoped they'd feed him. It wouldn't be French cuisine, but he was too hungry to care.

As he watched them work, settling blankets by saddles to make beds for the night, he realized he could make a break for it. They were busy. He might make it to the safety of the shadows before they had time to react. Obviously they weren't used to having a prisoner, or they'd have tied him to a tree.

Pleased he'd found a flaw in their plans, he shifted his weight, careful to make no sound. As he rose to his feet, the leader spun around, hand on pistol, and threw down on him fast.

"Go ahead." The husky voice challenged him. "You're more trouble than you're worth now . . . except to the buzzards."

Thor didn't move. The Wild Child Gang was as

sharp as he'd first thought. He held out his hands. "No point in getting jumpy." He sat down. "I'm hungry."

"You'll eat. *Last.*" The outlaw gave him a warning look, then turned back to the fire.

Two

Harmony Harper resisted the impulse to kick her hostage. Had he really thought he could simply sneak out of camp? The idea that he'd considered it was insulting at the least, dangerous at most. She didn't need the kind of trouble he brought, didn't want it, but he'd been all that had saved them on the train.

She still felt the terror that had gripped her when she had looked up to see the armed men. They might have shot one of the children, or her. At that moment, the full reality of what they were doing crashed in on her. It had never been so dangerous before. Now all she could think about was the harm that could come to them. How could she endanger their lives? Yet how could she not?

She was responsible for the children. She had to take good care of them. For months she'd done her best, but it never seemed enough. Now with this hostage in their midst, she didn't know what to do with him. She wished she'd never had to bring him along. But she had. The past was past. She must think of the future.

One thing for sure, she would not be gentle with this man. She couldn't afford to be. Besides, if there was one thing in this life she hated, it was rich, arrogant men. She glanced back at her captive. He didn't look quite so arrogant now. His face was sunburned. His clothes were dirty and torn. He was at her mercy. For men like him, she had no mercy. And with good reason.

She knelt to stir the stew. It bubbled. Satisfied, she ladled it into bowls, then passed them around to the children as they gathered near the fire. She counted. *Seven*. All safe. She lived in fear she would forget one or lose one on a train or have a horse go lame as they fled their crime. So far, they'd been lucky, as well as smart. But how long could it last, especially after a close call like today?

Putting stew into a bowl for herself, she hesitated as she remembered the hostage. He'd have to be fed, too. She got up and walked over to him. "Sit with your back to us." She didn't want him to see them when they pulled down their masks, although she wasn't sure it mattered at this point.

"If you'll untie my hands, I can eat better."

"No. Turn around so your back is to the fire." She stared at him hard, letting her scorn show in her eyes.

"Why?"

"Do as I say or you won't eat."

He shrugged and moved to face the tree rather than the children.

Satisfied, she glanced back at the campfire. "Go ahead and pull down your masks to eat."

The children quickly followed her words and began softly talking to each other as they ate. She watched them a moment, knowing they were too quiet for children, too cautious, too old before their time. But there was nothing she could do about it. Not now.

Reluctantly she moved to sit beside the hostage. "I'll feed you, but don't try anything or I'll have to shoot you. And if not me, then one of the children. They're well trained."

"I know. Impressive work back on the train."

She nodded, dipped a spoon into the stew, then lifted it to his lips.

He watched her a moment before opening his mouth. He took the bite quickly, then gulped it down. "Good."

She forced herself to remain calm and firm in the face of this much too intimate association with a man she could only hate. She fed him another bite, unable not to notice the sensual shape of his lips or the smoothness of his skin warmed by the light of the fire. His golden blond hair bleached light by the sun shone like bright metal in the firelight.

"Thanks." His intense blue gaze raked her and a puzzled expression entered his eyes.

She hoped he didn't see through her disguise. She wanted him to think her a child as long as possible. But she hadn't been this close to a man for a long time and it had a disturbing effect on her. She

29

hated the feeling and quickly turned her thoughts back to the job at hand. She fed him the rest of the stew, then stood up.

"Water."

She walked away, checked to make sure the children were fine, set down the bowl and spoon, then dipped water into a metal cup. She took it back and knelt. As she held the cup to his lips, her hand accidentally brushed his cheek. She jerked back as if stung. He needed a shave. No. She mustn't think of him that way. He wasn't one of them. He didn't have needs or desires or goals. He was *other*. He had to be or she could never treat him as a hostage.

"Enough!" She stood up.

"I want to talk with you." He gestured with his head for her to sit down again.

She remained standing.

"You can let me go in the morning. You're safe enough here. I haven't seen any faces. Even if I had, nobody's going to do anything to children except stop them and send them home. I promise not to tell and I'll be gone at dawn. What do you say?"

"I can't chance it."

"You can trust me."

"No." She turned away from him and walked back to the campfire. She must ignore him. She pulled down the scarf that covered half her face, relieved to feel cool air, and sat down. She ladled up more stew for herself, then gave seconds to the others who wanted it. She'd thought she

30

wouldn't be hungry after the scare on the train, but instead she felt ravenous.

As she ate, she looked at each child in turn, making sure each one was whole if not completely happy. She smiled, remembering the names they had chosen, abandoning their old ones when they had started their new lives.

The three Swedish girls, daughters of an immigrant family, had chosen Faith, Hope, and Charity. The smallest in size, daughter of a Chinese mother, had picked Star when she wished on a lucky one. Tara, thirteen and the oldest, had immigrated from Ireland and had named herself for her native land. Jasmine was East Indian and had named herself for a sweet scent. Blaze, the youngest at ten and of African-French ancestry, had vowed with her name never to forget what had set them on this path.

When their bowls were empty, Jasmine collected them and went to the pool to dip out water, careful not to dirty their water source. She was twelve, the most quiet, the one who always saw what needed to be done and did it. But she was used to work. They all were. Robbery was easy compared to what they'd done before, but still they wouldn't be doing it if they had a choice. Options. They'd had few before and now they had none, save robbing stages and trains.

Blaze began a soft song in her clear, high voice. The others joined, blending their voices as they had their lives for so many days and nights. Jas-

31

mine sat down near them and added her voice to the song.

As Harmony listened, she heard a rustling behind her. The hostage! Jerking up her mask, she whirled around. He sat in the shadows watching the children. She couldn't read the expression on his face, but she was glad the firelight and shadows distorted the girls' faces. For as long as she could, she wanted to keep their identities secret. She wished he hadn't looked. He wasn't accustomed to obeying orders, but what rich man was?

She should get up and do something about him. But what? She wasn't used to having a hostage. She could command him and point her pistol at him, but she didn't want to move. She was so tired. It had been a horribly stressful day. They were safe in their hideout. All would be well if not for the stranger. At least he wasn't trying to escape. For now.

They'd outrun their past, or thought they had. But the past followed. The anger remained, and the fear, the worry. She looked at the girls as she pulled down her mask. They were still alive, and free. What more could she ask?

Plenty more. But how could they get it? She shivered, realizing the nights were getting colder. But winters here would be nothing compared to those in Chicago. She didn't fear death from the cold, not here. But death still stalked them . . . in their nightmares, in their solemn eyes, in their memories. And in the form of Isham Turnbull.

She pulled her blanket more closely about her,

listening to the low voices of the children, never too loud, never too happy. They had grown up before their time. And no wonder. She glanced down and touched the jagged scar that formed a pink ridge across the back of her right hand. The wound had never had a chance to heal right.

Thrusting her hand out of sight, for she hated everything the scar represented, she looked into the campfire. The flames should have been comforting, light and heat on a cool night in the desert. But her thoughts had already twisted backward. These flames reminded her of others, bigger, hotter, wilder. Tears filled her eyes. Smoke filled her lungs. Screams filled her ears.

The fire roared out of control, consuming everything in its path. Women and girls, mothers and daughters beat against the locked door of the sweatshop. Harmony screamed for help, her voice joining the others. But no help came. They surged as a mass against the door, trampling each other in their desperation.

Harmony backed away from the group, deciding that way was hopeless. She glanced around, trying to think of some other way to escape. The yards of fabric and partially completed clothing went up fast as the fire licked its way through the large, windowless room. Where were the managers? The owner, Isham Turnbull? The firefighters?

But she knew, *knew*, their shop would be low on anyone's list of importance and their location on the South Side added to the problem. Would anyone ever even know or care?

At twenty-six, she was one of the oldest workers. She had a responsibility to think clearly, despite the fear clawing inside her. Several of the children she had trained ran up to her, coughing, their eyes streaming tears, their bodies shaking with fear. She held them against her as she stood in the growing inferno, desperate to save them, trying to think past the screams and the agony.

She remembered the tiny office, partitioned off from the main room and rarely used by the owner. She'd been in there the day before to stack some boxes. They'd been using the office as a temporary storeroom and she'd knocked over some boxes, making a mess. While she was putting things back in order, she'd noticed a small, painted-over window. Hope beat fast in her heart. She grabbed the girls, hurrying them with her away from the front door.

If she was wrong, she'd be the death of them, but if she was right they might escape alive. Inside the office, she realized the window was higher than she'd realized. But the smoke wasn't as thick. The children helped her stack boxes in a pile below the window.

She climbed upward, scraping her legs as some of the boxes gave way. Finally she reached the window. It was painted shut. Nothing she did would open it. The cries from the other room and the heat drove her to action. She wound her shawl around her right hand and broke out the window with her fist. She hardly felt the cut or noticed the blood.

One by one she helped the girls up and out, although several had mothers back in the shop and cried for them. She told them she'd get everyone else out that she could. Fortunately it was a first-story window, but even so the children had to leap to safety. When they were all outside, she climbed down and ran to the doorway. Smoke was fast filling even the office. She couldn't see far and the heat was so intense she dared go no farther.

She called, but it was now quiet in the sweat-shop except for the crackling of the fire. Tears ran down her cheeks. Surely they weren't all dead. She called again and heard a child cry for her mother. Replying, she got down on her hands and knees. She crawled into the inferno, coughing, calling, listening for the girl's voice.

When she found the child not far away, she called again, but no one else replied. Beams fell from the ceiling, crashing into the room. She couldn't wait any longer. She pulled the girl with her to the office and helped her out the window.

Weak, scared, in pain, they stumbled away from the building as the roof caved in, sending flames shooting into the darkened sky. Terrified, they ran into the alley, realizing they may have been the only ones to escape.

In the light of the fire, she saw police and fire-fighters at the front of the building. She left the children in a huddled mass in the darkness and hurried to get help. But she quickly realized nothing was being done for the sweatshop. They were trying to save only the nearby buildings. She heard

Isham Turnbull talking to the men in charge and rushed up to them.

Surprised, they turned to her. She begged them to unlock the front door and try to help the others inside. She explained that she and seven girls had escaped through a back window. And she asked for medical help for the survivors.

Turnbull turned on her in fury, screaming at her for lying, for causing the fire, wild to let everyone know there were no locked doors in his businesses. He blamed her for setting the fire, for otherwise how could she have escaped with her chosen few if no one else had.

Stunned, she denied his charges, begging them to unlock the front door, to send for doctors. She cried, tears streaming down her cheeks, even as she tried to be firm and forceful. Turnbull insisted she and the others be arrested for arson. He told them she was a disgruntled worker and labor agitator who would go to any lengths, even the deaths of innocent women and children, to get protective laws passed.

Shaking badly from shock and fear and anger, she could hardly stay on her feet. But she wouldn't back down. She turned to the police for help, but how could she expect them to believe the word of a poor, powerless young woman against that of an established, rich businessman? She saw the doubt in their eyes, the accusation. Turnbull had done his job well. When the police officer insisted she get the children so they could all be taken in for questioning, with no mention of a doctor, she knew she had lost. She turned and ran. And got the girls. And ran.

They knew the back streets and alleys of Chicago well so they escaped. But they were now hunted and they couldn't return to their tenements. They feared to go to a doctor even if they'd had any money. Eventually, they crouched in a dark alley and helped each other as best they could. But nothing could ease the pain, the loss, the agony of what they'd been through.

Harmony shivered, dragging her thoughts back from the past. The campfire had burned low. The girls had moved together in sleep. She hoped they had no dreams, for she knew the power and pain of nightmares. Many nights she couldn't sleep at all. In her dreams she tried over and over to save the others in the sweatshop. She never succeeded, but she never stopped trying, either.

She rubbed the scar on her hand. Turnbull had not been done with them that night of the fire. He wanted them silenced and death was the best way to do it. She and the children were hunted by the police and Turnbull's henchmen and hounded by the newspapers. The Chicago papers were full of news about the heartless woman named Harmony Harper who took it upon herself to martyr a hundred innocent women and children to gain sympathetic attention for the cause of labor reform.

Although she hadn't been an activist the night of the fire, she became one afterward. But only in her heart. First, she had to make sure the girls had food and clothes and minimum shelter. They couldn't get jobs. They hid most of the time. They were afraid to go to the law because Turnbull would know where to find them. They had no living relatives and friends.

Desperate to stay alive, they turned to crime. First they became pickpockets, stealing only from the rich. After Turnbull's men almost caught them several times, they realized Chicago was too dangerous for them.

They fled south and west. For a while St. Louis supported them. The girls could slip in and out of crowds unnoticed. And because of her petite size, she could appear as one of them. In fact, if she had been any bigger she'd never have gotten out of the sweatshop window alive. She owed her life to her size.

But Turnbull's men continued to follow them. In Missouri they decided to steal enough money to buy a ranch where they could hide out until the girls were older. For that, picking pockets wasn't enough. They were frightened the first time they robbed a stage, then a train, but they got better, more self-assured as they made a name for themselves as the Wild Child Gang.

The campfire burned low, but the flames of the Chicago fire burned bright inside her. She was more determined than ever to find a safe haven for the children, then return and bring Turnbull to justice. When that happened, her name and those of the girls would be cleared. And maybe sweatshop reform laws would be passed.

But they were still far from their goal. She had hoped this train robbery would be the last one, but they'd been interrupted and hadn't gathered nearly enough cash. Now they had a hostage to complicate everything. What was she going to do with him?

She jerked the mask up over her face, stood up, and stalked over to him. He glanced up at her, his blue eyes wary. How she hated his blond good looks, his well-fed, well-muscled body. What did he know of children starving even when working eighteen hours a day, seven days a week at exhausting, dangerous work? What did he know of being accused and found guilty by newspapers and the law simply because you were a woman or a child or poor? She kicked him hard.

"Tired of me already?"

"You're not in a position to make jokes."

"What am I in a position to do?"

She hesitated. His question made her stop and think. Yes, he could help them. And why not? She sat down, her hand resting on the butt of her pistol. "You're our hostage. We can do whatever we want with you."

"You're children. Are you going to add murder to your crimes?"

She shook her head. "We need money."

"I've heard that story before."

"No doubt." She took a deep breath, knowing she made her life more dangerous every moment. "If you want to go free, you have to provide a ransom."

"Ransom!"

"Yes. Enough money to buy and stock a small ranch."

"Oh, I get it. The Wild Child Gang wants to be cowboys after they've been outlaws. I'd say you all read too many Wild West novels."

"It doesn't matter why we need the money or the ranch." She hardened her heart to this handsome man. "You are our hostage and if you want to go free, you will get the money."

He narrowed his eyes as he watched her. "I can't trust you or your gang."

"We can go together into Las Cruces. You can wire for money from the local bank. When you get it, you'll give it to me and I'll let you go free."

"What if I don't have that kind of money?"

"You're a rich man."

"What if I don't want to buy my life?"

"I'm counting on your desire for freedom."

"I'd like to know more about the Wild Child Gang."

"Why?"

"You've got to admit pint-sized outlaws are a new twist on an old story."

"I don't owe you an explanation."

He leaned back against the tree. "You push me so far and no farther. I want some answers, some assurances, something to base my decision on when I make it."

She stood up. "Don't you want to live?"

"Yes. But giving you money might not be in the best interest of my health."

Wheeling around, she walked over to her saddlebag and pulled out a length of rawhide. "Stupid, arrogant, rich man." She walked back to him. "I'm tying you to the tree for tonight."

"Good idea if you want me here in the morning."

She wound the rope around him and the tree, suddenly aware of the faint masculine cologne he wore, of the thickness of his hair, of the fine cut of his clothes. Disgusted with her thoughts and him for his privileged life, she tied the rope, and stood up. He was a hostage, nothing more. And he hadn't even had the sense to accept a good offer when he heard it.

Walking over to her saddle, she glanced back. "I'll want an answer from you tomorrow. Just remember, it won't take much for you to be more trouble than you're worth."

He nodded. "And you remember that I'm your hostage and if you don't take good care of me I won't be worth a plug nickel."

"I'm sure you aren't worth a plug nickel, but your money should make up the difference." She lay down, pulled down her mask, and rolled herself in her blanket.

Tonight the ground felt too hard, the night too cold, and her body too lonely. The hostage had a way of getting under her skin that she didn't like. A rich man had used and abused them so she should have no qualms about returning the favor to another such man. But it was hard to reconcile the hostage with Isham Turnbull. They didn't seem the same.

Yet it didn't matter. She couldn't afford a conscience. Tomorrow the hostage would be out of her hair and they'd be rich enough to finally be safe.

Three

Thor slept fitfully. By dawn his hands felt numb and he wondered if he'd lost the use of them forever. He ached all over from the ride, from the cramped position, and from the chill that had invaded him. He'd thought longingly off and on all night of warming himself by the campfire or under a blanket.

He surprised himself. He'd thought he was tough. They'd called him the Viking, but he wondered if college had softened him or if he'd never been as rough and ready as he'd thought. These children, despite their size and age, made him feel like he'd been pampered all his life.

On the other hand, maybe being out of control made him feel vulnerable, made him notice all the discomforts of the outlaw camp. Or maybe he was so mad he couldn't think normal, or straight, or any other damn way. Hostage! He'd happily throttle the bandit leader the first chance he got.

But first he'd have to give them money. It made him furious. He'd have to do it. He saw no other way around the situation. But he'd make them pay plenty after he got the money back. He might not put the law onto them, but he thought they'd make excellent candidates for the Flora McCuskar Institute. Strict discipline and control would change their nasty ways. And he'd be happy to see it.

As the day broke bright and clear, he watched the camp come alive. The children stretched, groaned, glanced his way, quickly pulled up their masks, then headed for the privacy of the bushes back up the canyon. He could use some of that privacy, too, but he'd be damned if he'd ask.

What he would do was try to talk them out of their life of crime. He didn't figure it'd do much good, but he had to give it a chance. They were probably having too much fun to listen to him. Now they wanted to be ranchers, too. He didn't figure they had any idea how hard a life that was and he was going to make certain they never found out.

He watched the outlaw leader come back, build up the fire, then put something on to cook. He noticed in the light of day and with nothing else to do that the leader moved gracefully with a body more like a girl than a boy. For the first time, he wondered if some of the bandits were female. He'd assumed it was a rough and tumble gang of boys, but they'd been extremely quiet and helpful to each other now that he thought about it.

Sitting still, he watched as the Wild Child Gang gathered around the campfire, handing around mugs of water, nodding, talking low amongst themselves behind their masks. Could they be a gang of *girls*, outsmarting, outgunning the law of the West? He scoffed at the idea.

His sister Deidre was a suffragist, smart, determined, strong, but she'd always been feminine, too. He couldn't imagine her robbing trains, even full grown, even wanting the right to vote. He must be mistaken about these outlaws. But what if he wasn't?

Whatever had happened to ladies in restricting corsets, full-length gowns, and expensive silks? Dressed like that they couldn't run, much less rob a train. And they sure as hell couldn't get a man into this kind of trouble. A lady would never take a man or anybody else hostage!

He thought about women who gained the right to vote, equality under the law, the right to do or be whatever they wanted. There'd be no more ladies, maybe not even any ladies of the evening. What a different world for men. If there was one thing a man learned early in life, it was that to be a real man he must control the women in his life. If he didn't, how could he have all the finer things he wanted without the worry of losing them?

Maybe he'd better have a talk with Deidre the first chance he got. He could understand the idea of a few ladies voting the way their husbands wanted, but the idea of every woman in the country voting any damn way she chose was scary. And the idea of competing with women for jobs made no sense at all. Men had their place in life and so did women. He liked his male privilege and he intended to keep it, no matter what his suffragist sister thought.

He frowned, deciding he couldn't possibly have been kidnapped by a bunch of girls. His male ego couldn't tolerate the idea. He focused on the leader. "Hey, come over here. Untie my hands before they turn black and drop off."

"When you agree to wire for the ransom money, then you'll get breakfast and the rawhide around your hands loosened." Harmony walked over to him, her hand on the butt of the pistol in the holster buckled low on her hip.

"You can't get away with this. It's stupid. You're going to get caught. Criminals always do." He looked at the group, grown quiet and still by the campfire. "This may be a lark now, but think about it. Wouldn't you rather be home with friends and family, trusting those who love you to take care of you?"

"That sounds nice, rich boy." Harmony didn't even attempt to keep the acid from her tongue. "But we don't know about a life like that. The closest we can come is getting money from you."

"You're children! Your mothers and fathers must be sick with worry over you."

Harmony stiffened. "Shut up! You don't know what you're talking about." She glanced over her shoulder. The girls had moved closer to each other. In a moment, he'd have them crying. What did he know about pain and loss in his sheltered life?

46

Hate ran swift and straight through her heart. She kicked him with the sharp-pointed toe of her cowboy boot.

"Damn!" He frowned up at her. "Don't you know better than to hurt your hostage?"

"At this moment I would like nothing better than to put a bullet in your heart."

"Do it! Go ahead."

"That's not what I want, and neither do you." She knelt beside him. "If you don't keep quiet, I will gag you."

"Don't you see how you're leading these other children astray?"

"I told you before and I'll tell you again that you don't know what you're talking about. Now either shut up or I'll shut you up."

Digging the heel of his Wellington boot into the dry dirt, he realized he couldn't win. The Wild Child Gang was set on its course. Far be it for him to stop them. "Okay, I'll get you the money."

"What?" Harmony's heart suddenly beat so fast her ears rang.

"I said I'd get the money for you." He was surprised at the difference in the brown eyes watching him. They weren't actually brown at all, but liquid amber.

"When?"

"The sooner the better." Let them hang themselves. It was no concern of his now. "Loosen these ropes and feed me."

Harmony stood up and walked away from the hostage. She felt almost giddy with relief. They'd be safe, finally, absolutely, and they'd have hurt nobody except taking money from rich men who had stolen it from others. She sank to her knees beside the campfire, suddenly weak. Tears stung her eyes, but she forced back the emotion. They didn't have the money yet. But they were close, so very close.

She glanced up to see seven solemn faces turned to her. She smiled beneath her mask. She'd told them about the ransom while they walked to the bushes. They'd heard his words of agreement. They knew what it meant. She could see the relief in their eyes, but the worry, too. How did she get him in and out of Las Cruces without being caught? She didn't know.

Jasmine and Blaze came to her and knelt beside her, stroking her back.

"We'll be all right now. Don't worry." Jasmine's soft voice comforted. "We'll feed him while you get ready."

"Don't let him trick you." Harmony started to get up and do it herself.

Blaze put a hand on her shoulder. "I'll keep my gun on him while Jasmine feeds him. He won't get away."

Harmony nodded. She couldn't let them think she didn't trust them. They had all been in on this from the first, equals. She wouldn't change that now. Besides, they had all earned their spurs during the past few months.

While they spooned up oatmeal for the hostage, she took a bowl for herself, sprinkled precious sugar over it, then began to eat. Her mind ran fast. She would have to dress as a ranch lady. It was the best disguise possible and it had worked over and over in the towns. *Lady.* How had she come so far from the past?

Her mother had done her best to raise her as a lady, a girl who would grow up and marry and domesticate a household. She could read and write to a limited degree, she could sew, she could cook, she could speak fairly well, but she would never marry. *Never.*

She still had visions of her father returning home after drinking to take out his frustrations on a wife who didn't know how to complain, even that she could. He had beaten her, sometimes badly, sometimes with almost loving cruelty. She had protected her daughter, always, until Harmony had grown old enough to protest. Then her father had hit her as well.

When she was thirteen, her mother had died from a brutal assault by her father. There were no relatives to protest or help since both were immigrants. Harmony had left home after the funeral, taking her clothes and a gold locket with her mother's photograph in it. She had wanted nothing else from her father, not that there was much anyway.

She had tried working in homes as a domestic servant, but that was considered immigrant work now and after one job when the man of the house had tried to force himself on her she had returned to sweatshop work. Five dollars a week was not enough to live on so she had gone hungry most of the time. Some of the older girls had found a *friend* to help them. Some of them had also worked as prostitutes.

She had lived with several other girls in a cramped room till she had grown older, more experienced, and had gotten a slight raise in wages and a better job. At eighteen she had finally managed a tiny room of her own in a boardinghouse only because she cleaned there, too. It was worth the extra work. And food.

But Isham Turnbull had noticed her on the job in his shop. He was used to getting his way with the female workers he wanted. They had little choice but to give in to his demands if they wanted to keep their job. Most of them had desperately needed the work, no matter how bad or how poorly paid.

Harmony hadn't had children or parents or a husband to support. She had resisted. He had struck her, threatened to fire her, but she had still resisted. And had kept her job. She had decided she presented an interesting challenge to him, for he had kept coming back. And she had kept saying no. He had given her a slight raise, a better position, and still she had said no. But he had sworn she would eventually say yes.

She realized the oatmeal tasted like sawdust in her mouth. But she couldn't feel sorry for her life. She had lived to be twenty-six. She hadn't been beaten since she was thirteen. She hadn't been raped. And no man had ever called himself

50

her master. She had made her own way for thirteen years. And she would find a way to keep going, to find a home for these girls who had no family, no relatives other than each other. They were her family now and she would guard them fiercely no matter what she had to do.

Even if it meant she had to rob and steal and force a stranger to give her money to keep his life. Even that. But how could she think of turning the hot blue eyes of the hostage into the frozen blue of the dead? Yet, how could she not if he was her one chance to save her family? Somehow she must make this arrogant man do what she wanted. Even though he had agreed, she knew he would try to trick her at the first chance.

She finished her food, then glanced around. The hostage sat in front of the tree, his hands bound loosely in front of him. He finished the cup of water and handed it to Jasmine. Blaze sat on the ground in front of him, her pistol resting on her knee, her hands wrapped around its butt, her eyes never straying from his face.

Harmony couldn't help but smile. The children were so fierce. They wore boots, trousers, shirts, vests, hats, and bandannas pulled up over their noses. Each had a gun belt made to size and their own pistol. She'd hated learning to fire a gun herself, then felt worse training the girls. But the knowledge of how to defend themselves might be the single thing that kept them alive, not only during a robbery but in the desert as well for snakes and scorpions and other dangerous creatures lived there, too.

She knew she had done the right thing, but she still hated that she'd had to do it. She could put the blame at the feet of Isham Turnbull and she did, every day, every night. He wanted them dead for what they knew, but she would see him dead before she'd let him do it. *Hate.* She must never let go of the hate. She must never feel compassion for anyone who could help her reach her goal. She must keep alive the memory of the fire.

Rubbing the scar across her right hand, she nodded to herself. She would get the money today and the hostage be damned. Standing, she motioned Jasmine over to her.

Jasmine set down the empty cup. "What do you need me to do?"

"I want all of you to stay here."

Jasmine shook her head.

"Yes." She glanced at the others. "I'm going to take him to Las Cruces. He'll wire for money. When he gets it, I'll take it and let him go free. If I'm not back by sundown tomorrow, you'll know the plans went bad. Get out of here as fast as you can."

Faith, Hope, and Charity leaned forward as one. "No! We'll come after you."

"Don't go alone." Star's dark eyes blazed with emotion.

"I can't chance any of you getting caught." Harmony pulled Jasmine close and stroked her back. "You've got enough money now to get you to

California. Maybe you can get jobs there and disappear if you continue to dress as boys."

"We're not going without you." Tara stood up and walked around to hug Harmony. The others joined her.

Blaze glared at the hostage, then ran over. "You can't leave us!"

"Now, stop this!" Harmony stepped away from them. "We've taken chances before. We survived the fire. If our luck holds through today, we can hide out till Turnbull gives up."

"But we won't forget." Blaze held out her hand.

"Remember our sisters!" They clasped one hand on top of another until they stood with their hands together.

Harmony placed her hand on theirs last. "I'll be back, but if by some chance I can't make it, you must stay free to see that Turnbull is stopped from killing others." She swallowed hard, tears misting her eyes. "I don't care how long it takes. Five years. Ten. Twenty."

"Don't worry." Jasmine nodded. "I'll never forget my mother's screams as long as I live."

"I know you won't." Harmony let her hand drop and stepped back. "I want you to remember that whatever happens to me you must go on. Now, do you promise?"

After a long moment, the girls agreed.

"Okay." Harmony whirled around to face the hostage. He watched them with a frown on his face. He'd heard too much, but she'd forgotten him in the heat of the moment. Above all, she'd had to make sure the girls would escape even if she didn't get back. With their promise, she could put her own life at risk.

"I'll saddle two horses." Tara waited for agreement.

Harmony nodded, knowing Tara was the best of them with animals. "Jasmine, would you and Blaze take the hostage to the bushes? Faith, Hope, Charity, would you pack us food and water? Star, will you help to make me into a ranch lady?"

As they headed about their tasks, Harmony felt relief flood through her. As long as she stayed busy, she didn't have to think about all the pitfalls of her plan, of the danger to herself, or of the possible future of the girls without her to help them. She'd have plenty of time to think about all that on the ride to Las Cruces.

When everything was ready to go, she hugged each girl goodbye, took the reins to the hostage's horse, then started up the canyon. The girls ran beside the horses until they reached the end, then they stopped and waved until she was out of sight. She glanced back at the hostage. She'd blindfolded him and left his hands tied in front so he could grip the saddle horn. She wished she could trust him, but she didn't dare.

She let the horses find their way down through the rocks and growth of the hillside. When they reached the desert floor, she took a deep breath. They were in the open now. Anybody could see them if they happened to ride by. She didn't expect to see anybody in this lonely land, but she had to be careful to play the role from now on out.

Stopping in the shade of a piñon tree, she glanced down at herself. She wore a dark gray cotton split skirt with a green and gray shirt, and her usual black boots, black gloves, and the black holster to hold her Colt .45. On her head she wore a black hat to shield her from the sun. She'd pulled her hair back into a simple chignon and wore a black scarf around her neck.

She smelled the air. It was clean and cool in the early morning. She glanced upward. A few clouds broke the wide expanse of blue sky. No buzzards circled in the distance so nothing would be drawing predators, two or four legged. She was glad of that.

Glancing over at the hostage, she shook her head. They'd dusted off his clothes, but he still looked out of place and disheveled for a man of his style. She hoped his appearance wouldn't give them away.

"You might as well take off this blindfold." If something happened, Thor wanted to at least be able to see. Blindfolded, he was too vulnerable in the desert. "If you'll recall, I saw the way into the foothills."

He was right, but more than that she wanted them to appear as normal as possible. She reached over and untied the bandanna, noticing the heat of his skin, the thickness of his hair. What would he think when he saw her as a woman? She pushed the thought away as she tucked the bandanna into her saddlebag.

He glanced over at her, then froze in surprise. "Damn! You're a woman. I knew somebody had to be leading those children." He frowned. "They are children, aren't they?"

"Let's get going." She moved her horse forward, then tossed him the reins to his mount. "Don't try anything that'll get you shot in the back."

Touching his horse with his knees, he moved close to her. "You don't still think you can get away with this, do you?"

She frowned at him. "I'm going to stick so close to you in Las Cruces, you'll think you've grown another skin. And my pistol will be in your side every step of the way." She looked toward the Rio Grande. "Isn't your life worth more than money?"

Thor nodded. "Are all the outlaws girls?"

"Yes."

He groaned, shaking his head. If anybody ever found out, he'd never live it down. The Viking captured by a bunch of girls and one small woman. He wasn't going to tell a soul. He'd wire his family in Tucson and warn them he'd be late for the dedication. He sure as hell wasn't going to ask for help.

Harmony chuckled. "It's amazing what a woman can do when she sets her mind to it, isn't it?"

"It's more than amazing." He knew he was being a fool, but he'd heard them mention a fire, no folks anymore, and running from somebody named Turnbull. Could they be in trouble? Did they need help besides the money? If they really needed a man for protection, why didn't they just ask him? He'd never turn down a needy lady and children.

"You don't have to understand or like what we're doing. All you have to do is get the money, then go about your business."

"I'd like to know why you turned to crime. The girls don't seem mean."

"Don't underestimate us." She was glad to see the river drawing nearer. His questions were dangerous.

"Where are your menfolk?"

She glared at him. "Not every woman has a man in her life."

"Why not?"

Picking up the pace of her horse, she moved ahead to the river. When she reached it, she got down, letting her mount drink. She sipped from the canteen. The day was heating up now. She wanted to be in Las Cruces and back again. She glanced back up to the foothills. The girls would be going about their usual chores. She wished she was with them.

Thor dismounted, then dropped the reins so his horse could drink. He walked over to her.

She handed him the canteen, then stepped back. She hadn't realized he was so tall, so big, but she wouldn't let his size intimidate her. She hated seeing him drink where she had placed her mouth. It was much too intimate. But everything about this kidnapping had been too intimate.

Handing the canteen back to her, he wiped the back of his hand across his mouth. His blue eyes were warm in the sunlight. "You can untie my hands. I'm starting to want to see this thing through."

She shook her head and stepped back again. "Outside of Las Cruces. Not before."

"You're sure a little thing, aren't you?"

A chill ran up her spine. What if he leaped on her and overpowered her? What if he put her own pistol to her head and shot her dead? What if he went back for the girls? She turned and walked swiftly to her horse. How much was she really in control? She caught the reins, put her foot in the stirrup, and felt large, warm hands around her waist, lifting her up into the saddle.

Shocked, she dropped her hand to her pistol. He could have had it out and . . . the knowledge was there in his eyes.

"I think you'd better start trusting me." Thor held up his hands, the rawhide taut between them. "You need a *man* to help you."

She felt her face flush. "And you think you're that man?"

"I sure do. A little thing like you—"

"My size has nothing to do with anything."

"I spanned your waist with my hands."

"It doesn't matter."

He smiled. "Lady, this is the Wild West."

"And you seem to forget I'm the leader of the

Wild Child Gang, outlaws who have terrorized several states."

He shook his head. "But you need my money." He reached up higher, stretching the rawhide tighter between his wrists. "And if I'm not much mistaken, you need me."

"Oh, all right." She didn't know if it mattered anyway. She still had the gun. She pulled a knife out of her boot, then cut cleanly through the rawhide.

He grinned, showing strong white teeth. "Thank you, ma'am. You won't regret it." He tucked the rawhide in his pocket.

"I regret ever seeing you in the first place."

He mounted his horse, then moved close to her. "The name's Thor Clarke-Jarmon."

"Thor?"

"Old family name from Norway."

"I suppose you've been called a Viking before?"

He showed his teeth again.

"Just remember one thing. I'm the leader here, not you."

Four

They rode toward Las Cruces beside the Rio Grande. For the first time in her life Harmony allowed herself to think what it might be like to have a strong man like Thor Clarke-Jarmon on her side, by her side, a partner in life. She thought on it a while, then shrugged as she admitted she was unable to imagine such a thing.

But she could imagine such a handsome man, so healthy, so muscular, turning to her in passion. Desire she could imagine, although she knew she shouldn't. Yet she didn't want passion thrust on her. She wanted to share that, too, or perhaps even start it herself. She smiled, remembering how she had kidnapped him from the train. When had she become so bold?

Fear, hunger, desperation could turn a person into a predator. She could never go back to being the lady her mother had wanted her to be, or the dispirited worker Turnbull had forced her to be, or the frightened victim she had almost become after the fire. She glanced down at the silver spurs on her black leather boots. She wore them to remind herself that she ruled her own life now and she could do whatever she set out to do.

Glancing over at Thor, she felt sensuality curl deep inside her. What would it be like to take a man like him, seduce him, make him want you above all others? She shivered, although the sun was warm on her. He must have felt her thoughts for he turned to her, his blue eyes narrowed against the brightness of the sunlight.

"You never told me your name."

He'd been thinking of her. She threw back her head and laughed. It'd been a long time since she'd felt a surge of pure pleasure run through her. She had nothing left to lose so what did tomorrow matter? What did it matter if he knew her name? She probably wouldn't live to see the sunset. And she'd be damned if she'd let them put her in a cell.

"Did I miss the joke?"

"No joke. Relief. For the moment the girls are safe and I'm riding to my destiny." She patted the neck of her horse. "If anyone should ever wonder, I'm Harmony Harper. And I'm proud of who I am."

He looked puzzled. "Harmony?"

"Sure. Why not?"

"Something like Cactus Kate seems more accurate."

She laughed again, realizing she hadn't felt like laughter in months. Why she did now she couldn't imagine. Their danger was more real than ever.

Maybe it was the man beside her who made her reckless. And wanton. "You think I'm prickly?"

"Now that I think of it, prickly's too mild." He looked her over again. He'd known more beautiful women, but he decided he'd never known a more fascinating one. Her petite body held surprising curves. In the sunlight, her brown hair gleamed auburn. And her brown eyes turned amber when she grew intense. The delicate bone structure of her face, a small, straight nose set in a heart-shaped face made you want to stroke the pale skin, kiss the full lips.

"Yes?"

He jerked his gaze away as he felt himself harden. She was better than the fantasy she'd interrupted on the train, but not nearly as available. He glanced down at her boots. The silver spurs gleamed in the sunlight. Her skin was like silk, but she protected it with the sharp rowels of her spurs. If a man got past her defenses, he wondered if he'd ever be able to let her go.

Disappointed that he'd ceased to play their game, she looked out over the desert. They'd reach Las Cruces soon. How could she have thought of this man as anything but a hostage? She'd simply been alone too long.

"I'd like to try your silken spurs."

"What?" She looked around at him in surprise and was caught by the heat in his blue eyes, the desire. She felt a response in the fast beat of her heart. She couldn't look away for the life of her.

"Your spurs. No matter what you may say, I think they're silken."

An uncontrollable shiver ran through her. "Is it worth the chance?" Her voice grew husky. "They might be silver instead."

He moved his horse close to her. "I can handle either one."

Mesmerized by his words, by the heat in his eyes, by his nearness, she returned his gaze. "If you weren't my hostage, maybe you'd have the chance to find out." The moment the words were out of her mouth, she realized she'd broken the spell.

He looked away. "All you want from me is the money, isn't it?

She nodded, knowing she couldn't appear weak when the girls depended on her.

"My mistake." He thrust his horse into a gallop.

It didn't take her long to catch up with him. She felt surprise at his reaction. What did he think this was all about? Maybe his emotions were as mixed up as hers. No. She couldn't afford emotions. She had to have the money. That's all she wanted or needed.

He glanced over at her and slowed the pace of his horse. "You think you can stand alone, don't you?"

"I don't *think*, I know."

"Are you telling me you never had family and friends to support you?"

"Not since I was thirteen and my mother died."

"What about your father?"

She threw him a hard glance. "Let's just say there hasn't been a father in my life since I was thirteen." She felt the pain that always came when she thought of her father. He'd professed to love them over and over. What kind of love hurt and killed? No. She couldn't believe he'd ever loved them because she was afraid it was the only kind of love between a man and a woman that she could know herself.

"You were orphaned at thirteen?" Shock filled his voice. "Did relatives take you in?"

"My past doesn't matter anymore."

"It does to me."

"We're in the West. Nobody has a past here."

"So I've heard. But you have to admit the Wild Child Gang is bound to make a man curious."

"I don't have to admit a damn thing!" She didn't want to talk about her past or the girls. What did he know about pain and loss? She urged her horse faster for she could see Las Cruces getting closer.

He stayed with her.

"All we have to discuss is how and when to get the money. Nothing more." She had to put him in his place before it was too late.

"There's not much to discuss." Anger made his words clipped. "I go to the telegraph office and wire the bank in New Orleans to transfer money to the bank here."

"You forgot a small point."

"What?"

"I'll be with you every step of the way. If you

try to get help, I'll shoot you." She turned to glare at him with agate hard eyes. "I've got nothing to lose. Do you understand how dangerous that makes me?"

He watched her a moment. "You're dangerous, all right. To me. And you don't even need a gun to do it."

Her breath caught in her throat. "What do you mean?"

Moving closer, he captured her with his stare. "I want to know everything about you." His gaze raked her face, her body, then returned to focus on her brown eyes. "I want to know you inside and out."

She was astonished to feel herself blush. She wasn't used to this type of banter.

"You're the most fascinating woman I've ever met."

Shaking her head, she tried to drive away his words, the heat of his blue eyes, the sheer power of his desire for her. "I'm simply a woman trying to survive in a man's world."

He leaned closer still, watching the curve of her mouth, the way her pink tongue wet her lower lip as she spoke. He wanted to kiss her, but it was the least of his desires where she was concerned. "I want to help you and the girls."

She closed her eyes, willing away the sight of him. "I can't trust you."

"You don't need this ransom. I know a place in Tucson where the girls will be safe. Maybe you

65

could work there. I'd hang around and give us a chance to—"

"Stop!" Tears filled her eyes. "Don't do this to me. Who are you? What are you? Why should you help?" She looked directly at him. "And if you do, what do you want in return?"

He reacted as if slapped. "I'm a gentleman offering my services to a lady and children in need. To think of payment is an insult."

"Is this some kind of rich man's game to you?" She wanted to believe him, but she didn't dare. Besides, she didn't need a man to take care of them, as if one would. She needed his money, nothing more.

"Trust me, Harmony. Disband the Wild Child Gang. I promise you won't regret it. If you go on like this, I'm afraid for your life."

"No! You can't expect me to trust you or change my plans to suit your sense of honor. I don't need a knight in shining armor. I need the price of his steed."

Thor shook his head. Why had he expected this headstrong woman to listen to reason? But she was right. Why should she trust him? And what did he want from her? *Everything.* What did she want to give? *Nothing.* For the first time in his life he really understood why men needed women to depend on them. How else could they keep them?

"We're almost to Las Cruces." She pushed down all her emotions. "The plan still goes. You wire for enough money to buy and stock a small ranch."

66

He looked at her. "What if somebody recognizes you?"

"They won't. Would you?"

"What about me?"

"If somebody recognizes you, we'll tell them I rescued you and the gang got away."

"You've got it all figured out."

"If I don't, we're both dead."

She urged her horse ahead. There was no reason to talk anymore. She didn't want to think, or feel, or respond. She had to be absolutely cold and ruthless, just as she was during a robbery. And she *must* not think of Thor Clarke-Jarmon as a man, especially one with a name and a family and a past. Nor one who wanted her. He was the hostage, nothing more, nothing less.

As they rode toward the main street of Las Cruces, she took several deep breaths, then checked her Colt .45. She was as ready as she could get. She glanced over at the hostage. He watched her, silently, accusingly, but he didn't speak and his blue eyes were hard and focused. Good. He appeared just the way she wanted him.

When they entered the town, she checked the wide street, noting the number of horses tied in front of buildings, men lounging in chairs on the boardwalks, women shopping, and especially the sheriff's office. The buildings were wooden, narrow, with overhanging roofs over a long boardwalk on each side of the dusty street. A tumbleweed rolled along in the breeze. A dust devil swirled past, then subsided. All looked quiet, normal, not too busy, not too still.

As far as she could tell, they blended into the town, or they would have if her hostage had been dressed differently. For a moment, she had a strong urge to take him into a dry goods store and buy him cowboy clothes, but new clothing would be more noticeable than what he wore. At least she'd gotten him to remove his tie.

As they walked their horses side by side down the street, she held the reins in her left hand, letting her right arm dangle loose near her pistol. She had to be ready for anything, especially a break by the hostage. So far, he wasn't a problem, but she hated to think what was going on in his mind.

She had been through the town before, setting the layout and business locations in her mind. She'd also shopped there, bringing a different girl with her every time. Although she'd felt an inner tension then, it was nothing compared to what she felt today. So many things could go wrong. But if the hostage had spoken the truth, maybe he *would* actually help and not hinder the ransom.

When they reached the small telegraph office on the other end of town, she let out a small sigh of relief. So far, so good. She glanced over at the hostage.

He nodded, then slipped from his horse.

She quickly followed, then threw her reins loosely around the rail in front of the building. As she moved in close to him, she made sure he left his reins loose, too. She wanted to be able to escape quickly if necessary. With the girls in constant danger, she'd learned to think ahead. But now she figured she mostly needed to control the hostage. She put her left hand on his arm and felt a sudden warmth rush through her.

He glanced down at her in surprise, the heat that sizzled between them apparent in his blue gaze. He shook his head as if to dispel the momentary lapse of control, then held out his arm as a gentleman would for a lady he was escorting down the boardwalk.

Touching him disturbed her more than she wanted to admit, but she kept her right hand loose and near the .45 on her hip.

As he helped her up the step to the boardwalk, he smiled, then leaned close and adjusted her hat as if they were close friends or lovers. "If I get you the money, will you buy me a hat to replace the one I left on the stage?" His voice was low and caressing, his body large and warm.

She gripped the butt of her pistol. "Don't play games." Her voice came out in a harsh whisper. "We're in danger every moment we're in this town."

"The hat?" He lowered one hand to cup the side of her face, then stroked the smooth skin with his fingertips.

Closing her eyes, she felt a shudder run through her body. What was he trying to do to her? She'd never felt so out of control, so desperate to touch a man, so wanton. And she'd never felt this weak since the night of the fire. *Fire.* She shook her head to dispel the cloud of emotion. "No!"

"No hat?"

"No, you won't sidetrack me."

"Are you sure?"

"Shut up and get inside." She glared at him.

Surprisingly, he smiled. "I'm beginning to wish you'd kidnapped me for my body rather than my money."

She narrowed her eyes, then glanced around them. If she didn't stop him, he was going to get them caught. Everything still looked normal. Three men walked out of a saloon across the street. Something about them seemed familiar, but they were in the shadows and she figured they were probably people she'd robbed on a train. They weren't important, not now, not when she was so close to achieving her goal.

"Let's go." She pushed him toward the door.

"If we're going to keep riding around the desert, I do need a hat."

"All right! You can get a hat, clothes, whatever you want. Later. It has nothing to do with me."

He put his hand on the door, then stopped. "You sure you want to go through with this?"

She looked up at him, and nodded.

He pushed open the door.

"Harmony! Harmony Harper!" A voice hailed them from across the street.

She froze, gripping Thor's arm. Every nightmare she'd ever imagined flashed through her mind.

He pulled her closer as he wheeled around, reaching for the pistol that wasn't on his hip.

As she turned with him, she felt horror rush through her. "Oh no!" She drew her .45 as she clung to Thor, pulling him toward the horses. "It's Turnbull and his henchmen."

Thor frowned and stepped toward them.

"No!" She tugged at his arm. "We're outgunned. In town. Get on your horse."

Harmony pushed away from Thor as she watched the three men hurry across the street toward them. Two of them were hired guns, tall, muscled, dressed in a combination of Eastern and Western clothes. The other was of middle height with a slight paunch and hadn't adapted his clothing to Western heat at all. She wasn't surprised. No matter how hot he got, Turnbull wouldn't adapt. He was above it all.

She felt a swift rush of hate as she put a foot in the stirrup and swung up onto the back of her horse. She glanced to the side, making sure Thor was with her. She was a little surprised he'd mounted as well, but at the moment he had to realize he was in as much danger as she was from Turnbull's men.

As she wheeled her horse around, Turnbull stopped in the street, a gunman on either side.

"Stop!" Turnbull spread wide his legs. "I'm making a citizen's arrest."

"Hell if you are!" Thor turned his horse around and bore down on the men. He glanced back at Harmony. "Get out of here. Now!"

She didn't hesitate. She had to think of the girls first. She started back the way she'd come, but she glanced back. Why wasn't he right behind her?

Thor rode his horse close to the three men, kicked the gun out of one's hand, then made the other two scatter. He turned his mount around so fast the horse reared up, pawed the air, then came down in a run.

Shocked, she realized he was protecting her, giving her time to get away. No one had ever done anything like it for her before. Why now? Why him? And why didn't he try to escape?

She ruthlessly pushed the emotions and thoughts aside, as she concentrated on getting away. She glanced at the sheriff's office as she rode out of town. Nobody else was after them yet. She looked back and with relief saw Thor racing to catch up with her. She focused on the desert, then heard several shots. She glanced back again, but Thor still followed. Relieved, she kept riding back the way they'd come.

When he caught up with her on the outskirts of town, they rode together into the desert. She headed toward the Rio Grande and the route they'd taken after the train robbery, but she was afraid of going back to the hideout. Turnbull and his men would be able to mount horses and be after them in no time. She couldn't take a chance on leading them to the girls.

She glanced over at Thor. He looked excited, wild, and determined. *Viking.* Oh, yes, she could see it in him now. And, damn him, he was enjoying the chase. He caught her glance with his own and threw back his head to laugh. Maybe he didn't understand the danger, or maybe he did. For the first time she felt the pure pleasure of being alive, of having escaped death so narrowly, of being with someone who could share that feeling. And perhaps much more.

Suddenly she noticed the blood on the front of his shirt. Red against white. All happiness left her. Worried for him, she pointed at his chest.

He nodded, but didn't glance downward.

Of course he already knew. They were in worse trouble than she'd realized. If they didn't get him off the horse in some safe place where she could see how badly he was hit and bandage him, he'd lose so much blood there'd be no help great enough for him. Fear ran through her as she urged her mount faster and faster. How had this man come to mean so much to her?

Thor felt the pain in his chest, felt the wetness of his own blood, but he ignored the feeling. They had to get as far away as possible before the horses gave out. He knew they couldn't go back to the hideout. He only hoped Harmony knew another place. He should have felt afraid or worried or some such emotion, but instead all he could think about was that they'd escaped alive.

Now he had some answers coming to him. What the hell was Harmony Harper mixed up in? Who was the Yankee and his bodyguards who'd fired at them? What the hell was going on? And why was he fool enough to endanger himself?

He didn't want to admit it, but he felt more alive than he ever had before in his life. He glanced at the woman riding beside him. What he wanted to do this very moment was tumble her onto her back and throw up her skirts. But if he didn't get her to take care of his wound first, he wouldn't be much good for anything.

Harmony Harper. Wild Child Gang. Did this wild woman do anything halfway? He didn't think so. Imagining her wild in his arms made him want her all the more.

But he was going to have some answers first, if he lived that long.

Five

Harmony didn't slow her horse until she reached the Rio Grande. Once there, she paused in the protection of the growth along the riverbank. Thor hunched over his saddle, a hand to his chest. She refused to let the sight affect her, knowing if she became too worried she couldn't think straight enough to get them to safety.

Looking back down their trail, she saw the dust of pursuing riders. They'd gained a little time, for Turnbull and his men probably had to get their horses from the livery stable. They'd be even luckier if he hadn't involved the local sheriff, but she doubted that.

She looked back at Thor. His face was too pale. He must still be losing blood. She glanced up at the foothills where the girls waited in the hideout. They'd be worried, but they'd also be patient until tomorrow at sunset. Hopefully, they could join them by then. For now she had to get Thor out of sight and bandaged before he lost much more blood.

Moving close to him, she put her gloved hand

over his hands that held the reins and clung to the saddle horn. "Let me take the reins. I'll guide your horse."

He looked up, attempted a smile, then shook his head. "No. It'll slow us. I'm just resting."

"You're sure?"

"They're on our tail. Have you got a place in mind?"

"Come on."

She turned her horse into the river and moved north upstream. Their trail would go cold here if they weren't spotted. Right now they had a chance to ride the river with the trees and underbrush to protect them from being seen. But it couldn't last. Riding in the Rio Grande slowed them and made them vulnerable.

As they moved north, she kept glancing backward, watching, listening for Turnbull to spot them. But she couldn't see into the distance from the river and no sound alerted her to possible danger.

She passed the cutoff to the foothills leading to the hideout, but kept going. As they rode, the sun lowering in the west, she scanned the closer hills and rocks. As she searched, she thought, trying to remember a place that would make a good temporary hideout. Fortunately she had earlier scouted around the area, but she didn't want to stop too close to the girls.

When she thought they'd gone far enough to lose their trail in the water, she urged her horse out of the river and onto the western bank. They had to pick up speed now or risk being caught before they found shelter. She looked back at Thor. He followed, but she could tell he was in pain. She forced back the growing fear that made her chest feel tight. He'd be all right. He had to be.

As she scanned the area, she noticed a lone saguaro cactus near a jumble of rocks. She'd used that as a landmark before. Heading her horse toward it, she glanced back at Thor. He nodded. She kept her mount to a slow pace, not wanting to stir up any more dust than necessary. As they moved farther into the desert away from the Rio Grande, she could see the dust of the riders following them. They'd reach the river sooner than she'd expected or wanted. But maybe not soon enough.

She set her mount climbing up toward the rocks, then around them, keeping watch on Thor as they moved deeper into the hills. They passed the saguaro, but kept going, now lost to sight to anyone below. But she couldn't stop yet. They were still vulnerable. Finally, they reached the rock outcropping she remembered. As her horse moved around it, she breathed a sigh of relief.

What she'd remembered wasn't a cave, but it was the closest she could come. Rocks formed an overhang large enough to handle the horses and two people. Dark shadows in sharp contrast to the brightness of sunlight on pale desert beckoned her. But she'd lived out here long enough to know she wouldn't be the only one seeking shade.

She dismounted, dropped the reins, then crept into the shadow of the rocks. She waited until her eyes adjusted, then searched. She found three scorpions, scooped them up on the brim of her hat, then tossed them outside. Fortunately she didn't find any snakes. She hurried back out, led her horse inside, then went back for Thor. She helped him dismount. He leaned on her as she led him into the area, then helped him sit down.

When she had his horse inside with him, she stepped back outside. She found a tumbleweed and hurried back toward the river, following their trail. She couldn't see the dust of Turnbull and his men anymore. They were getting close, too close. At the river's edge, she started walking back up their trail, brushing it out behind her with the tumbleweed.

Even going as fast as she could, even knowing she couldn't see Turnbull, she still felt the sharp stab of fear. If they saw her now, they could pick her off with a rifle and find Thor. Maybe even the girls. Sweat trickled down her face, down her collar, in between her breasts.

She reached the rocks, then glanced backward. So far so good. She hurried, destroying the trail as she came around the rocks. And heard a rattle. She froze. No, not now. She moved nothing except her eyes and found the rattlesnake sunning itself on a rock high above her. She let out her breath. Safe.

Leaning down low, she continued her job, but watched the rattler until she'd passed its territory. As she rounded the first rock outcropping she heard the jingle of harness and froze. *Turnbull.*

They were nearer than she'd expected. But were they still in the river?

She wasn't safe, not yet. As quietly as she could, she continued her job, moving deeper into the rocks and sand, removing their tracks. Even if Turnbull came this far, he'd be unlikely to find their shadowy hideout. Yet it could be done. She swept away the last of their trail, then threw the sagebrush away.

Inside the shade of the rock overhang, she knelt beside Thor. He'd leaned back against a rock. She felt his forehead. No fever yet. She got the canteen off her horse, then knelt beside him again. She let him drink, then set the water aside.

"They're in the river nearby. We must be quiet." Her voice was hardly more than a whisper.

He nodded.

"I'm going to have a look at you."

He nodded again.

"But first the horses." She walked over to them, patted their heads. If they made any sound, they were all dead. She quickly hobbled both, then removed the saddles and bridles. As she worked, she kept glancing at Thor. He didn't look any worse. When she was satisfied the horses wouldn't be a problem, she washed her hands with water from the canteen, then knelt beside him again.

She put her hands to his chest, felt the stiffness of the fabric from his blood, and lost hope. He'd surely lost too much blood to save. No. She couldn't give up, not now. She pulled back his jacket, then gently undid one button after another until she could pull open his shirt. His chest was bared to her. Dark blond hair matted his chest, the skin tanned, the muscles hard. Twisted to one side over his heart was a gold medallion on a heavy gold chain.

"What do you think?" His voice was husky and low. "Will I do?"

Glancing upward, she caught the gleam of humor in his blue eyes. "How can you joke at a time like this?"

"I don't figure it's too bad or I wouldn't still be here."

"Don't waste your strength with talk." She took off her bandanna and wet it with water from the canteen, then pushed the shirt and jacket back farther as she looked for the wound. Shoulder. She shut her eyes as relief flooded her. She felt as weak as if she had lost the blood, not him. A hand on her shoulder made her glance up.

"That bad?"

She smiled, then shook her head. "No. It's a shoulder wound. You've lost blood, but you're lucky. The bullet grazed you."

"Good." He reached upward and pushed her hat so it hung from a cord down her back. He lightly brushed fingertips across her cheek. "You've got mud or dirt or something on you."

She trembled at his touch. In self-defense, she took his hand in hers. "Blood. *Your* blood."

His blue eyes darkened. "You're a marked woman now. *My* woman."

Heat stung her face. How could this man affect

her so strongly? "I believe you've got that all wrong, mister. You're *my* hostage."

"So you've got to keep me alive."

She nodded.

"You know what they say about captives."

"No."

"The captor becomes the captive." He touched her lips with his thumb, then pushed until they parted.

She touched the tip of his thumb with her tongue. She didn't know what made her do it, except that she'd suddenly had an overwhelming desire to taste him. She realized it was a mistake the moment she'd done it, for he inhaled sharply and looked as if he'd been burned.

Grabbing his hand with both of hers, she pulled it away from her face and held it out from her. She took several deep breaths, holding onto him as if she *could* control him, as if he were a lifeline, as if she could never let him go.

"It's no good, Harmony."

She glanced up, fighting back tears. Somehow he'd breached her defenses and she couldn't allow that. "I'm going to bandage your wound and you are not to touch me while I'm doing it."

"Or what?"

Not replying, she resolutely placed his hand on his thigh, then wet the bandanna with water again. As she cleaned the wound the best she could, she concentrated on it totally. She would not listen to her body or him. They hadn't escaped yet and to even think of anything else until they were safe with the girls was wrong. And, most of all, she wouldn't think of the way he had tasted.

When she could see the exact condition of the wound, she was pleased it was no worse. Getting up, she hurried to her saddlebags and pulled out a long clean cloth, a jar of salve, and returned.

"This will keep you from getting infected, I hope."

"Thanks."

As she applied the salve, she glanced up into his eyes. The fires were banked. She felt grateful. As she wound the cloth around his chest to hold the bandage in place, she couldn't help noticing the hard muscles, the smooth skin, and the heat of him. She felt hot with her knowledge of how much she wanted to hold him, stroke him, and let him do the same to her. But she couldn't. He was the hostage.

When she finished, she wiped her hands off on another cloth, then rinsed them with water. "Jasmine packed beef jerky and bread. We'd better eat. You need to keep up your strength."

"I'm hungry enough to eat about anything." But his gaze told her what he wanted to taste and it wasn't food.

While she traded the salve for food, she noticed him pull his shirt and jacket back into place. He'd be all right. It'd take a little time for him to heal and he'd be sore for a while, but he was a strong man and it wouldn't be long before he was fine again.

She brought back the food and set it on a clean

cloth between them. She didn't want to make the mistake of getting too close to him again. She wasn't nearly as tough with him as she needed to be, especially with Turnbull and no telling how many other men prowling around out there looking for them.

As she bit into a chunk of bread, she realized how hungry she was. She tried to relax. If they hadn't been found yet, they might be safe. But she wouldn't be sure until tomorrow when they made it back to the hideout. She hoped the girls were all right. This was the first night they'd been separated since the fire. She knew they could take care of themselves, but she missed them and worried about them.

Thor finished off a piece of bread and jerky, took a long drink of water from the canteen, then looked directly at her. "Are you going to tell me what that was all about back in Las Cruces?"

She avoided his gaze, took a deep breath, glanced around at the horses, listened for Turnbull, then set down the piece of bread she'd been eating. How much could or should she tell him? Did she owe him any explanation at all?

"I'm part of it now. The more I know the less dangerous it'll be for all of us."

She looked into his blue eyes. Maybe. Maybe not. Did she dare trust him? Did she dare not? He already knew so much that he held their lives in his hands if she let him go free and alive. But how could she possibly hurt him? Or anyone? She well knew the path of pain.

He leaned forward. "I want to help you and the girls. Trust me. I'm the one who got bloodied so you at least owe me a reason for it."

She did feel guilty about him getting shot, especially when he was helping her to get away. She sighed. She was so tired of fighting, of running, of protecting herself and the girls from every possible danger. Maybe she could trust him, at least with the truth.

Crumbling a bit of bread as she thought, she looked out at the rocks, at the shadows made by the sunset, at the stillness of the land. Safe. It's all she wanted. But they'd been seen by Turnbull now.

He leaned forward and took her hands, stilling the movements. "They're the ones who are after you, aren't they? Why?"

She looked back into his blue eyes, felt the heat of his hands, and wanted desperately to share the burden she had carried for so long. "It happened last summer in Chicago." She held tightly to his hands as she relived the fire, the smells, the sounds, the horrors, then the fear, the loss, and finally the turning to crime.

He listened quietly, his gaze never leaving her face, his hands never relaxing their grip. When she was done, he pulled her toward him. Caught by surprise, she fell against him, heard him groan in pain, then tried to pull away.

"No. I'm okay." He settled her against his good shoulder, an arm around her, her body molded to him. He held her hand, stroking the slim fingers.

"You aren't alone anymore, Harmony. You can count on me now."

She allowed herself to lean into his warmth, to savor his strength, his sureness, but she knew it couldn't last. Men were not to be trusted. Yet maybe for a little while she could pretend differently. She didn't really need him or anyone, but for the moment it felt good to rely on someone else for a change.

He fought the anger that had come with her words. He'd been a gentleman all his life, caring for the women around him, even if only fleetingly as they moved through his life. But he'd never before felt this overpowering fury that was aimed at the man who had so wronged this woman, the children she'd saved, and those who'd died in the fire. His anger went well beyond a gentleman helping a lady in distress.

But could he trust her words? Was she simply a clever outlaw, determined to outwit him and every other honest citizen?

As he stroked her hand, he realized he wanted to believe her, trust her, but his desire could simply be his body talking to him. He wanted her in a way he'd never wanted a woman before. But it wasn't an easy lust. It couldn't be bought and seven orphaned girls came attached. He was a fool for not running the first chance he'd had back in Las Cruces. But he'd reacted on instinct and that impulse had told him to protect the woman he wanted.

The first chance he got he'd hire a detective in

Chicago to find out the truth about this wild woman and her girls. In the meantime, he'd satisfy the yearning inside him. When he had what he wanted, he'd go on his way as usual. He turned to look at her. He'd never bedded an outlaw before.

She gazed deep into his blue eyes. Mesmerized, she couldn't look away. She felt his heat, her heat, their bodies demanding more than she could even imagine. He tilted his head toward her, his gaze focused on her lips. She wanted to move, to get away, yet more than that she wanted to feel his mouth on hers.

When he pressed hot lips against hers, she felt a flash of pleasure rush through her. She savored it for only a moment before the feeling turned to pain as she remembered the terror her mother had known with her father, the pain Turnbull had inflicted on her. She jerked back, moving out of his arms, and slapped him hard across his face. The sound cracked through the quietness of their refuge.

He lifted his hand to touch his face, then shook his head. "You could've said no."

She realized she was breathing hard, as if she'd run long and fast away from him. "You don't know." Her voice was low and hard. "Men think a woman like me and the other girls I've worked with are theirs for the taking because we don't have money and family and friends to protect us. Why should we need to be protected? Why should men be predators? Why should they keep us poor and mistreat us? All we need is to be paid enough money for a job well done so we can live a decent life."

"I'm not a predator. I give as good as I get." He flexed his wounded shoulder. "I don't even know how much I could do now anyway."

"It doesn't matter. You wanted to touch me."

"Any red-blooded man would."

She slapped him again. "Don't insult me or make light of me! I didn't succumb to Turnbull or any other man, even when it would have meant food in my belly, shoes on my feet, a warm coat in winter. And I won't succumb now so you will give me money."

"Don't hit me again, Harmony." He frowned. "I'm a gentleman, but if you persist in acting like anything but a lady I'll treat you that way. And I meant what I said as a compliment. You're a desirable lady."

"Lady!" She leaned forward, her brown eyes sparkling like agates. "I've never had the luxury of being a lady. And I won't be a harlot, either. I'm an outlaw, if you've forgotten. You're my hostage. And I've still got to get money to protect the girls. One way or another."

"I've never met a woman like you before."

"Of course you have. I'm no different from any other woman." She glared at him. "Men have taken from me and my girls, but men will pay in blood and money."

"My blood and my money?"

"If necessary, yes!"

"If Turnbull's at fault, he should pay."

"If?" She inhaled sharply. "What do you mean, if?"

"I mean I've got no proof except your word. And you're an outlaw."

She narrowed her eyes as she stared at him. "My word is all I have left. After twenty-six years of struggle, my honor is all I've got so don't you *dare* even think of disbelieving my word."

"I'm twenty-one."

Surprise made her hesitate. "You're younger than me."

"It doesn't matter. I'm a man."

"I didn't realize you're still—"

"I'm a *man*, damn it."

She took a deep breath. "You're too young to even consider touching me."

"If our positions were reversed, would you think I'm too old for you?"

"That's different."

"No, it's not." He reached out to take her hand.

She let him hold it, even after he stroked her palm with his thumb. She couldn't stop the shiver that ran through her. Why did he affect her? Why did he still fire her senses? She had one good reason after another to reject him, to distrust him, to thrust him from her life. Yet when he touched her, all reason fled, leaving only desire in its wake.

"I want to help, Harmony. Let me."

Jerking back her hand, she glared at him. "It looks like I'm stuck with you till I can get the girls away from the hideout and to a new place.

But I've got to have money. We'll be running low in no time." She clenched her fists. "I'd hoped that train robbery would be the last one."

"We can go to another town and wire for money."

"No! Now that Turnbull has seen us, he'll have men at every telegraph office in the area. And he'll have the law ready and waiting, too. They've seen my face now. And yours, too."

"I don't care."

"You can't do us any good now. After we've robbed another train, I'll take the Wild Child Gang farther West. And you can go your own way if you promise not to tell about us."

"You'd trust me?"

"I'll have to if I don't want to kill you."

He looked hard into her eyes. "Would you do that?"

She bit her lower lip. "I wish I could consider it, but I don't think I can."

Nodding, he smiled. "I can't turn you in, either. But I can get us help in Tucson."

"No."

"Harmony, listen to reason. There's no point in endangering yourself or the girls anymore. We can make it to Tucson if we don't take any well-traveled routes. Once there, we can—"

"No! I'm not part of your life. After the next train robbery, we'll go our separate ways."

"I can't change your mind?"

"My course was set in Chicago."

"Then I'll help you rob the train."

"What?"

"I said—"

"I heard what you said. You can't mean it. You'll be putting yourself on the wrong side of the law. Somebody might see you. It's dangerous." She hesitated, horrified at the thought of him being hurt again. "And you're wounded."

"I'm going, even if it's only to hold the horses."

Six

Harmony got up and walked away from him. She stood in the entrance, watching the shadows as day gave way to night. How did she deal with this Viking of a man? Why should he help? Why would he want to endanger his own life? It couldn't be for her. She had known all her life that she would never be the type of woman who excited men to great deeds or passions in her honor. She hadn't that type of stunning beauty or important family or any of the other necessary ingredients to provoke male action. And she'd never needed, wanted, or expected it.

So why did Thor Clarke-Jarmon insist he found her fascinating, insist he would help her and the girls, insist he wanted her? He must have some ulterior motive. Turnbull had always been like that. Maybe all men were. If that was the case, then she must be more cautious than ever.

She glanced back at him. He'd leaned against the rock to watch her. Perhaps she was making the situation too complicated. He was the hostage. He wanted to get free. If he thought desire would do that for him, why wouldn't he pretend to want her? But maybe his feelings weren't completely forced. He was alone with a presentable woman. She had indicated desire for him. What man wouldn't take advantage if he could?

Looking away, she realized she hated her thoughts. She wanted him to desire her for herself alone. But how could she suddenly think this way? He was five years younger than her, a wealthy man, a hostage. She was being foolish and she knew it. But she'd had so little of closeness in her life, so little of the luxury that would make her feel free enough to touch a man in passion that now she seemed to be going to extremes. And she mustn't do it. She couldn't endanger the girls.

She turned back to face him. "You'd better get some rest. You're weak. We get up at dawn."

"You'll have to join me. It gets cold out here at night. In my weakened condition—"

"Stop!" She put her hands on her hips, frowning. Was he this desperate for a woman? "We've both got blankets."

"It won't be enough without a fire." He gestured outside. "And you won't chance smoke from one, will you?"

"No. Turnbull may still be out there. I can't sleep anyway. I have to keep watch."

"You can't stay up all night. I said it before and I'll say it again, you can trust me."

"What about Turnbull catching us by surprise?"

"Maybe Indians could get up these rocks without a sound, but the three I saw in Las Cruces can't."

She walked over to the saddles, then untied their rolled blankets. "Use them both if you need the warmth." She shook out his, laid it across his body, then started to do the same with her own.

"I already spent one cold night on the ground. Do you expect me to do it again?"

She hesitated. He'd lost blood so he'd be vulnerable to the night air. She didn't want him to get sick. And she couldn't expect him to help keep watch in his weakened condition, even if she could trust him. What if he slipped away in the night to tell the law about the Wild Child Gang hideout? A reward had been posted and rich men always wanted more money.

Besides that, she needed to get some sleep herself. She walked back to her saddlebags and pulled out a length of rawhide. When she sat down beside him, he looked surprised. She ignored his reaction as she tied the rawhide around his wrist, choosing the arm with the wounded shoulder since he had limited use of it anyway. She'd just have to be careful not to hurt him.

"You don't need to tie me." He watched her with fascination when he realized she was tying the other end of the cord to her own wrist. "Forget what I said."

Glancing up, she frowned. "This is not some game to amuse a wealthy, bored gentleman. I don't want you sneaking off in the night."

"If you keep me warm, I'm not going to complain. Or leave."

She exhaled sharply. "This isn't personal."

"Certainly not." He grinned, showing even white teeth as he held up the blanket to make way for her.

She unbuckled her gun belt, then set it within her reach but away from him. She sat down stiffly near him, feeling his body heat, his strength, catching his scent. It was going to be a long night.

Placing the blanket over her knees, he patted her thigh. "Why don't we lie down?"

"You can, but I'm not—"

"I can't lie down if you don't and I'm feeling weak."

She didn't know if he was using her or not, but she didn't want him weak tomorrow when they rode back to the hideout. "All right." She placed her blanket on the ground, spreading it out for them, then turned to him. Caught by the humor and intensity in his eyes, she stopped.

He put a strong hand around her arm and pulled her with him as he lay down. She had no choice but to lie beside him, spoon-fashion, but she didn't let their bodies touch. Pulling the second blanket up over them, she lay stiff and unmoving, listening to the night around them.

"That's not going to do and you know it."

"Thor, it's enough."

"Say my name again." His breath was warm near her ear as he put his hand on her waist and pulled her back against him as he moved slightly forward.

When their bodies touched, heat leaped between them. She caught her breath as she felt his hand stroke her waist, making longer and longer forays up and down, his fingers dangerously close to touching her breast. She pulled the rawhide taut, then caught his hand to stop him. He changed his tactics by nuzzling her hair.

"You smell good." His voice rumbled low.

She felt vibrations run up and down her spine. "How can I sleep if you touch me?"

"I'd hoped you wouldn't want to sleep. Till later."

She flounced onto her back so she could look into his eyes. She immediately realized her mistake. He raised up onto his good elbow, a shadowy shape in the darkness. He stroked the loose hair back from her face, then traced the contours of her face, gently, sensuously, slowly.

"I must kiss you." He brushed her lips with his fingertips. "I won't hurt you. Trust me."

"No."

"Shhhhhh." He pressed a fingertip to her lips. "You want it, too. Don't fight."

"You're too young."

"I'm old enough for what we both want. What else matters?"

"You're my hostage."

"I know. And you've got to take care of me if I'm going to do you any good."

"You can't."

95

"I can and will do you a lot of good." He stroked lower to her throat, then lower still. When he cupped one breast, she gasped and moved her feet restlessly. The spurs jingled.

"Stop." She spoke without strength of conviction.

He rubbed his thumb across the fabric and felt the tip harden. "I'm doing what you want, what we both want."

She put her hand over his, stopping the tantalizing sensation. But it didn't stop the desire building in her. "I don't know what to say, much less do."

"Say yes." He pressed hot lips to hers, then raised his head. "I still want to find out if your spurs are silken."

She shuddered as passion raced through her body. Why should she fight this? She took a deep breath, trying to regain control. "You're the hostage."

"That's right. I'm yours to command. Tell me to love you."

Pushing her fingers into his thick hair, she pulled his face close to her once more. Wordlessly, she touched him as he had her before, tracing the strong contours of his face, then she pressed her lips to his mouth.

He groaned as he returned the kiss, then squeezed her breast, feeling the small softness ignite his body with need. Raising his head, he gazed down at her. "Kiss me. Hard." When he returned his lips to hers, he felt the tension in her body that told of her response to him. Empowered, he stroked her breast as he nibbled at her lips, causing her to moan and move restlessly.

"Thor, please, I—"

He took advantage of her words to deepen the kiss, thrusting his tongue into her mouth as he turned her toward him, pulling her against his chest as he wrapped a leg around her to hold her tight. With their wrists bound, he pulled her hand behind her back so that her breasts pressed against his chest.

Now he controlled her the way he wanted and he stroked her back as he thrust deeply into her mouth, tasting her sweetness, savoring her dangerousness. When he felt pain in his strained shoulder, he ignored it. Nothing could stop him from sating his desire for this outlaw woman.

She shivered, unable to believe the emotions that poured through her. She'd never been kissed like this, nor held like this before. She'd never let a man get so close, so intimate, and she couldn't imagine why she was doing it now. Yet her body craved him so badly she could do nothing except return the kiss, finding herself more bold, even in this, than she could ever have imagined.

When he finally broke the kiss, he gazed at her in wonder, for he'd never thought to need a woman as he needed this one. "I want you. Now."

She felt the hardness of his desire press against her. She felt the passion between them. And she felt the wildness of the night. They were safe from the chase for the moment, but they were not safe from each other.

"Trust me, Harmony."

"No!" She forced herself to push him away, then started to get to her feet, her spurs jingling. But she only got so far, no farther, for they were still bound by the rawhide. She pulled, but couldn't get away. She fumbled to untie herself, but she couldn't for he pulled back on the thong, drawing it tight.

"You can't get away so easily."

"I must. You don't understand. I have to think of the girls. I *can't* trust you, or any man."

Thor bowed his head a moment, took several deep breaths, then looked up at her again. "I won't touch you if that's what you want. Remember, I'm your hostage. But come, lie down beside me. We'll keep each other warm tonight."

She hesitated, searching for trust, not knowing if she even wanted it. No, she didn't want him to be good. She wanted him to be bad. She wanted him to overwhelm her senses, make her forget all her responsibilities, her past, her pain. She wanted to be so caught up in him that nothing else mattered, past, present, or future.

He took her in his arms and pulled her down to him again. She lay facing him, the rawhide binding them less than their emotions. When he took her hand, entwining their fingers, she felt tears sting her eyes. She hadn't known it could feel so good to share, to be so close, to be almost one with another. She pressed her face against his good shoulder, inhaling his scent, feeling the soft fabric against her cheek.

"Sleep now, Harmony. It's been a long, hard time for you. I'll keep watch a while."

She knew she should get up before she fell asleep or did something equally as foolish. As she moved her head, she felt something wet against her cheek. She sat up in alarm, the blanket falling away from her.

"Thor, you're bleeding again. We've hurt your shoulder." She touched his shirt. Yes, his blood had soaked through the bandage. Guilt flooded her. How could she have been so thoughtless?

He put a hand over hers and held it there. "It's nothing. If I lie still, it'll stop."

She could feel the beat of his heart, the movement of his chest, and his heat through her hand. She felt bound to him by much more than rawhide. It wouldn't do. "I don't like it. You could get sick or weaker if you aren't careful."

"Harmony Harper, I'm already weak. I've been that way since I first set eyes on a wild outlaw woman. What's a little more now?"

"Don't joke. Out here a wound is serious and you know it."

"What kind of wound are we talking about?"

"Stop it. You're hurt and it's no joke."

"If you'd stop stroking my chest, I'd hurt a lot less."

"Oh!" She jerked back her hand, but felt the tug of the rawhide and stopped. He enjoyed teasing her, making her feel guilty for everything that happened. If he hadn't been shot, she'd make him sorry. She'd make him pay for teasing her and pushing her and taunting her. She smiled to herself. And she knew just how to do it. She'd let him know how hard her spurs could be, after he'd felt their softness.

"Are you going to lie back down here or not?"

"Yes." Even to herself, she almost sounded meek. Good. Let him wonder. Let him be the one thrown off guard. And let him be the one to suffer. Tonight she'd sleep beside him, warm and safe. In the morning, when he was better, he'd see just what kind of outlaw woman had captured him.

"Harmony?"

She snuggled her bottom into the curve of him, feeling his heat, then his hardness. She smiled again. It might be fun to play with a man. She'd never done it before. She'd never had the luxury. But what did she have to lose? Wasn't she in control?

"I don't think I'm going to get a damn bit of sleep." He moved restlessly.

"You might as well since you're going to be a very good boy till your shoulder is better."

"And how do you think you're going to enforce that?"

"With my forty-five, of course."

He groaned and reached down to capture her breast with his hand. He rubbed a thumb over the tip till it hardened, then he bit her earlobe. "Getting sleepy?"

"Stop that." She pushed his hand away.

He chuckled. "What's good for the gander is good—"

"Don't make me get out my pistol."

"What about your whip?"

"I don't have one. With me."

"Doesn't every outlaw have a long black whip?"

"Perhaps."

"If you don't, then I'll put that on the list to buy when I get my new clothes."

"I think you're finally learning how to be a hostage. Yes, of course, you should buy the whip."

He nipped her earlobe. "You can talk as tough as you want, outlaw woman, but I know where you're vulnerable."

"And you also know the price you'll pay if you overstep your position as hostage."

He pulled her closer. "If before I met you, anybody had asked me if I wanted to be kidnapped by a wild outlaw woman, I'd have said no."

"And now?"

"I wouldn't have it any other way."

She chuckled, a deep warmth spreading through her. What did this man do to her? Why did she feel so bold? And what was she going to do about it?

Taking his hand in hers, she stroked each finger, noticing the length, the strength, then lifted his hand to her lips. She kissed the palm, then teased it with the tip of her tongue.

He groaned. "If this is punishment, I want more."

She smiled in satisfaction. It felt good to have power. Yes, she had power with this man. Maybe she had more control than she'd ever realized. Why had Turnbull chased her all the way from Chicago if he hadn't felt threatened by her? They'd been on the run, hiding out, robbing when necessary, but still feeling like victims. Now that she thought about it, the Wild Child Gang had power, too. People were afraid of them. *Power.*

As she lay there thinking, feeling Thor tickle her ear with her hair, she heard a sound down in the rocks nearer the river. Fear raced through her. She held her breath to hear better. Again. Rocks fell. Somebody cursed. *Turnbull!*

Thor gripped her hand, then put a fingertip to her lips. They lay absolutely still, listening hard.

"The damn bitch ain't gonna be up in those rocks."

"If we don't get her tonight, she will have escaped again." Turnbull's voice, with its Midwestern accent, carried loudly through the still night.

"You're not gonna get her now. It's too dark."

"I can't believe she escaped. Again. We were so close back in Las Cruces."

"And where'd she stash the girls?"

"She must have a hideout somewhere around here if we could find it." Turnbull's voice held frustration.

"We won't tonight, boss. Best thing's to hire more men. You can't count on the law."

"You're right about that." Turnbull's voice turned

mean and angry. "I will handle Miss Harmony Harper and those girls myself. If she gets another chance, she will lie and try to convince everyone I locked the front door to that shop."

"Did you?"

"Fool! What the hell does it matter? What counts is that I won't be blamed for the fire. The problem is troublemakers like her. They are to blame for labor unrest in Chicago, New York City, Boston, everywhere. You name it and there is some labor organizer trying to put us out of business. If we paid what these lazy workers wanted, there would be no jobs at all. Idiots!"

"We'd better get on back, boss. The sheriff's bound to be at the river by now."

"I hate to go. I feel strongly that she is hiding somewhere around here. I was so close today." Turnbull's voice lowered. "Did you notice that man with her?"

"You bet I did. He kicked the hell out of me and I won't forget."

Turnbull chuckled. "You can do what you want with him when we catch him."

"Thanks. I got a knife that knows what to do with troublemakers."

"I bet you do." Turnbull's voice turned cold. "Do you think she's whoring with him?"

"Could be."

"Then you can use your knife on her, too, when we catch him."

"What about the girls?"

"Make it quick and clean. I have a soft spot

103

for children. But you can both have Harmony after I'm done showing her what a real man is like." Turnbull's voice turned mean. "Remember, it is her fault a hundred women and children died. She deserves to get what is coming to her and if the law won't catch her, I will."

"Right, boss."

"It's only a matter of time now." Turnbull's voice quieted. "Come on, let's get back to Las Cruces."

Harmony lay stiff and quiet as she listened to them ride away. When she couldn't hear them anymore, she sat up and hugged her arms around her stomach. She felt so cold she didn't know if she could ever get warm again. Turnbull! How had the man tracked them this far? She'd tried everything to lose him. Would she and the girls never be safe, never have peace? No. At least, not until they had enough money to hide out somewhere safe.

Sitting up, Thor rubbed her shoulder. "That man seems to think you're a murderer. And a labor agitator."

She dropped her head, covering her face with her hands. She was neither. But how could she win? How could she hope to outsmart Turnbull with all his money, all his connections, all his power? Why had she ever felt powerful? She'd always been at the mercy of others. Why did being in the arms of one man make her think she could suddenly overcome years and years of servitude?

"A man who's got something to hide, something to cover up is a dangerous man."

"You believe me?" She hesitated when he didn't immediately respond. "Or Turnbull?"

"It's not what I believe. It's what the law, the newspapers, and men like Turnbull can make others think. But from my viewpoint, I can't think why you'd lock the door or how you'd even do it."

She turned and gripped his hand. "You're not sure?"

"I want to believe you. You saved the children. But like I said, it doesn't matter what—"

Jumping to her feet, she jerked his hand upward. "After what I told you, how can you question me? I told you. My word is all I have left."

He stood up, too. "Harmony, listen to me. I want nothing more than to believe you. I can't think of any reason you'd do it, or why you'd save the girls if you did. But he's got a point. Agitators *are* threatening some of the workplaces. If there was a big fire and the cause of it got laid at the feet of an employer, then there'd be hell to pay in the newspapers and magazines, not to mention the police. I can understand his viewpoint."

She slapped him hard. "You coward! You disgusting—"

He jerked her against his chest. "I told you not to slap me again."

Trying to get free, she suddenly realized how strong he was, how far away her gun was, and how truly vulnerable she was to him physically even with him injured. But she was too furious to care. "How dare you question me or any other

105

worker? What do you, son of a rich family, exploiter of the workers, know about not making enough to stay alive, or the unsafety of the factories, or of seeing children ruin their eyesight, their health before they're grown?" She threw back her head, glaring at him. "How the hell would you know?"

"I know. And care. I've seen it, too. My family pays more than a living wage."

"Maybe. Why should I believe you?"

"And why should I believe you?"

They glared at each other, caught in their struggle. In the distance a coyote howled and broke the tension.

Thor pulled her against him, then stroked her hair. "If we turn against each other, we'll never get out of this alive. Remember, they want me now as much as they want you and the girls."

She didn't respond, for she was too overcome with emotion. She'd been a fool to ever think she had any power or any control over this man or any other. Turnbull had her on the run just the way he wanted and if she wasn't careful he'd have her destroyed, too. She needed help, but she didn't know how to ask for it.

Thor tilted her head back with one hand to look at her face in the pale moonlight that filtered into the cave. He pressed a gentle kiss to her lips. When she still didn't respond, he hugged her against him, ignoring the pain in his shoulder. "Forget the past. We have one goal and that's to stay alive. Later we can prove whatever we need to the other. Okay?"

Taking a deep breath, she pushed back from him. "How's your shoulder?"

"It hurts like hell, but not as bad as what you're going through."

"I'm used to it. Nobody's believed me yet. Why should you?"

"We'll get out of here, then we'll find a way to prove you innocent."

"You'd help?"

"Remember, I'd like to keep my skin whole, too."

She nodded. "I'm sorry I got you into this mess. It's not fair."

He stroked her cheek. "But then how'd I ever have found out what it was like to be hostage of a wild outlaw woman?"

"Maybe you could have lived without the experience."

He shook his head. "No. I'm your hostage till you let me go. And I wouldn't change that, not for any damn thing."

Seven

After a restless night of too much heat from Thor and too much cold from the desert, Harmony had Thor in the saddle and headed for the Wild Child Gang hideout before the sun had broken the eastern horizon.

If she'd been honest with herself, which she refused to be, she'd have accepted the reality of the physical cravings he awoke in her. Instead, she fought her desire as they rode down from their rocky shelter into the desert.

Although they stayed away from the Rio Grande, it didn't make her feel any safer. Turnbull and his hired guns, as well as the local law, could still be scouting the area for them. By now the railroad might have its own investigators in the field. Any which way she looked at the situation, they were in trouble. And still without enough money to escape for good.

Why she should suddenly crave a man in the midst of all her problems was beyond her ability to understand. What's more, she didn't want to deal with it. She glanced over at Thor. He looked better today. She'd put more salve on him before they'd left, grateful the wound hadn't started bleeding again. But he was still hurt. All she needed to go along with seven homeless orphans was a wounded, arrogant hostage. Would the horror begun back in Chicago never end?

As they reached the foothills leading to the hideout, the sun rose, turning the desert a rosy hue. She stopped her horse near a juniper tree and glanced back. She felt relief that no one was following and that she could see no dust trail coming toward them. For a moment, she allowed herself to enjoy the beauty of the sunrise, then stiffened as Thor put his hand on hers and squeezed.

"No matter how many times or places you see the sun rise, its always different, isn't it?"

"Not in Chicago."

"What do you mean?"

"I worked from before dawn to after sunset, just like a lot of others. Only since we've been on the run have I been able to enjoy the beauty of a sunrise. We had to become outlaws to have time for pleasure."

"I'm sorry your life has been so rough."

"I didn't mind the work, none of us did. It was the fact that no matter how long or how hard we worked we could barely make enough to stay alive."

"We don't do that to our workers, I promise."

She shrugged. "It doesn't matter, not here, not now, not anymore." She knew it did, but she couldn't seem to deal with the truth today. She wanted Thor to remove his hand from hers and yet she wanted him to come closer still. Even now she could feel the imprint of his body against hers, the hardness of his arousal, the intensity of their desire. Would she never be able to get this man out of her senses? And should she even try?

"It does matter, not only for your sake but for other workers and for the health of our nation's economy as well. Men like Turnbull should be stopped."

She felt a catch in her heart as she turned to look into his eyes. "Do you really think there's a chance to do that?"

He nodded, squinting into the sunlight. "Maybe not all men like him all the time, but look at the growing power of the Grange and other unions. If the workers band together, they can force changes. That's their best chance for making changes."

"You aren't afraid of too many demands?"

"A lot of workers have a long way to go before they can even imagine that, don't they?"

"Yes. But that's not what Turnbull and his ilk shout to anybody who'll listen."

"We aren't listening." He squeezed her hand again, then took up his reins.

"No, not anymore."

She urged her horse forward, anxious to see the girls and make sure they were all right. She knew they must have been worried about her and about their future. She would reassure them, then they'd make new plans as a group as they always had.

But they had to be safely away from Turnbull before they could possibly plan ways to stop him.

As they rode farther into the foothills, moving upward, she saw the flash of a mirror, the pattern repeated three times.

"What the hell's that?" Thor leaned forward in his saddle, watching to see if the light appeared again.

"The girls have a guard posted. It's the signal for all's well but somebody's coming."

He slanted a glance at her. "I suppose you came up with that idea?"

"No. The credit goes to Faith, Hope, and Charity."

"Smart bunch of girls."

"That's right. Every single one of them."

A moment later they rounded the piñon tree leading to the mouth of the box canyon. To Thor's astonishment, girls leaped out at them from all sides.

"You're caught!" Blaze grabbed Harmony's leg, put her foot on top of Harmony's boot, then vaulted up behind the saddle. "Let's go!"

Harmony laughed, happiness filling her at the sight of her friends.

"Are you okay?" Jasmine stroked the nose of the horse Harmony rode.

"Yes. We're both fine, but Thor is slightly wounded." She took a deep breath. "We ran into Turnbull and two of his gunmen in Las Cruces."

"No!" Tara stepped closer and put an arm around Jasmine's waist. "We were so worried."

"We thought you'd never come back." Blaze put her arms around Harmony's waist and hugged her hard. "We love you."

"We took care of ourselves, but we were horribly worried." Star looked up at Thor and frowned. "Was it his fault?" She placed her small hand on the butt of her pistol.

"No. He helped." Harmony glanced around at the questioning faces. "Truly, he did. Now let's get back to camp. We're starved and we have lots to tell you."

The girls took off at a run and disappeared into the mouth of the canyon. Blaze clung harder, pressing her face against Harmony's back.

"They were ready to kill me if I'd caused you harm." Thor's voice held wonder.

"We're family." Harmony patted Blaze's hand. "We've seen too much death. We don't intend to lose another one of us to some man's greed."

"I'll remember to watch my back."

"And your front. Don't forget you're still hostage of the Wild Child Gang." Harmony clicked to her horse and moved forward.

"How could I?" Thor followed her into the canyon. Little had changed since they'd been gone. The horses looked rested. A campfire burned low and the girls had gathered around it to prepare food. He hoped it'd be tasty and filling because he felt hungry enough to eat a horse and chase its rider.

When they stopped their horses and dismounted, he watched Harmony gently lift Blaze down, kiss

112

her on the forehead, then turn to the other girls and hold out her arms. They rushed to her and they all hugged, murmuring to each other, obviously so close and so connected that they didn't need anybody or anything else in the world.

He felt like a damn third wheel. Why had he ever thought Harmony needed him for anything? He was sick of being made to feel like a fool by a young woman and a bunch of girls. He hoped to hell nobody ever found out.

Turning his back on them, he walked over and sat down by the fire and dished up a bowl of some kind of stew. He blew on it to cool it, then took a big mouthful. Surprisingly, it was good. They'd used dried jerky, beans, peppers, and fresh spring water. It was filling enough to take the edge off his hunger. But what he really craved was a thick, juicy steak. Maybe with that in his stomach, he'd be able to get his mind off the delectable Miss Harmony Harper. But he doubted it.

He watched them while he ate. When they were done hugging and kissing, Harmony sat down beside him. Jasmine dished her up a bowl of stew, handed it to her, then the others joined them in the meal. He supposed it was their breakfast, or leftover dinner. Whatever it was, he spooned up another bowlful.

When their appetites were sated, Jasmine and Tara picked up the empty bowls and carried them over to the spring to wash. While they were busy, Harmony glanced around the group, feeling the warmth of love she'd only known once before with her mother. She savored the feeling. Then she looked at Thor. Something else entirely tugged at her heart when she thought of him. It wasn't love. At the great age of twenty-six, a confirmed spinster, she suddenly craved a man. And it couldn't have been more inconvenient.

When Jasmine and Tara returned, the girls turned to look at Harmony. She smiled, trying to put a cheerful face on the situation, but it didn't do any good. They were sharp enough to know they were in trouble again.

"You're sure it was Turnbull?" Tara twisted her hands together.

"Yes. No doubt. If Thor hadn't kicked one of his gunmen in the face to give me time to ride away, I might have been shot or captured."

Seven faces turned solemnly toward Thor and considered him.

"Do you want to join our gang, is that it?" Jasmine watched him with steady dark eyes.

"He's a man. He can't!" Blaze pointed at him.

"He's too big. And so blond." Star frowned at him.

"Blond and big is good." Faith, Hope, and Charity smiled at him. "He'd be a normal size in Sweden."

"Not in China." Star put her hands on her hips.

"Girls, please! Thor got wounded as we fled from Las Cruces after helping me escape."

"Now he's weak besides big." Blaze glanced around the group, her point made.

"I'm not that weak. And I'm still strong. The

bullet just grazed me." Thor realized he was defending himself to the girls and clamped his mouth shut. What the hell did he care what they thought of him? Once more, he was thankful none of his friends or family could see him. Everything he'd ever believed in was getting turned upside down and if he wasn't careful he'd be sucked into believing it himself.

"We didn't have a chance to send for the money." Harmony wanted to get their attention off Thor.

Blaze jumped up and paced. "What are we going to do?"

"We'll have to rob another train." Tara clasped her hands.

"Or stage." Faith, Hope, and Charity leaned closer together.

"But what about Turnbull, the law?" Jasmine looked to Harmony.

"We have the train schedule. They didn't find our hideout and I don't think they'll expect us to strike again so soon or in the same area. What do you think?"

"We've got to have the money?" Blaze sat down near Harmony and put her arms around her.

"Yes. I'm afraid so. We've got to have more money to get farther west, try to outrun Turnbull. It's not safe to stay here any longer." Harmony glanced around the area. It'd been a good place. She hated to leave. But they had no choice.

"Can't *he* get some money?" Blaze pointed at Thor.

"We tried. Turnbull saw both of us. I'm sure the sheriff has a description of Thor by now."

"And he wasn't wearing a hat." Jasmine shook her head. "They'll have a real good description."

"It looks like we don't have a choice if we want to stay free and alive, do we?" Faith put her arm around Hope and Charity leaned toward them.

"No." Harmony focused on the group. "But we need to vote on it like we always do. Everybody who agrees, raise their hands."

All the girls agreed, then looked at Thor as he raised his hand, too.

He cleared his throat. "Well, what do you expect? I'm a wanted man now thanks to you. I'm part of the Wild Child Gang whether you want me or not."

"You're the hostage." Tara glared at him, then turned to Harmony. "That's right, isn't it?"

Harmony turned her hands palm up. "He's offered to help. He'd have gotten us the money, I believe, if he could have."

"We can't have a big man on the train. He'd give us away for sure." Star frowned.

"I agree." Harmony smiled, trying to satisfy the group. "But what are we going to do with him?"

"He could hold the horses." Hope looked at her two sisters who nodded in agreement.

"The horses?" Thor felt insulted. "I'm the best one of the bunch of you to rob a train. I'd intimidate them all a hell of a lot more than any one of you." He realized he was defending himself again, and all to be part of robbing a train. His

116

mind was getting twisted there was no doubt about it.

Blaze looked around Harmony at him. "But they can't tell us apart. Anywhere we went with you, they'd recognize us."

"She's right." Harmony looked at Thor. "I suppose you could stay out of sight and hold the horses."

"What if we can't trust him?" Star's dark eyes held fear and worry. "What if he ran away with the horses while we were on the train?"

"Somebody will have to stay with him to help hold the horses." Jasmine glanced around the group. "It's too dangerous to leave him here alone anyway. He could escape."

"Okay. He can go, but only to hold the horses." Harmony looked at each girl in turn. "Are we in agreement?"

They all nodded their heads.

"Look, this is stupid." Thor finally twisted his mind back to normal. "I know a place in Arizona that takes in children. You could go there. Maybe Harmony could work there." His statement was met with stony silence. "Trust me, it's a nice place, run by good people. And you might even find families to join."

Blaze jumped up and walked to put her arms around Faith, Hope, and Charity. "We *are* family. We don't want some people telling us what to do, making Harmony go away, maybe separating us to live with strangers."

"That's right." Charity frowned. "Besides, we have a job to do."

"Yes." Hope leaned toward the fire. "We have to stop Turnbull and prove ourselves innocent."

"We'll never rest easy till we do that." Faith's blue eyes glittered with purpose.

Thor glanced around the group. Children weren't supposed to be like this, especially not girls. "Look, I promise to help. I've got influential friends and family. Put the problem in my hands and go back to doing what little girls do."

"What's that?" Blaze moved toward him. "We've worked eighteen hours a day, seven days a week in a sweatshop since we could. That's what little girls do. Is that what *you* want us to do?"

"If they go back to that, they'll be too worn-out to stop Turnbull and men like him." Harmony reached out to Thor. "Even if they could get jobs with him following them, they—"

"Stop!" Thor threw up his hands. "That's not what I mean. I thought you'd spend your time choosing pretty clothes, going to parties, learning how to read and write and do fancy needlework. You'd have pretty dolls." He was stopped by the incomprehension on their faces.

Harmony squeezed his hand, then shook her head. "You've lived in a different world than we have so don't try to put your values and dreams onto us. They won't fit. Or work."

"But I want you all to have the best. You deserve it."

"We deserve to get justice and revenge." Blaze

knelt beside Thor. "That's what we want and need."

"And freedom." Jasmine frowned.

"That's why we'll rob another train." Harmony saw the confusion on Thor's face, and sighed. "I've told you all this before and it's still true. We no longer trust anybody to help. We take care of ourselves and as soon as this robbery is done, we'll be on our way. We'll let you go then because you won't know where to find us."

"But if you tell anybody about us, we'll be back to gut you once we're done with Turnbull." Star picked up a piece of burning wood and held it high. "This is our torch and we'll keep it burning till we've seen justice done."

Thor shook his head. "All right. What the hell do I care what happens to a bunch of outlaws. I'll hold the horses, then I'll go my own way. But when the Wild Child Gang gets caught, don't send any telegrams asking for my help because I'll remember how you don't need it." He glared at them, then got up and walked away.

He stopped by the horses, wondering how the hell he'd been so lucky to get involved in this mess. His shoulder ached, his temper was bad, and he had nothing to do. The girls would make all the plans for the robbery. They sure as hell wouldn't ask his advice. And why should they? They'd been doing damn good on their own. In a short time, they'd made full grown men perfectly useless. Except for one thing.

Glancing back over his shoulder, he focused on

Harmony. He could do something for her all right, something she'd never forget. But how did he get her away from the girls? He wished they'd never come back. If he'd kept her in the rocks a few more nights, she'd have been his for as long as he wanted her. Now he'd have to fight seven revenge-crazed children to get near her. And she wasn't even a mother!

Cursing under his breath, he examined one horse after another, thinking he'd find something to do, something they'd overlooked, but the horses were as well taken care of as the girls themselves. Hell, when they said they didn't need him, they meant it. But why should he care? In a few days he'd go on to Tucson and nobody'd be the wiser. The girls didn't have to worry about him revealing their identities. Fact of the matter was, he'd pay *them* to keep quiet.

When he felt a hand lightly touch his arm, he wheeled around.

Harmony smiled at him, shaking her head. "They're something, aren't they? I'm proud of them. They've been through so much, but they're not defeated."

"I admire their courage, but they need a home, a place where they can go to school. They need to be secure."

She dropped her hand. "Why do you think we're trying so hard to get enough money to buy a place of our own? We haven't been able to yet. And now here's Turnbull." She glared at Thor.

"Don't you see, we have to stay alive before we can even think of doing anything normal."

"I see that, but—"

"Your talking about dolls and pretty clothes and school and families hurts them. Don't you understand that? Most of them had maybe *one* doll in their lives and *one* change of clothes. And they lost that when we had to flee."

"All right. I'm sorry. I didn't realize."

"Of course not. You're a spoiled rich man. You're used to getting anything you want. Well, we aren't. We're used to using our wits to survive. That comes first. Nothing else."

He grasped her shoulder, letting his fingers bite into the flesh. "I'm not insensitive. I told you I'd help. But I've had enough of you accusing me of crimes I've never committed."

Jerking away from him, she stepped back. "I think you should lie down and rest your shoulder today. Sleep will do you good."

He started to protest, but she held up her hand to stop his words.

"We're going to hit the train tomorrow. We'll be up at dawn and I want everybody resting today." She gazed back up the canyon. "If all goes well, we'll be out of here in two days, heading toward California. And you can go back to your pampered life."

"I'm not pampered. I just completed college. I'll work like everybody else. My family works. That's the way it is." He wished he didn't feel a need

121

to keep explaining himself, but she had a way of getting under his skin and making him defensive.

"Your sisters and mother?" Her voice held scorn.

"Yes. My sister is a suffragist."

"How nice she has the time."

"Yes, it's nice. She's working hard so women can get the right to vote."

"I don't need to vote. I need a good job, a safe home, and food for these children."

"She's working for that, too. She and my mother are taking over the family shipping firm. They're employing women as typists."

Harmony's eyes lit up. "I always wanted to do that. It sounds so modern, so clean, so important." She glanced away. "But it requires training and that takes money I don't have. Besides, if I step out of my rabbit hole Turnbull will be down on me so fast it won't be funny."

"Harmony, I'll help." He didn't know why he didn't give up, but something in him couldn't. He put his hands on her shoulders and turned her so she had to look into his face. "Damn it, let me help. You can become a typist. The girls can have a good place to live. Why do you have to be so stubborn?"

She shrugged his hands away. "I'm not stubborn. I'm smart. If you'd been through what we have and if your life was in as much danger as ours, you wouldn't trust a stranger, either."

He started to say more, then stopped. "Have it your own way then."

"Thanks, that's so good of you." She turned away, feeling her heart beating fast. Why couldn't she even be civil to this man? Maybe he really could help. But maybe he would lead them into a trap. No, for the girls' sake, she couldn't trust him or what he made her feel.

"Harmony?"

Glancing back, she stopped.

"When you come to your senses, I'll still be here."

She almost smiled. "You're more stubborn than I am."

Eight

Late the next afternoon, Thor sat on his horse by the juniper tree leading down into the desert. The Wild Child Gang surrounded him. He'd left his tie, vest, and coat back in the hideout. He wished he had a hat to help conceal his face, but they had no extras and one that would fit the girls would be too small for him anyway.

He glanced up at the sky. It was another beautiful, clear day. Never could he have imagined himself riding off to become an outlaw. But he could never have imagined a woman like Harmony or children like the girls, either. In a short space of time his life had changed drastically.

"Thor." Harmony held out her hand to him, fingers closed around something clasped in her palm. "We want you to have this back."

He held out his hand, palm open and up. She laid his gold watch in his hand. Their fingers touched and heat leaped between them. She quickly pulled her hand away as his fingers closed over the warm gold of his pocket watch. He was

124

touched by the gesture. "Thanks. My father gave it to me and I hated to lose it."

"I guess you're one of us now, at least till the robbery is over." Harmony glanced into the distance. "We'd better get moving."

He checked the time, noticed the watch had been wound, then tucked it into his pocket. Without a vest there was no way to wear it normally, but he didn't need to do that now anyway. He was simply glad to have it back.

Returning the watch to him showed the distance they had covered since the girls had first kidnapped him. He knew how much the Wild Child Gang needed the money the watch could bring, but they also knew how much it meant to him. They weren't nearly as heartless as they pretended to be and he was glad to have proof of that fact.

He looked around at the faces of the girls. "I'm ready as I'll ever be."

Harmony led the way into the desert. Thor rode beside her. And the girls followed close behind. They headed toward the Rio Grande, then rode along its bank back toward Las Cruces.

He didn't know his way around the area, but Harmony seemed to know exactly where she was going. He supposed she'd scouted around before he ever met her. Any smart outlaw would have. And that's exactly what she was even if he didn't always accept it as fact.

As they rode, he noticed Harmony kept a close watch toward Las Cruces and the girls stayed alert, too. They kept impressing him, but it was because he kept forgetting they were professionals. They did their job and did it well. He should never forget the fact. That's how they'd taken him hostage in the first place. They were changing his opinion of women, and fast.

After they'd ridden close to an hour, Harmony led the way across a narrow gorge, then up a slight rise into the shadow of a group of windswept juniper trees growing around large boulders.

She stopped, dismounted, dropped her reins, then hurried to the edge of the trees. Glancing around, she motioned for them to join her. He followed her example, then knelt beside her on the warm desert sand. She pointed. Before them lay the snaking tracks of a railroad. Not too far, not too close. It wasn't the same place as before, but the locale was similar. And a good choice.

"Now comes the hard part." She pulled on her black leather gloves, touched the black silk scarf that hung below her chin to make sure it was still there, then glanced up at the girls. "Let's get the timber in place as quickly as possible."

"What's going on?" Thor wanted to help them no matter what.

"In order to get the train to stop as it's leaving Las Cruces, we must put something on the rails. We've always used fallen limbs and small trees before, letting the horses drag them into place." Harmony glanced back toward Las Cruces.

"Why don't you do something different this time?"

"How? Why?"

"I'm along." Thor flexed his shoulders, felt the pull of the wound but ignored it. "Let me earn my keep. I can carry some of these boulders down and wedge them into place. I can guarantee a train will stop for them or be stopped."

Harmony glanced at the width of his shoulders, the size of his arms, even his hands. "Go ahead. It's a good idea. But we'll bring down some timber, too. Remember, there's no time to lose."

"Okay."

He picked up a rock nearby and felt a surge of pride when he noticed their shocked stares. Finally he'd impressed them. There were a lot of uses for strength they'd never considered and he was glad to show it to them. He lugged the rock into place, set it down, then returned for another.

He noticed the girls worked well together, leading down two horses to get tree branches into place. They all worked quickly and quietly. By the time he'd rolled the fifth rock into place, he was sweating and sore. His shoulder ached. If he wasn't mistaken he'd torn open the wound and it'd started to bleed again. But he wasn't about to tell anybody.

Harmony dusted her hands together, looked down the length of the tracks toward Las Cruces, then turned to him. "We're set. This looks good. Thanks for the help. If they won't stop for this, they won't stop for anything."

Thor followed her gaze. "I thought I heard—"

"Train!" Harmony clutched his arm. "They're early."

Pure animal instinct took over as he jerked her to him. "I'm not letting you into this kind of danger."

"Let me go!"

"No, Harmony. I'll do it. Let me put my life on the line." He didn't know when he'd felt such a surge of energy rush through him. He felt powerful enough to do anything. And he couldn't for the life of him let a woman and children endanger themselves.

She pushed against his chest. "Get back with the horses. They'll see us and all will be lost."

"Harmony, come on!" Blaze motioned for them to follow as she and the other girls led the horses toward the safety of the junipers.

"Thor, be reasonable. We know what we're doing. You don't." She struggled against his strong hold on her.

"What if something happened to you? What if you're shot? I won't be there to—"

"Stop! Let me go this instant. You're going to get us shot right here in the middle of the tracks."

He glanced back over his shoulder. He couldn't see the train, but its vibration shook the ground and its sound grew loud.

"They'll see us and shoot us!"

"All right. We've got to move." He picked her up, amazed she felt so light, then ran toward the trees. She struggled against him, but he held on tight, savoring the warmth of her body, the curves that fit against him so well. When they reached safety, he set her down.

128

She started to hit him. "You big oaf!"

He grabbed her hands and held them still, watching her struggle but unable to compete with his superior strength. Yes, there were a lot of good ways to use a man's muscle. "I told you not to hit me again."

Furious, she glanced at the girls. "He's gone wild. Don't listen to him or pay him any attention. Get your masks up, check your guns, make sure they're loaded. When the train stops, run out there and get on board as fast as you can. This time, don't linger. If somebody gives you too much trouble, go to the next one. And be careful."

"I'll rob the train." Thor kept his grip on Harmony. "I don't want you getting hurt."

Jasmine put her hands on her hips. "Listen here, mister. We work as a group. We make decisions as a group. And no big man is going to come along and think he can order us around."

"That's right." Blaze put her arm around Jasmine. "You agreed to help hold the horses."

"You can't go back on your word now." Star glared at him.

Thor shook his head. What the hell was he going to do? He couldn't let them go into danger. Yet he had given his word, hadn't he? Glancing up, he saw the train. It started to slow down. Whatever he decided, it had to be done now.

"You're bleeding, Thor." Harmony pulled against his hold. "If you go with us, you'll make it all the more dangerous for us. Besides, one man can't rob the train on his own."

He finally let her hands loose, then looked at each girl's face in turn. He couldn't stop them, not all of them at once. "You can walk away from this. Right now. I promise to get you help."

Faith, Hope, and Charity pulled up their masks, and the other girls followed.

Thor felt his gut churn. "Listen to reason!" He wanted desperately to stop them, but he didn't know how. And they were right. He couldn't rob the train on his own.

"Star stays with you." Harmony nodded to the smallest of the group. "Shoot him if tries to stop us."

Star pulled out her pistol and aimed it at him.

"I can't believe this. You're children, girls! I could break any one of you in half with my bare hands." He had never felt so frustrated and yet at the same time so worried about those who were trying to control him.

"That's why we all wear an equalizer." Harmony turned her back on him. "All right, girls. Remember the fire. Remember Turnbull. Remember the Wild Child Gang."

Thor watched them run out of the trees and toward the train as it slowly pulled to a stop. Picking a car, Faith, Hope, and Charity boarded together, Jasmine and Blaze took the next car, and finally Harmony and Tara disappeared into the last one. He clenched his fists. Everything was too quiet. The tension was almost thick enough to cut. He glanced down at Star. Her jaw was set.

"They *never* get hurt or caught." She holstered

her pistol, then glanced at the train. "I don't figure you can do any harm now."

"I wanted to help."

"We help ourselves."

As they silently watched, Thor resisted the urge
to check his watch. Minutes seemed to stretch into
hours. He felt desperate to take Star's gun and run
down there and help, but he knew at this point
it'd only confuse matters and maybe get them all
caught or killed. He couldn't afford to throw off
their concentration.

He wanted to pace, but he didn't dare make a
sound or movement. Instead he clenched his fists,
glanced down at Star, then back at the train.

"Has it been too long?" He could hardly get
the words out past the tension locking his throat.

"I don't know." She hesitated, touched the butt
of her pistol, then looked at him. "Maybe."

"Hell and damnation."

"Quiet. They'll be running out soon. We must
hold the horses still till they're all in the saddle,
then we follow them out, watching their backs.
Understood?" She turned hard dark eyes on him.

"Yes." He rubbed his damp palms against his
trousers, watching the train. Why the hell was he
taking orders from a child?

"Soon now."

Faith, Hope, and Charity jumped down from one
of the cars, then ran toward the trees. Relief
flooded him, but none of these girls was Harmony.
He watched and waited. Blaze and Jasmine jumped
from the next car and followed the others. He was

surprised how fast they moved. A grown man would have a hard time catching them and he would have slowed them down. He was impressed despite himself.

It was going to be okay. He'd worried for nothing. He glanced at the horses, checking to make sure all was in order. They'd be riding out of here fast and soon. Suddenly he heard a shot, followed by several more.

Harmony! Energy pulsed through him. The time for waiting was over. He grabbed Star's pistol, took several steps forward, then glanced back. "Get the girls out of here fast. Go back to the hideout. I'll deal with whatever's happened on the train."

"Wait!" She took off her mask and tied it around his head, making sure the lower half of his face was covered, then put her small hat on his head, tied it under his chin, and turned down the brim.

"Thanks." If he looked like a fool, he didn't care. He had no more time to lose. He ran from the trees and came upon the girls. As they passed, he hollered to them. "Keep going. I'll take care of it." Much to his relief, they kept moving toward safety.

He ran as hard and fast as he could, then grabbed the railing on the car that still contained Harmony and Tara. He swung up onto the porch. Pistol in hand, he crouched, then slowly opened the door. Shots rang out, flying into the wall of the coach and over his head. He didn't respond.

He didn't want to call attention to himself if he hadn't been seen.

Glancing around, he saw frightened passengers hunkered down in their seats. Worst of all, Harmony and Tara were trapped behind a seat, with Harmony returning fire at somebody in the front. How had this happened? What was he going to do? And who the hell was shooting at them?

Then he noticed the blood or Tara's shirt and the way she slumped against Harmony. One of the girls was hurt! His blood pounded in his ears with rage. Some idiot had shot a child, *his* child. There'd be hell to pay now. He felt like kicking himself all over the West. He should never have trusted them to pull this off alone, not with so many people alerted to them. But he'd think about that later. For now he had to rescue them. And quick.

He focused on the front of the car, trying to see who was doing the shooting, but they were concealed behind a seat. He'd fix that, but first he had to let Harmony know she had help. And give himself away at the same time. Fortunately she wasn't too far away.

He pitched his voice just for her. "Wild Child, get out! I'll cover you." His words drew everybody's attention. And revealed his opponents. One raised his head to fire several shots at Thor. And he recognized the man. One of Turnbull's hired guns. That explained a lot. He'd never forget that face. Or the one that turned around to gaze at him in wonder and relief . . . Harmony.

She nodded, then put an arm around Tara. She holstered her pistol, knowing she'd need all her strength and concentration to get Tara out of the train and to safety. But Thor had only six bullets, or less. He'd have to make every one of them count. She gave him a quick nod, grateful he'd ignored her warnings.

As Thor fired at the front of the car over the heads of the passengers, she helped Tara to her feet and hurried toward him. She heard the return fire before she felt the bullet hit her. She took the blow, felt the sting of pain, but kept going. Nothing could stop her now.

When she reached Thor, she realized she'd never been so glad to see anybody in her life. Now if they could only escape alive. She pulled Tara with her, past Thor, and out the door. She collapsed to the floor, but knew she couldn't give into the weakness that had overcome her.

She jerked Tara's unfired pistol out of her holster and handed it to Thor. As he fired into the train, she ignored the pain in her arm and helped Tara down the steps to the ground. She didn't know how they'd make it to the trees, but as she looked up she saw Star galloping toward them leading three horses. If she'd been glad to see Thor, she was even happier to see Star.

Thor didn't know how the hell they were going to get out of the situation alive. He'd be out of bullets in no time, but maybe Harmony and Star could make it to safety. He'd give them the chance anyway. He'd hold down Turnbull's men as long as he had ammunition.

He glanced to the side, hoping to see Harmony and Tara on their way to the trees. Instead he saw Star riding toward them. These girls were braver than any bunch of combat soldiers. He'd never been so proud or so terrified they'd be shot. Yet Star was going to save their lives, even his own tough hide. He fired several more bullets into the front of the train, wishing he could put a slug into Turnbull, tucked the pistols in his trousers, then slammed the door shut.

He jumped to the ground, took Tara from Harmony's arms, set her in the saddle of one horse, then lifted Harmony into the saddle of her own mount. As he swung onto the back of his horse, the girls were off and riding fast for the junipers. He dug heels into his horse's flanks, then leaned low over his mount's neck. As he rode hard after them, he heard more shots ring out.

Looking back, he saw Turnbull and his two gunmen standing on the porch. Damn! Not thinking he had a chance in hell on a moving horse, he jerked out a pistol, aimed behind himself and pulled the trigger. The three men dropped to their knees. The sight gave him a great sense of satisfaction even if he hadn't hit them. Moments later he reached the safety of the trees, then raced after the Wild Child Gang.

He caught up with Harmony, Tara, and Star as they rode fast across the desert. He glanced behind. Nobody followed and if there weren't any horses on the train they'd probably be able to make it safely to the hideout. But what if Turnbull and his men were traveling with horses in one of the cars? That thought made him put heels to his horse. The desert was no place to be caught in the open.

Ahead he could see the other girls riding hard and fast toward the Rio Grande. He wished the hideout was closer. His shoulder was hurting and bleeding, but he knew he could continue. Glancing at Harmony, he noticed blood spreading over her shirtsleeve. Damn! She'd been hit, but not badly from the looks of it. Then he focused on Tara. She clung to the saddle horn, the reins loose in her hands, her head bowed. She was losing a lot of blood and fast. Fear for her life and fury that she'd been shot gave him renewed energy.

Riding close to Tara, he leaned over and plucked her from the saddle, pulling her into his lap and cradling her to his chest. Star noticed his action and turned her horse so she could take the reins and lead Tara's horse. Harmony turned haunted eyes on him and nodded.

Tara's weight and size surprised him. The girls were all so big in spirit he usually thought of them as big in body. She was frail in his arms and he could feel the warm wetness of her blood soak through his shirt to his skin. But the wound didn't have to be bad. It could be in the side or shoulder or hip. She was young and healthy. A gunshot wound didn't necessarily mean death.

But his heart beat fast in his chest and he felt

guilty. He should never have let the children go into danger. He didn't care how many times they had done it before and come out alive, there was still the chance that a robbery would go bad. Now it had. How could Harmony have led them into so much danger? He cast an angry glance in her direction.

She'd gotten them all into this mess, and now she was wounded, too. Still he couldn't accept her actions or even her reasons. He knew the circumstances, knew Turnbull was on their trail, knew the girls had to escape, but he couldn't stop the anger or the guilt or the horror from riding himself as hard as he rode the horse. He *should* have stopped them.

Jerking down the black mask so he could breathe better, he noticed the others had already done the same. Experience. He cursed. What the hell were they all thinking of, riding about playing outlaws? He didn't know when he'd done anything so stupid. But if he hadn't been along, what would have happened to Harmony and Tara? He refused to think about it. What was done was done.

When they reached the Rio Grande, they turned north and followed it. The other girls were still safely ahead. They should make it to the hideout even if their smaller group didn't get that far. He didn't know how much longer the horses could keep up the pace and he feared the sheriff in Las Cruces might have been notified by telegraph. But there was nothing he could do but keep on riding.

He watched Harmony turn her horse into the

137

river. He followed, slowing his mount to a walk, careful of the dangerous bottom. If they could once more lose their trail, they'd be hopefully safe. But they had to hurry. Tara had grown more still, not moving at all. How much blood could she lose and live? Yet they couldn't stop to bind the wound. Hopefully it had stopped bleeding on its own by now.

He glanced down at her too still, too white face and felt a powerful emotion grip him. How could any human hurt an innocent child like this? How could any man overwork her or starve her or hunt her down to kill her because she carried knowledge?

Cursing as they moved up the Rio Grande, he pulled her tightly against his chest. "It'll be okay, Tara. I'll never let anybody hurt you again."

Nine

Harmony didn't cry. She wouldn't let herself cry. She hadn't since the fire and she wouldn't now. She glanced behind her. Thor still carried Tara in his strong arms. She was glad of that, knowing the child couldn't have ridden alone. Would Tara live? She didn't even want to consider that question, but it nagged at her.

Finally she turned her horse, leaving the waters of the Rio Grande behind. As she rode west, picking up the pace again, she glanced to the south. As far as she could tell, no one followed. She looked toward the foothills. The other girls were now disappearing into its safety. She felt a deep sense of relief. At least some of them would make it. And if their luck held, they would be there shortly, too.

But nothing could ease the pain in her heart for Tara. What had gone wrong? After all this time, how could it have happened? Yet she knew only too well. *Turnbull.* The moment she'd seen his face on the train she'd known they were in trouble. But why had he been on that train, in that car? Why hadn't he stayed in Las Cruces where he'd last seen her?

She could only suppose he'd put two and two together and come up with the Wild Child Gang. In fact, news of them may have been what had brought him so far West. Perhaps that's why he was on the train, hoping to catch them. And he had.

The moment she'd seen him, she'd tried to get Tara out, but his gunmen were too fast. As they'd run for the door, a bullet had hit Tara. When Tara had staggered, she'd pulled her safely behind a seat, protecting both of them. But it had been a trap. They'd been pinned down by Turnbull's men and unable to run for the door.

She hated to admit it still, but Thor had been a welcome sight. He'd proved his loyalty. He'd put his life on the line to save them. But why? Turnbull would hunt him down, too, if he got a chance. Why would this stranger whom they'd taken hostage help them? The thought ran over and over in her mind as she rode closer to the foothills.

But that question couldn't block out her worry for Tara. Until now the robberies had been like a game. They'd been so successful, so sure of themselves that perhaps they'd become cocky. No. They'd done what they had to do to survive, but being the Wild Child Gang had not seemed real. Sometimes they'd turn to each other, laughing, and point out the fact that *they* were the notorious outlaw gang.

Now Turnbull had changed that. He'd turned it bad and dangerous just like he had the sweatshop in Chicago. With Tara wounded, it was all too real. And she'd been hit, too. Fortunately, the wound hadn't stopped her. It felt painful, but she knew it wasn't too bad. Yet it could have been much worse. Then what would the girls have done?

Had she been careless of all their lives? She shivered, and glanced back. Thor, Tara, and Star kept coming and no clouds of dust revealed followers. Yet nothing could ease her worry about Tara and their decision to rob trains. Had she been wrong? The girls had wanted to do it. There hadn't seemed another way to survive. But now?

She forced it all from her mind. She had to concentrate on gaining the safety of the hideout, then make sure Tara was all right. Later she could think about the consequences of their actions. She would deal with the guilt then.

When they were close to the foothills, she slowed her horse. If she pushed the animal any farther, she'd be without a horse and so would the others. Besides, they were near enough now to be safe. She hoped.

Star rode up beside her. "I'm going on in and make sure they've got water boiling for Tara. And you." She reached out and gently touched Harmony's bloodied shirtsleeve. "Are you okay?"

"Yes. I'm fine. It's just a graze. Go on. We'll bring Tara."

Star nodded, glanced back at her friend, then up at Thor, cocking her head to one side.

"I've still got your hat, don't I?" He jerked the strings to untie it, then pulled it from his head and handed it to her. "Thanks. I'll get you a new one. I must've stretched yours all out of shape."

"Just take care of Tara." Pulling Tara's horse behind her, Star disappeared into the foothills.

Harmony looked at Thor as he rode up beside her.

He frowned. "How the hell could you take children into a situation like that?"

"Don't!" She focused on Tara. "How is she?"

"As if you care."

"I don't want to hear it! I feel bad enough as it is. Let's just get to the hideout." She glanced behind her. Shock swept through her. "Thor, quick! Get into the hills. I see the dust of riders."

He didn't pause to look back until he had dug his heels into his tired mount, sending it forward. As they rounded the juniper, he looked back and saw the dust cloud moving fast beside the Rio Grande. Cursing, he kept on going to make sure they were completely out of sight.

Harmony followed him, then stopped in the shelter of the juniper. "Get Tara to safety. I'll guard the entrance." She dismounted, then pulled a rifle from its saddle holster.

"Hell if you will."

"Thor, they may have seen us."

"I don't think so. We were in the shadow of the foothills."

"We can't take a chance."

142

"Get on your horse and come get Tara. You take her in and see to her. I'll guard here."

She hesitated, but only a moment. "You're sure?"

"Who's the better nurse and who's the better shot?"

Setting the rifle against the juniper, she mounted her horse, then rode to his side. He set Tara gently in her arms, then handed her the reins to his horse.

"Take them all. If it goes bad, a horse won't help me a damn sight."

She nodded, hoping against hope they hadn't been seen, then tied the reins of his horse to her saddle horn. Starting into the hills, she glanced back. Thor had already picked up the rifle and climbed to a spot in the rocks to give him a good lookout point. For the third time that day she was glad of his presence.

As she rode toward the canyon, she glanced down at Tara who murmured and moved her head. Taking heart, Harmony stroked the girl's hair and whispered comforting words. But inside she felt more like crying than ever. How had it all come to this? *Turnbull.* She had to stop him. And soon.

The distance from the juniper tree to the entrance of the box canyon seemed to take forever, but she finally reached it. Star came running up to her and took the reins of Tara's horse and led it away. As she rode down to the campfire, she noticed Jasmine and Blaze busy around the fire. Faith, Hope, and Charity tended the horses.

143

She smiled tiredly. She couldn't have asked for better friends. They knew what had to be done and did it. And she felt grateful. When she drew near, Star hurried over and took the reins from her. Jasmine left the fire and held out her arms to take Tara. Harmony dismounted quickly, then helped Jasmine carry Tara to the fire. They laid her down on her blanket, then covered her with another. She moaned and tossed her head.

"Tara. You're safe." Harmony knelt over her and stroked back her wild red hair. "We're back at the hideout and we're going to take care of your wound. Don't worry. You're safe."

"Smoke. Hurry. Did they get the door open? Mother!" Tara tossed her head back and forth, struggling against the blankets.

"Tara, there's no fire. You're safe. We're here with you. Don't worry now." Harmony stroked Tara's face, then glanced up as the girls grouped closely around them.

Faith, Hope, and Charity knelt beside Tara. "Is she going to be all right?"

"I hope so." Harmony shook her head to steady her mind. "I want all of you to go on as usual. I'll take care of Tara. Later we should eat. We've got to keep up our strength and get out of here as soon as possible."

When the girls didn't move, Harmony glanced at Blaze, realizing she had to get them past their fear and worry so they could help themselves. "Will you help me?"

"Yes. But where's the hostage?"

"He's guarding the entrance." Harmony almost told them about the cloud of dust, but stopped herself. They had enough to worry about without that.

"We'd better check on him later." Star reached out to stroke Tara's hand.

"Girls, you did fine today. We got out alive." Harmony pulled down the blanket that covered Tara. Blood soaked the left side of the girl's chest.

"And we made a little money." Jasmine pointed toward a saddlebag.

"If only Tara is okay." Faith put her arms around her sisters.

"I won't let anything else happen to her. I promise." Harmony took a deep breath, then glanced at the girls. "We wouldn't have had this problem except Turnbull and his two gunmen were on the train. One of them shot Tara."

"No!" Star's voice blended with the gasps of shock and horror that came from all the girls.

"How did he know?" Charity turned to her sisters.

"I don't know." Harmony unbuttoned Tara's shirt. "But we got away and we'll keep getting away. Now, let's take care of ourselves and the horses."

"Water's boiling and I've got our medical supplies right here." Blaze pulled a saddlebag forward.

"Good." Harmony looked at the bloody area of Tara's cotton chemise, but she couldn't tell how badly the girl had been hurt. "Please get me a wet cloth."

Blaze handed her one, but remained silent.

Harmony washed away the blood, holding her breath, then gave a sigh of relief. Tara had been hit from behind in the side, in the fleshy part under her arm. As far as she could tell the bullet had gone cleanly in one side and out the other. The bleeding had slowed. She wouldn't have to dig for a bullet. It should heal all right if Tara didn't get an infection.

Harmony looked up and smiled, feeling tears sting her eyes in happiness and relief. The girls hugged her as they clustered closer to Tara.

"She'll be fine. It's a clean wound in her side." Harmony wiped away the tears, realizing that to cry in happiness washed away the pain.

"Tara's lucky." Blaze handed Harmony another clean cloth.

"How long will it take her to heal?" Jasmine put a hand on Harmony's shoulder.

"I don't know, but she'll need peace and quiet and rest."

"And a real doctor?" Star leaned over Tara to get a better look at the wound.

"That would be good, but where can we go?" Harmony glanced around the group. "And I'm not sure how soon we can move her."

"We can kidnap one." Star put her hands on her hips. "We can bring him here."

Harmony shook her head. "It's too dangerous. Please, no more hostages." She looked sternly at the group. "She'll be all right. Let me do what I

146

can, then we'll rest and talk about what we're going to do later."

"What if Tara gets a fever?" Faith frowned. "People can die of that."

"I know." Harmony turned back to Tara. "We'll take care of her no matter what we have to do. Okay? Right now the best thing we can do is take care of ourselves so we can take care of her."

The girls nodded, then reluctantly moved away to finish their tasks.

Harmony cleaned the wound as best she could, disinfected it with a powder, then wrapped it in bandages. When she could do no more, she closed the shirt and covered Tara's chest with the blanket.

Blaze patted her hand. "Now you do what you told us. Clean up. And we'll eat."

Smiling, she clutched Blaze's small hand with hers. "You're right. Thanks for reminding me." She pulled the child close and hugged her.

Not long after, they sat down together. Sunlight faded as the day gave way to night. Harmony wasn't hungry, but she accepted the bowl of stew, her mind torn between Tara and Thor. She hadn't heard any gunshots yet so she assumed the riders hadn't seen them or hadn't gotten close enough yet. She wanted to go and check, but she wanted to settle the girls first.

She forced herself to eat, not tasting what she put in her mouth. The girls ate, but kept glancing at their wounded friend. Tara slept peacefully now, but Harmony dreaded the idea of her getting sick with fever. They could use a doctor. They'd never had the price of one in Chicago. And once on the run, they'd never been able to trust one. Could they now? She didn't think so. But if Tara developed a fever, she'd brave whatever it took to get her help.

As soon as she'd finished her stew, she set the bowl aside and ladled more into a clean bowl. "I'm going to take this to Thor and see how he's doing." She picked up a canteen of water.

"You ought to let us dress your wound." Blaze looked at her in concern.

"Thanks. I'll take care of it later." She stood up, balancing the bowl of stew. "If Tara wakes, see if she'll eat liquid from the stew."

"Don't worry. We'll watch her." Jasmine moved closer to Tara and stroked her forehead.

"I'll be back soon."

As Harmony walked rapidly away from them, she felt more tense than ever. She didn't want to confront Thor. She knew what he'd have to say about the robbery. She already felt guilty enough without him reminding her of what she should or shouldn't have done.

When she reached the mouth of the canyon, she glanced back. She was going to have to get help for the girls. She could *never* take them into that kind of danger again. And she was going to have to ask Thor for that help and she hated to put herself at the mercy of a man again. Yet she had to do what was best for the girls.

Her resolve grew as she walked down the trail, passing cactus, hearing rustling in the rocks. The night came alive in the desert after the heat of the day, but she was used to that after so many nights outdoors in the West. What she wasn't used to was a man like Thor.

No matter what, she wouldn't owe him. She wanted the girls free even if he gave them help. She had nothing to offer him, other than what they'd stolen and they'd need that to escape southern New Mexico. She had no jewelry save the gold locket with her mother's photograph inside. She couldn't bear to part with that and it wouldn't be worth enough for him anyway.

As she walked, she grew bolder, remembering that she was part of the Wild Child Gang. She wasn't a sweatshop worker anymore. She'd proved her worth as an outlaw woman. And something else. She'd been unable to forget the heat in Thor's eyes when he'd touched her. He wanted her. And men paid for that. She ought to know. She'd seen a number of her friends take a gentleman friend to help them survive. She'd never done it. Now she had to think of the girls. And, even if she didn't want to admit it, she didn't think letting him touch her would be so bad.

Just before she reached the juniper tree, she stopped. And listened. Before she could move, a hand clasped her arm. She gasped.

"They rode on by." Thor's voice sounded husky.

"I brought you stew." She thrust it at him as she stepped back from the heat of him.

"Thanks." He started eating hungrily.

"Do you think we're safe?"

149

"For now."

"Good." She let out a sigh of relief, then clenched her fists. She had a lot to say and she didn't want to say any of it. "Thanks for coming to our rescue back at the train. Thanks for helping the girls. And thanks for watching down here so I could get them safely settled."

"I wanted to do it. No thanks are needed. How is Tara?"

"The bullet went through her just under the arm. It's a clean wound. I've bandaged it. I think she'll be okay if she doesn't get a fever."

He nodded, quickly finished the stew, then set aside the bowl.

She handed him the canteen of water. "I need to talk with you."

He drank greedily, then wiped his mouth with the back of his hand and set the canteen beside the bowl. "Did that busted robbery finally knock some sense into your head?"

"Yes, if you must know the truth. And I suppose you have a right to gloat. But the fact of the matter is we'd never had a problem until today. And we've been desperate." She swallowed hard. "Turnbull made the difference."

"His two *gunmen* made the difference. I wonder why they were on that train? Was it a setup?"

"I don't know. I just want to get the girls far away." She took a deep breath. "You're not going to make this easy, are you?"

"You've given me a hard time of it. Why should

I let you off the hook? Tara's lying hurt back there. She could be dead. You could be, too."

"You were wounded in Las Cruces."

"I'm a man."

"So?" She took a deep breath to still her growing rage. She needed this man. She mustn't let him upset her.

"That makes a difference whether you want to believe it or not."

"Oh, I believe it." She put her hands on her hips. "I know exactly how men hurt women. And nobody stops them."

"If you're talking about that fire, then—"

"Yes! And everything else." She paced several steps, desperate to control her temper.

"Harmony." He held out a hand. "I don't know what we're talking about, but only one thing matters right now. You can't take those girls back into danger."

"I agree."

"You do?"

"Yes." She took a deep breath and turned back toward him. In the shadow of the rocks around them, his face was all planes and angles. She couldn't quite make out the expression in his blue eyes and she didn't want to, either.

"Then you'll let me help?" He moved toward her.

She held up a hand. She didn't want him to touch her. *Yet.* "I'm willing to make a bargain with you. The girls and I don't want to be beholden to you."

"But I—"

"Please, hear me out." If she didn't say it quick, she'd never have the nerve to say it. "You mentioned a place they could stay a while. You said you had friends there. I'd like to leave the girls there, but only till I've had a chance to catch Turnbull and—"

"Forget Turnbull!"

"No!" She stepped toward him, her eyes blazing. "I will leave the girls there for a while, but I have nothing to pay the fees and we won't take charity."

"There are no fees. It's a place for women and children without homes."

"It's *your* place, not mine." She swallowed hard. "I'm willing to exchange your use of my body for the children's room and board and schooling until I can—"

"You're willing to do what?" His voice carried loud in the night as he grabbed her shoulders and jerked her toward him.

She winced as pain shot through her. He was touching her wound, but she wouldn't let him know it hurt. "I said I was willing to trade my body for—"

He held her tight. "I heard that. You don't know what you're saying."

She panted slightly from the pain and his nearness. "I won't owe you, Thor. I want this to be a fair and square deal."

He pulled her against his chest, wrapping his arms around her as he shut his eyes to hold back

152

the anger. Why would she think he was the kind of man who'd demand payment, that kind of payment, to help children? He'd offered to help over and over. Now she insulted them both. But his thoughts were distracted by the scent of her hair, the warmth of her body, the feel of her curves pressing against him.

Feeling himself respond, as he always did to her, he set her away. "The Flora McCuskar Institute is being established with help from my family for people like you and the girls. They won't demand payment and neither will I."

"You don't want me?"

"Damn!" He turned away, then stepped from her to keep from taking her into his arms again. "I want you all right, but—"

"Then it's a deal." She held out her hand. "Thor, please. Leave me some honor."

He wheeled around. "That's what I'm trying to do. I don't want you to turn whore for me."

She dropped her hand. When he put it that way, it sounded so wrong. She started to walk away, but before she'd taken more than a few steps she was in his arms and he was kissing her face, covering her eyes, her nose, her lips with hot, hard kisses. She trembled with wild sensations, then lifted her hands to encircle his neck, drawing his head back down to hers so she could touch his lips with hers.

Groaning, he deepened the kiss, thrusting his tongue into her mouth, tasting her, teasing her, wanting desperately to bury his need deep inside her and never let her go. He stroked down her back, her curves tantalizing, seductive, till he reached her hips and drew her tightly against him.

As his body spoke of its own deep need, his mind argued with his initial reaction. Why the hell was he fighting her offer? A week ago he'd have accepted what a woman wanted to give him. Why was he suddenly trying to protect her from himself? It made no sense because no matter Harmony's offer she wanted him as much as he wanted her. He'd stake his life on that fact.

As their kisses grew more feverish, he became determined to understand her motive. Maybe her offer was a way of salvaging her pride, of becoming his lover without taking responsibility. If that was the case, then he should be glad to oblige. But he didn't want her this way. He wanted her free and willing, acknowledging her desire for him openly, honestly.

Yet perhaps it was simply a deal to her. A working woman like Harmony may have used her body repeatedly to get what she wanted. That thought made him see red. The idea of another man, or men, having gone before him made him hurt all over. He wanted to bust heads at the thought. This outlaw was *his* wild woman and he'd tame her like no man ever had and when he was done she wouldn't ever be able to remember another lover, much less want one.

He ended the kiss in a savage fury and thrust her from him. Pushing his hands into his pockets to keep from touching her, he frowned. "Okay. We'll do it your way."

She put a hand to her lips, touched the swollen, burning feeling there and wondered if she'd just made the most dangerous mistake of her life.

Now, she wondered, who wore the spurs?

Part Two
Pistol of Fire and Ice

Ten

Harmony rode into Tucson, Arizona Territory a day after Thor. She hoped. For safety's sake, they had agreed to travel separately. Faith, Hope, and Charity had gone with him, for all the world looking like his daughters. Star, Tara, Jasmine, and Blaze had traveled with her, starting out a day later to give Tara longer to heal and to put distance between their two groups.

But none of their plans meant she trusted him. They'd simply run out of choices. The girls hadn't wanted to go to this place called the Flora McCuskar Institute. Yet they were terribly worried about Tara and with Turnbull in the area none of them felt safe. They needed a safe hideout and without money to buy one, Thor's suggestion made the most sense. If he didn't betray them or try to use them in some way, maybe they would be all right. At least that was what they had all agreed upon.

Now Harmony wasn't so sure. She was tired, dirty, and worried. Tara was still weak and in pain. She badly needed rest and a place to finish healing. They all needed that. But they were putting their lives in the hands of strangers and she was putting her body into the hands of Thor Clarke-Jarmon. Away from him and in the light of one day after another, the idea that she could actually let him touch her seemed unreal. Yet she had been the one to offer herself. She had been the one to insist.

Now she feared her trade for freedom might end up being the very thing that tied her to him. She couldn't forget his warm blue eyes, the strength of his body, the determination to stand by her and the girls, and the way he had kissed her, molding her body to his long length. She shivered, hating to see him again and yet aching to be with him, too. Her emotions made no sense, but perhaps she was too tired and too worried to think clearly.

One thing she knew for sure. She *must* take the girls to the Flora McCuskar Institute because that is where Faith, Hope, and Charity awaited them. Or at least they had better be there or Thor would know fury like he'd never known it before. If she didn't like the institute or the people there or anything about it, she would take the girls and leave. Somewhere, someplace, they would find safety. And freedom.

As they rode, passing adobe structures with chickens scratching in the dirt around the houses, she kept a close watch for anyone who might be the law. But they saw few people. To the north a mountain rose high into the sky and she wondered if it might make a safe hideout.

She glanced at the girls. Tara slumped in the saddle. They couldn't stay on the run any longer. But what if Turnbull or the law awaited them at the institute? What if Thor had betrayed them? She felt a shiver of unease run through her. They were all so tired even their horses would have trouble making a fast getaway. Touching the pistol on her hip, she knew she'd use it if necessary.

As they rode into the dusty town, she noticed the train tracks. She'd heard Tucson was a railroad center. It didn't matter to her now except she didn't want anybody recognizing them as part of the Wild Child Gang. Turning down a side street, she moved away from the tracks and deeper into the town. Adobe buildings gave way to rough wood, then to colorful Victorian houses that looked out of place in the desert.

The Flora McCuskar Institute was located in one of the Victorian homes, but she wasn't going there yet. She glanced down at her black clothes, trousers, shirt, leather vest, and boots with spurs. She'd worn her usual outlaw clothes, as had the girls. They were practical. Now she realized how out of place they would be inside a fancy house. But she couldn't let it bother her.

She took a deep breath and kept riding. She turned down another street, leaving the Victorian houses behind. She pulled her horse to a stop and looked at the girls as they clustered around her.

"Do you think we should all go in at once?" Star glanced around uneasily.

"No." Harmony touched Tara's shoulder, relieved

when the girl attempted a smile. "I think I should take Tara to the house. The rest of you could wait here."

"There's a cafe over there." Jasmine pointed. "We can get something to drink and wait. What do you think?"

"I think that's smart." Harmony looked from one tired face to the other. "If we don't like the institute, you know we don't have to stay."

Blaze nodded. "And if they double-cross us, they'll wish they hadn't."

"I'll take Tara in now." Harmony hesitated. "But if I'm not back soon, you'll know there's trouble."

"Then what?" Star moved her horse closer.

"Tomorrow morning you head out for California."

"No!" Jasmine leaned closer. "If you're not back by sundown, we'll know we've got to get you out."

"We've got some money. We can hire somebody to help us." Blaze narrowed her eyes.

"One thing for sure, we won't abandon you." Jasmine crossed her arms over her chest. "We're the Wild Child Gang and we take care of each other."

"But girls, I want you safe." Harmony knew they'd always made group decisions before, but she didn't want them to do anything again that put them in danger. But was that possible with Turnbull after them?

"If one's safe, we're all safe. If one's in danger,

we're all in danger." Star patted Tara's hand, then glanced at Harmony.

Harmony sighed. She couldn't argue with them, not now. She had to get Tara help. And she had to check on Faith, Hope, and Charity. Besides, she didn't really expect any trouble. She was simply being cautious. "Okay. I'll be back as soon as I can. But if I'm not, don't come yourselves. Hire somebody." She looked at Tara. "Ready?"

Tara sat up straighter. "I'm okay. Don't worry about me. I can keep on going."

"It's not much farther now."

Harmony waved goodbye as she rode away with Tara at her side. She glanced back to see Star, Blaze, and Jasmine stop their horses in front of the small cafe. She hated to be separated from the girls. What if she didn't get back? What if Turnbull and the law were waiting for them? No. She wouldn't think those thoughts. They'd be safe.

She turned onto the street of Victorian houses and started looking for the Flora McCuskar Institute. She had a description of the house and its location. Tara rode close as they continued down the street. As the houses became smaller and farther apart, they kept riding until they came to one built at the edge of town.

Harmony tensed as they rode closer to the house. It was a painted lady. Bright turquoise trimmed the pale yellow wood of the three-story building, accented with lacy woodwork, a porch, a balcony, and a sign hanging from the roof over the porch. Carved in wood and painted in turquoise and yellow, the sign read, FLORA MCCUSKAR INSTITUTE.

"Do you think it's safe?" Tara moved toward Harmony.

"If it isn't, we'll know soon enough."

They started up the circle drive that curved in front of the house. Suddenly its front door banged open. Faith, Hope, and Charity raced down the steps to the drive, calling and waving their hands.

Relief rushed through Harmony, then amazement. She'd never seen the girls dressed as they were now. Each wore a pastel shade of yellow, blue, or green in a sprig patterned skirt and solid-colored blouse of the latest style. Their thick blond hair had been pulled back from their faces, then left to hang down their backs. They weren't recognizable as sweatshop girls in gray, patched dresses or outlaws clad in black.

If Thor had meant to disguise them, he couldn't have done better. But she couldn't keep from feeling guilty. She could never have done so much for them. How could she have ever thought she could take care of seven girls alone?

But she had. And they'd taken care of her. They were still alive and safe. Nothing else mattered. She pulled her horse to a stop, then jumped down and ran to them. They hugged each other, tears misting their eyes, then turned to Tara. She held out her arms to them. They ran to her and helped her down and enfolded her in hugs and kisses.

Hope finally stepped back, glanced around, then frowned. "Where are the others?"

"Is something wrong?" Faith clutched Harmony's hand.

"Turnbull?" Charity looked from one to the other in fear.

Harmony shook her head. "No. Everything's all right. We made it safely here. We didn't want to take any chances in case the law or Turnbull had found out you were here."

Faith nodded.

"Come inside." Hope tugged on Harmony's arm. "It's really nice."

"I've got to get the others." Harmony turned back toward her horse.

"Let us." Charity smiled. "Faith can take you inside and I'll take Hope to get the others."

Harmony put an arm around Tara to steady her. "They're at a little cafe not far from here and north on the next street over. It's called the Rainbow Kachina."

"I'll get them." A low, masculine voice interrupted them.

Turning around, Harmony felt her breath catch at the sight of Thor. "You didn't need to creep up on us." He looked good, dressed in black trousers with a white shirt open at the throat. She realized she'd missed him more than she'd thought possible. It made her defensive.

"You wouldn't have heard a stampeding herd of mustangs with all that noise."

She hated to admit it, but he was probably right. Worse, she hated to admit the sudden shortness of breath she felt in his presence. It had been only a week or so, but in that time he seemed to have grown taller, his eyes a deeper blue, his hair blonder, and his body more tempting.

Faith, Hope, and Charity turned to him. "We want to go."

Thor shook his head. "Best thing for you to do is show Harmony and Tara around."

Harmony felt as if she was losing control to Thor. "I'll go get them. I know where they are."

"You're tired."

"The girls expect me to get them and I'm going." She turned to Faith. "Why don't you take Tara on inside so she can get to bed."

Faith nodded. "Okay, but hurry back. We've got lots to show and tell you."

Harmony hugged her tightly, then turned back to her horse. As she mounted, she noticed Thor swing into the saddle of Tara's horse. "Don't you trust me to come back?"

"Leader of the Wild Child Gang. What do you think?"

She gave him a dark look, then turned her horse around, noticing he kept pace as they rode back down the street.

"You weren't taking any chances, were you?" Thor moved closer and put a hand over her gloved one clutching the saddle horn.

"Did you think I would?"

"I was as surprised as hell you trusted me to get Faith, Hope, and Charity here."

She pushed his hand away. "I had no choice."

"You're a hard woman, Harmony Harper."

"I'm a hunted woman, a wanted woman, and—"

"A wild woman."

"I'm driven by the past."

"I'd like to see you driven by something else."

She glanced at him and felt the heat of his blue eyes. "I suppose you expect me to stay in your room. For the girls' sake, I wish—"

"I'm staying at the Blue Coyote Hotel. You're staying with the girls."

"Thanks."

He covered her hand again. "I'm not going to embarrass you, Harmony. I was raised a gentleman. I may not always act like one, but where your children and my family are concerned you can trust me to do the right thing."

"It won't be for long."

"What? Me?" He tightened his grip.

She glanced into his eyes again. They burned with blue fire. "I mean I'll leave the girls at the institute only long enough for me to find a safe place for us and take care of Turnbull."

"I told you to forget Turnbull." His voice turned hard.

"And I told you I'd never rest easy till that man was brought to justice and our names cleared."

"Out here it doesn't matter. Nobody has a past. I promise the girls will never be hurt."

She wished she could trust and believe him, but she couldn't. "Let's talk about this later. Right now I only want to get the girls and make sure they're safe."

He squeezed her hand, then let it go. "Okay. We'll get you settled in first."

Turning her horse down another street, she scanned the area for the cafe. When she saw it up ahead with the girls' horses tied out front, she sighed in relief.

Thor smiled. "Afraid they'd be gone?"

"I take nothing for granted, not anymore."

As they rode up to the cafe, Star, Blaze, and Jasmine hurried outside, looking happy. They stopped abruptly when they saw Thor. For a moment they appeared glad to see him, then their expressions changed as if they obviously remembered he couldn't be trusted.

Harmony glanced at Thor. He looked disappointed they had greeted him so cautiously. For the first time she realized he might have come to care for the girls. But could it be possible?

"Come on back to the house." Thor smiled. "We've got some feather beds, new clothes, and ice cream waiting for you."

"Clothes?" Jasmine stepped closer, her dark eyes showing interest.

"Ice cream?" Blaze moved toward her horse. "I've never had any."

"And maybe a new doll or two." Thor watched them closely.

"Dolls?" Star put her hands on her hips and glared at him. "Do you think we have time for *dolls?*"

Thor glanced around in confusion. "I . . . well, I saw them and I . . . well, they looked lonely."

He shrugged. "I thought I knew just the girls to give them a happy home, but maybe not."

Star mounted her horse. "We wouldn't want them to go to a bad family."

"That's right." Blaze moved close to Thor. "We'll keep the dolls."

He grinned. "I'm sure they'll be grateful."

As the other girls mounted, Harmony smiled at Thor. She couldn't imagine why he was being so thoughtful, but she was glad. Dolls and ice cream. She stopped smiling. When they left, would the girls be hurt to leave it all behind? Was it better to have had luxury once than never to have had it at all? She didn't know. But she did know that having known her mother's love had helped her through the lonely years.

As they rode back toward the Victorian houses, she felt chilled as another thought struck her. What if this was all part of the bargain, her body for the girls safety and happiness? She didn't want to believe it, but what other reason could Thor possibly have? She'd never known a man to help women and children. Why would this one unless he had a good reason.

She felt her heart grow heavy. She mustn't let her emotions cloud her reason. She had a job to do and she would do it just as she always had before. Thor was part of that job now and she would try to please him until she could go safely on her own way. She didn't know why she wanted their relationship to be free from outside forces.

Life didn't work that way and she knew it. She had to pay for everything she got.

When they came to the circle drive leading to the front door of the institute, she took a deep breath. She wouldn't let herself be intimidated by the rich people who ran it or by Thor's passionate interest in her. She glanced at the girls. But most of all she mustn't let herself feel she was losing the Wild Child Gang to those who could care for them better.

Despite the hard words to herself, all of those feelings grew as they rode closer to the door leading into a new life. She held back her horse. She didn't want to go on, didn't want to fit into a new world, didn't want to deal with different people. She wanted to go back to her old world, despite its danger. Turnbull! He'd thrown her out into the cold again and she hated him more than ever.

Stopping at the front of the house, she took a good look at the Victorian building. A few steps led up to a single front door set to the left of center. A cut glass design framed the door and was set in the door light above. On the right was a partially enclosed porch. The left side of the house was set at an angle so the window on each floor partially faced the street. Three small windows gleamed from the third story set under a steep roof.

She thought it looked very much like something she might have seen in a better part of Chicago. But it was not the type of house she had ever set foot in before.

170

"Harmony?"

She glanced down to see Thor standing beside her horse, a hand outstretched to help her down. The girls had dismounted and were staring up at her. As she looked around, the front door opened. Faith, Hope, and Charity stepped out, then bounded down the steps toward her. Following them, two women walked onto the porch and waited. They were beautiful, with tall, slim bodies and blond hair. They were clothed expensively and elegantly in linen dresses. Their contrast to her couldn't have been greater.

Harmony glanced down at herself, then back at Thor. She would *not* be intimidated. She let him help her from her mount, his hands spanning her waist as he lowered her to the ground. He stepped back, offered her his arm, and smiled. She tried to look pleasant, but her face felt frozen.

She noticed two Mexican or Indian men come from around the side of the house to take the horses and lead them away. She wasn't used to anyone doing for her. Again she took a deep breath, then put her hand on Thor's arm. Maybe her early training as a lady would finally be useful.

They walked up the steps, the girls clustered around them, and stopped in front of the two women.

"I'd like you to meet my mother, Alexandra Clarke-Jarmon, and my sister, Deidre Clarke-Jarmon. This is Harmony Harper." He glanced to the side. "And Star, Blaze, and Jasmine."

Blaze stepped forward, her hands on her hips. "You can't take our guns."

"That's right." Star moved close to her friend, frowning at the two elegant ladies.

Alexandra smiled. "I wouldn't think of it. I've lived on a ranch long enough to know how important a pistol or rifle can be. But perhaps you'll allow us to place them with the other weapons while you're inside."

"You've lived on a ranch?" Jasmine moved closer. "You don't look like it."

Deidre laughed. "These are our town clothes. Thor'll tell you we don't always dress this way."

"We're going to have a ranch some day." Star looked toward Harmony. "It's a good place to grow up."

"You're right about that." Deidre turned a moss green gaze on Harmony. "You're a little bit of a thing, aren't you?"

Harmony raised her chin, but knew it was useless to try and appear any bigger with this tall family. "Lately, it's served me well."

"Really?" Deidre looked interested.

Relieved Thor hadn't told them the truth, she cast about for some explanation for their appearance. "We've been traveling a long way."

"I'm so sorry. How thoughtless of us." Alexandra stepped back into the house and held open the door. "Please come inside. The men are out getting some supplies, but they'll be back later for dinner. Would you care to see your rooms and freshen up before then?"

The girls looked to Harmony for guidance.

"That would be nice." Harmony gestured the girls in ahead of her, then stepped across the threshold, feeling Thor's hand possessively on the back of her waist. She glanced at the stairs that led straight upward, then to the right at a spacious parlor. "This is lovely."

"Thank you." Deidre laughed softly. "We're trying to make it more adaptable to children and comfortable. I hope we've succeeded."

Harmony took a closer look at the parlor. It was more beautiful than anything she could have imagined. Decorated in bright floral print and dark wood, it had white lace at the windows and on the tables and furniture. Pretty, clean, and comfortable, it was not had easily.

"If you'll come upstairs, we'll show you the other rooms." Alexandra started up the stairs, with Deidre and the girls following her up the staircase.

Harmony put a foot on the carpeted stair, then stopped. How could she hope to fit in here? How could she ever hope to pay for so much home? She glanced up at Thor.

"Do you like it?"

"Thor, I don't think we can stay here."

He raised his eyebrows. "Why not? Isn't it good enough?"

"Oh, yes. It's *so* good."

"I'm sorry there's not enough space for each girl to have a room of her own."

Harmony looked shocked. "Of course they wouldn't have their own room."

173

"Faith, Hope, and Charity are in a room on the second floor. I thought since Star and Blaze are small they could share a room with Jasmine, then we'd put Tara in her own bed till she heals. They'll take up the second floor. It has a bath. Then you can have the suite at the top."

"A suite? I'd have the entire third floor to myself?" She could only stand and stare at him.

"Yes." He gently stroked her cheek. "I hope you'll be happy there."

"How could I not?" She shook her head to clear it. "But what about other children?"

"The place just opened. We missed the dedication, but I smoothed that over with my folks. They've hired a teacher with nurse training from back East to live in a room on the first floor they've turned into a bedroom. She hasn't arrived yet. Your suite will normally be reserved for a mother with children, but feel free to stay as long as you want."

She held on to the bannister for support. She'd never been given this much kindness or consideration, not since the death of her mother. And she'd *never* been offered this type of luxury. She'd never even imagined it for herself. She knew some of the rich in Chicago donated money to run boardinghouses for working women, but those establishments weren't cheap and they had long waiting lists. Besides, they only took in single women who were teachers or typewriters or saleswomen.

"I can see you're still confused. There is a good reason for the Flora McCuskar Institute to exist.

174

If you'll wait till dinner, you'll be given an explanation by those who know more than me. Will you wait?"

She nodded.

"Good." He put an arm around her waist and pulled her close. "I've got a lot I want to show you." He placed a quick kiss on her lips. "But we'll start with the suite and the clothes I got for you. I hope they'll fit. I've only had since yesterday and—"

"Thor!"

"What?"

"Clothes?" She frowned.

"You and the girls must have something to wear that will disguise you in town. Right?"

"I suppose so." She felt more and more out of control, not only in this house but in his arms as well.

"So we went shopping this morning." He grinned. "We didn't get much, I promise."

"I hate to think what you bought."

She started up the staircase, her heart beating fast. Whatever happened, she couldn't let herself get used to this type of luxury, not the house, not the gifts, not the man. She couldn't afford them, not on her own. She didn't need or want them anyway. All she and the girls needed was a simple, clean, safe place of their own.

Until they got it, this would do.

Eleven

Thor stood in the parlor, looking out a side window at the cactus garden Dee Dee had planted. Mentally he corrected himself. His little sister wanted to be called Deidre now that she thought she was all grown up. *Women.* The cactus reminded him of Harmony, prickly on the outside but soft and succulent on the inside. He knew how to reach the inside of a cactus, but how the hell did he reach Harmony?

The days without her had been long and frustrating, in more ways than one. Surprising himself, he had enjoyed the company of Faith, Hope, and Charity, especially when he'd taken them shopping. They'd obviously done without for so long that whatever he bought them was prized beyond anything he could have imagined. He'd valued little the way they did the one change of daywear, underclothes, and nightgown he'd bought them. So little for so much thanks. It made him feel humble and he was unaccustomed and uncomfortable with the feeling.

But it was nothing compared to the feelings

Harmony aroused in him. He'd worried about her the whole time he'd ridden to Tucson, about Tara, about all the girls. What if Turnbull caught them, or the law? Anything could have happened to them on that long ride. His only comfort was that they weren't robbing trains or stagecoaches, or at least he'd hoped not. He knew the Wild Child Gang had been on their own for months, but that was before he knew and cared about them. Now he worried and it wasn't like him, not at all.

When Harmony had ridden up, looking tired and dusty but very real, he'd wanted to run and take her in his arms. And that was only the beginning of what he'd wanted to do with her. Yet she'd immediately argued with him when he'd tried to help. Why did she have to be so independent? Why did she have to be so prickly? He knew there had to be more to her past than she'd admitted so far and he intended to find out just what. If he understood her better, maybe he could reach deep inside her and take what he wanted.

Right now he wanted to talk to her, to be alone with her, but he was waiting to give her a chance to bathe and dress. He couldn't wait much longer. His thoughts were running more rampant as he waited, imagining her taking a hot, scented bath, imagining her skin soft and supple as he touched every single inch of her. He could almost smell her scent, feel her curves. . . .

"Thor, would you like—"

He spun around, sharp disappointment rushing

through him when he realized the feminine voice belonged to his sister.

"I thought you might like something to eat." Deidre walked toward him, a smile on her lips.

"No!" He realized how gruff he sounded and tried to change it. "I mean, I'm not hungry. I'm waiting to talk with Harmony. Do you think I can go up to her suite now?" He hesitated. "Will it hurt her reputation if I go up there?"

Deidre stopped beside him and placed a hand on his arm. "When did you ever care about a woman's reputation?"

He frowned. "Harmony's special. I mean she's had a rough time of it. I don't want her hurt." He forced himself to look out the window again, trying to remain calm. If he didn't watch himself, he would sound like a smitten schoolboy.

She chuckled. "If I didn't know you better, I'd say you had finally met your match. Is that right, Thor?"

"She needs help, that's all. She's taking care of seven children and they aren't even hers."

"Are you going to tell us what happened? How did you meet her? What—"

"It's her story to tell. We met on the train coming out here. That's all I can say." He looked down into Deidre's moss-green eyes. "You may be right. I think she's a match for any man, even if she is a little slip of a thing."

"From that pistol on her hip to those silver spurs, I'd say she can hold her own."

Thor nodded. "I'm going up to see her."

Deidre pressed her fingers against his arm. "The suite has a sitting room. Is that proper enough for you?"

He looked a little embarrassed. "Yes, if it is for you."

"You know me, I've never been impressed with propriety, especially not for women. As far as I'm concerned, being a lady is much too confining for my tastes."

"Speaking of propriety, when are you going to marry Hunter?"

Deidre smiled. "I have lots of other things to plan besides a wedding. There's college, Clarke Shipping, and until recently the Flora McCuskar Institute."

"Not to mention woman suffrage."

"That goes without saying." She paused. "I want you to know Hunter has made my life complete. I can't tell you how wonderful being in love is for me. A partner makes all the difference in life."

"I can see the change in you."

"If you need any help with Harmony, let me know."

He stepped away from her. "I'm *not* in love. If I was going to be that foolish, wouldn't I pick someone more suitable?"

Deidre shook her head. "The one you love is the one most suitable." She held up her hand before he could speak. "I know. You're not in love. Now, go on up there and—"

"We're going to discuss the girls." As he walked from the room with his back straight, he heard her chuckle. Dee Dee always tended to think she knew everything, but this time she was completely wrong. He had a business arrangement with Harmony Harper, nothing more.

As he walked up the stairs, he decided he didn't understand women nearly as well as he'd thought he did. Except in bed. Once he got Harmony there, he'd be in control. He'd take what he wanted, then move on as he always did. Beyond that, he didn't need to understand a woman.

Smiling at his decision, he reached the second floor and heard the girls talking and laughing behind closed doors. The Wild Child Gang was safe. *Finally.* A doctor would arrive soon to look at Tara. With medical care, rest, and proper food she should be as good as new. Now that he had the girls under the protective roof of the institute, he felt relieved. He didn't know when he'd begun to feel responsible for them, but how could anyone not want to help seven orphaned girls?

Starting up the last flight of stairs, his mind returned to Harmony. How could any man not respond to her? In the beginning he'd thought he'd known more beautiful women, but now he couldn't imagine any woman comparing to her in any way. He didn't know what it was about her, but she'd managed to fascinate him from the first. She was a challenge he was bound to conquer.

He reached the landing and stopped. She was behind the closed door. Did he knock? Would she respond or ignore him? Should he open the door, not giving her the chance to say no? He frowned.

He wasn't used to indecision. What was it about this woman that made him unsure?

"Oh, no!" Thud. Harmony's voice carried through the door.

Thor's indecision vanished. Something was wrong. Striding down the hall, he turned the knob, and thrust open the door so hard it banged against the inside wall. He stepped into the room, his fists clenched, looking around for Turnbull or some other source of trouble.

Instead, all he saw was Harmony standing in the middle of the sitting room. She stared at him in shock. She wore the robe of peach silk he had bought for her. It was too big. She'd rolled up the sleeves, but the hem pooled around her feet. Belted around her tiny waist, the fabric emphasized her perfectly formed but small body. The hard tips of her breasts thrust against the silk. Finally, he focused on the wild tangle of dark brown hair that cascaded around her face, over her shoulders, and down her back to below her waist.

He didn't move. He couldn't. He'd never seen her so near to nakedness and he'd immediately hardened in response. He wanted her with a sharp twist of pain.

"What are you doing in here?" Harmony crossed her arms over her breasts as if in protection or concealment. Her face turned rosy.

"I heard you cry out." Remembering his initial fear for her, he glanced around the sitting room. "Are you all right? Turnbull?" He desperately forced his mind to other matters, hoping his body would follow.

"Of course I'm all right." She turned away, presenting her back to him.

He groaned, trying to stifle the emotion that gripped him when he saw the rounded contours of her hips. If he'd wanted her before, now he felt heat flame through him until he could hardly withstand the assault she made on him from across the room.

She looked back, an eyebrow raised. "What's wrong with you?"

Grimacing as he tried to smile, he could only think how badly he hurt, ached for her.

"You don't look well." She turned and stepped closer, tripping on the hem of the robe and reaching out to stop her fall.

He caught her hands, trying to keep her away from him. He'd come to talk, not seduce her. But she'd lost her balance and she continued to fall ever nearer until he found her against his chest, his arms wrapped around her. And he gave up the fight. Pulling her closer still so he could feel her softness, her curves, yet her strength against him, he turned his face into her hair. Damp and clean, her soft tresses smelled like wildflowers.

"Thor?"

Starting to speak, he realized he couldn't. He cleared his throat. "I . . . I didn't realize you were so small."

"What!" She pushed away from him and stepped back, anger expressed in her face.

Surprised, he wondered what he'd done wrong, but more than that he ached to have her back in his arms. "I thought you'd been attacked."

"No. I'm fine, or almost. Were you trying to insult me by saying I'm small?" She glanced down and pulled the fabric more tightly over her breasts. The movement only served to emphasize their shape and size.

He realized she'd misunderstood him, completely. "Harmony, how could you think I'd insult you? You're beautiful. You're perfect. I've never seen such a wonderful body." He picked up her hand and sized it against his own. He could hardly believe her fingers were so small, so delicately shaped, and so very different from his own. "You fascinate me, that's all."

"You mean you don't think I'm too small?" She stroked his long fingers, obviously amazed at the size and strength of them.

"Hell no! I told you, you're perfect." He noticed the scar on the back of her right hand and stroked it with his thumb. "How did you get hurt?"

"The fire. It's nothing." She jerked her hand away. "I'm not beautiful." She squared her shoulders as if for his rejection.

He frowned in puzzlement. "How can you say that?"

She stared at him. "I've looked in a mirror lately even if you haven't."

"Harmony, don't say that about yourself. Any man would want you. I *need* you."

Tossing her head, she smiled. "You're flattering

me, but I like it anyway." She hesitated, stepped closer, and put a hand on his chest. "You aren't bad yourself, for a great big brute of a man."

"Great big brute?" He looked angry, but felt anything but fury flow through him. "I've been told I'm the best to ever warm a woman's bed."

"You've been with a lot of women, have you?"

He realized his mistake. This wasn't the time or place for references. "I'm a man so there've been a few women."

"How many?" She leaned closer, smiling slightly.

Smelling her, seeing her, touching her made him feel wild, aggressive, made him want to stop talking and do nothing but meld their bodies. But she'd asked him a question. What was it?

"So many?" She turned abruptly and walked away from him, her hips swaying.

"So many what?" He couldn't look away from her hips, imagining his hands holding them, imagining the dark, moist depth they hid, imagining . . .

"Women!"

He shook his head and glanced up at her face for she had turned to look at him over her shoulder. "I can't remember any other women when I'm with you."

She frowned. "You don't want to tell me."

"I don't know." He realized his mistake immediately, for she turned to face him.

"You've been with so many women you've lost count?"

"No!" He crossed to her in two strides and took

her in his arms. He pulled her face against his chest and held her even though she struggled slightly before becoming still against him. "Remember, our pasts don't matter. We're in the West. We're together."

She raised her face to look up at him. "You don't want a virgin, do you?"

His breath caught in his throat. *"Virgin? Don't tell me that."* His heart pounded hard and fast. To be the only man to ever have her made his blood boil with desire, but it couldn't be true.

Nodding, she buried her face against his chest and put her arms around his waist to hold tightly to him.

He pulled her arms away and pushed her back so he could look into her face. "You've never been with a man?"

She nodded. "You like experienced women, don't you?"

He dropped her hands, turned, and walked toward the door. "This isn't going to do."

Running after him, she caught his arm and held on tightly. "I can't help it. Our bargain still stands. You didn't say anything about virgins."

He turned around. "I can't do it. It'd be wrong."

"Wrong!" She stepped in front of him and punched him in the chest with the tip of her finger. "You just don't want me. Go ahead and admit it. Go ahead! You don't like tiny, inexperienced, sweatshop worker women. You want ladies and lots of them." Finally, she turned away. "You don't want me."

185

He took a deep breath. "Harmony, come back here."

"No!"

"Come here!"

"You don't—"

"If you'll come here, I'll prove I want you."

She looked at him suspiciously. "How?"

"Walk over here and I'll prove it."

"You think I'm not good enough for you."

"You're too good. You're an angel, a saint. I'm the desperado here."

"No. I'm an outlaw and—"

"Would you get your shapely bottom over here. *Now.*"

She didn't move.

"It's part of the bargain."

"All right, but I don't believe there's anything you can say or do to change my mind." She walked over to him, but watched him cautiously.

"Stand in front of me."

"How close?"

"Damn it! Stand close enough to touch me."

She stopped right in front of him, pulled the sash on her robe more tightly around her waist, squared her shoulders, then looked up at him. "Prove it."

He picked up her right hand, turned it over, then lifted it to his lips. He kissed the palm, then teased it with the tip of his tongue.

She shivered, then jerked back her hand. "That proves nothing."

He took her hand again and pulled it to his

chest. He pressed it hard so she could feel the beat of his heart, then he moved her hand slowly lower until he reached his belt buckle. Maintaining eye contact, he lowered her hand till he pressed it against the hardness that bulged against the front of his trousers. He held her hand there as he watched her eyes grow wide, then soft, then darker with what he hoped was desire.

Keeping her hand against him, he leaned forward and captured her mouth, kissing her softly at first, nibbling at her lips, tracing their outline with his tongue, then delving in deep to taste her more fully. She met his thrusting tongue with her own, then moaned and clutched at the hardness in her hand. He groaned in need and frustration, then pulled back, pushed her hand away, and stepped away from her. He took several deep breaths, trying to control himself. Much more of this and he wouldn't be able to stop.

She put a small hand on his back and gently massaged. "Then our bargain is still good?"

"No."

"What?"

He reluctantly turned to face her. "I'm not going to take advantage of you, Harmony Harper. Don't get me wrong. I'd like to do it. I should. But I want you free and willing. I don't want you as payment."

"You mean you *don't* want me free. You want me to owe you and your family. It'd be just like the sweatshop and Turnbull. We'd *never* be free. We'd always owe you and your family. Forever."

She stamped her bare foot. "I won't have it. I'll leave."

He jerked her to him, holding her arms in a tight grip. "You're not leaving. If I have to keep you and the girls locked up here, you'll stay till Tara heals and you can find a safe place to go, if you must." He shook her.

"Let me go. You're just like all the others."

"What others? I thought you said you were—"

"There've been other men who wanted me, tried to take me. Turnbull!"

"Did he touch you? What did he do?" Anger flooded Thor, making him see red. He shook his head, trying to control the emotion overpowering him. "Tell me!"

"He's come after me, hasn't he? Let me go. You're hurting me."

He dropped his hands and walked over to the balcony to look out over the landscape in back. The French doors were open and a warm, dry breeze swept over him. He took deep breaths. It didn't help to cool him or his anger. But nothing would until he'd made sure Turnbull could never touch or hurt Harmony again.

She watched him gaze out the open balcony doors. "I think it has come down to one fact for Turnbull. He will either have me and break me to his will or he will kill me. There will be no in-between. Not with him."

Thor turned back. "He's not going to have you. That is a fact. And he's not going to hurt the girls."

"But you won't have me either, will you?"

"I want what's best for you. And the girls." He moved closer to her again. "Promise me you won't try to leave till Tara is well. At least give me that."

"Why should I? You're an oathbreaker."

"Don't say that. It's not true. I simply don't want to hurt you." He glanced down the length of her. "I'm too big for you anyway." He tilted his head to one side and smiled. "I might hurt you. Inside."

She blushed and looked away. "I won't break."

Putting strong arms around her, he felt her shiver against him. "I can't stand to see you hurt anymore. That's why I rushed in here when I heard you cry out. What happened?"

"I'd washed my hair, but it was so tangled I couldn't get a brush through it. I got mad and threw the brush against the wall." She chuckled. "See, I'm no angel."

"You're an angel with spurs."

"And you've been a hostage too long."

"Or not long enough." He cleared his throat, then glanced around. He strode across the room, picked up the brush, then lifted a straight-back chair. He carried it over to the balcony, then set it down.

"What are you doing?" She followed him out onto the small balcony.

"Sit down. I'm going to brush your hair."

"Oh, Thor, no." She glanced around. "Somebody will see and—"

"I don't care. Do you want you hair brushed, or not?"

"Yes, but—"

He lifted her into his arms and set her down in the chair. "Now sit still." He pulled her long, wild hair over the back of the chair, then lowered the brush to take a long sweep through her tresses. It caught.

"Ouch!"

"Sorry." He frowned. "How'd it get in this state anyway?"

"Outlaws don't get pampered."

"You will now." He started again, but more gently, fascinated with the thick beauty of her dark hair, letting one hand run through it while the other brushed. "You've got more hair than I've ever seen on a woman."

"And with your vast experience, you'd know."

"I have a mother and a sister. And friends. For your information, I haven't bedded every woman west of the Mississippi."

She glanced up at him. "With the ability to brush hair like that, I'm surprised you haven't."

"What about my pretty face?"

"That doesn't hurt, but I think I'm more impressed with what you've got lower down."

"And I thought I'd impressed you with my abilities as a lady's maid."

Reaching behind her, she found his belt buckle, then moved lower to capture him. When he hardened against her hand, she smiled in triumph. And squeezed. "That's what impresses an outlaw."

"If you don't stop that, you'll never get your hair brushed."

"I thought you weren't interested in me." She continued to stroke him.

"I'm interested." His voice sounded strained as he kept brushing her long hair. "But I'm a gentleman."

"That's too bad." She stood up and turned to him. "Because I'm no lady." She pushed him against the wall and leaned into his long length, then tilted her head back and gave him a calculating gaze. "I'm an outlaw and I take what I want."

He set her back from him, frowned, and handed her the brush. "Remember, I'm doing this for your own good. I'll see you at dinner." He turned and strode to the sitting room door and opened it.

"See you later, hostage."

He slammed the door shut behind him.

Twelve

Harmony stood on the balcony, letting the cool evening breeze caress her body as she tried to stop thoughts of Thor. Even though it was nearly time for dinner, she could still smell his scent, sense his presence, remember his nearness. And her boldness. How could she have touched him so? How could she have been so wanton? Yet she reminded herself that she was an outlaw woman. She did what she wanted to do. She took what she wanted. Did she want Thor? It didn't matter. They had a bargain.

She'd see him again soon. Would she be embarrassed to look into his face in front of others, his family? Could they tell how intimately she had touched him? Could they tell he wanted her? No. She was letting her imagination run wild. She had kidnapped Thor, not the other way around. He was helping her and the girls. And she was repaying the favor. Nothing more, nothing less.

She took a deep breath and reminded herself that she would not be intimidated by Thor or his rich family and friends. She was part of the Wild

Child Gang, Terror of the West. And she had the newspaper headlines to prove it. If Thor excited her sometimes, it was simply part of the thrill of the chase, the hunt, an outlaw's game. It was nothing at all to overwhelm her or make her heart beat fast.

Good. That was better. She had to get herself under control. She had to stop letting Thor's presence twist her mind and emotions, making her forget her goals and the needs of the girls. Nobody had ever affected her this way before and she didn't know how to deal with it except to push her reaction into a tiny box and close the lid. Unfortunately, the lid kept popping open.

She shut the doors to the balcony and turned back to the sitting room. She'd never stayed in such a lovely place before. The French furniture with its delicately carved wood and silk upholstery seemed much too fine to use. A chaise lounge near the balcony beckoned to have a body reclined on it, but she hadn't yet touched it. And the colors. Forest green and burgundy dominated the draperies, the upholstery, and the carpet. It was almost too beautiful to be real.

She walked into the bedroom and couldn't help but admire the matched bedroom set of gleaming golden oak. Delicate embroidery covered the top of the tall dresser. Perfume bottles and a celluloid set of powder container, brush, comb, and hand mirror were laid out on the vanity table.

Stroking the smooth wood of the vanity, she thought about workers like herself who had made everything in the room. Jobs had been provided by the people who had bought all this. But what type of working conditions and pay had been involved? She could have enjoyed the luxury if she had known that the workers who had made it had been well fed and housed. But she couldn't be sure.

She glanced at herself in the mirror above the vanity, hardly recognizing the young woman looking back. She'd pulled her hair into a neat chignon at the nape of her neck. She'd powered her nose and put fragrant perfume on her wrists. That hadn't changed her much.

It was the clothes that made the difference. *Silk.* She had never worn it before. Now she wore a corset of ivory sateen trimmed with brown lace and silk ribbon, hooking up the front. Over it she wore a matching silk cover with ruffled drawers. On top of all that she had slipped on a soft ivory silk petticoat trimmed around the bottom with brown satin ruffles.

The luxury didn't stop there. She stroked the rich dark amber color of the watered silk skirt, then glanced in the mirror at the ivory silk blouse. The colors made her hair and eyes gleam like jewels. Even to herself, she looked almost pretty. Thor had chosen well. He'd even found sizes to fit her. She only hoped he'd bought it all from a local seamstress and not at a shop that sold merchandise ordered from merchants who used sweatshop labor.

But if all her clothing hadn't been taken from her to be washed, she would have worn something of her own. She didn't want to owe Thor any more than she already did and she couldn't be sure of the workers who had made the clothing. Yet after her bath, she hadn't had the heart to put on dirty clothes and she would have been out of place at the dinner table without the new finery.

She turned from the mirror and sat down on the bed. She slipped on silk stockings, shuddering at the cost if she snagged one, then pulled on soft leather slippers of dark brown. Last, she lifted a dark amber fedora vest of net and lace to place around her neck, letting it drape to her waist. If she hadn't known better, she would have thought a lady stared back at her from the vanity mirror. But she was only too aware that a sweatshop worker could have lived a year on what she wore.

Abruptly she turned away. She was an outlaw on the run. She was no lady. And she was no longer a sweatshop worker. The clothes were borrowed, nothing more. She mustn't let herself be distracted by fine gifts and luxurious surroundings. She must remember the fire, the choking smoke, the cries of the dying. Hate and revenge were her twin companions until Turnbull was brought to justice. And she must never forget it, not for a single moment.

She stepped into the bathroom. A bathtub with floral designs painted on it dominated the small room. After so long in the desert, she didn't know when she had enjoyed anything so much as her earlier bath. It seemed hard to imagine how she had come from that one train robbery to this house in Tucson. *Thor.* Yes, he'd brought her, turning her path from the first moment they'd met. Yes, he'd made her bold and passionate. But he would not take her freedom. She'd hold him to their bargain.

She turned and quickly walked through the suite to the main door. Hesitating there, she took a deep breath, then opened the door and stepped outside. All was quiet on her floor. She shut the door behind her, then took the stairs down to the second level. Here, silence also reigned.

She felt fear. What if something had happened to the girls? What if Turnbull had somehow sneaked inside and stolen or hurt them? She wasn't used to being separated from them. They'd been together constantly since the fire until Thor had parted them. Maybe the Flora McCuskar Institute wasn't a good idea after all.

But for Tara's sake she knew this was where they needed to be. Earlier she'd checked on Tara after the doctor had come and gone, explaining that Tara would be as healthy as ever if she rested and ate nourishing food for a few weeks. Yes, the girls had to stay at the institute. Where else would they get a doctor's care, a safe place to live, and good food to help them grow strong and straight?

She hated to depend on Thor and his family, but it wasn't forever. It was simply a matter of time before she finished with Turnbull and made it safe for the girls to come out of hiding. She pushed her fear aside. No harm could come to them here.

Walking down the hall, she paused outside of Tara's room. She heard murmuring inside. Surprised, thinking Tara would be asleep, she quietly pushed open the door.

All the girls sat on Tara's bed, surrounding Tara who leaned back against several pillows covered in ivory and trimmed with blue lace. They stopped speaking the moment they saw Harmony, looked guilty, then held out their arms to her. She shut the door behind her, then walked over to them, giving each a hug as they made a place for her on the bed with them.

She sat down, not caring if she wrinkled her skirt, knowing she needed to be near them, wanting to make sure they were all right. "I thought we'd agreed to let Tara sleep." She hadn't the heart to say more. They looked so happy and healthy and safe.

"We wanted her to see our clothes before we went down to supper." Jasmine fluffed the ruffles around the collar of her white dress.

"Dinner. That's what they call it here." Star lifted her chin to elevate her nose in the air. "Supper's not good enough for them."

"I don't care what it's called just let me eat." Blaze turned to Harmony.

"We're used to eating when we want." Faith glanced at her two sisters who nodded in agreement.

"But we're not on our own anymore." Harmony understood their feelings. After being free for so long, this change was going to be harder than

197

she'd realized. "And we're safe here from Turn-bull."

"I don't want to eat at some fancy table with bunches of forks and knifes and glasses and plates that if you broke one it'd take a year to pay for it." Blaze clenched her fists, frowning.

For the first time Harmony imagined not a wooden table in the kitchen, friendly and warm near the stove with pottery plates and a three-pronged fork, but a table set with Irish linen and terribly expensive crystal and china. There'd be so many courses of food and so much silver and everything else that she wouldn't know much better than the girls how to use it.

"Tara had her food brought up on a tray." Star pointed to the empty plates stacked on a tray pushed onto a nearby table.

"How are you feeling, Tara?" Harmony reached out to stroke the girl's face, pleased to see her color better.

"Good." She glanced around the room. "I've never been in a place like this or been treated like this before." She turned back to Harmony. "But I miss the horses."

"You'll be riding again in no time." Harmony desperately wanted the girls to be comfortable. They were working class. What did they know of rich society? And why should they? They were equal in all ways except money. Besides, no one needed more than a fork, a plate, and a glass to eat a good meal. As she well knew, most of the time back in Chicago there would never have been enough food to fill one plate or the restraint to eat it with a fork. They'd always been hungry until they became outlaws.

"Did you see our dolls?" Tara pulled a beautifully dressed doll with a painted china face from under the cover. "We all got one to match the color of our hair."

Harmony held the doll and looked her over, realizing it must have cost a great deal. "She's beautiful. What did you name her?"

Tara laughed and the others joined her. "Harmony."

"We all named ours Harmony." Blaze tickled Star and they both laughed harder.

"So we agreed to call them One, Two, Three . . ." Faith began.

"Four, Five, Six . . ." Hope continued.

"And Seven." Charity finished, then laughed even harder.

Harmony couldn't resist laughing, too. "But there are so many other names to choose."

The girls stopped laughing and looked at her solemnly.

Tara squeezed her hand. "But none means as much to us as Harmony."

Harmony felt tears fill her eyes, but she wouldn't cry in front of the girls. They needed her to be strong. She pulled them close, hugging them tightly against her. Who cared about silk finery when they had love like this? She had done the right thing in bringing them here. And she would do the right thing when she found them a small place of their own.

"Do we have to eat downstairs?" Blaze pulled away and frowned.

"Thor had trays sent up to us last night and this morning," Faith said. "We didn't have to talk to anybody or use fancy stuff or anything."

"If we have to go downstairs, I'm not hungry." Star glanced around the group.

"Me neither." Jasmine's stomach rumbled and she rubbed it hard.

Harmony looked at them in concern. "You're going to have a good dinner." She hugged Jasmine. "As to what and where, I'll go down and see about it." She smiled at them. "Don't worry. I'll see you don't go hungry."

As she started to get up, she heard a soft then louder knock on the door. They all froze, watching the door as it slowly pushed inward.

Thor stuck his head around the corner, then smiled. "I wondered where everybody had disappeared. What happened to all those starving outlaws?"

The girls glanced at each other, then moved closer to Harmony.

Concerned, Thor stepped inside. "Isn't anybody hungry? Juanita cooked all afternoon." He focused on Harmony. "Is something wrong?"

"Why don't we leave the room a moment?" She stood up and walked over to him. Glancing back, she nodded at the girls, then stepped outside.

He followed Harmony with a puzzled frown on his face. "What's going on?"

Putting a fingertip to her lips, she moved downward until she stood halfway between the floors.

He stopped close to her. "What's all the secrecy?" He looked her over from head to toe, his frown disappearing. "I picked the right size, didn't I?" His blue eyes darkened. "I knew I'd never forget."

"Yes. Thanks. I won't keep the clothes when I go, but—"

"They're yours. The skirt was altered in length. We can't take it back."

She pressed her lips together. One more thing to owe him. But she'd think about that later. The girls came first. "Thor, I should have thought about this before. The girls have spent most of their lives working in a sweatshop or living on the trail in the West. They don't know *how* to eat at a fancy set table."

"Damn!" He ran a hand through his thick blond hair. "I never thought of that."

"Could we have food sent up on trays tonight?"

"Sure. Tomorrow we can have a picnic outside and they can eat breakfast at the table in the kitchen. Would that be okay?"

"Yes. Thanks."

"If they want to learn special table manners, I know Deidre would be happy to teach them."

"I think they should learn so they'll be comfortable wherever they go in life. My mother taught me the basics, but I'm not sure I can handle a really fancy table setting, either."

Placing a fingertip under her chin, he tilted up her face. "Just watch what I do tonight. If you want lessons later, I'll be happy to oblige."

"I don't intend to need them in the future." She stepped downward to get away from him. She couldn't think straight when he stood this close. All she could think about was the heat and hardness of him when she had touched him earlier. She felt her face grow warm. She mustn't think about what had happened or she'd never get through the evening.

"Don't be too sure."

"If you'll tell the housekeeper, I'll explain to the children."

"I'll tell Juanita. You won't be long, will you?"

"No." She glanced upward. He dominated the stairs above her and he didn't seem inclined to move out of the way. She took a step toward him. He didn't move. Instead he watched her, his blue eyes growing hotter by the moment. As she tried to brush past him, he put an arm around her waist, pulling her against him.

"You weren't so anxious to leave me this afternoon."

She shivered at his touch, feeling his heat transfer to her. She raised her chin, trying to look determined. "I thought you wanted to get away from me."

"Just trying to save myself." His gaze lowered

202

to focus on her lips. "What am I going to do with you, Harmony?"

Pushing away from him, she frowned, determined to keep her body from turning traitor in his arms. "You're going to let me by, then get some food sent up for the girls."

"I see you're still the outlaw leader. You're not done ordering me about, are you?"

Suddenly she wanted to order him to bed, to strip for her, to make her experience everything he'd made her body crave, to make the past go away forever. But she was Harmony Harper, sweatshop worker, and he was Thor Clarke-Jarmon, rich, spoiled, and dangerous. She reached up to stroke his face. "You're still my hostage, aren't you?"

"Yes." The word came out in a growl as he pulled her tightly against his long body.

She stroked lower to his chest, feeling the hard beat of his heart. Her own heartbeat increased, but she wouldn't let her feelings overwhelm her. "The girls need their dinner."

"Later." He lowered his head to press hot lips against her mouth.

She moaned, fast losing any control at all. When he started to deepen the kiss, she pushed against him with her fists. "No." Her voice came out in a husky whisper.

"Yes."

She kept her hands pressed against his chest. "Everyone's waiting for us."

He glanced down the staircase and shook his head. "Damn. I can't take much more of this."

"You'll take whatever you have to take, hostage."

Shaking his head, he stepped back. "You've got a wicked tongue."

"And it's a good thing." She pushed past him, forcing her body to move as naturally as possible. But she really only wanted to run back to him and fling herself into his arms.

At the top of the stairs, she glanced down. He watched her with hooded blue eyes. They seemed bound by a cord that pulled tighter and tighter. No. She wouldn't let her thoughts run wild. She forced herself to turn her back on him, walk down the hall, and slip into Tara's room.

The girls looked up, their faces expectant.

Smiling, she sat down in a small rocker near the bed. She was hot and prickly all over. "Thor's going to ask the housekeeper to send food up for all of you. Tomorrow you'll have breakfast in the kitchen, then a picnic outside. Okay?"

Star clapped her hands.

"When do we get our own clothes back? This fancy stuff won't last long on horseback." Blaze glanced around the group for agreement.

"And we aren't giving up the horses," Star said. "They're not going to make us into prissy missy ladies."

"I like my new dress." Jasmine smoothed the watered silk and toyed with the lace edges. "I don't think being a lady is such a bad idea as long as we can be outlaws, too."

"Dresses are fine for in here." Star bunched the

skirt of her new dress in her fist. "But look at that. It'd be a mess in no time outside."

"How long do we have to stay here?" Charity pulled her sisters closer as she glanced around the room.

Harmony followed her gaze. Wallpaper in ivory with rows of blue sprigs covered the walls. Blue drapes, bedspread, and a blue and ivory floral carpet accented the rest of the room. The Jenny Lind spool furniture suited a girl's room with its warmth and practicality. "Don't you like it here?"

"It's beautiful." Jasmine ran her hand over the bedspread. "But we were happy in the hideout."

"That's right." Blaze hopped down and hugged Harmony. "We don't care where we live so long as we can be together. We're family, remember?"

Harmony held her close. "Yes, I remember." She stroked Blaze's head. "But we need a safe place right now. And Tara needs a doctor."

Blaze stepped back. "You won't leave us, will you?"

She hugged Blaze close again and glanced over her head. "We're all in this together."

"We won't be put in foster homes." Faith held on to her sisters. "We'll run away first."

"No foster homes." Harmony looked from one face to another. "Later we'll get a house of our own like we always planned."

"And we get to keep the horses?" Blaze smoothed down her skirt.

Harmony couldn't help smiling. Blaze's yellow dress was already sadly wrinkled and soiled. This type of clothing wouldn't last long around her. And she wasn't sorry. She didn't want the girls changed. She didn't want them made into something they'd never been and didn't want to be. She wanted them to always be themselves and she was trying hard to give them that chance.

Standing, she smoothed down her own silk skirt. "Look, I miss my trousers, too. I miss the freedom we had in the hideout. But it was dangerous. You know that. Tara's better and we want to keep her that way."

Blaze sat back down on the bed.

"We're a family. We love each other." Harmony kissed Tara's cheek, then touched each of the others. "Nothing can ever change that. Right?"

The girls nodded.

"I'm going downstairs and eat with Thor's family. You have fun up here. Change into your nightclothes if you want. But get to bed early. Outlaws have to rest when they can."

She opened the door and glanced back. They'd lost so much so fast in the fire that she realized they now hated to let her out of their sight. She understood their fear, but she couldn't help them if she stayed with them. She blew them a kiss, then shut the door behind her.

As she walked down the stairs, she tried to still her thoughts and make herself ready for what awaited her downstairs. She didn't want to meet Thor's family again. She didn't want to eat a fancy dinner. She wanted to be sitting next to a campfire, a stew bubbling, and the children singing.

Until now, she hadn't realized how much her freedom had come to mean to her.

Now not only did she fear Turnbull, but she feared Thor taking over her life. Either one of the men could take her freedom, leaving her powerless. Turnbull wanted to kill her, but Thor wanted to possess her. Somehow she had to escape both their desires while saving the girls and providing a safe home for them. As for herself? Maybe someday she would have time to explore her own wants and needs, but that day had yet to come.

Thirteen

Thor glanced up as Harmony entered the sitting room. He smiled as he walked over to her, trying to ease her tension. She and the girls had been so much in command as outlaws that he'd never considered the possibility they would be uncomfortable in a simple drawing room or dining room. From what he now knew of their background, he realized it made sense. But they could learn. He wanted to be Harmony's teacher in more ways than one.

Looking into her warm brown eyes, he wondered if she knew how much he enjoyed playing her hostage game. She was like no other woman he'd ever met. She kept him fascinated, annoyed, aroused, and protective. Even when she was dressed as a lady as she was this evening in clothes he'd chosen and bought for her, he could still sense the boots and spurs she was never without, at least not mentally and emotionally. What was he going to do with her? How could he possibly touch her, even when that was what he most wanted to do?

She'd never been with a man. The fact both excited and infuriated him. He'd feel like the worst sort of heel if he took her virginity, knowing he would be ruining her later chances for marriage. But how could he say no if she kept insisting on keeping their bargain? It was going to take more strength than he had or wanted to have, for every moment he was with her he wanted her more.

He took her hand and tucked it into the crook of his arm, then turned toward his family who had stood up at her arrival. Feeling a tremor in her hand on his arm, he covered it with his own large one and walked with her over to his family.

"Harmony, you've already met my mother and sister. Now I'd like you to meet my father, Jake Clarke-Jarmon, owner of the Bar J Ranch in Texas and the Jarmon Plantation in Louisiana. I'd also like to introduce you to Deidre's friend Hunter and his father, Alberto Cazador Raimundo de Santiago, from Raimundo Rancho in southern Arizona. This is Harmony Harper."

She smiled pleasantly at the group, but reserved her acceptance.

"Please call me Alberto. My full name is too much for anyone." The older gentleman, obviously a Spanish grandee by his dress and manner, bowed slightly from the waist. He had thick white hair and mustache, dark blue eyes, and a strong, straight build.

"Thank you. Please, all of you, call me Harmony."

"I'm only sorry my mother, Flora McCuskar,

isn't here to meet you," Hunter said, looking very much like a younger version of his father except his hair was still a lustrous black. "She loved children. We've created this institute in her name and for her memory. I know she'd have been proud to have your seven girls staying here."

"I regret I didn't have the chance to meet her, but I'd like to thank all of you for allowing us to stay here. I promise it won't be for long."

"Nonsense." Alberto leaned forward. "This institute is here to provide everything a child could need for as long as he or she should need it. Surely you won't take away the privilege you've granted us by allowing us to help your little ones."

Raising an eyebrow, Harmony glanced around the group. She'd never heard such a pretty speech. He made it sound as if she was doing them the favor. It must be the grandee upbringing. "Thank you. Thor told me all of you would be kind and generous. I can see that it's true."

Deidre stepped forward and slipped her arm through Harmony's, tugging her away from Thor. Deidre looked a great deal like her mother, with blond hair and green eyes. She wore a simple gown of green silk with a small bustle in back. "Don't let my brother monopolize all your time. We can have some woman-to-woman talk. By the way, are you a suffragist?"

Thor laughed and tugged Harmony back toward him. "Not every woman is a suffragist."

But Deidre stood her ground. "Every woman

needs the right to vote, among other rights, and I want to discuss it with Harmony."

Trying to appear interested but wanting to get away from the intensity of both of them, Harmony kept a smile on her lips. They had no idea what it was like to survive a sweatshop fire. Their battles would be mental, not emotional and physical. She'd like to tell them so, but she was their guest and the girls depended on their charity.

"Deidre, Thor, stop!" Alexandra clapped her hands. "Harmony, please don't pay any attention to my son and daughter. They're both spoiled and want their own way on everything. Now both of you let Harmony go. She'll think neither of you has any manners at all."

Jake chuckled, putting an arm around Alexandra's waist. His thick blond hair looked windblown and his blue eyes crinkled at the corners with laughter. Tall and muscular, time had treated him well. "You tell them, darling. They never listen to anyone but you, my iron-fisted Yankee."

Alexandra poked him in the chest with the tip of her finger. Although now in her mid-forties, she had hardly changed, simply adding a few strands of silver to her strawberry blond hair and laugh lines around the outer corners of her green eyes. "Who has the iron fist in this family?"

Jake laughed. "Not us, that's for sure."

"I'll let her go if you will." Deidre glared at Thor, keeping her hold on Harmony's arm.

Thor glared back. "You go first."

"No. You."

"I don't trust you—"

"Stop!" Harmony pulled away from them. "Really, you're both worse than the girls." Then she realized what she'd said and looked down at her feet. How could she overcome her social blunder? Instead she heard laughter. Glancing upward, she saw the entire family laughing and hugging each other.

"I think you've met your match, Thor." Hunter slapped him on the back. "My piece of advice is when you've found a fiery woman, don't ever let her go." He looked over at Deidre and for a moment they shared a heated gaze.

"I agree." Jake lifted Alexandra's hand to his lips, then turned it over and slowly, lingeringly kissed her palm.

Alexandra smiled seductively at her husband, then glanced at Harmony. "And when you find the right man, lasso him, hog-tie him, whatever it takes till he knows just which woman has branded him."

Everyone laughed.

As the tension broke, Harmony suddenly felt more at ease. These people weren't at all what she'd expected. They were warm and loving and kind and considerate. And they cared desperately about each other. They reminded her of her mother and she felt warm inside. They were a family, just as she'd had with her mother and just as she had with the girls. She was glad for Thor. She glanced up at him, pleased to be at the institute.

He smiled at her and put a hand around her

waist, pulling her closer to him. He leaned down and placed his mouth near her ear. "Are you going to tie me up again?"

She playfully hit his shoulder. "Whatever it takes to control you, hostage." But she spoke for his ears alone.

He nodded, a warm light in his eyes, then turned back to his family.

"I think dinner must be ready by now." Alexandra looked at Harmony. "I hope you don't mind, but we don't stand on much formality here. Carlos, Juanita, and their son, Julian, take care of the place. Juanita cooks the meals for the institute and since your girls are the first residents she's just now deciding how to handle it all. For tonight she's putting food on the sideboard so we can help ourselves."

"That sounds perfect." Harmony smiled. It wasn't going to be nearly as bad as she had imagined.

With Thor's hand warming her back, she followed the family into the dining room. The room was simply decorated with a green leaf pattern on ivory wallpaper, a carpet of similar design on the glossy wooden floor, lace draperies on the windows, and a long wooden table with matching chairs in the center. She guessed the table would seat twelve, but tonight it was set for seven with a green cotton tablecloth and matching napkins, green glassware, and a limited amount of silverware.

Alberto glanced at Harmony. "You'll notice we

213

designed everything to appeal to children, to make them comfortable. I had special dishes and glasses made in Mexico. They're sturdy and pretty and I've got plenty in case they break." He chuckled, obviously very much involved with the institute.

"Dad's got his own place in town." Hunter clasped Alberto's shoulder. "We've been staying with him, but he spends most of his time here overseeing everything."

Alberto winked at Harmony. "I've been doing a lot more than overseeing. I've put my hands to any task that needs doing. What do you think of the place?"

"It's wonderful and beautiful." Harmony glanced around the room again. "It's perfect for children. The girls like it here, only they miss their horses."

"I understand," Alberto said. "While we have room to keep a horse here for the carriage and another for riding, we had to board your eight horses at a local stable."

"Perhaps we should sell them. They'll need to be ridden and the girls might not have time." Harmony hated the thought of selling the horses, but how could she expect the institute to keep up the expense of boarding them.

Alberto looked horrified. "I wouldn't think of selling the horses. They're special to the girls and children should grow up knowing how to ride."

"Spoken like a true rancher." Jake laughed.

Everyone joined him, although Harmony wasn't quite sure what was so funny. But she smiled anyway. All she could think of was the cost of keeping horses in town. Out in the country it hadn't been much problem since the animals could forage for food and water, but this was entirely different.

Alberto focused on Harmony again. "I think children, even if they live in town, should grow up around animals. A dog, a cat, horses, maybe even a goat for milk and chickens for eggs would be good. We have enough room here out on the edge of town. The children could care for the animals. They need responsibilities of their own. We might even move the horses down to my ranch or to one closer to the institute. Don't worry. It'll all come together in good time."

"Especially when Miss Bonita Sonneberg, teacher and nurse extraordinare, arrives from Boston." Alexandra smiled at Harmony. "Miss Sonneberg has a degree in both areas, plus several years of experience. Alberto was very lucky to get her for the institute."

"Lucky!" Alberto snorted. "To lure her West, I'm paying her top wages."

"And she no doubt deserves it, too," Deidre said. "But I wonder if her photograph had anything to do with your decision to hire her?"

Alberto looked furious. "Young lady, I chose the most qualified applicant. If she is also a very intriguing-looking lady, that is not my concern."

"I'm just teasing. You're doing a wonderful job with the institute and you know it." Deidre placed a kiss on Alberto's cheek, then linked arms with Hunter. "Now, I don't know about the rest of you, but I'm starved and the smell of this food is driving me wild."

"You're already wild." Hunter led her to the sideboard.

Harmony followed them in line, with Thor right behind her. She picked up a plate from the stack at the end of the sideboard, delighting in the brightly colored design that had been handpainted on each plate. She watched Deidre uncover dishes, then put food on her plate. The food was not what she was used to in Chicago, but she had seen and eaten some of the Mexican dishes since coming West.

She realized these people, despite their wealth, seemed to appreciate and pay well for the skill and labor of those they hired. With this realization, she relaxed even more. The food looked delicious and she felt starved, too. She took something from each bowl and platter, then glanced up at Thor. She hoped she didn't appear greedy. But his plate was fuller than hers so she felt better.

They carried their plates to the table and sat across from Deidre and Hunter. Soon Alberto sat at the head of the table with Alexandra on his left side and Jake at his right.

Thor looked from Harmony's face to her plate, then back again. He smiled in understanding. "You might as well learn to like Mexican food because in south Texas, New Mexico, and Arizona, it's the best of the best." He pointed. "Those are tamales, both sweet and hot. Frijoles or beans seasoned just right. Use the corn tortilla like a fork or spoon.

216

And go easy on the peppers till you're sure you can handle them."

"Thanks." Harmony decided to start with the beans, thinking they'd be safest. They were delicious and seasoned like nothing she'd ever tasted before. She smiled around the group, nodding her approval.

"Great food, right?" Deidre ate quickly, watching Harmony. "If you haven't had this before, you must be from back East or . . ."

"Chicago." Harmony felt her heart beat fast and set down her fork to take a drink of water. They'd want to know about her. It was only natural. How much should she tell? How much would be safe to tell?

"I've never been there," Hunter said. "But I hear it's quite a city."

"That's where the cattle get shipped after we drive them up to Kansas," Jake said. "I was there a few times."

"I grew up in Chicago." Harmony lost her appetite. "I suppose like most cities it has some beautiful areas, but ugly places as well." She swallowed hard, deciding she wasn't going to pretend to be something she wasn't. "I worked in a sweatshop there."

"Really!" Deidre leaned forward. "How brave of you."

Harmony blinked in surprise. "It wasn't a choice. I had to have a job. I have no family. The girls worked in the shop, too. But we escaped."

Deidre dropped her fork and gestured with her

hand around the table. "There. Didn't I tell you? Children are being worked to death in sweatshops and not just in Chicago." She focused on Harmony again. "But you got away. I've heard not many ever do. You are a living testament to the determination of a woman to save herself and others. I'd love to have you come back East and speak to woman suffrage groups. What do you say?"

Harmony looked horrified. She'd never spoken in public before and the thought terrified her, almost as much as Turnbull. Robbing trains was one thing, but speaking to a group of strangers was quite another.

"Deidre, can't you wait till Harmony's eaten dinner to try and intimidate her? You're going to ruin everybody's digestion." Thor frowned at his sister.

"I'm not trying to intimidate her. I'm thrilled to meet a sweatshop worker."

Alexandra turned to Harmony. "You must understand Deidre is working to help all women and children and men gain equal rights under the law in jobs, working conditions, and housing. She is driven in part by my own life when I was near her age."

Jake squeezed Alexandra's hand.

"You see, I inherited Clarke Shipping Company in New York City, but legally I didn't gain control until I was twenty-one. My parents died when I was a child and they left me in the care of Jake's grandfather, Olaf Thorssen, who died when I was twenty. The men in my family tried desperately to make sure I never took control of the company.

218

They didn't believe a woman should have it. I survived, thanks to Jake's help."

"It took more than my help, darling. Your own courage and determination saved you." Jake squeezed her hand once more, then lifted a forkful of beans into the air. "But I'll admit that first attempt of yours at cooking almost killed me and Uncle Lamar." He put the beans into his mouth as he chuckled.

"Oh, I'll never hear the end of that." Alexandra glanced around the table, laughing. "My children have heard this story many times, but I'll repeat it for those of you who haven't if you want to hear about it."

"Please tell," Alberto said.

"I came from a very pampered life to the Bar J Ranch in the wilds of South Texas. Jake decided I should earn my keep by cooking. Of course, I didn't know how. He gave me beans and told me to put them in water and cook them. I did. What he failed to tell me was to wash them first. When he and Lamar bit down on those beans, we all heard the sound of crunching rocks. You've never seen two men rush outside so fast." She chuckled and lovingly glanced at Jake.

"An easy mistake to make and very funny." Alberto laughed, then continued eating.

Harmony felt the tension in her stomach ease as the conversation moved away from her. She quickly ate to make up for lost time. She could get to like it here, enjoying the company, the food, the surroundings.

When they were all finished, Alexandra stood up. "Why don't we retire to the parlor. Deidre, would you help me with the coffee?"

"I'll help." Harmony stood up.

"No. You're the guest, at least for tonight." Alexandra smiled warmly at her. "Go ahead and relax. Deidre will help."

As the two women walked into the kitchen, Thor led Harmony into the parlor. She'd seen the room briefly when they first arrived, but she hadn't realized how really comfortable and charming it was till she and Thor sat down on an overstuffed settee. She didn't know if she'd ever been so full or so content before.

While the men settled into chairs, she looked more closely at the room. A hand-hooked carpet in multicolors covered most of the wooden floor. Floral chintz drapes had been pulled back from the windows, revealing lace curtains. The furniture had been upholstered in bright colors of floral or solid chintz. Several matching round pillows had been thrown here and there for comfort. She could imagine the children playing here, for the furniture looked made for fun.

Alexandra walked into the room and set a tray down on a low table in front of Harmony. Deidre followed with a plate of small cakes and cookies. As Alexandra poured coffee into brightly painted pottery mugs, Deidre handed them around with dessert. When everyone had been served, Alexandra sat by Jake and Deidre took the chair near Hunter.

"Okay, now I want to find out more about Harmony." Deidre leaned forward. "Thor has been absolutely secretive about how he met you. On à train. How? When? Why? And please don't say you can't tell or some such thing because I'm dying of curiosity."

Harmony couldn't help but smile at Deidre. She seemed so young and eager and so sure of success. It was a wonderful quality, one Harmony didn't think she'd ever felt and probably never would. She couldn't blame Thor's family for their interest, especially since they were taking care of the girls for a while. She glanced around her. These people weren't like the robber barons of Chicago who financed their gilded lives with tenements and sweatshops, but they still lived very special lives and she wasn't sure they knew it.

"Oh no! You're aren't going to tell." Deidre looked disappointed as she took a sip of coffee.

"It's not that." Harmony felt her dinner grow huge and heavy in her stomach. No matter what, she still couldn't completely trust them. "I'm not sure where to begin." She glanced at Thor. He was trying to give her a message with his eyes, but she couldn't understand it. "We did meet on the train. The girls and I were traveling westward and he helped us out of a . . . problem."

"What kind?" Deidre leaned closer still.

"Oh, well—" Harmony glanced at Thor and realized he was afraid she was going to tell them that she and the girls had kidnapped him. She couldn't help but chuckle. He'd never live it down in his family if they found out.

221

"What's so funny?" Alexandra nibbled a cookie.

"The way we met." Thor took control. "She had her hands full with seven girls and they all got sick at once on something they ate. I happened to be sitting near them and in self-defense I helped them down the car so they could hang their heads over the railing outside."

Deidre laughed, her green eyes twinkling. "Oh, Thor, I'd like to have seen that. I bet you were mad."

"You have no idea." He gave Harmony a dark look. "When I realized she needed a place for the children to stay, I thought of the institute and offered your services."

"That's so sweet." Deidre smiled at Hunter. "My brother can be thoughtful when he wants—"

"Something?" Hunter laughed.

Embarrassed that the implied suggestion meant her, Harmony felt her face heat so she quickly tried to explain the situation better. "Really, I think it was all in self-defense like he said."

"Seven sick little girls is a lot." Alberto chuckled. "But how did Tara get hurt?"

Harmony choked on the coffee and coughed. As Thor patted her back she realized how lying was making the situation worse and worse. But she couldn't tell them about the Wild Child Gang. They'd never help outlaws. And she wouldn't want them to know the truth in case Turnbull or the law came to call, questioning anybody and everybody.

"Another accident on the train. A stupid,

drunken cowboy started target practice." Thor took over again.

"That's terrible." Alexandra looked at Harmony in concern.

"He won't do that again." Thor set down his mug of coffee, untouched.

"We're so glad you came to us for help." Alexandra smiled at Harmony. "And I'm glad my son was able to help you and the girls on the train."

"I'm lucky to have met Thor and come to the institute." Harmony knew she was going to have to tell some of the truth in order to make sure the girls were kept safe. "The truth of the matter is that I'm in a difficult situation. What happened with Thor and the train is behind us now." She glanced at him, letting him know she was thinking about the Wild Child Gang. "But we still have a problem."

"What is it?" Deidre sat back in satisfaction. "I knew it. You're a labor activist, aren't you?"

"In a way I suppose I may be. You see, the girls are all orphans because their mothers and relatives and friends died in a sweatshop fire. We lived, but we got blamed for the fire. That's why we fled Chicago."

"How tragic. I don't know how you kept on going. You have my deepest sympathy," Alexandra said. "As we've mentioned before, if there's anything at all we can do to help please tell us. Believe me, I know how cruel this world can be. And you've been very brave and strong."

Harmony found the sympathy and the looks of concern on their faces almost harder to bear than Turnbull's cruelty. She could fight meanness, even understand it, but this took her breath away and made her feel weak with longing to be protected. But she mustn't let these feeling overwhelm her. She must continue to fight.

Thor squeezed her hand.

She appreciated the support, but pulled away as she focused on Alberto. "Yes, I still need help. If it's all right with you and the girls, I'd like to leave them here so they'll be safe while I go back to Chicago and clear our names. I hope to put the man responsible out of business and behind bars."

Deidre jumped to her feet. "I'll help you get justice."

Harmony looked at her in astonishment.

"Sit down, Deidre." Thor frowned. "If anybody's going to help, I will."

"You?" Deidre sat down, but stared at her brother. "When did you care about woman or labor suffrage?"

"Don't you have enough battles of your own without having to get involved with Harmony's problem, too?"

"I don't expect you to understand, but Harmony and I are part of the same sisterhood. Sisters help each other."

"Well, so do brothers, or husbands, or fathers." He cleared his throat. "You know what I mean." Lover is what he'd thought, but he hoped no one

FREE BOOK CERTIFICATE

4 FREE BOOKS

ZEBRA HOME SUBSCRIPTION SERVICE, INC.

YES! Please start my subscription to Zebra Historical Romances and send me my first 4 books absolutely FREE. I understand that each month I may preview four new Zebra Historical Romances free for 10 days. If I'm not satisfied with them, I may return the four books within 10 days and owe nothing. Otherwise, I will pay the low preferred subscriber's price of just $3.75 each; a total of $15.00, *a savings off the publisher's price of $3.00.* I may return any shipment and I may cancel this subscription at any time. There is no obligation to buy any shipment and there are no shipping, handling or other hidden charges. Regardless of what I decide, the four free books are mine to keep.

NAME _____

ADDRESS _____ APT _____

CITY _____ STATE ____ ZIP _____

TELEPHONE ( ) _____

SIGNATURE _____

(if under 18, parent or guardian must sign)

ZB0693

. . . .

Fill in the Free Book Certificate below, and we'll send your FREE BOOKS to you as soon as we receive it.

If the certificate is missing below, write to: Zebra Home Subscription Service, Inc., P.O. Box 5214, 120 Brighton Road, Clifton, New Jersey 07015-5214.

FREE BOOKS

TO GET YOUR 4 FREE BOOKS WORTH $18.00 — MAIL IN THE FREE BOOK CERTIFICATE TODAY

4

FREE BOOKS

MORE PASSION AND ADVENTURE AWAIT... YOUR TRIP TO A BIG ADVENTUROUS WORLD BEGINS WHEN YOU ACCEPT YOUR FIRST 4 NOVELS ABSOLUTELY *FREE* (AN $18.00 VALUE)

Accept your Free gift and start to experience more of the passion and adventure you like in a historical romance novel. Each Zebra novel is filled with proud men, spirited women and tempestuous love that you'll remember long after you turn the last page.

Zebra Historical Romances are the finest novels of their kind. They are written by authors who really know how to weave tales of romance and adventure in the historical settings you love. You'll feel like you've actually gone back in time with the thrilling stories that each Zebra novel offers.

GET YOUR FREE GIFT WITH THE START OF YOUR HOME SUBSCRIPTION

Our readers tell us that these books sell out very fast in book stores and often they miss the newest titles. So Zebra has made arrangements for you to receive the four newest novels published each month.

You'll be guaranteed that you'll never miss a title, and home delivery is so convenient. And to show you just how easy it is to get Zebra Historical Romances, we'll send you your first 4 books absolutely FREE! Our gift to you just for trying our home subscription service.

BIG SAVINGS AND FREE HOME DELIVERY

Each month, you'll receive the four newest titles as soon as they are published. You'll probably receive them even before the bookstores do. What's more, you may preview these exciting novels free for 10 days. If you like them as much as we think you will, just pay the low preferred subscriber's price of just $3.75 each. *You'll save $3.00 each month off the publisher's price.* AND, your savings are even greater because there are never any shipping, handling or other hidden charges—FREE Home Delivery. Of course you can return any shipment within 10 days for full credit, no questions asked. There is no minimum number of books you must buy.

else had followed his line of reasoning. His mother was looking at him with a little smile on her lips that didn't bode well. Like Deidre she always thought she knew everything. Unfortunately, she usually did.

"Please don't argue." Harmony realized she had to stop this before it got out of hand. "Deidre, I thank you for the offer, but this is dangerous. I wouldn't dare involve anybody else. I want to leave the girls here where they will be safe. When I'm done, I'll want them with me again. That's all. Is it okay?"

"You can leave the children here for as long as you like." Alberto looked sternly at Harmony. "But we couldn't possibly let you go off into a dangerous situation without proper help and support."

"I'll help her if she needs it." Thor frowned at everyone in the room.

"Thank you." Harmony felt amazement rush through her. She could hardly believe she was being offered so much help and concern. How could these people be so generous, especially with total strangers? Maybe it was because they had so much or so much to give to others, not only in money but in love and happiness, too.

"I don't know anyone in Chicago, but I'm sure I could get a name for you." Deidre set her coffee aside. "I really would like to help."

Unfortunately their generosity made Harmony feel she was losing control of her life. Once more. If she wasn't careful, she'd be swathed like a newborn baby. She couldn't let that happen. They didn't understand the danger, or Turnbull, or how she had to do it on her own if she could ever respect and rely on herself in the future. She would *not* lose her freedom, not even for help.

Thor glared at Deidre. "I told you I'd help her."

"Please, I can't tell you how much it means to me for you to offer help, but only I understand the situation." Harmony took a deep breath. "If you will keep the girls here so I can rest easy in my mind about them, then I'll go on alone. That's all I want."

"You're going nowhere alone." Thor took her hand and held on hard. "If you insist on going to Chicago, then I'll take you."

Harmony started to protest.

"We can discuss payment later." Thor squeezed her hand. "You can hire me as bodyguard if you insist. I'm sure you can use one."

Deidre chuckled as she glanced at Hunter. "You'd better beware of bodyguards, Harmony. They get awfully good at their job."

Harmony looked from one to the other, confused but aware of an undercurrent of emotion or meaning. Suddenly she couldn't take any more. She wasn't used to having her plans and actions questioned. And she wasn't used to having to explain herself. She'd been on her own a long time. And she liked it that way. She stood up.

"Thanks for the warning. And dinner." She smiled at the group to take the sting from her quick retreat. "If you don't mind, I'm feeling tired so I think I'll go on up to my room. Thanks again

226

for everything. When I've had a few days to rest and make plans, I'll know more what I want to do."

Alberto stood and bowed to her. "Put your mind at rest. We will take the very best care of your girls. And we stand ready to help you in any way we can."

She smiled her thanks, then quickly walked across the room. She heard Thor follow, but didn't look back. As she put a foot on the bottom stair, she turned to face him.

He stopped near her. "You haven't changed your mind even after seeing how good life can be here?"

"It is good here, but until I settle my past I have no future at all. Surely you understand."

"I understand you're stubborn, but so am I." He leaned forward and placed a warm kiss on her forehead. "We'll talk about this later. Now get some rest."

She raised an eyebrow. *"You* get some rest." She started up the staircase, then glanced back.

He saluted her, his blue eyes warm and bright.

Fourteen

When Harmony awoke the next morning, she realized she had slept late. Sunlight streamed in through the lace curtains covering the windows. She sat upright, her heart beating fast. What had she missed? Were the girls all right? The horses? What about Turnbull? Was there enough food for breakfast? Had Tara gotten worse in the night?

And then she remembered why she had slept late. For the first time in her life that she could remember she had the luxury of not having to get up before dawn to work, or help, or nurse, or clean. She dropped back against the soft sheets and inhaled deeply. How clean the room smelled with the faint scent of the desert coming in through the partially open window.

For the moment she didn't have to do anything, absolutely nothing. She stretched the long muscles of her arms and legs. She had slept well, with not a single nightmare to wake her. She didn't know when she had felt so wonderful. She was clean, just a little hungry, and safe. Someone else had taken over the responsibility of the girls for a while.

Until this moment, she hadn't realized how much pressure she had been under to keep them all safe and fed and happy. Now that the pressure was gone she could feel how great the tension had been. How had they survived to this point? She shivered. They could have been caught or hurt so many times during their long escape from Chicago. But here they were in a safe house, with loving, caring people around them. *Rich* people. Had she actually come to believe there could be people with money who cared about others besides themselves?

She hadn't wanted to believe Thor could care. She hadn't wanted to believe he was more than an overgrown spoiled brat looking for a good time. She hadn't wanted to trust him or his family. But seeing them together, understanding their love for each other, and being made a part of it had affected her. She wanted the family closeness they shared and she wanted it forever.

Suddenly her mood changed. She wasn't part of this family. And she never would be. She sat up, swinging her feet over the side of the bed. She was too different to ever be accepted as one of them. If she stayed much longer, she'd destroy herself by always reaching out to take whatever crumbs they were willing to drop her. She could become so dependent, so willingly their slave for her own happiness as well as the girls' safety that she would never be able to leave.

She stood up and pulled on the peach robe that matched the nightgown she wore. *Silk.* She stroked the soft material. She had never thought to wear it and she wasn't sure she ever would again. She mustn't let physical comfort dim the reason she was at the institute. She mustn't forget the fire. Or Turnbull. She'd almost believed in Thor's fantasy life. But it wasn't real. Not for her.

Turnbull was somewhere in New Mexico or Arizona, maybe even in Tucson. And he was searching for her and the children. He knew they were nearby. He wouldn't give up now that he was so close. He wouldn't give up at all. He had to get rid of them for good, one way or another.

She pushed her long hair back while she walked to the bathroom. As she used its comforts, she realized how easily she could become accustomed to this luxury, too. Turnbull lived this type of life and he'd left it for the wilds of the West. That's how much he wanted to catch her. Otherwise he'd never have left his comfortable, powerful base in Chicago.

Stepping out of the bathroom, she glanced around the room. How she'd like to stay here and never, ever leave. But that was a fantasy, too. A fantasy that belonged to a weak woman, not the leader of the Wild Child Gang, not her mother's daughter. But for a moment she wished she were weak, for then she would cling to Thor and his family for as long as they would let her.

She walked across the room, appreciating the loveliness of the decor, something Thor's family took for granted. Voices and laughter drifted through the window from the backyard. She stopped to look outside. And smiled. The girls were having a picnic lunch just as Thor had promised. His family had gathered and appeared to be having as much fun as the girls.

Feeling a sharp stab of jealousy rush through her, she glanced away. Could she be so easily replaced? Maybe it would be best for the girls if she left them here and never returned. What could she ever offer them that could compare to this? How could she ever afford to give them even a part of this type of life? Yet was it best for them?

None of them had ever had the chance to go to school. They'd worked as soon as they were able and stopped only because of the fire. Even if they had worked strictly in the home, she doubted if any of them would have gone to school. Nobody she knew considered it important for girls to read or write or do their sums. Boys went to school, not girls. That's what her father had always said and it had made him mad when her mother had read a newspaper or tried to teach their daughter to read.

She pulled her mother's gold locket from between her breasts and felt its warmth in her palm. Her mother had braved his violence to teach her. Now she could read, not really well but good enough to get by, and she could sign her name and print fairly well. She'd been teaching the girls on the trail and all of them could sign their names now. They could also read a few headlines. But how could she compare to a college-educated lady, a real nurse and teacher?

Maybe she'd been living in a dreamworld all along. Maybe her mother had put too many fancy ideas in her head. Maybe all her dreams were fantasy. She dropped the locket back under her nightgown. She would *not* feel sorry for herself.

She and the girls had survived the fire. They were a family. They wouldn't abandon each other and they'd find a way to get what they needed from life. Yet she would have to leave them for a while. She had to find Turnbull and take him back to Chicago for justice.

Maybe again she was thinking too big. Maybe nobody would take her seriously. But she *would* do it, if not for herself then for the memory of the women and girls who had died. And for her mother who would have left her father before he killed her if she'd had a proper education so she could get a good enough job to support herself and her daughter. She'd do it for all the women who needed help and couldn't get it.

Looking back out the window, she smiled at the happiness she could see there, then she noticed Thor had disappeared. He probably had business or friends or something elsewhere. She felt another stab of jealousy. What was wrong with her? He had his own life. He did whatever rich young men did. They partied, she supposed. He'd mentioned graduating from college so maybe he worked for his father now or maybe not.

Now that she thought about it, she didn't know

what he did or what type of goals he had. He'd been on his way to attend the opening ceremony of the institute, but he'd missed that. Now he had no reason to stay. Maybe he'd go back to his family's ranch or their plantation or their place in New York City. Why would he want to stay here with some young girls or go with her on a dangerous mission? He probably couldn't wait to get back to his real life.

She shuddered at the thought of the way she'd offered her body to him. He could buy or have given to him the very best of women. She wasn't the best. And she wasn't even young anymore. At twenty-six she had reached the age most women married, but she wasn't interested in that. How could she have been so bold, so confident? But that was when she'd been leader of the Wild Child Gang. Here she was simply a woman in need. What a change. And what a difference it made in her.

Turning, she quickly crossed the room. She couldn't stay here. At this rate, she'd be helpless in no time and then nobody would want or need her. And she'd be unable to help herself. She'd never let that happen. She would get dressed and go into Tucson and search for answers. A man as prominent as Turnbull had to leave a trail somewhere. It was up to her to find it, but not let him find her. To do that she would dress like a lady. She laughed without humor. What a perfect disguise. He would never recognize her.

She took out the clothes she had worn the night

233

before and tossed them on a chair near the bed. Before she dressed she would make the bed and leave everything as neatly as possible. She didn't want someone cleaning up after her. She'd had to do plenty of that herself in the boardinghouse. She'd had enough of other people's dirt to last her a lifetime.

As she lifted the covers on the bed, she heard a sound in the sitting room. Whirling around, she saw Thor stop in the doorway.

He glanced at the bed, then back at her. "You getting that ready for me?" His blue eyes turned darker as he let his gaze trail over her body, examining the peach robe that exposed more than it concealed.

Without conscious thought, she pulled the robe tighter over her breasts. She felt vulnerable, exposed, then grew angry at herself. In the desert she had never felt this way. She had been aggressive there. Leader of the Wild Child Gang. She stepped toward him. "Did you come to collect?"

He shook his head. "I wish I had. No, I came to check on you. I saw you watching us from the window. I expected you to join us, but you didn't."

"I thought I'd go into town."

"I wanted to thank you for bringing the girls here. My family is having a good time making a fool of themselves over them."

"And you?"

"I already did that so I guess it runs in the family."

She smiled. "And I thought we were the fools, or like pigs in a field of corn."

"Do you really like it here?"

"It's lovely. And I like your family, too."

"Good. You won them over last night. Deidre is so impressed she can hardly wait to get back to New York City and tell her friends about you. Mother is treating the girls like the grandchildren she keeps hoping I'll have. I thought that was up to Deidre now that she's come of age, but the way she's going with college and the shipping firm and woman suffrage I doubt if we'll see any children from her before she's thirty. I keep trying to get Hunter to make an honest woman of her, but—"

"Deidre will do what she wants when she wants."

"Don't I know it. It's beginning to look like I may have to be the one to provide my parents with grandchildren."

She chuckled. "I don't think you can do that all by yourself."

"I know."

For a moment silence filled the room as she struggled for breath. She could hardly think for the heat in his eyes or the predatory stance of his body. What did he mean? Surely not her. She was completely wrong. He must be thinking of the girls as children. She inhaled sharply. "The girls are my family, Thor. I'm not leaving them here forever."

"You can stay with them." He stepped into the room.

She took a step backward. "I have to go to Chicago. If I don't, I'll never be able to live with myself and Turnbull will never stop hunting us."

He didn't stop until he stood in front of her, within easy reach if he wanted to touch her. "I'm used to getting my way. You know that, don't you?"

She nodded, unable to speak for his nearness made her hot and wild and confused.

"I'm starting to want you in a way I've never wanted any woman before."

Forcing herself, she shrugged. "At twenty-one, that's not long."

"Long enough." He reached out and captured a strand of her long dark hair. "I even like all those girls of yours."

"We don't live in the same world."

"Now we do."

She shook her head, pulling her hair out of his hand. "I'm going to Chicago. You're going back to whatever life you live."

"Now that I'm out of college, I'm going to run the plantation. I'll have a lot of experienced help at first, but it'll all be mine in time. I love the land there. And the people. I need a lot of workers. I know plenty of people who can supervise, but I don't know so many who can lead workers."

She raised an eyebrow in puzzlement. "I don't understand what you mean." She could hardly listen to him, for his presence in the bedroom, so

236

close to the bed, so early in the morning was doing strange things to her mind and body. When had she come to want him so much?

"Job. I was thinking about you being somebody the workers could come to with their problems. You're experienced, you can lead, and you can learn." He took a fistful of her hair and pulled it toward him, then let it slowly slip through his fingers.

"You're offering me a job on Jarmon Plantation?"

"Yes. The girls would like it there."

She lost the strength in her legs and abruptly sat down on the bed.

"Are you okay?" He sat beside her, then took her hand and rubbed it. When it was warm, he started on the other. "Harmony?"

Lowering her head, she inhaled deeply. He'd given her the answer to all her worries. A job. But could she trust him? And could she even do the work? She jerked her hand away. "Would it pay enough to provide well for the girls?"

"They'd have everything they want, education, horses, friends. I think they'd like the South. If you didn't want to live on the plantation, you could live in New Orleans. But I'd rather you lived in the house."

"With you?"

He nodded, his blue eyes dark and serious.

She jumped up and paced away from him before she pulled him into her arms. Of course he didn't mention marriage, not to a woman like her. She'd

237

have been shocked if he'd even considered it. Why should he? Anyway, she wasn't interested in marriage. It had destroyed her mother, as well as other women she'd known. As far as she could tell, marriage was a dangerous state for women. They lost too many rights and were too much at the mercy of their husbands, who seemed to have very little.

"What do you think about the job?"

She twisted her mind to his question. "If it was a job, it'd be strictly a job." She turned back to face him. He sat on the bed, still, so very still. "I'm going to pay you back for the girls staying here, but then we'd be even. Right?"

He stood up and walked over to her. "We could go to Louisiana now. Turnbull would never find you. You wouldn't owe me for the girls staying at the institute. We'd have time to get to know each other. And it'd be strictly a job."

Biting her lower lip, she shook her head. "It's a fantasy. It's too perfect. Life doesn't work that way."

"But you want to come with me, don't you?"

"Yes!" She turned around and walked over to the window where she could see the girls laughing and playing with Thor's family. She turned back, safely across the room from him. "But I won't. I have to make my stand, here and now, or I'll never be able to live with myself or the girls." She inhaled deeply. "The fire. You weren't there. You don't wake up in the middle of the night, sweating and gasping for breath, hearing the cries of women and children burning alive. And all so somebody rich could get richer."

He crossed the room in several strides and took her in his arms. He held her close as she shivered and clung to him. "I'm sorry. I don't, can't know what that was like, but I understand your need. Deidre taught me that much. And I've seen you struggle to survive. I'll never think of women the way I did again."

Pushing back, she looked up into his face, then raised her hand and traced his features. "You're too young for me, too innocent, maybe even too good. I don't want you to ever understand."

He cradled her head against his chest. "It's too late for that, Harmony. The offer in Louisiana still stands, but if you're going after Turnbull so am I."

She pushed away from him. "I can't take you into that type of danger. If I'm hurt or killed it doesn't matter. The girls will be all right here. And so will you."

Frowning, he crossed his arms over his chest. "It matters if you live or die. And if you hadn't noticed, I'm twice your size. You've been protecting the girls so long you think you have to do that for everyone. Trust me, I can take care of myself. And you as well."

She threw up her hands and paced away from him. "Thor, you don't know what you're saying. Why are you doing this?"

"How the hell should I know? Why don't you put it down to a bored rich boy. Make me happy.

Say you want me to come on your vendetta. Deidre would never get over me helping somebody in her own chosen area."

"Is that all it is to you?"

"If that's what you want to believe."

"I don't know what to believe."

"Well, believe this." He strode across the room, took her by the shoulders, and pulled her close. He glared down into her eyes. "There is no way I'm letting you go after Turnbull alone. If you're hell-bent on going, then we'll go together. When we're done with him, then we can plan our lives."

"In Louisiana?"

"Yes." He lifted her face with the tip of one finger and placed a hot kiss on her lips. "I've been waiting a long time for you and didn't even know it."

"I pay my debts and I don't succumb to my bosses."

He shook his head. "You've run free for too damn long. It's going to take a powerful man to bring you home and keep you there."

"Why don't you get out your lasso, partner?"

He grinned, showing strong white teeth. "I've already got you roped and you don't even know it."

"Wrong. I kidnapped you. I tied you up. *You're* roped and don't know it." She glared at him.

"I haven't tried your silken spurs yet, but when I do you'll know who's wearing the lasso around their neck."

"We already know."

"Do we?" He put an arm around her waist, his

hand hot through the silk. "Do you want me to show you?"

"I thought you were afraid to try."

He growled and put the other arm around her, drawing her against the long, hard length of him. When he pressed his mouth against hers, he felt her shiver against him. He nipped at her lips, heard her protest, then soothed them with his tongue. "Open your mouth to me."

Reaching upward, she twined her hands around the back of his neck to pull him closer. "Is the rope tight enough?"

He thrust his tongue into her mouth, tasting her sweetness, taking all she would give, then demanding more as she stroked deep into him, making him groan and rub his hands over her back, then lower until he cupped her hips and drew her against him, feeding his hardness with her softness. When she moaned and pulled him tighter yet, he broke the kiss and raised his head so he could look deep into her dark brown eyes.

Tenderly he touched her swollen lips. "I think we must look like a couple of drovers who missed their cows and lassoed each other."

She lowered her lashes, then mischievously looked up at him. "I think you might look good in a collar."

"Only if you're holding the leash."

Smiling, she opened her eyes wide, feigning innocence. "I thought you wanted to be the boss. I thought you wanted to wear the spurs."

"I've had it all. Now all I want is you."

She stepped back and shook her head. "Not with the boss, I don't."

"I'm not your boss." He growled and reached for her.

Moving just out of his reach, she shook a finger at him. "You can't have it both ways. Either I pay off the debt or you become my boss."

"Damn!" He looked frustrated a moment, then he grinned. "I want it all. Why should I change my life now?"

"Because—"

"No!" He walked across to the open doorway, then looked back. "Get dressed and meet me downstairs. I'll take you into Tucson and show how to go about getting what you want."

"Turnbull?"

"Isn't that what you want above all else?"

She hesitated. At the moment, she wanted Thor above all else. But that wasn't practical. She'd played all she had time for right now. She had to get serious. It was simply that Thor brought out something in her that made her want to tease and flirt and drive him wild. But it was his fault. If he didn't seem to enjoy it so much, she wouldn't dare.

"Isn't it?" He took a step toward her.

She held up a hand to stop him. "Yes. I want Turnbull."

"Then let's start hunting him down." He frowned. "The sooner that man is off your mind the sooner you can think about other, more pleasurable matters." He turned on his heel, then stopped and glanced back again. "By the way, Deidre sent up a copy of that book she gives anybody who'll stand still long enough. You don't have to read it. Just thank her. That's enough."

She followed him as he walked through the sitting room.

At the door, he looked back. "You've got fifteen minutes. Be downstairs by then or I'll come after you."

"What makes you think I'll follow your orders?" But he'd already shut the door by the time she'd finished her sentence.

She walked over to the door and locked it. He wouldn't be making another surprise entry. She glanced around and saw the small volume on the chaise lounge. For the first time she sat down and found the piece of furniture wonderfully comfortable. She picked up the book and read aloud, *"Vindication of the Rights of Women* by Mary Wollstonecraft."

Opening the book, she turned to the first page and started reading. Fascinated, she leaned back. The book was about women's lack of rights, but it had been written almost a hundred years before. So long ago and yet so little change for women. She wanted to read more, but she didn't read well enough and she needed to go into Tucson. Later, she promised herself, she would find a way to read the book and share it with the girls.

Standing, she set down the volume. Some day soon she would learn to read well. She would go to school, maybe with the girls. She would become

243

educated, maybe get a good job and help other workers just as Thor had suggested. Had he been serious? Would it be a real job? Did she dare even think about it? Harmony Harper, a labor organizer? No, she couldn't think about it.

She walked back into the bedroom. There was no point in thinking about her future after Turn-bull. She must focus on revenge first. She had been lulled by beauty and peace, but her anger still raged deep inside. Until it was sated, she had no future. No job, no happiness, no love. Not even passion.

Thor Clarke-Jarmon was a luxury, a fantasy she could not afford. When she went to Chicago, she would go alone. He would stay safe with the girls and his family.

And anger would go with her.

Fifteen

"Thank you for the book, Deidre." Harmony stood on the front porch of the institute. She smiled as she gazed up at Thor's sister. Clarke-Jarmon blood. Harmony Harper with her dark hair and short stature didn't fit in with their tall, blond beauty. Harper blood. It was just as good.

"Vindication of the Rights of Women is my favorite book in the whole world." Deidre gave a bright smile. "When you've read it, I'd love to discuss it with you. And my offer still stands for New York City. If you don't want to speak to a group, I'd be delighted for you to visit. You could stay at the house and attend some suffrage meetings with me."

"Thank you, but I've got so much to do right now."

Deidre nodded. "Of course you do. Labor organizations like the Grange are changing working conditions for everyone. Now is the time for women and children to stand up for their rights so they won't be excluded."

"But I'm not—"

"If you bring that sweatshop owner to justice, you'll have the credentials to lead workers any-where you want." Deidre's eyes turned to green fire. "Harmony, you're needed! You saved those children. You saved yourself. If you can do it once, you can do it again. Please don't turn your back on the Cause. I'll help any way I can."

"Thanks, but until I know justice is done, I can't think about the future."

Deidre narrowed her eyes. "You're right. Focus. It's one of my greatest problems. That's what I like about you. You see the job and you do it, quickly, quietly, efficiently. How I wish I were more like you."

"Like me?" Harmony blinked in astonishment.

"Everyone takes you seriously right from the first, even if you are petite. And you've got that great voice that would calm and organize a herd of raging longhorns."

"I do?"

"Oh my yes. Of course you noticed the way you had my entire family eating out of your hand last night. And, believe me, they aren't easy people to persuade. You're a straight-shooter and they like that. Everyone does."

"I'm not quite that honest, Deidre. You're mak-ing me out to be much more than I am."

"Spoken exactly as I'd expect. True leaders don't need fanfare and worshipers. They go about quietly getting the job done, only later noticing the masses who are following. You're a born leader, Harmony Harper. A woman born for her time. We need you.

246

And don't think for a moment that anyone will let you drift back into obscurity."

"What if I told you I've been on the wrong side of the law?"

"Oh, that Wild Child Gang stuff."

Harmony opened her eyes wide in surprise and horror. Had Thor betrayed them?

Deidre grinned. "It's just a guess, but you all arrived sporting pistols, wearing trousers, and looking tough enough to take on the West. I simply *knew* who you had to be. I mean, the stories have been in *all* the papers. You're celebrities. You could probably sell your story to a New York paper for lots of money. In fact, a friend of mine, Simon Gainesville, works for the *Tribune*. Why don't I ask him to see what his paper would think about buying your story?"

"I didn't say I was part of the gang." Harmony's mind whirled. Sell her story? What about the law? But what about the money she could desperately use?

"You don't have to say it. I guessed. Mother agrees."

"Oh no!"

"But we haven't discussed it with anybody else. That was a nice story about meeting Thor when the girls were sick, but I don't believe it for a moment. It was a holdup, wasn't it?" Deidre leaned closer, fire in her eyes. "How I envy you. You're just about the most exciting woman I know. I think the only one who comes close is Old Nate, a one-armed sailor about near a hundred years old who runs a tavern in the Bahamas. What a woman! You two would make great friends. I hope you can meet some day."

"Bahamas?" Harmony wanted to cover her ears. She didn't know when she'd heard so much so fast. And it was all so wild! How could this beautiful, rich, educated young lady be in awe of her, plain little Harmony Harper?

"Yes. New Providence is gorgeous. You've never seen such clear turquoise waters or bright white sand."

"Chicago has a beautiful lake."

"Tropical islands. You should get Thor to take you there when this is all said and done. Maybe Hunter and I can join you. For that matter, we should get Mom and Dad to go, too. That's where they met."

"Wait! You're running away here. This is the farthest I've ever been from Chicago. I can't even imagine a place like the Bahamas."

"It's safe now. Don't worry about that."

"You mean it wasn't?"

"Wreckers. You know, they lure ships onto rocks to tear out their hulls, then salvage the cargo on the shore. Clarke Shipping lost several ships that way."

"That's horrible. What about the crew and passengers?"

Deidre nodded. "Dead."

"Is there no way to end greed in the world?"

"I don't much think so and that's why we must work to stop it hurting innocent people." Deidre glanced up at the institute. "Yes, after this is all set up and before Hunter and I move to New York City and start college next winter, we all deserve a vacation in the Bahamas. The only person who might give us any trouble is that nasty Captain Sully, but Old Nate sent word they haven't seen hide nor hair of him. He might even be dead."

Harmony shook her head. "Captain Sully?"

"Don't worry about him. If he sets foot on New Providence Island again, Old Nate will see he wishes he hadn't."

"If I knew what you were talking about, I could say I was relieved." Harmony shook her head.

"Trust me on this one. You don't want to know." Deidre glanced up. "Oh, here comes Thor. He's such a bear about you. He wants to keep you all to himself." She cast a sly glance at Harmony. "Listen, he's had his own way too long. He needs a good, strong woman to get him in line."

"I don't mean to sound unfriendly, but I'm leaving for Chicago soon. Alone. I suppose you'll be going to New York and Thor back to Louisiana."

"And Mom and Dad to Texas."

"The fact is, I may never see any of you again."

"Oh, how can you say that!" Deidre looked stricken. "We're just getting to know each other and Thor needs a woman like you." She frowned. "Okay, I can see I'm rushing this. I tend to do that. Before you go, I'll give you my address in New York and the name of someone reliable in Chicago." She took Harmony's hand and squeezed.

"I adore the girls and I can't wait to see them all grow up to be suffragists. On the other hand, maybe we'll have equal rights by then and woman suffrage will simply be a brief note in history. That'd be best, wouldn't it?"

Harmony nodded. This young woman simply took her breath away with her energy, enthusiasm, determination, and great love for humanity. She *would* like to get to know her better and she *would* like for the girls to spend more time with her. But she realized Thor's family had gathered for a very special occasion and soon they would all part and go their separate ways. She'd been lucky to meet them all here and now because there might never be another opportunity. She felt sad and glad all at the same time.

Deidre squeezed Harmony's hand. "Please, don't be sad. I know you have a great responsibility on your shoulders, but remember you have friends, some you've never even met yet, to help you. And if you need me, I'll come to Chicago with you."

"Hunter'd never forgive me if I took you with me." Harmony squeezed Deidre's hand back, then let it go. "And Thor would be even worse."

Nodding, Deidre looked up as her brother drove the institute's surrey around to the front of the house. "You can trust him to help."

"He has already."

"Oh, look, there're the girls. I've got to run now."

Harmony glanced up to see all the girls dressed in their Wild Child Gang gear, without the masks, ride up with Thor's family. They were going for a ride out to a local ranch to look at cattle and see about a place to keep the horses so the girls could ride whenever they wanted. She wished she was going with them. She already felt sad and lonely to see them riding off with others. But she had to carry out her plans to find Turnbull, or the girls might not live to ride horses many more days.

"I'll see you later." Deidre waved to everyone waiting on her. "Don't forget to think about selling your story. If not to the newspaper, then maybe to a book publisher."

"I have to clear our names first. And, remember, I never said we were the Wild Child Gang."

Deidre laughed. "Of course you didn't. I wouldn't expect you to incriminate anyone. And don't worry. I have complete faith in you to accomplish whatever you set out to do." She planted a quick kiss on Harmony's cheek, then ran down the steps to mount her horse.

Harmony waved as she watched them ride away. After being the most important person in the world to the girls for months on end, suddenly they had others to love and care for them. It was hard to give up that special place in their lives. It was hard to share them. But she'd known it had to happen someday. She'd simply never expected it to happen so soon.

"Are you coming with me, or not?" Thor looked at her impatiently from the surrey.

How confident they all were. Thor had a wonderful family, a wonderful life. She was glad for him and glad to have shared it for a few days. If nothing else, she would always have the memories.

Hopefully the girls would learn a great deal here at the institute. Maybe they could even learn to trust, to have confidence in themselves, and to expect good in life. Maybe they could be children for a while. She hoped so because it was all something she could never have for herself. The most she could hope for was to get justice for her friends and find a good job. If she did that, life wouldn't be so bad, especially not while she shared it with the girls.

She gazed at Thor. If anyone could distract her from thoughts of losing the girls, it was this man. What would it be like if he really belonged just to her? Maybe that's why she had kidnapped him. Maybe she had wanted him to be hers for a while. Whatever the reason, she had learned from him, enjoyed him, and would be sad to lose his company.

Already she was seeing the end to her brief way of life as leader of the Wild Child Gang. She had to go on, but the future was unknown and filled with danger. Thor offered her sanctuary in Louisiana, but how long would it last? He was young and men were fickle. She had to have security for herself and the children. Nothing less would do.

"Harmony, what's keeping you?"

She curved her lips into a smile. She must stop her sad thoughts. She had a few more days here and she should enjoy them completely. They would never come again. She quickly ran down the steps, moving toward Thor in the brightly painted surrey with FLORA MCCUSKAR INSITUTUTE lettered on its side.

Yet Deidre's words came back to her, maybe to mock her. Both brother and sister saw her as a labor leader. She didn't understand how they could. It was true she had counseled other sweatshop workers, finding ways to make their lives a little less hard, sometimes talking to Turnbull for them, but she had always considered it simply what a friend and more experienced worker did. Could that add up to being a labor leader?

She had no idea. And she supposed it didn't matter. She had only one single goal right now. Stop Turnbull. Maybe Deidre was right. She could be single-minded. In fact, she didn't know how else to be, especially when the lives of others depended on her.

As she reached the surrey, Thor jumped down and walked with her around to the other side. He helped her up, letting his hands linger around her waist as he smiled at her with warmth, then he went around to sit beside her. He picked up the reins and started the horse forward.

As they rode down the street, Harmony thought of how different Tucson was from Chicago. And it wasn't simply the land and size. It was the wild spirit of the West. As Thor had once said, here no one had a past. Did she and the girls fit in better than Turnbull and his gunmen? Is that why he'd had so much trouble finding them? For the first time she didn't feel like so much of a stranger. Maybe she had always been wild at heart. She liked the idea, for it was in direct contrast to what she would have believed of herself as a sweatshop worker.

"The girls will be okay. Don't worry. You can trust my family to take care of them."

"I do. It's just that I wish I had gone with them."

"We still can."

"No. I can't wait any longer. Turnbull could already be in Tucson."

"And what if he's not?"

"He's somewhere close by. He recognized us on the train at Las Cruces. How far away could we be from that point?"

"In theory, the gang could've gone back to El Paso or south into Mexico or north into Colorado."

"Yes, but Turnbull's no fool. He followed our trail. We'd gone as far south as we could in the States, then turned west. And what is the next biggest town west after Las Cruces?"

"Tucson."

"You see my reasoning?"

"Yes. But it doesn't mean he isn't still hanging around Las Cruces."

"I agree. And that's why I have to find out where he is. And soon."

"You can count on me to help."

"I know. But I'm not sure how to go about any of this."

"We probably should have asked Deidre. She and Hunter tracked down the wreckers who were preying on Clarke ships."

"Really? I'm impressed." After all the praise Deidre had given her, she should have saved some for herself. Anybody who had done that deserved it.

"But I hate to ask her anything." Thor raised his hat and ran a hand through his hair. "She's such a know-it-all."

"You two like to fight, don't you?" She paused, thinking. "I can't imagine what it would be like to have a brother or sister, someone you're so close to that no matter what you say or do the other always understands and accepts."

"I don't think it's that easy." Thor clicked to the horses. "But we've always trusted each other to guard the other's back. I guess that's saying a lot."

"I think it is."

They rode on in silence, basking in the warm afternoon, looking at Tucson as they neared the heart of the town.

The main street wasn't all that far away from the institute and Harmony thought it looked just as rough and ready as she had expected by its reputation. Yes, it had a certain civilized air to it as seen in the Victorian house area where the in- stitute had been built, but it still had plenty of bars and bordellos and dance halls mixed in with the merchants and bathhouses and barbers.

Tumbleweeds rolled down the dusty main street. Horses were tied to the hitching posts out front of the buildings built side by side and fronted by roofed porches and long wooden boardwalks. Men lounged on wooden benches in front of the businesses. Women strolled along shopping, talking with friends. Proprietors glanced out their front doors to check the weather or the time of day or to look for patrons.

Harmony felt amazed at how normal it looked, while somewhere within the town's depths could lurk Turnbull and his men. But she didn't think he'd recognize her. She glanced at Thor. For asking questions, he could come in handy. He or his family were probably known around here. And he was a man. He'd be much more likely to get answers to questions even though she hated to admit it.

"I'm staying at the Blue Sage." He pointed to a three-story hotel, painted a sand color and trimmed with blue. "It's one of the best places in town. If Turnbull's here he might be staying there."

"Would you check? Could you ask around?" She hated to ask his help, but she needed it and he had offered. "Or should we start at the sheriff's office? Turnbull would surely go there first."

"I agree, but we should check the train depot and livery stables, too."

"Good idea. What about the newspaper office? Most of the Western papers have carried stories about the Wild Child Gang." She chuckled. "Most of what they printed about us wasn't true."

"But it sold papers?"

"I guess so."

As they laughed together, their gazes met and held till they both felt the heat and glanced away.

"I think you ought to be careful here, Harmony. Don't forget the Wild Child Gang is wanted by the law in the West. You're wanted by the law from Chicago. And Turnbull would like to get to you first."

"I think my disguise as a lady is good enough."

"It's no disguise at all."

She smiled, touched by his remark. At this rate, he was going to destroy her resistance and she'd never want to leave him. Louisiana. How could she even think of making her home so far from her beginnings? Yet Chicago had only bad memories for her now, except for her mother.

"Don't get mad, but how about if I leave you at the Drover Cafe? It serves plain, good food and ladies go there. You'd be safe. I could head over to the jail, see if a man like Turnbull had been in asking questions, then maybe go to a couple of the saloons. If I don't succeed, then you could go to the newspaper office." He glanced at her. "If you go into the saloons or sheriff's office, you'll cause enough talk to bring Turnbull running if he's in town."

"And all because I'm a woman?"

"Yes. A lady's got her place out here and that's

a plain, simple fact no matter how right or wrong."

"What would these good men think if they knew the Wild Child Gang was all female?"

Thor threw back his head and laughed. "Hell, they'd think the same thing I did at first. It couldn't be true, then embarrassed at how you'd tricked us all." He squeezed her hand. "The world's changing, Harmony. Women like you and my sister and my mother are seeing that it does, but men want the comfort of thinking they control the women in their lives. They aren't going to give it up easily."

"I know." She thought of her father. "But the price of that control can be the destruction of what they love."

"Few will see it that way."

"And you?"

He slanted at glance at her. "Between you and Deidre, I understand women better than I'd ever thought possible. I want the girls to grow up strong and smart and free to make their mark on the world any which way they choose. But somebody else like you is going to have to walk the path first."

"I'll need help if I'm to walk it."

"You've got it. Didn't you know?" He cleared his throat. "You won't be the first. Women have been fighting for their beliefs a long time. Deidre can give you all the names. Joan of Arc comes to my mind. Men underestimated her, then killed her for their fear. I don't want you to be a martyr."

"I won't, not if I can help it." She looked away from him, not wanting to believe what she read in his eyes or heard in his words. She also didn't want to think of herself as a leader or a martyr. She was simply doing what must be done.

"Good. So what do you think about having a cup of coffee at the cafe while I ask around?" He pulled to a stop in front of the Drover Cafe.

"As much as I hate to admit it, I think you're right. But instead of waiting here, I'd like to look around a little, maybe do some shopping for the girls, maybe even ask a few questions."

He frowned at her. "You'll be careful and meet me back here soon?"

She nodded and started to step down.

"Wait." He wound the reins around the brake, jumped down, then hurried around the back of the surrey. He held out his arms to her and when she came into them he held her longer than he should before letting her slowly slide down the length of him. "You're sure you'll be okay?"

"Yes." His nearness made her want to forget everything except being alone with him. "You be careful, too."

"I'll give you some money."

"No!" She walked away from him. "I still have some." When she stepped up on the boardwalk, she glanced back to watch him drive away.

On her own again, she turned to see what businesses were in the area. She noticed a dry goods store not far away and started for it. As she passed people, she saw they watched her, checking out her clothing, perhaps her general appearance. Could they possibly tell she was part of the Wild Child Gang? No, not unless it was written on her forehead, which it wasn't. She hoped.

Stepping inside the store, she realized it was cooler and darker than outside. The floor was rough wood. The merchandise was displayed here and there with very little order. It was far different from the Chicago stores like Marshall Field. But at least she could afford to buy something here.

Today she had a little extra money. She wanted to buy the girls something to remember her by when she was gone. As she looked around she quickly realized Thor's family could buy them much more and much finer things than she could ever afford. She had to save most of what money she had to pay for her trip back to Chicago.

Sighing, she picked up one item, then another. Finally she found herself standing in front of the candy jars. Candy would be a special treat that wouldn't last, but one they had rarely had a chance to enjoy. As she tried to decide what kind and how much, the proprietor walked over to her.

"Can I help you, ma'am?"

She glanced up into the weathered face of an older man. He looked at her hard behind tinted glasses.

"I want to buy eight twists of candy."

"Yes, ma'am. What kind?" He began twisting squares of white paper into cones.

"Two twists of each. Lemon drops. Horehound drops. Peppermint sticks. Licorice sticks."

She glanced around again while he filled her order. She would like to leave a thank-you gift for the institute. It would be good if it was something future children could enjoy, too. She wandered through the store again, trying to make a decision when she saw the perfect gift. Books.

Hurrying over to the area, she picked up each volume to read its contents. She found a few of the Red Line Edition of the Poets, the Arlington Edition Standard Classics, and the Hurst Popular Classics. She had to admit she didn't know much about the books, but she wasn't satisfied until she found the Alcott Works for girls. The single volume had been beautifully bound and cost ninety-nine cents. It was a lot of money for a single book, but she wanted to give something that would last.

She carried it to the counter and laid it down beside the twists of candy. The proprietor totaled up the cost and she tried not to think of the expense as she paid the amount. As he wrapped it all together, she decided to do a bit of prying on her own.

"I've heard the Wild Child Gang might be headed to Tucson. Have you heard?"

He snorted. "They're seen everywhere and by everybody, mostly by whiskey-soaked cowboys who don't have nothing better to do than brag about how they'll catch the gang." He turned and spat tobacco in a spittoon on his side of the counter.

He pointed at what he'd just wrapped. "This here's the best way to catch the Wild Child Gang."

"What do you mean?"

"They're a bunch of runny-nosed brats, aren't they? Candy'll catch them faster than the law."

"I see what you mean."

" 'Course I'm right. Any fool can see that."

"Are you planning to catch them right here in Tucson?"

"No, ma'am. That gang's too smart to come into Tucson. That'd be like digging their own grave. But they've been spotted all over Arizona." He leaned closer. "Don't you read the papers?"

"Not lately." She picked up her package.

"Careful where you take that candy. You'll have the Wild Child Gang nipping at your heels."

As she left the store, his laughter followed her. She smiled to herself. If he only knew how close he was to the truth. But she was glad to hear there'd been so many different reports. Maybe it would keep Turnbull confused. While he was chasing ghosts, she would catch him.

She quickly walked down the boardwalk and pushed open the door to the Drover Cafe. Only a few customers sat at the round oak tables covered with blue-and-white-checkered tablecloths. Curtains in a matching fabric had been pulled back to expose glass windows. She hesitated, unsure what to do. She had eaten in only a few cafes in her life. She'd never been able to afford them until she'd left Chicago.

"You meetin' somebody, ma'am?" A tall, big-boned woman in a gray dress and a long white apron walked up.

"Yes. I'd like a table."

"Near a front window?"

"Yes, thank you."

When she was seated, she glanced up and smiled. "Coffee, please. And do you have any of the town's newspapers I could read?"

"Sure. I keep them for the customers. You want a whole week's worth?"

"Yes, please."

Harmony watched the woman walk away and breathed a sigh of relief. So far so good. People thought her simply a lady shopping for her family. She set the package on the table near the window, then glanced outside for Thor. He wasn't in sight so she turned back. The waitress set a stack of newspapers, then a cup of coffee on the table.

"Anything else you need, ma'am, let me know."

"Thanks."

While she waited for the coffee to cool, she checked the papers. Starting with the current date, she glanced through the paper, checking the headlines for any mention of the Wild Child Gang. Three days back, she stopped in shock. The headline read, WILD CHILD GANG IN FLAGSTAFF!

She could hardly believe her eyes as she slowly scanned the article, stumbling over many of the words. As far as she could tell, it seemed the Wild Child Gang had attacked a group of drunken cowboys returning to their ranch north of Flagstaff. Suddenly she realized what was going on in the

West. People were blaming the gang for losing their money in gambling or some other way so they wouldn't be responsible or embarrassed themselves.

As she read on she learned the cowboys had all sworn they'd recognized the Wild Child Gang because of their size and viciousness. The law had taken down the amount of lost money and horses, then sent out a report. She set down the newspaper. What if Turnbull had read the article? What if he had believed it? What if he had gone to Flagstaff searching for them? What if he was there right now seeking their hideout? Her mind whirled with possibilities.

Where was this place called Flagstaff? She read through the article to discover the small town was located in northern Arizona. It would be easy to assume the gang had fled to a more isolated spot after the shootout on the train. Why they would call attention to themselves by robbing cowboys made no sense, but she hoped Turnbull wouldn't think of that point.

Taking a deep breath she leaned back in her chair and glanced up. Thor was walking toward her. He looked good, almost too good. Handsome, golden, tanned, muscled. Suddenly she found it hard to breathe. Her skin flushed. When he sat down and reached for her hand, she lost all track of thought.

"Sorry. Turnbull and his men were here a few days ago, asking about the Wild Child Gang. The sheriff had no answers for them. And he hasn't heard from them since."

She squeezed his hand. "It's okay. I think I know where they are." She pushed the newspaper toward him.

He read the headline, then looked back at her, a puzzled frown between his eyes.

"Do you know how to get to Flagstaff?"

Sixteen

"What have you got in the package?" Thor glanced in the back of the surrey where he had earlier put Harmony's package.

"Surprises for the girls. I bought them twists of candy."

"They'll love it."

"They've had so little chance to be children. I thought it would make them feel young and special."

"Good idea. They'll have a great time eating it."

"I bought one for you, too."

He raised his eyebrows. "For me?"

"Aren't you part of the Wild Child Gang?"

"True enough. What flavor do I get?"

She chuckled. "You have your choice of lemon, peppermint, horehound, or licorice." She stepped closer to him. "What is your favorite flavor?"

He put a fingertip to her lips. "You."

Licking his finger with the tip of her tongue, she smiled seductively as he pulled back his finger to suck the tip, tasting her.

"You're bad, Thor."

266

"Not out here where everybody can see us. If I had you alone, it'd be a different story."

"What kind?"

He started to reply, then noticed a horseback rider watching them as he rode by. He looked away from Harmony, took a deep breath, then glanced back, his blue eyes hooded. "Did you buy candy for yourself?"

Surprised, she shook her head.

"You don't think of yourself enough. Didn't you ever get to be a child?"

Her brown eyes widened, then she lowered her lids. "It doesn't matter now. I'm twenty-six and—"

"What's your favorite candy?"

"Thor, I said it doesn't matter anymore."

"Tell me, what kind?"

She rolled her eyes. "I don't know. Okay?"

He frowned. "You don't know?"

"Well, I've never had much. Maybe on special occasions. My mother would save to . . . I don't want to talk about it." She turned away and started to step up to the surrey.

Thor's hands were warm and strong around her waist as he helped her up. When she was seated, he squeezed her hands. "I'm sorry. I didn't mean to bring back painful memories."

"It's all right. I'm being silly. If you must know, I like lemon."

"Sweet and sour. That's my Harmony."

"I'm not *your* anything."

"Wait. I'll be right back."

She watched him jump up to the boardwalk,

267

then take several long strides down it to disappear inside the dry goods store she'd been in earlier. What had he forgotten? She looked away. Why had she gotten so upset about the candy? It was silly and it didn't matter anymore. She had a lot more important matters on her mind.

She thought back to their afternoon. Over delicious apple pie and strong coffee, they'd made plans about Turnbull, then they'd gotten the information they needed with a few questions placed here and there in town. She knew where to find Turnbull now and she knew what to do with that information. She was ready to start a new life, anxious in fact.

What she didn't need to do was discuss her childhood, or lack of it. It simply didn't matter anymore. Something like that could never be brought back or changed. And she had no need to do it. Sometimes Thor reminded her a lot of the girls. He was five years younger than she was so maybe that accounted for it. She just wished he'd hurry.

She glanced over her shoulder in frustration, then gasped in astonishment. Thor hurried toward her with the whole glass jar of lemon drops from the store, only now it was completely full. He grinned at her, then strode the last several steps to her side.

Plopping the jar in her lap, he placed a quick kiss on her lips, then rounded the surrey to sit down. As he picked up the reins, he glanced at her and winked.

"Thor! What is this?" She glanced over her shoulder. "You didn't steal it, did you? That man's not coming after us, is he?"

"Relax." He reached over and tapped on the glass lid. "Have one."

"Thor! You bought this? All of this? For me?"

He laughed in pleasure. "Yes, for you, just for you. Happy Birthday!"

"It's not my birthday."

"Happy Fourth of July!"

"It's not that day, either."

"Thanksgiving?"

"No."

"Christmas?"

"No! Stop it."

"Then Happy Harmony Harper Day. That's all the excuse I'll ever need to buy you something."

Harmony couldn't speak. She looked down at the gift. She pressed her lips tightly together. If she wasn't careful, she was going to cry and make a complete fool of herself.

"You do like lemon, don't you?"

She nodded, then took the lid off the candy jar. She reached inside to take out one of the pretty yellow drops. She put it in her mouth and tasted the delicious flavor she'd had so seldom in her life. She couldn't help but smile. She blinked back her tears, then glanced at Thor. "Thanks. It's been a long time since I've had a present."

"You like it and won't take it back?"

Grinning, she hugged the jar tight. "I like it and I won't take it back."

269

"May I have one?"

"You want me to share?"

He laughed. "I didn't know you were greedy."

"Only when I get the chance." She leaned the jar toward him.

"I'll remember that." He glanced at the candy jar, then at her. "You pick one for me. I've got to drive."

She selected the best piece, then handed it toward him. He opened his mouth. Smiling, she put the candy against his tongue and felt his lips close around her fingers. She looked into his eyes and felt the heat of his blue gaze penetrate her, deep, so very deep. Her heart beat fast. Her limbs felt weak. She had to force her hand away from his mouth.

Thor smacked loudly. "That's good." He let his gaze travel up and down her body. "Are you going to share *all* your candy with me?" As he waited for her answer, he turned the horses and headed home.

She shook her head. "Now that you've had one, all you can think about is more."

"I'm as greedy as you are." He slanted a glance at her. "Do I get more?"

"Only if you say 'pretty please.' "

"If I say 'pretty please,' will I get more than lemon drops?"

"Maybe. If you've been very, very good."

"Or very, very bad?"

She laughed. "Oh very well, I'll suppose I'll have to share."

270

"That's what I wanted to hear."

When she glanced at him, laughter filling her eyes, she noticed his face was serious and his blue gaze hot and hard.

"Stop looking at me! You're going to drive into somebody."

"They'll watch out."

She put her arms around the lemon jar and pulled it to her chest. "You're not going to endanger my candy jar."

Thor gave her a sly smile. "I wouldn't think of it. Right now, I can't decide if I'd rather be a lemon drop or a candy jar."

She put her nose in the air and looked away from him. "I'm not listening to you anymore. You're just trying to make me react foolishly in public."

He gently stroked her hair. "No matter how hard you try to suppress it, you've still got the child inside of you. We're going to bring Little Harmony out to play no matter how deep she's buried."

Suddenly tears blurred her vision. "Stop! Thor, just stop. You know I don't have time for this. I can't play. I can't tease. I've got to catch Turnbull."

"You can do both, and you know." He caressed her face, then turned back to watch the street as they continued down it at a leisurely pace.

"Don't you understand? I'm afraid. I don't want to be hurt. Not ever again."

He glanced at her. "I'm afraid, too. I don't want to be hurt."

"You're safe, Thor. You've got money and family to protect you. I don't have any of that."

"You have the girls. And yourself."

"But I'm vulnerable."

"So am I."

She frowned at him. "I don't see how."

"You can hurt me."

Looking away, she tried to calm herself. Why was he telling her these things about himself? They couldn't be true. She couldn't mean anything to him. He was using words to reach her and she couldn't let him. She had to get away from him before he did touch something deep inside her. She was afraid if he did she would shatter and she would never be able to put the pieces back together again.

"Harmony, don't shut me out." He reached to touch her face again.

She wouldn't look at him. She held on harder to the jar of lemon drops. "Please, I can't take anymore." Her voice was soft and husky.

He stroked her face again, then dropped his hand. "Deidre and I are both too pushy. We're spoiled. We're used to getting our own way. My parents will take the blame for loving us too much."

"No. It's not possible to love too much." The moment she'd said the words, she wished she hadn't. What had ever made her say such a thing? It was foolish nonsense and she knew it. "I mean, you can't love a child too much."

"I know what you mean."

She glanced at him in horror. But there was no triumph in his eyes. Instead, his blue gaze was almost dazzling in its intensity and understanding and acceptance. She couldn't stand to look long into his eyes and so turned to stare blindly at the buildings they passed. She cleared her throat. She should say something, but she felt speechless, her body aware of him at every level. Somehow he'd struck deep, so deeply she didn't know if she would ever be able to get him out of herself again.

Knowing she should feel horrified at the invasion, she didn't. Instead, she felt, like him, almost a relief, an acceptance, even a happiness. And then she saw the institute looming ahead and shut down all her feelings. What had gotten into her? Where had her mind been going? Her emotions? So he'd given her a jar of lemon drops? The price meant little to him, hardly anything at all. It should mean just as little to her.

She straightened her back as he pulled into the circle drive and stopped in front of the house. Nothing had changed for her, absolutely nothing. She was set on her course and that was that.

Thor turned to her and tipped back his hat. "We'll get Turnbull. And we won't rush anything else."

Taking a deep breath, she looked at him. "Thanks for driving me to town and helping to get the information. And thanks for the lemon drops." She smiled, forcing herself to return to their banter. "But I'm keeping them all in *my* room."

He followed her lead. "Good. I'll know where to get what I need."

She hesitated, wondering if he'd meant more than he'd said, then shrugged. She didn't care. She started to step down, but he was around the surrey and helping her down before she got far. She even let his hands linger around her waist longer than necessary before stepping away from him. After all, she wouldn't be with him much longer.

He picked up her package and they walked up to the front door as Juan came from around the house to lead the horse and surrey to the stable in back.

Harmony watched the horse and surrey a moment, realizing how glad she was that her own horse was being kept in the institute's stable. The girls could do without having their horses nearby, but she couldn't afford to be without her horse, not now.

As they reached the front door, it burst open and seven laughing, talking girls threw themselves at Harmony and Thor. Pulling the jar of lemon drops to one side and holding it against herself with one hand, Harmony hugged the girls in return, sharing kisses and laughter. When they finally quieted down, the girls all pointed at the candy jar and asked if it was for them.

Putting a stop to the questions, Thor led them all inside. "I bought the jar of lemon drops for

Harmony. They're all hers, but she might share if you ask politely."

"Oh, please . . . please, we're starving after riding all over Arizona." Star laughed, tickled Blaze in the ribs, then they both giggled.

Thor's family walked in to join the group, also laughing at the girls' antics.

"We had a wonderful time." Deidre hugged Jasmine. "They make me want a dozen of my own."

"I'd be happy to oblige." Hunter pulled Deidre to him and nuzzled her neck.

She laughed, putting her arm around him.

"You can all have a lemon drop." Harmony glanced around the group. "Thor was extravagant. But I am going to keep them in my room."

Everyone laughed.

"I don't blame you," Alexandra said, then glanced up at Jake. "It's so good to have children around again, isn't it?"

He nodded, smiling just for her.

Harmony took the lid off the jar, then held it for each girl as they selected a single piece of candy. As they put it in their mouths, they rolled their eyes and smacked out loud.

Jasmine took two. "I'm going to run upstairs and take this to Tara." As she bounded from the room, everyone looked after her in approval.

But Harmony wasn't done. She carried the jar to Alberto. He selected a lemon drop, popped it in his mouth, then winked at her. She went on to Alexandra, Jake, then Deidre and Hunter. Finally, she held up the jar to Thor. He picked out one, then put it in his mouth, his gaze never leaving hers. And she knew just what he was thinking because she, too, remembered when she had given him the first one and felt his mouth close around her fingers.

To distract herself from the memories, she looked back at the group. "I bought a gift for the Flora McCuskar Institute in thanks for all it has done for us and all it will do for needy children."

She handed the candy jar to Thor, then pulled the paper-wrapped book from her package. She walked over to Alberto and handed it to him.

"Thank you, but you didn't need to buy us anything." Alberto smiled in pleasure.

"I wanted to do it and I hope it's something girls who live here will enjoy for many years to come."

He tore off the paper, then laughed in surprise and delight. *"Alcott Works.* What a perfect book to buy for the institute. And it is a beautiful edition. Thank you." Alberto took Harmony's hand and kissed the back of it. "You are a jewel among women."

Harmony blushed, then stepped back to Thor and took her jar of candy and package. She wanted to give the paper twists to the girls in private.

"Did you have a good day in town?" Deidre looked pointedly at Thor.

"Yes, we did." Thor returned her gaze with a

cool one of his own. "Did you find a place to board the horses?"

"Yes. A good ranch," Alberto said. "We left the horses there, but I think the girls won't be completely happy until we make a place for them nearby. Isn't that right, girls?"

They nodded and laughed and hugged each other.

"I'm worried about the cost." Harmony frowned at the girls. They shouldn't place an added burden on the institute because of their horses.

Alberto waved the suggestion away. "The girls need to ride. If I buy some land around here, down by the Santa Cruz River, then the animals will have water and food. And the girls will have a good place to play. I'll start looking into it tomorrow."

Harmony realized he was enjoying himself and that making the girls happy, providing a safe haven for them meant more to him than she'd realized at first. He took this institute and the children it sheltered very seriously and obviously no expense was to be spared in making it the best. He'd even hired a fine educator for them. Once more she felt she could never do as well for the girls, but she had love to give them and plenty of it.

"I think we are all probably tired after our big day." Alexandra glanced around the group. "Why don't we rest and freshen up until dinner, then we can meet here again. What do you say?"

"Good idea." Alberto gazed at the girls in concern. "You're not too tired, are you?"

They all shook their heads, carefully sucking on lemon drops.

"You can go on upstairs and I'll be up in a moment." Harmony smiled at the girls as they hurried from the room and made their noisy way up the stairs.

Alberto walked over to Harmony. "I'm on my way back to my house now." He glanced at the others. "Are you coming?"

"I'll see you this evening." Thor reluctantly moved away from Harmony.

As Alberto started to the front door with the others, Harmony grasped his arm and held him back. When Thor and his family were outside, calling for the surrey, she turned to Alberto. "I want to thank you personally for what you're doing for the girls."

"No need to thank me. It's my pleasure." He smiled warmly at her.

"I also want to tell you that I may need to leave unexpectedly."

He raised his eyebrows in surprise.

"I'll be all right, truly." She smiled to reassure him. "But I'm concerned about the girls. I wonder if there is some way you could make sure they were well protected."

"They are safe here." He looked confused.

"I know the institute will take good care of them. It's not that. I was thinking of something unusual. If somebody thought of them as a danger, they might want them completely out of the way."

"Killed?" Alberto stepped back in shock.

"I'm sure they'll be safe here, but just in case I thought maybe an extra guard would help."

"My dear, I had no idea your trouble was so serious or had followed you so closely." He shook his head in concern.

"I don't think anybody will know the girls are here, but just in case I thought I should warn you. I wouldn't want anybody to get hurt because of us."

"Don't let it worry your mind another moment. I'm an excellent shot myself and so are the others. But when they are gone, I'll ask several of my men to come up from the ranch and watch the house. How does that sound?"

"Wonderful. Thank you so much. As soon as the danger is over, I'll let you know so this can all go back to normal." She hesitated. "If you don't want this possible danger affecting the institute, I can still take the girls and go."

"I wouldn't hear of it." He straightened his shoulders. "My family has been on this land for generations. We know how to deal with strangers."

She smiled and stood on tiptoe to place a soft kiss on his cheek. "Thank you."

"As I've told you before, it's my pleasure." He bowed slightly to her, then left the house.

She walked to the door and waved to them as the surrey drove away. It was odd to see them leave, but Thor was staying at a hotel and the rest of his family was staying with Alberto. Somehow it seemed as if they should all be here as one big family. But, of course, there wasn't room at the institute and it wasn't their home anyway.

When the surrey was out of sight, she shut the door, feeling oddly lonely. The house seemed too quiet, too big, too empty. How could she think of leaving the girls here? But how could she take them with her?

She had to stop thinking so much. She walked from the room and hurried up the stairs, clasping the candy jar and package. As she passed the landing on the second floor, she heard the girls talking with each other. Smiling, she went on to the third floor, then walked inside her own suite and shut the door. She set the package on the chaise lounge beside the book Deidre had given her, then carried the jar of lemon drops into her bedroom.

Finally alone, she sat down on the bed, then set the candy jar on the nearby table. Fluffing the pillows behind her back, she leaned against them, then took off the lid, selected a lemon drop, and popped it into her mouth. She rolled it around, hearing it click against her teeth as she enjoyed the sweet tart taste. What luxury to have an entire jar to herself. She would *never* have thought of buying a whole jar, even if she'd had the money. It would take someone like Thor to think of such extravagance.

But she'd have to leave the candy jar behind. She couldn't put off leaving Tucson any longer. She'd learned enough this afternoon to know what she had to do next. She had to go before Turnbull disappeared or she used up the last of their robbery money. And she couldn't put off telling the girls much longer.

Yet she wanted them all to have one more night together, one more night as a family. She wanted it for the girls, but most of all she wanted it for herself. Tears blurred her vision. She wouldn't cry. She'd had more than she'd ever expected in her life. She didn't fit into Thor's world and never would. She'd made him a part of her life for a while, then lived in his world for a little time, too. But it couldn't go on forever and she knew it.

She stood up, touched the jar of lemon drops, then crossed the room to look out the window. She couldn't think of Thor and his family. She must think of the fire. And Turnbull. Anger flooded her. Yes, she must seek only revenge.

Nothing more, nothing less.

Seventeen

Harmony awoke the next morning to the singing of birds. She wished she felt as happy as they sounded. Night was giving way to day, but it wasn't yet light enough to see well. She lay still a moment, enjoying the luxury of the soft, clean bed in the beautiful, safe house.

She couldn't stay in bed any longer. She wanted to be gone by the time anyone came to the institute. She forced herself to sit up. She lit the lamp beside her bed, then paused as she noticed the jar of lemon drops. Reaching for one, she stilled her hand. No, that life was over.

Standing up, she quickly made the bed. Fortunately she didn't have much to do. She'd packed her saddlebags the night before after Thor and his family had left and the girls had gone to bed. She'd raided the kitchen for food and filled her canteen with water. She didn't have much to take with her, but she didn't need much on the trail.

She walked over to the chair where she'd laid out her outlaw clothes. Slipping off her silk nightgown, she put it beside the matching robe and ran her fingers over the soft fabric. She wouldn't take any of her new clothes with her. She already owed Thor too much.

Shaking her head at her reluctance to leave the institute, she stepped into the bathroom and used its comforts one last time. She thought of the long, lingering bubble bath she'd had the night before. Her skin was still soft and clean and fragrant.

She pulled her thoughts back to the job at hand and left the bath. She dressed quickly in her plain cotton chemise and drawers. At least she wouldn't have to wear a corset again for a while. She pulled on her black shirt, buttoned it up the front, then slipped into her black trousers and fastened the black belt around her waist before pulling on the black leather vest. She tied the black silk scarf she had worn as a mask around her throat. Finally, she pulled on her black cowboy boots, hearing the jingle of the spurs. Silken spurs. Thor was wrong. She couldn't afford to be soft or silken.

Picking up her black hat, she glanced around the room a last time. She noticed the jar of lemon drops, started toward them, then stopped herself. She didn't need any along to remind her of Thor.

She walked into the sitting room. Her saddlebags, holster with the loaded .45, and canteen lay on the chaise lounge. She threw the saddlebags and holster over her shoulder, then the canteen. She picked up the package that contained the candy for the girls. As she turned to leave, she noticed the book Deidre had given her. She picked it up. *Vindication of the Rights of Women.* She hesitated, then tucked it into her saddlebags.

As she shut the door to the suite quietly behind her, she noticed the birds' songs had increased in volume. Dawn would be here soon and she must be on her way. She hurried down the stairs to the second floor. Taking a deep breath to steady herself, she opened the door to Tara's room and found the girls all snuggled together in the same bed.

She smiled, shutting the door quietly behind her. How she loved them. Family. This is what it was all about. She had to make sure other girls and women weren't hurt or killed. A vision of the girls safe and healthy and happy would go with her. It was what she had fought for so long. It drove her now.

"Girls. Wake up." She moved toward the bed, then set her saddlebags, holster, and canteen down in a chair. And placed her hat beside them.

Tara awoke first, yawning. Slowly the others opened their eyes. When they saw Harmony, they held out their arms and called for her to join them. She did, hugging and kissing them as she sat down on the bed.

"I'm so much better." Tara beamed at the group. "I dreamed of lemon drops." She laughed.

Harmony chuckled. She was relieved to see the results of Tara's good care. She'd be okay now. "Did they tell you there's a whole jar of lemon drops in my bedroom?"

Tara nodded, then licked her lips.

"You're all welcome to them, but first I have a surprise for each of you."

"Really?" Jasmine touched the package, then quickly withdrew her hand.

"What is it?" Blaze moved closer.

Harmony opened the package to reveal the eight twists of candy. As she heard the girls moan in delight, she glanced around at them. "I wanted to give you something more, something lasting, but I thought you'd like this best."

"What kind of candy is it?" Star bounced on the bed.

"There are eight, two of each kind. One is for Thor. You can give it to him later."

"Later?" Hope asked.

"When you have time. Now quickly make your choice." Harmony pushed the twists toward them.

"Oh, peppermint." Star took a twist.

"Licorice for me." Jasmine grabbed her twist.

The girls quickly made their choices, then hugged Harmony before tasting the first of their own personal candy.

As Harmony watched their happiness, she sighed. How she wanted to remain with them here in this safe, cozy haven. But she couldn't and she had to tell them now.

"Girls, you know I love you, don't you?" Harmony hoped to ease into the situation.

The light and laughter left their eyes at the seriousness of her voice. They grew still, concern on their faces.

"I learned a lot in town yesterday. Thor and I

asked questions. From what we could tell, Turnbull and his gunmen took a train to Phoenix, then a stage to Flagstaff two days ago."

"Where's Flagstaff?" Blaze asked.

"North of here in the mountains, about as far from here as it is back to Las Cruces, except it's all uphill."

"Then we've lost him?" Jasmine's voice held hope.

"For now." Harmony steadied her resolve. "But he'll find out soon enough we aren't there."

"Won't he ever give up?" Star's eyes filled with tears. "Hasn't he done enough?"

Harmony squeezed Star's hand. "You've all been brave and strong and patient. You must be that way a little bit longer. Turnbull has to be taken in for justice. I know where he is and I'm going after him."

"We'll help you capture him." Charity straightened her shoulders.

"No. I'm sorry. I know we've done everything together, but we can't take a chance on another of you getting shot."

"I'm sorry." Tara began to cry. "I didn't mean to get hit. I tried as hard as I could to be a good outlaw. I only slipped up that once. You aren't going to leave me behind because of that, are you?"

"Oh no." Harmony pulled Tara into her arms and held her close, patting her back. "It's not your fault. None of it is. And you'd never have gotten shot if not for Turnbull. It was his man who did it. You know that."

She let Tara lean back against the pillows. "None of you is to blame for anything we have gone through. Turnbull is wrong. He did it all. But it will be dangerous to get him. I don't want to put a single one of you in danger ever again. I'm going after him myself. And I'm leaving you here where you'll be safe."

The girls simply gazed at her in stunned silence.

"That's why you're dressed like that, isn't it?" Blaze asked.

"Yes. I'm leaving in a few moments. I want you to know I love you. I'm doing this to protect you. As soon as Turnbull is behind bars and our names are cleared, I'll send for you and we'll be a family again."

Blaze blinked hard, obviously holding back her tears. "What if Turnbull's men shoot you? We won't be there to help you."

"You may never come back." Star frowned, then rubbed at her eyes.

"We're a family. You said so yourself." Faith put her arms around her sisters. "You don't leave family."

"Girls, please understand. I need you to be strong and stay here for me."

"Why?" Jasmine bit her trembling lip as tears slowly slipped down her cheeks.

"If you're along, I'll be so worried about you I won't be able to concentrate on Turnbull and his men. And I might get hurt."

"You don't think we're good enough to help you

287

now." Blaze jumped up and glared. "You think Thor's better to help you."

"I'm not taking Thor with me."

Blaze threw herself against Harmony and hung on tight. "I don't want you to go alone. He'll kill you just like he did everybody else."

Harmony held the crying girl against her, not knowing how to reach them or reassure them.

"I don't want my candy anymore." Faith shoved it aside. "You don't love us."

"I do. Please, I'm doing this so we can be a family but safe and happy and without fear that Turnbull will find us. I will not endanger any of you again. Alone, I may be able to stay safe. With all of you along, I can't be sure. Don't you see it's for the best?"

Blaze raised her head. "You're not taking Thor?"

"No."

"You'll be safer alone?" Faith asked.

"Yes."

"And we're still your family?" Star put her arms around Harmony.

"Yes."

"And you promise to come back?" Jasmine asked.

"Yes. Or send for you."

"And we can have our own place?" Hope asked.

"Yes."

"And candy?" Charity asked.

"Yes. Sometimes."

"Will we have to be real good while you're gone?" Blaze sat down on the bed.

"Yes. I want you to learn all you can from the teacher who's coming here."

"You're our teacher," Faith said.

"This one has a college education. She knows lots more than I do."

"Nobody knows more than you do, Harmony." Star smiled as she wiped away her tears. "You're the leader of the Wild Child Gang."

"I wish we could go back to the desert and be a family again." Jasmine looked wistful.

"It was good then," Blaze said.

"Before Thor came." Star frowned.

"It wasn't his fault." Harmony stroked Star's hair. "What we did could only last for a little while before the law caught up with us. I had to kidnap Thor that day or we'd have been caught. After that, it was only a matter of time."

"He's not so bad." Blaze nodded to the group, then looked at Harmony. "Is he?"

She smiled. "No, he's not so bad. He brought us here and it's a good place for a while."

"Why isn't he going with you?" Star asked.

"I want to keep him safe, too." Harmony picked up the leftover paper twist. Licorice. She smiled. "Will you give this to him when I'm gone?"

The girls nodded, but continued to look concerned and unhappy.

"You're leaving now?" Blaze's dark eyes narrowed.

"Yes. I came to say goodbye."

289

The girls threw themselves against her and held on tightly.

"Please don't cry. I promise I'll be careful and we'll be a family again. You must promise to be good and learn, but have fun, too. And you can eat my lemon drops."

Star raised her head, tears in her eyes. "How can we have fun with you gone?"

"You must." She lifted their faces so she could look into their eyes. "Now I want to see you smile. Think, I've finally located Turnbull. I'm going to get revenge for us all. Remember, I'm part of the Wild Child Gang, Terror of the West. I know how to do a lot of things I didn't back in Chicago."

Blaze nodded, then straightened her shoulders and dried her tears. "Turnbull better watch out. We're the Wild Child Gang and we always will be. Won't we?"

"That's right." Harmony looked from one to the other. "We'll always be the Wild Child Gang."

She stood up, knowing if she didn't leave now she never would. She put her saddlebags, holster, and canteen over her shoulder. She put her hat on her head and started for the door. The girls jumped off the bed and followed, pressing themselves against her.

"I need you to be brave and strong. You're the Wild Child Gang. When Alberto comes over today, tell him I've gone to right a wrong, but I'll be in touch as soon as I can."

"Please take us with you." Jasmine clung to Harmony's hand.

"I need you all to be safe for me. You'll do that, won't you?"

They nodded, tears in their eyes.

"Please stay here. I want to go down alone. It'll be easier for me that way." She smiled, then hugged each one hard.

Finally, she opened the door, stepped outside into the hall, then shut the door behind her. As she took the stairs downward, she told herself over and over that she wouldn't cry. She had to be strong, too. But she couldn't stop the pain of leaving the girls behind.

She walked into the kitchen. Juanita was already at work. She'd hoped to leave before anyone but the girls saw her. Now it was too late.

"Breakfast?" Juanita glanced at Harmony's clothes, then back up at her face.

"No thank you. I'm leaving early. I just need to saddle my horse."

Juanita frowned. "Stay here. I have biscuits and coffee. You shouldn't go out on an empty stomach. Carlos will saddle your horse."

Before Harmony could protest, Juanita had slipped out the back door. She took off her hat and set it with her saddlebags, holster, and canteen down by the door, then sat down at the kitchen table. Maybe it would be best if she ate first. The food smelled good, although she didn't know how she could be hungry with such strong emotions churning through her.

291

A moment later, Juanita slipped back inside and quickly set the table for one. She put a plate of biscuits near Harmony, then added butter and preserves.

"I can help." Harmony started to get up.

"This is *my* job and I do it well." Juanita spoke with dignity. "All you need to do is eat."

Harmony glanced up. "You like your work?"

Juanita nodded as she set a cup of coffee in front of Harmony. "Yes. I run the house. My husband and son take care of everything else. We live together near here. It is a good life. Mister Alberto is a fine man."

Harmony nodded, pleased to hear Alberto was a good employer. She ate as quickly as possible. The food was wonderful. She'd miss it. When she'd eaten two biscuits, she lifted the cup of coffee to her lips. "I'll be gone for a while. I hate to leave the girls, but I must. It would ease my mind if I knew you were taking special care of them."

Juanita crossed her arms under her ample breasts. "I will watch them closely and make sure they eat well. Don't worry for them." She hesitated. "You're going with Mister Thor?"

"No. I'm going alone. I have to take care of something from my past." She abruptly set down the coffee and stood up. "I've got to be going."

"Mister Thor is staying at the Blue Sage."

Harmony put on her hat, then picked up her saddlebags, holster, and canteen. She opened the back door, then looked back. "Thanks. But Thor's got his own life to live."

She hurried down the back steps. Carlos and Julian held her saddled horse for her. She quickly threw the saddlebags behind the saddle, tied them in place, then added the canteen. She took the reins from Carlos, then stepped up into the saddle. She placed the gun belt across her lap. As soon as she got out of Tucson, she'd strap it on.

"Thanks." She smiled at them. "If you'd take extra care of the girls while I'm gone, I'd be grateful."

Carlos hit his fist against his chest over his heart. "Do not worry for the little ones. We watch over them."

"Mister Thor is at the Blue Sage." Julian rubbed the nose of her horse, then stepped back.

"Thanks, but I have to go alone."

She turned her horse. As she started around the side of the institute, she glanced upward. Seven faces were pressed to the window in Tara's room. The girls waved. She blew them a kiss as she clicked to her horse and rode to the circle drive in front. She didn't look back as she reached the street and kept going. There'd have been no point anyway since she couldn't see for the tears in her eyes.

After a while, she pulled a handkerchief out of her pocket, wiped her eyes, and blew her nose. It would never do for her to be weak. Not now. She had to keep going. Only when Turnbull was brought to justice could the girls be truly safe. But it was harder than she'd ever imagined to leave them. Yet she felt better after talking to Alberto, then Juanita, Carlos, and Julian. They'd take care of the girls for her, she felt sure of that. She couldn't be leaving them in a better home.

Now she mustn't keep thinking about the girls or the institute. She had to turn her mind to the task at hand. She rode toward the main street. And toward the Blue Sage Hotel. They hadn't had to tell her where Thor stayed. She knew only too well.

Tucking her handkerchief back into her pocket, she focused her mind. She had everything she needed. She was ready to go. She had only one more thing to do in Tucson before she left.

Riding down the main street, she noticed the town looked sleepy and quiet. Good. She wanted to catch Thor before he'd gotten busy with his day. As she rode up to the Blue Sage Hotel, she felt her stomach tighten. Maybe she shouldn't have eaten after all. She stopped her horse in front of the hitching post, then took a deep breath and glanced around. It wasn't too late to back out. No. She was still leader of the Wild Child Gang and she didn't walk away from responsibilities.

She slung her holster over her shoulder and got down. She tied her horse to the hitching post, then walked into the hotel, her spurs jingling. A sleepy young man sat behind the register. She walked up to him, and smiled.

He abruptly woke up as he glanced over her, then returned her smile.

"I'm here to surprise Thor Clarke-Jarmon. I'd like a key to his room."

The young man shook his head. "I'm not supposed to do that."

"Thor is a friend of mine. He'll want to see me."

"I can sure understand that, but—"

She slid money over the counter. "No one needs to know." She handed him more money. "Would you take breakfast up to him in two hours?"

Finally, he smiled knowingly. "Yes, ma'am. I could sure do that." He handed her the key. "If you don't mind my saying so, he's a lucky man."

She gave him another smile, then took the key and headed up the stairs. Her heart was pounding so hard she could hardly breathe, but she continued down the hall. Thor's room wasn't hard to find. She stopped outside his door. He should still be asleep. They'd all stayed up late the night before. He wouldn't be expecting her. She had surprise on her side. If only she could calm her nerves.

Glancing around, she noticed the place was as quiet as she had expected. Perfect. This shouldn't take long, then she'd be on her way. She slipped the key into the lock, then turned it. She heard a grating noise and stopped. She waited and when she heard nothing from inside, she pulled out the key and turned the knob. She pushed on the door. As it swung inward, it squeaked. She stopped, holding her breath, then slipped through the narrow opening.

Thor lay naked on his back in a big brass bed, all the covers kicked off except a white sheet that covered his lower body. One arm lay outstretched, the other curled near his head. His hard-muscled chest moved up and down as he breathed. A gold medallion on a long gold chain nestled in the dark blond hair that curled over his chest and down his stomach before disappearing beneath the sheet.

Harmony felt hot all over. He lay naked under the sheet, completely vulnerable to her. Now. But not when he awoke. She had surprise on her side. She had to use it while she could. But should she? She could still leave. He'd never know she'd been there. But heat coiled inside her. She wanted to see more of him. She wanted to completely expose his bronze, muscled body.

But her desire wasn't why she was here. She had a job to do. And she would do it. She quietly shut the door behind her, then locked it, leaving the key in the lock. She took off her hat, set it and her holster on a nearby table, then walked over to the bed. She looked down at him. He seemed younger in sleep, his blond hair tousled around his face. His lips looked darker and fuller than usual and amazingly sensual. He was only twenty-one. He was still so young. Yet he was a man. He'd proved that over and over.

She shook her head at herself. She mustn't take this personally. She mustn't get involved. She reached into her pocket and pulled out two lengths of rawhide. She had tied him before and she would again. Only this time she couldn't turn a gun on him. She knew him too well. This time she must do it while he slept.

She was glad the bed was brass. The bars would make her job easier. She leaned over and tied one end of a piece of rawhide to the head of the bed, pulled on it to make sure it was tight, then gently eased the other end around his wrist. He moved his head restlessly and she stopped, holding her breath. When he was still again, she tied the rawhide, making sure it was tight.

Smiling at her success, she straightened. She was half done. The other arm would be harder to reach, but she could do it. She walked around the bed, noticed the jingle of her spurs, then moved cautiously, quietly, to the head of the bed. She didn't want to awaken him until she was ready.

She leaned over to tie one end of the rawhide to the bed. Fortunately she had a good length because she had to pull it down to his outstretched arm. She eased the end around his wrist, but he groaned. She stopped and stood completely still. He moved his head, then his legs restlessly. She didn't have much time. He would awaken at any moment. She quickly jerked the rope taut and tied it.

"What the hell?"

She straightened. She cast a quick glance at her second tie. She wasn't sure of it, but she'd run out of time. She focused on Thor and took a deep breath.

He looked at her with intense blue eyes, a puzzled frown on his face.

She put her hands on her hips. "It's time to pay my debt."

Eighteen

"My spurs." Harmony stepped up and put one booted foot on the bed. She lifted her heel and flicked the rowel of the spur with a fingertip. It whirled round and round. "You wanted to know if my spurs were silken or silver. I think now is the time to find out."

He looked from the spur to her face. "That spur is the first thing I ever noticed about you."

"And it'll be the last."

"You damn near broke my hand when you stepped on it back on the train." He frowned. "What do you mean, last?" He pulled on the wrist bound above his head. "And what the hell is going on? Didn't you get enough of tying me up when I was your hostage?"

"I guess not." She shrugged, determined to carry out her role as leader of the Wild Child Gang. If she didn't allow herself to feel anything, she could maybe, just maybe, get through this. "It seems to be the only way I can get you to do what I want."

He pulled against the bonds with both hands.

298

"Harmony, what the hell are you doing? Let me loose."

She put her foot back on the floor. "I told you. I'm here to pay my debt. Remember our bargain?" She glanced down at her body, then back up at him.

His eyebrows rose in surprise, then lowered as his blue gaze darkened. "I thought we settled that when I found out you're a virgin."

"It means nothing and you know it. A deal's a deal. I'm going to pay you for helping the girls, then we'll be even. I want it that way before—"

"Before what?"

"Never mind. One thing at a time."

He jerked hard against the rawhide thongs, then grew still. "This won't work if I don't agree."

She arched an eyebrow, then leaned forward and placed a small hand on his chest. She wanted to ask him about the gold medallion he wore, but she had no need to know more about him, not now. It would soon be all over between them. She kept her hand above his heart till she heard it beat faster.

Smiling, she guided her hand slowly downward, feeling the coarseness of his hair, the smoothness of his skin as she moved ever nearer the white sheet. She didn't watch his face. Instead, she stayed attuned to his body. As she reached the edge of the sheet, it started to rise.

"Damn! Stop that." He kicked restlessly against the sheet, but only succeeded in lowering the white fabric precariously over his hips. "You can't mean to *seduce* me."

She glanced up at his face. "Why not?"

"It's not done this way. At least, not by women like you." He frowned. "I mean, you need help." He jerked against the rawhide. "You're a virgin. You don't even know what you're doing."

"I wish you'd quit throwing that in my face like it's some kind of disease. In a few moments, I won't be one and that'll be the end of it."

Thor closed his eyes and took a deep breath. When he spoke again, his voice was low and calm. "Harmony, you can't do this. It's probably not possible and you wouldn't want to do it even if it was."

"Why not?" She traced the muscles of his flat stomach and broad chest, then reached up to pull her black silk mask over her nose. She was an outlaw, nothing more. And he was her hostage. "If you like, shut your eyes and imagine I'm any woman you want."

"No!" He thought back to the fantasy she'd interrupted when she'd kidnapped him on the train. He no longer wanted another woman, not even a perfect fantasy woman. He wanted Harmony Harper. He looked her up and down, excited by her outlaw outfit as he'd been from the first. Damn her!

"All right, be difficult if you want." Her voice was muffled by the mask. "I hadn't counted on your help anyway."

"You *can't* do this without my help."

300

"There's no more need to discuss this. If you don't stop distracting me, I'm going to gag you."

"What?" He flung his head back and forth as he pulled on the rawhide. "This is ridiculous." But he noticed the length of rawhide on his left wrist gave slightly. He smiled to himself. She wasn't as much in control as she thought.

"Thor, I told you to be quiet. I'm trying to concentrate. I've never done this before."

"Well hell, I've never done this, either."

She threw him a dark glance. "I believe you have."

"Not like this, I haven't."

She set her foot on the bed and unbuckled her right spur. She pulled it off and held it up for him to see. It sparkled in the diffused light coming in through the sheer white curtains over the window. She hit the rowel with a fingertip. It whirled around, then stopped as she shook it, making it jingle.

"I see you've given this some thought."

"You've admired my spurs from the first, Thor Clarke-Jarmon. I want to prove to you now that they are solid metal. Silver."

"Not silken?"

"No." She frowned at him, then leaned over and slowly ran the rowel of the spur down the center of his chest from his throat to his navel. When his body trembled in response, she smiled in triumph. But she wasn't done yet. She used the spur again and again, crisscrossing his chest lightly, then harder as she moved ever lower. Her results

301

were rewarded when the sheet peaked high in exactly the right place.

"You are a wicked woman." Thor's voice was rough with tension and emotion.

"Thank you. As leader of the Wild Child Gang, I have a reputation to uphold."

"I won't ever question it again." He shifted his legs, dragging the sheet downward till it caught against his erection. "But you'll have to use more on me than your spur to achieve your goal."

"Yes, I know." She put her foot back on the bed and replaced the spur on her boot. "But you do agree that my spurs are silver?" She leaned over him and placed a hot, hard kiss on his lips.

Thor groaned. "I'm not in a position to disagree, am I?"

She teased his mouth, running her tongue around the outer edge, then nipping his lips with her teeth. When he parted his mouth, she delved deeper, pushing into his hot depths as she explored him at her leisure. While she kissed him, she used her hands, running them through the soft, thick hair of his head and down across his chest, moving ever closer to his erection. Finally, she slipped her hand under the sheet and grasped his hard length, amazed at his size. Startled, she broke the kiss and stared into his dark blue eyes.

"If you came here to torture me, you're doing a damned good job of it." He pulled at his bonds, desperate to either stop her or crush her under him. He couldn't take much more of her touch.

And he was beginning to wonder if she was a virgin. With all her tricks, how could she be?

She smiled and tugged on him.

He closed his eyes and cursed. "Harmony, back away now while you can . . . while I can still stop."

"You have no control in this. I am determined to pay my debt, then leave your life forever."

He snapped open his eyes. "You're what?"

She bit her lower lip and removed her hand. She hadn't meant to tell him so soon. She didn't want him distracted. "You won't have to worry with me after this. I'm going after Turnbull, but I'm leaving you tied up here till I'm well away."

"You can't!" He glanced at the strip of rawhide binding his left wrist. It had definitely loosened. But could he get free in time?

"It's not your fight, Thor. You go on back to your plantation. I'll settle with Turnbull, then send for the girls."

He jerked against his bonds, thrusting with his feet against the brass rungs of the baseboard. The sheet shifted to reveal his tanned, muscular thighs.

Glancing downward, she looked at his body, slowly moving her gaze upward. She focused on the hard length of him, then touched him again, gently moving her hand up and down. She knew she was supposed to put him inside her. She'd lived in enough cramped conditions to know what women and men did when they had sex. But he was so long, so wide, simply so big. And she was so small. She felt afraid he was going to hurt her.

"Harmony, if you don't stop doing that, you're not going to get your wish."

She stopped her movement, but didn't remove her hand from his heated flesh. "Why not?"

He looked her over, from her black silk mask to her black leather vest to her black boots with her silver spurs. He realized he no longer cared if she was a virgin or the most experienced madam in New Orleans. He was beyond rational thought. "I want you. You proved it, all right?" He swallowed hard. "I can't take much more if you keep touching me like that."

Her brown eyes shifted from his face downward, then she nodded and withdrew her hand.

He jerked on his bonds again, then kicked the metal of the baseboard hard. If she wasn't careful, he was going to tear the bed to pieces and come after her. But that would spoil her game, wouldn't it? She wanted to be in control, needed it. He understood that need. Anyway, who was he to stand in her way of pleasure? He cursed. It wasn't pleasure she wanted. It was duty. He pulled against the rawhide again. And the left bond slipped a little more.

"I'm going to make this quick, Thor." She unbuckled her belt and pulled it loose. She flung it to the floor, then unbuttoned her trousers and loosened her drawers. Glancing at his face, she reddened slightly. "I don't think you should watch."

"I shouldn't *what?*"

She walked across to the washstand and picked up a towel. She carried it back to him. "I mean it's not like we're going to be really intimate. I'll just cover your eyes so I'll be more comfortable." She dropped the towel across his face, leaving his nose and mouth free.

"Get this damned towel off me." He kicked outward.

"Now be quiet. And still. I'm just going to straddle you." She put a knee on the bed, then tossed a leg over his hips. "There now." She patted his chest. "We'll be done here in a moment."

Thor tossed his head and the towel slid to one side. "Harmony, I'm warning you—"

"Stop that!" She slapped his chest, then readjusted the towel, tucking its sides under his head.

"Get this off me. Untie me!"

"I'm going to gag you if you don't stop giving me orders. I'm the one wearing the silver spurs." She leaned back, twisted her legs inward and ran the rowels down his sides.

He shuddered. "Damn! You don't know what you're doing. Stop it!"

Taking a deep breath, she raised herself and slid her drawers and trousers downward. For a moment she hesitated. How could she do this? She shivered. He didn't even really want her. She was using his body. No, he *had* wanted her out in the desert and they'd made a bargain. She had to remember that. It didn't matter how she felt. It didn't matter that she was shaking inside and out, that she'd never felt so wanton or so excited or so hot-blooded for a man. She would have him, this once. And she could live on it forever.

She reached behind, searching for his long length and was surprised to discover he wasn't as hard as before. She looked around. She could never get him inside now. What had gone wrong? Perplexed, she frowned. It was probably the towel. Maybe he needed to see. She shivered. It'd make it all so much more intimate if she could see into his eyes. Well, she wouldn't look. She knelt, a knee on each side of his wide chest, and pulled off the towel. She tossed it to the floor, then gazed at the top of his head.

"I guess you can look."

"Unbutton your shirt. Show me your breasts."

"Is it really necessary?"

"Yes, if you want to fulfill your bargain."

She sighed, but quickly, with trembling fingers, unbuttoned each button, then pulled her shirt apart.

"More."

"I don't see why—"

"Yes you do."

She unhooked her chemise, then pulled it apart until she could feel cool air against her breasts. She knew her mother's gold locket nestled between her breasts, but she also knew Thor probably didn't even notice it. She dared to look down. His gaze was locked on her breasts. His expression made her nipples harden and the heat deep in her center spiraled outward, making her burn all over. Then he was looking into her eyes and she couldn't breathe for the wildness washing over her.

"You're beautiful." He started to reach forward to touch her, but was stopped by the rawhide. He jerked hard against his bonds. "Damn it to hell. Untie me so I can feel you."

She shook her head, suddenly anxious to get it over with. She couldn't take much more. She felt extremely weak. And she couldn't feel that way now. She couldn't feel anything. Reaching behind her, she found his erection, hard and hot and ready. She smiled and lifted herself. She glanced downward to position herself exactly over him, then settled onto his tip. He felt huge. How could she ever take him inside?

He frowned. "Why the hell if you're going through with this, don't you untie me and get out of your clothes? This is driving me wild."

She rubbed against him, feeling her own wetness as she tried to get him inside. She wondered that she could think or move or do anything except throw herself against him, rip off his bonds, and let him take over, let him bury himself deep inside her. She'd never wanted anything so much as she wanted him, right now, this moment. But she couldn't trust him, no matter the heat of her body or her desire. "Be still. I'm trying to make this work."

"You're too damn small. Look at the difference in our sizes." But he couldn't be still. He was desperate to tear the clothes off her body and bury himself to the hilt in her moist heat. He pulled at the rawhide, kicked out with his legs, then thrust upward with his hips, hardly aware of his actions.

"Oh!"

He stilled. "Harmony?" He could feel himself inside her, but not all the way. He was blocked by the proof of her virginity. So he was her first man. Damn! If he'd been crazed before, now he was burning with desire. Sweat beaded his forehead. He couldn't last much longer. If she moved in the least, it'd all be over. Yet he couldn't stop now. It was already too late.

She smiled, then leaned forward and pulled his head down to place a hot kiss on his lips. Her breasts brushed his chest, leaving a trail of fire between them. She straightened her back, lifted herself slightly, then bounced down hard, spearing herself on his erection. She cried out in pain, feeling him go in deep, deep, all the way inside her.

Grinding his hips upward, he couldn't get in far enough, feel enough of her. He pulled hard at his bonds, braced his feet against the brass rungs, then moved as best he could inside her. She caught the rhythm instinctively and moved with him, drawing him into her. If she was anything, she was a natural, virgin or not. He couldn't wait a moment longer. He exploded deep inside her silken heat, feeling her ride him, taking his pleasure into her, and he cursed even as his passion was at last fulfilled.

As the tension eased from his body, he relaxed against the bed, breathing hard, sweat beading his skin. She straddled him, her heat enclosing him still. And he was painfully aware that he wanted her all over again.

"Is that it?"

"Damn you! What the hell did you expect?"

"It hurt."

"Of course it did." He frowned, pulled against the rawhide and felt the left one give way. He stilled, realizing he'd gained his freedom. But too late.

"I thought that's what you wanted."

He exhaled harshly. "Are you going to ride me all day or get off?"

She hesitated. "I wanted to be good for you."

"You were! I just hope to hell nobody ever finds out I was kidnapped by a bunch of girls and a half-pint woman, then had my manhood taken by that same half-pint woman."

She leaned down and placed a soft kiss on his lips. "Is that what I did?"

"For the moment, it seems."

"You don't have to be so grumpy about it. And you don't have to insult my size."

"I could have made it better for you."

"It was just fine, except for the pain. But that's over now."

"Just fine isn't good enough for me. I damn well have a better reputation than that."

"Do you want to try again?" Her brown eyes narrowed in concern. "But it'll have to be quick. I've got to get on my way."

He growled. "Just get the hell off me or you won't have a choice. And I can guarantee you it'll be quick."

She felt him getting hard inside of her. "Oh, Thor." She moved, testing her inner muscles as she tightened around him. He felt good, so very good inside her. She wanted to keep him there forever.

"Hell! Get off me, Harmony."

"Oh, all right." She eased up off him and gasped when she saw the blood on her thighs. No wonder it had hurt, but it had felt good, too. She'd been moving somewhere, toward something, some feeling that she had wanted desperately to reach. But she hadn't reached it. He had. And that was enough. She was paying the debt, not him.

Stepping to the floor, she picked up the towel and wiped herself dry. Her virginity was a small price to pay for the girls' safety and happiness. She just wished, well, that her first time could have been different, lasted longer. No, she'd done what she had set out to do. Now she must be on her way.

She buttoned up her trousers, pulled her chemise together, then slowly put herself back together. When she was all buttoned into place, she slipped her belt back on, then walked over to the window and glanced outside. It was still early morning. How could so much have happened so fast? How could she leave him now?

"Harmony, come here."

She glanced at him. He lay still in the bed, but his body gave him away. He still wanted her. She hated to leave him in that condition, but there were plenty of other women for him. She was just a passing fancy. She walked over to him and sat down on the bed by his chest. She stroked his damp hair back from his face.

"I've got to go, Thor. You won't be tied up for long. A young man downstairs is bringing you breakfast in an hour or so."

He shook his head. "You're going to leave me tied up here, looking like a fool for some stranger to find?"

"It can't be helped. I don't think you'll come after me, but in case you get that wild notion I want my trail to be cold." She reached down and pulled the sheet up to his chest. "I'm sure there are plenty of other women to take care of your needs."

"How can there be when you're the one who makes the need?"

She cocked her head to one side. "I don't understand. I'm not beautiful or educated or a lady or any of the things you should want."

He shook his head. "You're gorgeous, smart, a lady when you want to be and an outlaw when you want. You seem to be everything I need."

She put a fingertip to his lips. "Quiet. I'm leaving now and you go on back to your life. It's best this way. I have to take care of Turnbull." She touched her heart. "I can't feel anything here except hate till my friends are avenged."

"I don't believe you."

"It's true." She stood up. "I came to say goodbye and pay my debt. I've done both of those so now I must be on my way. It's a long ride to—"

"Flagstaff?"

"No." She shook her head. "I think that story was a ruse. Turnbull is still in Las Cruces. I think

311

I should go back there. But it doesn't concern you. Not anymore." She walked to the end of the bed, her spurs jingling.

"Harmony, if you get killed what will the girls do?"

"They're safe at the institute." She stopped by her holster and leaned down to pick it up.

"I've made a decision about your spurs."

She glanced at him over her shoulder. "Yes?"

"Your spurs are silver, all right, but they're silken, too. They're smooth to the touch unless you turn the rowels against me, then they're hard."

"Silver, Thor. All silver." She drew her gun belt around her hips. Now that she was leaving Tucson, she could wear it again. She buckled the gun belt, then adjusted it into place. She put a hand on the cold metal of her pistol. "Maybe some of your Southern belles wear silken spurs, but not me. Mine are solid silver."

She put on her hat, walked to the door, unlocked it, clutched the key in her fist, then opened the door. She glanced back to see Thor still tied to the brass bed. Good. It was where she wanted him for a while yet.

"Life wasn't meant to be lived alone." He watched her with hooded eyes.

"You have your family and I have my girls."

"That's not what I meant."

"I'll let you know if I need another hostage."

"You've got a job waiting for you at Jarmon Plantation."

"Thanks, but I'm going back to Chicago." She

didn't want to leave. She could hardly stand the thought of never seeing him again. But she had to go and now, for she couldn't talk any more over the lump in her throat.

Raising her hand in a final farewell, she shut the door, locked it, then walked away, her spurs jingling, jangling as she moved quickly down the hall.

Part Three
Spurs of Silver and Gold

Nineteen

As Harmony rode northwest along the Santa Cruz River, she didn't look back toward Tucson. She didn't want to remember what she'd left behind. The sun felt hot and she was grateful for the protective black hat she wore on her head. She remembered Thor's lack of a hat when they'd ridden to Las Cruces. He'd gotten slightly sunburned. She smiled, then stopped the direction of her thoughts. She *wasn't* going to think about Thor, or his family, or the girls. Her mind was set on Flagstaff and Turnbull.

She was already warm and she'd get hotter before the day was done. It would be cooler as she neared the mountains of northern Arizona. Maybe she'd even see snow. Chicago had snow. It'd be fairly cold when she took Turnbull back for justice. Would there be ice on the edges of Lake Michigan? How strange the weather and land would seem after the heat and dryness of the desert.

She didn't want to wait. She wanted it to be over now, just like it was over with Thor. She'd paid her debt and gone her way. It should have been simple, but her body kept remembering how it had felt to be joined with him. She realized now how much more she had needed and wanted from him, but she had stayed in control and that was the important thing. She couldn't allow anything, anyone, to touch the frozen anger of her emotions.

She had gotten away before he had bound her to him with passion. She hated to think of a woman's loss of control if love joined desire. She shivered, despite the warmth of the day. Maybe it was part of what had bound her mother to her father before he had turned mean. Sex and death. She feared becoming like her mother, bound to a man for all the wrong reasons until he finally killed her.

No. She wouldn't think about her past or Thor. She was caught up with the future, not the present or the past. She forced herself to focus on the landscape around her.

The Santa Cruz River snaked its way northwest as far as she could see. And that was far, so far she couldn't exactly judge the distance. She was used to Chicago's buildings and lake and rivers. She didn't know if her eyes would ever completely adjust to the wide expanse of desert that stretched as far as she could see. North of Tucson rose a majestic mountain, purple and hazy in the distance. It could be far away or near. She couldn't tell for sure.

She wished she could get to Flagstaff quickly

and easily, but it would be a long, hard ride. No train was available north, except a limited line from Tucson to Phoenix, then from Prescott to Flagstaff. The distance from Phoenix to Prescott made it unworkable. Anyway she wanted the freedom of her own horse and she didn't want anybody to be able to trace her movements.

Maybe traveling alone by horseback was for the best. She needed time by herself to gather her strength and put Thor and his family from her mind. When she confronted Turnbull she must be totally focused.

As she rode onward, she realized she wasn't used to being alone. In Chicago, someone had always been nearby in the crowded sweatshop or boardinghouse. After the fire, she and the girls had been constantly together. She'd never had the luxury of being completely alone before. Now she wasn't sure it was a luxury. The silence of the desert grew louder the farther she rode from Tucson. What if she fell off her horse? What if the animal went lame? What if she was attacked by outlaws?

No. She touched the pistol on her hip. She wouldn't let fear overwhelm her. There would have to be ranches or small towns along the way. Other travelers used the road as well. She'd already passed a wagon as well as a buggy. She could hold her own with any outlaw or desperado who thought she was easy prey. But she missed the girls more than she could have imagined and she had only started her trip north.

Sighing, she patted her horse's neck, wishing they could go faster. She wanted Turnbull behind bars. Now. As long as he was free, the girls were in danger. She frowned, thinking of Turnbull and his gunmen having fun in Flagstaff. Anger rushed through her. She changed her vision. Now she saw Turnbull brought before a judge and jury. He begged for mercy, admitting his crime. The jury had no mercy. Turnbull was convicted and put in jail. She personally locked the door and threw away the key. Yes, every effort was worth her revenge.

She rode onward, controlling her thoughts as she controlled the horse beneath her. The land didn't change, remaining stark and majestic around her. When the sun was directly overhead, she knew she needed to rest her mount as well as herself. She glanced toward the river, hoping to find shade to shelter in the noonday sun. Up ahead she saw several cottonwood trees growing near the river. The branches curved outward, casting the ground under them in shadow.

She urged her horse faster to quickly cover the distance. When she reined in under a tree, she was glad to see grass growing along the riverbank. She knew her horse had to be tired and hungry, too. She stepped down, noticed the soreness of her muscles, then led her horse to the river. While the animal drank, she took off her hat and fanned her face. The cool air from the river felt wonderful.

When her horse started grazing, she knelt and cupped her hands to drink from the river. The water was cool and as wonderful as the air. She splashed water on her face, then took two biscuits and jerky from her saddlebags and sat down under a tree. She leaned back against the trunk and sighed in relief. She hated to admit it, but she was sore in a way she'd never been before. She owed that feeling to Thor. If he hadn't been so big, she'd have had no problem. Remembering the size and strength of him, she felt heat flush her skin.

Grabbing her hat, she fanned her face, then took a bite of jerky. As she struggled to eat it, she forced her mind away from Thor. He was the past and she lived only for the future. She focused on the beauty of the river, of the distant mountains, of the vast desert.

Once more she felt the loneliness of her mission. She wondered what the girls were doing, if Deidre had given anyone else a copy of her favorite book, if Thor had long since had his breakfast. No. She wouldn't think of what she'd left behind or of what might have been. Fire. Women and children screamed as they tried to escape. She must think only of hate and revenge.

She finished eating, then walked down to the river. She took several long drinks from cupped hands, then took off her black scarf, dipped it in the water, then walked back to the tree. She sat down again and wiped her face with the cool scarf. Leaning back against the tree, she heard a rider in the distance. She felt to make sure her pistol was in place. She didn't think she was very noticeable from the road, but she didn't want any unexpected trouble.

Watching her horse graze, she realized she was anxious to get on her way again. But the sun was still high and hot. She should let the animal rest and the day cool a little before starting out again. Besides, she was sore from sitting in the saddle.

As she cooled her face with the scarf, she heard the rider draw near and stop. Trouble. She set her scarf carefully on her hat, then quietly slipped out her pistol. Not rising, she turned, aiming her pistol toward the road and keeping the tree in front of her as protection.

A large man dressed all in black sat a black horse. He stared in her direction. When he saw her looking back at him, he lifted his hat in a salute. She recognized the handsome face and blond hair. Thor!

"You can put down your gun, Harmony." He made no attempt to approach her.

"What the hell are you doing here?" She jumped up and stepped out from behind the tree. She kept her pistol aimed at him.

"I don't think using a road is a shooting offense."

"You followed me!" She walked toward him.

"You're damned right I did." He turned his horse off the road and approached her. "Are you going to put that gun away or do I have to take it away from you?"

"As if you could." She slipped her pistol back

in its holster. Whatever happened, she couldn't use a gun on Thor. "What are you doing here?"

"You guessed right the first time. I followed you."

"How? And so fast?"

He stepped down from his horse, then led the animal past her to the river to drink. "Looks like you need a little more practice tying rawhide."

"I was in a hurry. You almost awoke before I was done." She frowned as she followed him to the river. "I worried the left one was loose."

"But you forgot about it in the heat of the moment." He let his blue gaze roam slowly down her body, then back to her face. He smiled.

"Why did you follow me?"

"Gentleman that I am, I thought you needed some more lessons. I wouldn't want to leave a lady in distress."

"Distress!" She shook her head. "Of all the bigheaded, outrageous ideas."

"Glad to see me?"

"No! You can go back the way you came." She sat down under the tree and picked up her scarf to cool off her heated face. "I don't need you. For anything."

"Did I ever mention that in addition to being beautiful and smart and courageous, you're also bullheaded?"

"Don't try to flatter me."

"I wouldn't think of it." He chuckled. "You never give up, do you?"

"Thor, you weren't there. The fire." She stopped herself, not wanting to think about it.

"I never did get around to sending a telegram to Chicago to find out about Turnbull."

She glared at him. "Maybe a gunshot wound was proof enough."

"Maybe. Most likely I came to believe you, even though you'd kidnapped me, tied me up, and used me."

"That's what outlaws do. What did you expect?" He chuckled again.

"I don't see a damn thing funny about this."

"You. You're absolutely relentless. Frankly, I pity Turnbull. There's no way in hell that man's got a chance."

"You're right about that. He's going to jail." She stared at Thor. "And you're going back to Tucson. If you want, I'll share my food with you, then you can be on your way."

He hunkered down in front of her. "You don't seem to understand, Harmony. I'm as relentless as you. And I'm spoiled. I'm used to getting what I want."

She rolled her eyes. "No doubt."

"I guess there's more Southern gentleman in me than I realized. I'd never be able to respect myself if I didn't help you and the girls. And my family wouldn't respect me if I didn't, either."

"That's silly."

"No, it's not. And it's what I want to do. I thought a lot about you riding out here. You're as stubborn as they come. And you're loyal, maybe too much for your own good. Nothing is going to stop you going after Turnbull, not even when you don't have to anymore. You're set and that's that. The best thing I can do to get what I want is to see this thing through to the end."

Her breath caught in her throat at the intensity in his blue eyes. "What do you want?"

"You." He smiled, a rueful twist of his lips. "You branded me, Harmony Harper. I guess you're stuck with me now."

She stood up and walked to the river. "This is unreal. You don't know what you're saying. You don't know Turnbull. How can you possibly want *me?* In your type of life, I'm nothing."

He walked over to her and took her hand. He kissed the palm, then stroked it. "In my life, you're everything."

For some silly reason, she had trouble seeing. She jerked her hand out of his grasp. "You're trying to make me believe in fantasy. I won't! You're trying to make me weak. You won't!"

"I told you I was willing to wait till you had Turnbull behind bars. And I will."

She glanced up at him suspiciously. "Thor, I'm going into danger. I want you safe, like the girls."

"You can't keep everybody else safe and put yourself in danger time and again." He looked out across the desert. "There comes a time when you need to accept help. You did it at the institute. Do it now, with me."

"You're determined to get under my skin, aren't you?"

"That's not where I'm determined to get."

"We're talking about Turnbull."

"No. We're talking about us." He looked back at her. "You can't stop me from following you, from dogging your steps every inch of the way to Flagstaff and Chicago. But I'd rather be your partner, part of the Wild Child Gang till we put Turnbull behind bars."

"I don't understand."

"I know. You're so frozen with hate you can't let yourself feel or understand anything except anger." He stepped closer and gently pushed a strand of hair back from her face. "But you'll get beyond it, I promise. And when you do, I want to be there."

She inhaled sharply. "I've always lived with anger. I don't know anything else."

"What about the girls? Your mother?"

"I tried to protect them." She frowned. "But don't you see? My mother got killed. Tara got shot. You were hurt, too. No matter how hard I try, I can't seem to keep the people I love safe. It's best if I go on alone."

He put his arms around her and pulled her against his chest. He held her tightly until she leaned into his warmth. "I can take care of myself. And you, too. Give me the chance. Trust me that much."

Leaning back, she looked up into his eyes. "You're going to do this no matter what I say or do, aren't you?"

"Yes."

She sighed. "You're too big for me."

He chuckled. "In what way?"

"Every way!"

"We're perfect together, if you'll give me the chance to prove that, too. Trust me, Harmony. I can make you happy. I can keep you safe."

She looked up at him again. "But can you let me be free?"

"That's the hardest of all."

"I have to be independent."

"My mother and sister taught me that about a woman if nothing else."

She pushed away from him, walked along the riverbank, then turned back. "I don't think you understand. I don't think you can. But it doesn't matter, not now. It looks like you've kidnapped me this time. I can't seem to get rid of you no matter what I do."

"Now you understand."

"And I can probably use some help. You've proved useful in the past."

"I dressed the part. Did you notice?"

She nodded. "Black. Like me. Yes, you're part of the Wild Child Gang." She looked him over more closely. "Your clothes look new. When did you get them?"

"As soon as I got untied, dressed, and out of that bed, I started getting ready to follow you. It wasn't as quick as I'd hoped since I had to get a horse and trappings, plus food and clothes."

"Weren't you worried you'd miss me?"

"No. I knew the road you'd take and I knew I

could give you an hour or two head start and catch up with you at noon or dusk."

She shook her head. "I think you're more stubborn than me."

"I'm a man with a mission. And I'm smart enough to know a good thing when I find it."

"If you're thinking of me, I'm *not* a good thing. I'm trouble."

"Outlaw woman. My kind of trouble." He took her hand and kissed the palm once more. "You didn't give me much of a chance this morning, Harmony. I want to make it up to you. I want you to know the pleasure between a man and a woman. Pleasure we can share."

She pulled her hand away. "I don't know, Thor. The debt's paid now, isn't it?"

"Did you think one time paid it?"

"Well, yes." She glanced up at him in surprise. "Didn't it?"

He shook his head. "That's part of why I had to come after you. You still owe me."

She frowned. "I don't see how."

"Virgins' aren't the most fun."

"Oh!" She stepped backward. "I couldn't help that."

"I know." He followed her. "That's why I want more."

"Now?"

"Later. Tonight." He put his hands on her shoulders and drew her closer.

She shivered. "I thought once was enough."

"How long are the girls going to stay in the institute?"

"Weeks, probably."

"See. Once isn't much of a bargain."

"I think this is a trick."

"Why?" He tilted her chin up so he could press a soft kiss against her lips.

She trembled. "I'm not sure this is a good idea."

He toyed with her mouth, teasing her lips with his tongue and teeth. "Why?"

Gasping for air, she tried to pull away, but he held her still. "We never agreed on how many times."

"Do you want to do that now?"

"I think it's too late for that."

"Do you?" He drew her against his chest, placing one large hand around her waist while thrusting his long fingers into her hair.

"I mean, the bargain was made without that—"

He closed his mouth over hers, then delved deeply with his tongue into her hot, soft mouth. He felt her tremble against him, then her arms slowly crept around his neck and she pulled him down to her. As their heat mingled, their bodies strained to merge until he grasped her hips with his hands and pulled her into his hardness. He groaned with need, desperation rising in him.

Finally, he raised his head to look into her desired, darkened eyes. "The bargain holds till you're done with Turnbull."

"So long?"

"Won't the girls be at the institute all that time?"

"Yes." She took a deep breath. "It's not fair. I can't think clearly when you kiss me."

"That's the least of your worries." He placed a hot, hard kiss on her lips again, then pulled her back against him. Suddenly he stopped and stepped back, dropping his hands to his side. "If I touch you a moment longer, I won't be able to stop till we're done, really done this time."

She felt her face flush. "I'm not sure about the bargain, Thor."

"If you get pregnant, I'll marry you."

"Oh!" She looked shocked and stepped back from him. "How can you even suggest such a thing?"

"Marriage?"

"No! I mean, a child. I already have seven daughters. Anyway, I would never force a man to marry me."

He shook his head. "What then?"

"It's the bargain."

"Damn it all to hell, Harmony. We made a bargain. Now stop trying to get out of it."

She squared her shoulders. "I don't think this is quite fair, but you have a point. All right. We continue the bargain. But I never thought you'd want more than once with me."

"Why not?"

"You could have so many more beautiful, talented women. Southern Belles."

He shook his head. "By the time we're done,

you're going to know beyond a doubt that you are the most beautiful, talented, intelligent woman in the world. And you'll know exactly why I want you."

"But Turnbull comes first."

"You won't let this go now? We can lose him in Louisiana."

"No. The girls' names must be cleared. The dead must be avenged."

"We've got no choice then." He glanced at the horses, then up at the sky. "Let's get back on the road. If I stay with you any longer, we won't get anywhere this afternoon. And the sooner we've got Turnbull the better."

"We must get to Flagstaff before he leaves."

"You're sure he's there?"

"It makes sense. You know we found out he bought a train ticket to Phoenix. With that newspaper article in hand, I'm counting on him and his gunmen taking a stage on to Flagstaff." She clenched her fists. "I just know that's where he is. I can feel it in my bones."

"Okay. I believe you. Let's get going." He turned toward his horse.

"Thor, if I have a child, it's mine. I won't burden you with it."

"Damn!" He turned around, grabbed her shoulders, and shook her. "I don't want to hear another word. Do you understand? We have a bargain. I'm staying with you, in every way, until Turnbull is in jail. After that, it's a different story."

She shook off his hands. "You don't have to

331

get upset. I just wanted you to know how we stand. It's a bargain. Nothing more." She took a deep breath. "My word is the most I've ever had and I've always kept it. You don't have to worry about me breaking the bargain."

"I'm not worried. I'm going to be with you every moment, every step of the way."

She nodded, then walked over to her horse. "When it's all said and done, I'm sending for the girls and you're going to the plantation."

Thor swung up onto his horse. "If ever a woman tried a man's patience, you do. You can only control so much in your life, Harmony. And you sure as hell can't control me." He clicked to his horse and started for the road.

She hesitated as he rode away, then turned to pick up her hat and scarf. When she had them securely in place, she mounted her horse. She took one last look at the river, realizing she wasn't alone anymore. Thor. How could she trust him? How could she not?

Shaking her head at herself, she rode out from under the cottonwood trees and joined him on the road. As they moved steadily northwest, she glanced over at him and took a deep breath. "Hostage."

He returned her stare, then smiled. "I brought the rawhide, *hostage*."

Twenty

"If I don't miss my guess, we'll be in Flagstaff tomorrow by nightfall." Thor led the way downward from the plains of north central Arizona into a rocky pass. Sunlight glinted from the western sky.

"But couldn't we be there today?"

"Maybe, if we kept to the main road. But we're taking a detour. I want you to see this country. There's nothing else like it."

"Thor, we don't have time for sightseeing."

"We have time for this. We'll make camp early and get some rest. We need it after so many days on the trail. And we'll need it for our climb up to the Mogollon Rim tomorrow."

"I think you're making this more difficult than it needs to be. If we just kept on riding north—"

"It'll be worth the extra time and effort. Trust me."

"I guess I don't have much choice."

"That's right, *hostage*." He chuckled.

She cast him a defiant look, then concentrated on the ground between her horse's ears. The past several days had seen the landscape change from the low desert of cactus with cottonwood trees along the riverbanks, to the higher central plains, still wide-open spaces but with mountains to the east and west. She also now saw more juniper, piñon, and cottonwood trees and fewer varieties of cactus.

They had seen few people along the route. Sometimes predator birds circled the sky and snakes and lizards sunned themselves on rocks, but towns and ranches were in short supply, at least along the road they traveled. She hated to admit it, but she'd been grateful for Thor's company every step of the way. She'd been lonely outside of Tucson, but she'd known nothing of the wild, empty land that awaited her north of Phoenix.

Now Thor wanted to take the long route. He wanted to show her something special. She didn't want to take the time. She wanted to get to Turnbull. But she also didn't want the time alone with Thor to end. She'd found he made a good companion, funny, thoughtful, considerate. They hadn't pushed their horses, as if they needed the time to gather strength for the coming confrontation.

She also hated to admit to herself that she missed their physical closeness. She'd expected him to seal their bargain their first night on the road. But when she'd gotten off her horse at the end of the day stiff and sore he'd understood without her saying anything. After that, he'd given her a gentle kiss in the mornings and evenings. And nothing more.

Surprised at herself, she realized the more she was in his company the more she wanted him. But she didn't want to admit it, especially to him. She'd become so aware of his body that she could almost feel his skin under her hands, his lips on hers, and his hard body pressed against her. She shouldn't want him, but she did. And she wished they were going straight to Flagstaff. Any more time in his company and she wasn't sure she could control herself. She'd be the one demanding he make good on their bargain.

She didn't want that. She didn't want any more reminders of him when they parted. As it was, she could never forget their one time together. She also couldn't help but wonder if he no longer wanted her. Maybe he had simply been a gentleman before, claiming she was the woman he needed above all others. Now that she was thinking clearly, she didn't know how she could ever have considered believing him.

Hating her thoughts almost as much as the delay, she forced herself to look at the land around her. They were coming out the other end of the pass, sand under their horses' hooves, a brilliant blue sky overhead, and sandstone flecked with red along their sides.

The girls would have enjoyed seeing this part of the country. They had been fascinated with New Mexico. She wished they were along. She missed them and couldn't help wondering what they were doing, if they were happy, if they missed her, too.

But she had done the right thing in leaving them behind.

As they rode onto the lower land, she gasped in astonishment. Tall, windswept mesas of a deep red color rose from the flat desert sand. Some were shaped like chimneys, others were broad with flat tops, one even looked like a coffeepot. She stared in awe at the stark beauty around her. Nature had worked its wonder here. Thor was right. She'd seen nothing like this before.

"What do you think?" Thor turned to watch her face.

"It's like something out of a storybook."

"I wanted to share it with you. I've seen it only once before."

"I'm glad we came." And she was. She only wished the girls were with her. She'd probably never be back to Arizona, but she would carry this fantastic memory with her forever.

They rode on, the scene slowly changing but remaining much the same as the red rocks altered their shape in accord with no law but their own. The sun continued its descent in the west as they came to a trading post set at the edge of a narrow stream. Red rocks towered around the area, but up ahead she could see trees in riotous fall colors. How could the land have gone from desert to red rocks to forest so quickly?

Thor glanced at her and grinned. "And you thought you'd seen the best, didn't you?"

"Where are we?"

He led them past the trading post and on down

336

beside the gurgling stream. "They call it Oak Creek Canyon. Amazingly, it's set in the heart of some of the driest land in the country. They even grow apples here."

"It's beautiful." The area looked more like something in northern Illinois, but in contrast to the surrounding land its beauty was even more astonishing.

As they rode on through the trees, watching sunlight play on the stream, Thor reached over and squeezed her hand. "We'll have time to rest here."

"I'm glad." She smiled at him, suddenly feeling relaxed. They needed the rest. He was right. And she would like nothing better than to bathe in the stream. Maybe they could even get some fresh food at the trading post. They continued riding and she wondered how much farther he wanted to take them. She was ready to make camp. Anyplace here would do fine.

"Look up, Harmony."

She pulled her horse to a stop beside him. Looking upward over a deep gorge, she was unprepared for the sight of a narrow waterfall that plummeted hundreds of feet from the plateau high above them. The waterfall was stunning, as was the wildness of the land that spawned it. She glanced around. From the floor of the gorge, the land rose abruptly to form a new shelf, much much higher. The exposed earth was sand colored with red here and there. Piñon, mesquite, and tall pines grew along the top of the ridge.

"We're going up there tomorrow."

"What!" She felt her heart beat fast. "There's no way up there."

"We'll follow one of the mountain trails."

"Thor, this is beautiful, but I'm not sure it's worth the climb out. I'm not even sure it's possible."

He chuckled. "The horses will do the climbing, although we may need to lead them part of the way."

"I think we'd better go back the way we came."

"Too late now." He moved his horse close to her and held her hand. "Magnificent, isn't it?"

"Yes." She wouldn't have wanted to miss this sight, but she couldn't imagine finding a way across the gorge and up the side of the steep cliff. It was a sheer drop. If the land changed so much here, what would it be like at the top? "Have you ridden up there before?"

"Yes. We can make it. And you'll be glad we did."

She wasn't so sure she would be, but she'd followed his lead on this journey. Now was not the time to stop, although that was exactly what she'd like to do.

"Come on. You've got one more sight for tonight."

"I don't know if I can take any more."

"Sure you can." He chuckled as he turned his horse around. He headed back the way they'd come.

She followed, once more entranced by the lovely stream and variety of trees, from oak to cottonwood to apple. After a while, he turned off the road and hit a narrow trail. Up ahead came the sound of water, louder than the stream. She could only wonder what they would see next. When they came out into an open area, she realized she couldn't have anticipated this sight, either.

Water cascaded down the smooth surface of white rock. The waterfall was as wide as three wagons and as long as a dozen placed back to front. The water had worn the rock smooth over countless years as it ran from the plateau above into the stream below. And the water wasn't deep. It was a thin layer over the smooth rock. At the bottom it fell into a pool of blue water.

"What do you think?" Thor gestured toward the unusual waterfall. "They call it Slide Rock."

"Why?"

"You can find out later." He shifted in the saddle. "Let's get down and let these horses rest."

She didn't care about the mystery of Slide Rock. Its beauty was enough to satisfy her. Besides, she wanted nothing more than to get off her horse and rest.

Thor dismounted, then put his hands around her waist and helped her down. He held her close for a moment, their heat mingling. "From now till morning this is all ours." His blue eyes turned darker as he lowered his head and placed a hot kiss on her lips.

She understood his promise and felt a shiver run through her. Tonight he would seal their bargain

339

with their bodies. And she couldn't protest. She needed him as much as he needed her.

"Let's get our campsite ready before it's dark." He stepped quickly but reluctantly away from her.

She led her horse behind him as he urged his horse down the side of the waterfall to the dark pool at its base.

He unbridled her horse, then let the animal drink with his horse while he removed the saddle. He glanced around, obviously searching for a good campsite, then carried her saddle and bridle to a secluded area behind several rocks under an ancient oak tree. He dropped the saddle and bridle to the ground.

Following him, she smiled in delight. "It's a wonderful place to camp. Clean, cool, plenty of water. And privacy." She glanced around to make sure their camp couldn't be seen from the trail or Slide Rock. "Do you think it's safe?"

He nodded. "This isn't Chicago. Remember the hideout in New Mexico?"

"Yes."

"This is just as safe. There aren't many people around here anyway."

"What about the trading post?"

"I'm going there now."

"What?" She felt alarmed. She'd be alone out here without him. She immediately clamped down on that feeling. She'd made it on her own a long time before she met Thor.

"Worried about me?" He cupped her chin with the palm of his hand. "I'll be fine. I'm going to see about getting us some fresh food. You might want to take the time to clean up while I'm gone. You're safe here. Trust me."

She nodded, realizing she was coming to trust him too much. She followed him from behind the rocks and watched him mount his horse and ride back through the trees. He was right. She knew only too well how few people were out in this country. The owners of the trading post wouldn't have any reason to come here, especially this late in the day. Turnbull was in Flagstaff. She could be sure he hadn't taken this scenic route. And maybe they shouldn't have, either. Could they afford the time?

Looking at Slide Rock, she shook her head. She had to stop questioning everything they did. They were here now. It was beautiful beyond imagining. They needed to rest, to be together one last night. Who knew what tomorrow would bring. Thor was right. She would bathe, relax, then eat and sleep well. Beyond that she didn't want to think.

She watched her horse graze, moving down the river away from Slide Rock. The animal wouldn't go far and needed to eat. She needed to do a few things, too. She walked back to their campsite, untied her blanket from the back of her saddle, then rolled it out on the ground. She set the saddle at the top of the blanket as a pillow, then untied her saddlebags. She took out a bar of soap and a comb. She set a clean shirt and a set of underwear beside the comb on her blanket.

Taking off her boots, she looked around. She

didn't expect anyone to be around, but she wasn't taking any chances either. She unbuckled her gunbelt and laid it over the saddle. Next she slipped off her vest, then her trousers and shirt. Finally she stood in her chemise and drawers. The air felt cool off the nearby water as the sun descended in the west. She knew the night would get cold, but for now the air was perfect.

Carrying her .45 in one hand and her soap in the other, she walked in bare feet over the dead leaf and pine needle-strewn ground to the pool at the base of Slide Rock. Her horse was out of sight. She sat down on a ledge of sun-warmed rock. She dipped a toe in the water. It felt cool and wonderful. She wanted very much to take off the rest of her clothes and savor the water all over her body. But she hesitated.

Frowning at herself, she remembered she was leader of the Wild Child Gang. She did what she wanted to do. She didn't worry about other people surprising her, not even Thor. Besides, she'd keep her pistol near at hand. She set the .45 on the rock along with the soap, then stripped off her underclothes. She set them beside the pistol, then slipped into the water. It was more delightful than she could have imagined. The past days of heat and dust disappeared from her mind and body.

She quickly washed out her underclothes with the soap, then used the chemise as a cloth to wash her body. Last she washed her thick hair, then wrung it out. Soap suds spilled over the top of the low rock formation and ran downstream, leaving the water around her once more pure and clear. She moved to the shallow end of the pool, braced her feet against the rock bottom, and leaned back against the warm rock surface. Laughing in pleasure, she splashed water upward into an arch. For a moment it made a rainbow in the late afternoon sunlight.

She didn't know when she'd felt so free, so happy, so content. Maybe being alone wasn't so bad after all. She had no responsibilities except herself. Shocked, she stopped her thoughts. Guilt ran through her. How could she even think of being happy when so many ghosts cried out for vengeance? How could she think of enjoying her time with Thor when so many women and children had died horrible deaths? What right did she have to happiness?

Losing all interest in the water, she started to get out when she heard a twig snap nearby. She reached up and grabbed the pistol, aiming it in the direction of the sound.

Thor stepped from the trees with his hands raised. "One of these days you're going to shoot before you look."

"I'm sorry. But with Turnbull in the area I can't be too careful." Her voice trailed away as she realized she had risen from the water and Thor was staring at her exposed breasts. Suddenly modest, she started to drop back into the water, but remembered the pistol. She couldn't get it wet. She quickly set it aside, then slid down in the water to her chin.

Thor chuckled as he walked nearer, leading his horse. "I'm ready to join you."

"Thor, I—"

"It's about time, don't you think?"

"I don't know. I was thinking about all my friends in the sweatshop."

"Don't!" He set a bulky flour sack down on the rock near her clothes, then hunkered down beside her. He pushed damp hair back from her face. "You're doing all you can possibly do to right a wrong. Let it go for one night."

She wished he wasn't so close. When she gazed into his blue eyes she couldn't think of anything but his nearness, the feel of his strong fingers. Was he right? Could she let it go for one night? Thinking only of him, she nodded.

"Good. I brought some bread and cheese and apples in that bag. Sound good?"

"Yes. I'm starved."

"I thought you'd like it. Let me set my horse free to graze with yours downstream, then we can eat." He stood up.

"Wait! If we're going to eat now, I'll get dressed."

"No." He picked up her wet underclothes. "You stay right where you are." He walked over to his horse.

"Thor! Bring my clothes right back here."

Ignoring her, he set her clothes on his saddle, then unbridled and unsaddled his horse. As the animal took off to join the other horse, Thor looked back. "I'll be right back." He crushed her underclothes in one hand and tossed the saddle over his shoulder with the other.

She watched him disappear into their campsite. She looked down at her nude body only partly concealed by the water, then back at the bag of food. Her stomach rumbled. Maybe she could get something to eat before he returned. She reached up and opened the sack. The food smelled wonderful. She picked up an apple and bit into the crispy fruit. Its flavor exploded in her mouth. As she chewed, she moaned in delight. After living on jerky and beans, this was wonderful.

"Save some for me."

She splashed back into the water, realizing in shock that he walked naked toward her. "Thor!"

"Yes?" He eased down into the water beside her, his body big and bronze. "Can I borrow your soap?"

She nodded, realizing her appetite had disappeared at the sight of him. If he'd been seductive prone on the bed, he was even more appealing now. She felt hot and hungry, but no longer for food. What did this man do to her?

He emptied the contents of the flour sack on the rock, then used the sack to scrub down his neck and shoulders after he'd soaped himself all over.

She watched in fascination, forgetting to eat her apple. She couldn't seem to get enough of watching him, of being with him. She hated the thought of ever sharing him with anyone again.

He glanced at her. "Why don't you help?"

Shaking her head, she smiled. "I'd rather watch."

"This time only." He grinned, then quickly finished washing himself all over before tossing the bag and soap up on the ledge. When he turned to her, his eyes were dark with purpose.

She bit into her apple, suddenly desperate to slow what was bound to happen. She had a frightening feeling that he was going to bind her to him with something stronger than rawhide. And how could she ever deal with that?

"You're going to fight all the way, aren't you?" He leaned against the rock, letting his feet brace against the bottom of the rocky outcropping. The water lapped low on his chest, turning the blond hair darker. The gold medallion around his neck gleamed in the light.

"Do you want something to eat?"

"Sure do." He picked up a hunk of bread and cheese, then began eating, all the while watching her.

She could feel the water lapping against the upper slope of her breasts and she wondered if the water was clear, if he could see very much of her, if it even mattered. She finished the apple, but it no longer had any taste. She continued with bread and cheese, but they could have been paper for all their taste. She was vitally aware of him, only him, nothing else really mattered. When she saw him eat an apple with his strong white teeth, then toss the core over his shoulder, she knew the time had come. She couldn't put off the bargain any longer. And she didn't want to anyway.

Taking a deep breath, she turned to him. He held out his hand and she took it, trusting him oddly enough in this one thing. Perhaps she had come to trust him finally and completely. But she didn't want to think about that now. His eyes were filled with heat and mischief and she felt herself respond deep inside to his sensual power.

He stood up, pulling on her hand. She hesitated, unable to turn away from the sight of his naked body. He was as beautiful as his surroundings. Primitive. He belonged here, an animal among the wilderness. But did she?

She let him draw her from the water, felt it cascade down away from her, saw the glimmer of desire in his eyes at the sight of her, and felt herself respond. But where was he taking them?

He dropped her hand and ran up the slope beside Slide Rock. He motioned for her to follow. She hadn't expected this. She had anticipated the bargain, but not this playfulness. He stood at the top, beckoning her. She glanced around, then down at her nudity. They were alone. What did it matter?

She hurried toward him, feeling as if he had finally drawn her into his fantasy. Nothing else seemed real, not Turnbull, not Chicago, not the girls. Where was he leading her? Could she, would she ever want to return? When she reached him, he pulled her against the hard heat of his body, then he knelt, pulling her down with him. She followed his movements, leaning over to let the water swirl through her fingers. For the first time, she realized moss covered the rock, making it slippery.

Laughing, he gently pushed her into the water. Caught by surprise, she slid onto the rock, then felt herself caught by the water and the next thing she knew she was zipping fast downhill. She heard him behind her, laughing still. Oh yes, now she understood the name, Slide Rock.

Yet happiness and excitement bubbled up inside her and she laughed, too. She felt exhilarated, free and happy as she plummeted downward. She heard him right behind her, splashing and laughing and playing like a child. No wonder he had gotten along so well with the Wild Child Gang. When she reached the pool at the bottom, she slid into it, splashing and sending up a cascade of water. She quickly stepped aside and turned to watch Thor, big and bronze and powerful, slide down to join her.

"What did you think?" He slicked his wet hair back from his face, his blue eyes alight with mischief.

She poked him in the chest with the tip of her finger. "You're bad!"

He threw back his head and laughed even louder.

"No fair!"

"Caught you by surprise, didn't I?"

"Naughty boy!" She poked him again, harder.

He stopped laughing, his eyes suddenly dark with desire. He lifted her into his arms and laid her against Slide Rock. The water gently cascaded around her. "You're so small, so perfect. I've wanted to see you this way from the first. Your body is truly beautiful."

She smiled, relaxing against the moss-softened rock. He made her *feel* beautiful. It was a rare and wonderful moment. She gazed up at him, caught in his spell, in his fantasy of her. Late afternoon sunlight glinted in his golden hair. His muscles rippled as he reached out to touch her, letting his hand discover the peaks and valleys of her body. He moved lower until he reached her soft mound. Hesitating there, he gently massaged.

"You aren't sore anymore?"

Unable to speak for the feelings coursing through her, she shook her head.

"Will I need to bind you?"

She couldn't keep from smiling despite the heat he was building deep inside her. She shook her head again. She was willing, only too eager for his touch.

He continued the discovery of her body with his hands, then lowered his face and seared her mouth with hot kisses. He was all fire compared to the coolness of the water around her. When he lingered on her lips, teasing, arousing, then delving deep inside her mouth, she moaned and reached up to run her fingers through his thick hair.

Groaning, he deepened the kiss, then nibbled down her neck to her shoulder where he bit her, sending chills through her body. She moved restlessly under him, feeling the heat he had built in her ignite into fire. She was warm and willing and wet where he had first breached her defenses. This time there was no defense against him, no longer any need. She wanted him, more with each passing moment. She felt desperate in her desire for fulfillment.

"I want this to be good for you, Harmony." He cupped her breasts with his hands, then teased each taut peak with his mouth, sucking, nibbling, causing her to moan and groan and writhe up toward him. She ran her hands up and down the corded muscles of his arms, then rubbed at the thick hair and muscles of his chest.

"Thor." She could say no more as he covered her mouth again, plunging inside her, making her hot, then cold, then wild with desire. She felt on fire all over, inside and out, with her core blazing and burning and demanding. She couldn't stand much more, although she didn't know exactly what she needed and wanted. But Thor knew.

He left her mouth, raked her body with his gaze, then parted her legs and stepped between them. "I won't hurt you this time."

Looking at the size of him, the hardness, knowing his burning heat, she doubted he could keep that promise. But she no longer cared. She knew more this time and she knew she wanted him inside her despite the price she might have to pay. Only he could put an end to her tender torment. She touched him as she had before, stroking his erection, pulling him toward her.

"Wrap your legs around me." He put his hands under her hips and raised her up to meet him.

When he pushed against her soft folds, she moaned and shuddered. "Thor, please help me. I need you."

As if her words released him, he pushed hard and slipped inside. He groaned, his body trembling with restraint.

She could feel his heat, his hardness as he moved deeper into her, so deep she didn't see how he could ever be separated from her again. To her surprise, she felt no pain, only a growing pleasure. He was as hot and hard inside her as the water was soft and cool around her. She felt abraded by the sensations inside and outside her body. And she felt the quickening of desire grow ever stronger as he thrust inside her, slowly at first, then gaining speed and force. This was different, so very different from before. But how could she have known?

"Look at me, Harmony."

She hadn't realized she had shut her eyes to better concentrate on the feelings of her body. Now she opened them and gazed into the dark blue turbulent sea of his eyes. But she couldn't keep from noticing his lips. They were full and red and sensual from kissing her. She shivered in response, feeling the heat of him inside and out. But it was not enough.

"I want to watch your expression when you finally know pleasure."

Glancing away, she realized he embarrassed her.

In fact, she felt jerked back to reality, torn from the fantasy he had created. What was she doing here in the open wilderness with Thor? Anyone could see them. Where was her control? She started to move away, but he thrust into her, long and hard and deep, faster and faster. She shut her eyes as her focus slipped back to the sensations of her body.

She moaned, tossing her head back and forth, felt herself slide against the slick moss and wrapped her arms around his neck, digging in her nails as he rode her harder and harder. She clung to him, her legs wrapped around him, until she thought she would explode from the tension, the fever building ever higher within her.

"Now, Harmony, look at me."

Wild with desire and need, she flung back her head, her brown eyes wide with wonder. He thrust hard inside her and she shuddered around him, the sensation moving from the inside out as she took him with her into the fulfillment of their passion. He pressed his lips to hers as he continued the ride, thrusting deep in her so there could never be any doubt as to their union. She clung to him as the wave of pleasure washed over them both.

In the aftermath, she lay limp in his arms, the tension and fear and loneliness of a lifetime released through him, by him. Tears filled her eyes, but she blinked them back, refusing to let him know the extent of her seduction.

He lifted her in his arms and sat down in the shallows of the pool. Water from Slide Rock gently caressed them as it spun into the pool, then continued downstream. The light grew dim as the sun slipped below the horizon, painting a purple and magenta sunburst in the sky. Birds chirruped in the treetops. Water sang in the stream.

And Harmony raised her head to look at the man who had given her so much. "I didn't know."

He smiled.

"I thought it was a simple physical act, like sneezing."

"Sometimes it is."

She looked puzzled.

"Trust me, I'll never let you know it any other way but like this."

Twenty-one

In the afternoon of the next day, Thor pointed out the town of Flagstaff in the distance. Harmony stood up in her stirrups, anxious to share the first glimpse of the town she'd come through so much to find. As far as she could tell, it looked like a typical Western town. But it was special. Somewhere within its borders was Turnbull and his gunmen. And she could hardly wait to get there.

They'd ridden through pine forests growing straight and tall in the high desert since attaining the heights of the Colorado Plateau that morning. Just as she'd anticipated, it hadn't been an easy climb. But it had been exhilarating, almost as exciting as Thor turning to her over and over throughout the night before.

Her body was sensitive today, for he hadn't been able to get enough of touching her, inside and out. She felt branded with his heat and passion. She slanted a glance at him. Perhaps he felt the same way, for she had returned his desire with a wildness of her own. She had surprised herself with her need. She also realized that if she'd known the value of his body when she had first kidnapped him, she might have made him a pleasure hostage. It wouldn't have been hard to do, knowing him now.

But she must put from her mind what they had shared. She must focus on finding and catching Turnbull. She must remain strong, even though her body was sensitive and she found it hard to breathe. She had the beginnings of a headache. Thor had told her that she was bothered by the height of the plateau. He'd also said it might take her a month to adjust to the altitude. She didn't have a week much less a month. She would simply have to ignore the irritation.

Twisting her mind away from her body, she focused on the town. Flagstaff was overshadowed by the magnificent land around it, for it had been built at the southern base of a majestic mountain range, white crowning its jagged peaks. The dark of pine covered most of the mountains except near the base where the leaves of aspen trees had turned yellow and orange. Buffalo grass grew tall and thick in the meadows and she could imagine a colorful carpet of wildflowers in the spring and summer.

Thor pointed toward the mountain range. "Americans named it the San Francisco Peaks. But long before that the peaks were home to the Hopi's kachina spirits. I suppose they still are."

"And the Hopi?"

"They live high on their three mesas as they always have. What have we got to interest them?"

"I wish we were going to be here longer." She was inspired by all she had seen in Arizona and by these tales of the Hopi. She realized how limited her life had been in Chicago. There was a richness, a vastness in the world that she had never experienced until forced to find a new life. Now she feared returning to her former world. What if she could never escape again?

"Flagstaff has a train depot. It's connected to the northern route. But it took the Atlantic and Pacific a long time to build tracks from Winslow to Flagstaff because they couldn't get enough workers to build a bridge to span Canyon Diablo."

"I suppose the Hopi didn't help."

"Hell no! The Navajo weren't anxious to help Americans scar their land, either. As it ended up, Mormon colonists mostly built it because they wanted the line into Flagstaff badly enough. They did the same thing up in Utah."

"Then we'll be able to take trains from there all the way to Chicago?"

"Looks like it."

"That'll help. I'd hate to try and take Turnbull in on horseback. I doubt if he can even sit a horse."

Thor turned to look at her. "Capturing Turnbull may not be so easy. He's got two hired gunmen with him."

"I know. But right's on our side."

"When the hell did that ever make a difference?"

"It must. At least this one time."

"I think we ought to go into Flagstaff at dusk. It'll give us a better chance of slipping in unseen. The last thing I want is for Turnbull to get the drop on us. We can get a hotel room, then ask questions around town."

"I don't know if I can wait. It's already been so long. I want to race into town right now and find him."

"Don't rush it. You've been an outlaw. You know waiting for the right moment is half the game."

"You're right, but I wish you weren't."

She sighed, watching Flagstaff get closer as they continued riding toward it. She wondered if some day maybe a hundred years from now the land would be sacrificed to the demands of a city of people, like Chicago. She didn't know if she could ever go back to living in such close contact with so many others, no matter if she had better living conditions. She'd gotten used to land around her. The West had changed her. Thor had changed her. But she couldn't go on until she'd gone back.

"What else can you tell me about Flagstaff?" She wanted to make the time pass more quickly.

"The area originally drew people for its natural spring, then it was a railroad construction camp. Now it's a growing center for cattle, sheep, and lumber. That is, if you don't count how the Indians have always used the land."

"I guess most don't."

"Not Americans."

"It doesn't seem fair to the Hopi and Navajo, does it?"

357

"No. And it's not. But as you well know, life isn't fair."

"Turnbull." She glanced to the west. The sun was bright in the sky. Later, it would create a beautiful sunset. She didn't think she'd ever seen more glorious sunsets than she had in New Mexico and Arizona. Maybe it was due to the flat land. She didn't know.

"We'll get him. Just give us time."

"Is it late enough for us to ride on into town?"

Thor turned to her and smiled, his eyes lighting with the special knowledge of all they had shared the night before. "You can't wait, can you?"

"No. Why don't we ride straight to the sheriff's office and see if Turnbull's been in asking about the Wild Child Gang."

"What if he's not in Flagstaff?"

"Don't even say it. He's there. I can feel it in my bones."

"Okay. I'm tired of being cautious. Let's go get him."

They rode onward, increasing the pace of their horses, and soon reached the town that had been built along Santa Fe, a street that paralleled the railroad tracks. They followed the road, the buildings increasing in size and density as they neared the center of town. Most of the buildings were built of lumber, but a few were made of brick. They passed the train depot, several saloons, a hotel, and a mercantile store.

Thor stopped his horse in front of the sheriff's office, stepped down, and tossed his reins over the hitching post. He gave Harmony an encouraging look, then stepped up to the boardwalk and disappeared inside the building.

She glanced around, watching for any sign of Turnbull or his gunmen. What she saw were mostly men, Americans, Indians, Chinese, and who knew how many immigrants from other parts of the world. Flagstaff was a busy town, obviously a growing center of the vast area around it. Turnbull could be anywhere within it.

Soon Thor stepped back outside, nodded to her, then mounted his horse and headed back down Santa Fe.

She paced him, carefully and casually following his example. She didn't want anyone to think they were doing anything out of the ordinary.

Down the street, Thor moved his horse close to her. "Turnbull and his gunmen are in town. They've been asking questions in the saloons, on the street, at the train depot, and in the hotels. I don't think we have to work hard to find them. They're looking for us."

Harmony felt a chill run up her spine as if somebody had seen her, somebody who wished her ill. "Thor, let's get out of here." She set her spurs gently to her horse's sides.

"No!" He hurriedly caught up with her, putting a hand over her hand holding the reins. "Don't cause anybody to notice us."

"I just realized Turnbull could have a gun on us this very moment." She hesitated, thinking. "All this time I've planned to search for him. But he's looking for us and has been for days. He already thinks we're in the area, but protected in a hide-out." She swallowed hard. "I don't think we should change his mind."

"Why?" Thor frowned.

"How long do you think it'll be before the sheriff lets Turnbull know a man looking like you asked about him?"

He nodded thoughtfully. "Turnbull's been working with the law all along, hasn't he?"

"Yes. He's had the backing of the Chicago police. We can't catch him by surprise."

"You're right. We should have thought of it sooner. Let's stop for supplies, then get the hell out of here."

"Supplies?"

"We ought to get Turnbull to follow us. He'll think we're leading him back to the Wild Child Gang hideout. Remember, he doesn't want just us."

She shivered. "He wants the girls, too. And he can't get them unless he lets us live."

"For now. If we get him to follow us out of town, then we've got the upper hand."

She cast him an appreciative glance. "You think like an outlaw."

"I was taught by the best."

They continued down Santa Fe until they came to a dry goods store. They stopped in front of its hitching post. Around them, the town was quiet.

"I'll go inside." Thor glanced down the street. "If something goes wrong, save yourself."

"No. We'll go in together."

360

"It'd look more normal if only one of us went inside and the other stayed outside to guard."

She resisted looking behind her, although she still felt as if a rifle was aimed between her shoulders. "You're right. Go ahead. We can use some food anyway."

He stepped down, flung his reins over the hitching post, then moved cautiously up on the boardwalk. He glanced in both directions, then walked inside.

Straining all her senses, Harmony waited for trouble while she kept her gaze on the doorway and her hand on the pistol at her hip. She almost hoped Turnbull came to her now. She'd like to shoot him dead in the street and be over with it. That way she'd never have to go back to Chicago or confront the law there or her memories. But that wasn't the way to do it and she knew it. She had to clear their names.

Time seemed to stand still as she waited. Every sound in the street or on the boardwalk made her stiffen. Her senses felt raw. Her headache raged. She realized they had to get out of town and find a hideout or a place they could defend before it grew dark. She wished they were in southern New Mexico where she knew the area better. Here she would have to rely on Thor. She hoped he knew his way around.

Just when she thought she couldn't stand the tension any longer, Thor stepped outside, carrying a bag in one hand. He looked in both directions, then walked without hurry to his horse. He mounted, gave her a nod, then started down Santa Fe. She followed, hoping they hadn't miscalculated and the next thing she felt was a bullet in her back.

"Look cautious but casual." Thor turned his head from side to side. "If Turnbull or one of his men is watching, we don't want them to think we know they're in town."

"I feel like they've got a gun aimed at my back."

"So do I."

"And they probably do."

"Right." He glanced at her. "I'm going to head out of town where we'll have some room to move around but cover from trees and hills. Do you trust me enough to follow?"

"You trusted me in New Mexico. We're both alive. I'll follow you now."

Thor nodded, his eyes constantly shifting. "But you didn't give me much choice." He had tried for a light tone of voice, but failed.

She smiled, but the movement felt forced. Each time she saw somebody move on a boardwalk, she tensed, ready to dodge a bullet. It wouldn't do any good. By the time she could react, Turnbull would have a slug in her.

They rode east along Santa Fe and the railroad tracks. As the buildings became fewer and farther between, she let out a sigh of relief. The tension in her shoulders eased, but she still felt watched. She glanced back, unable to resist. A wagon followed, as well as several riders. But none of them had to be Turnbull and his gunmen.

"How will we know if they follow?" She moved her horse closer to Thor.

"We won't, for sure. I doubt if they'll let us see them, not until it's too late. They can follow our trail."

"Not after dark."

"The light stays a long time out here."

"How far are we going?"

"I've got a place in mind. If they haven't seen it before, it'll distract them and we'll be ready."

She wished they were already there. She hated the waiting, the tension, the endless possibilities of the things that could go wrong. What if Turnbull had outsmarted them both? What if he didn't see them and follow? What if he waited for them to come to him? The questions were endless and she finally forced them from her mind. They had decided on a course of action and they would follow it to the end.

After a while, Thor turned north and headed up a rough road that skirted the eastern edge of the Peaks. She followed and they rode in silence, listening to the sounds around them and for anybody who might have followed. As they continued, she glanced behind, but didn't see anyone on their trail. Yet she remained tense, despite the beauty of the land around them.

As the sun began its descent in the west, Thor turned east onto a narrow trail that cut into a forest. Before she followed, she glanced back at the

Kachina Spirits Peaks. She wondered if the Hopi kachina spirits were watching her and if they would smile on her quest. She hoped they would, for she needed all the help she could get. She shook her head at her fancy. Arizona affected her in strange ways.

She felt the breath of death on the back of her neck and hurried to catch up with Thor. She glanced down as they rode and realized their trail on the soft sand would be easy to spot. Yes, Turnbull and his gunmen would soon find them, if they followed.

After riding down the trail for some time, Thor stopped. She rode up beside him and gasped in surprise. Stretching out before them the land lay in black waves from a mountain that had in some distant past become a volcano that was now a gaping red mouth above black cinder and lava flows that spread outward toward the north. All around the plateau of the volcano rose trees, windswept and stunted. Gnarled piñons spoke of wild wind and burned soil. But the setting sun tinted the volcano a beautiful rosy hue.

She sat speechless with surprise.

"What do you think?" Thor finally turned to her.

"I've never seen anything like it. To come from the richness of Oak Creek Canyon to this terrible, awesome beauty is almost overwhelming."

"That's what I'm counting on."

She finally looked at him.

His blue eyes narrowed. "There's cover in the hills over there. I'll make sure they lose our trail at the edge of the lava flow, but they won't notice that first."

"No. They'll see the volcano."

"And we'll see them."

"We've both got rifles."

"Right." Thor smiled, a grim twist of his lips. "Come on."

She followed him back down the narrow trail. He dismounted and so did she. He led his horse back through the trees, then toward the windswept hills to one side of the lava. She followed. When he led his mount back into the hills, she went right behind him. Finally they stood together out of sight.

He pulled her against his chest and held her tightly for a moment. He leaned back, then gently stroked her face and placed a tender kiss on her lips. "I'm going to rub out the trail from the lava to here. While I'm gone, get out the rifles. There's extra ammunition in the bag I bought in Flagstaff."

"Be careful."

She watched him run back down the path. He was in danger because of her. Had she made a great mistake? They could be in Louisiana by now. They could be safe. Turnbull would eventually give up and return to Chicago. The girls were finally happy and safe. Was revenge worth endangering everything she had fought so hard to achieve? Was it worth Thor's life? Or hers?

All the anger and hate she had felt for so long, that she had lived on so long seeped out of her.

She felt limp, as if she had lost a vital part of herself. She leaned against the rocky surface of the hill for support. She thought of the fire, of the screams, of the death, and of her nightmares. But it all seemed farther away. Less real. The sweatshop fire would always be with her, but she realized she no longer needed anger to motivate her, to keep her running when she only wanted to curl up and rest.

Suddenly she stood up straight, feeling a new strength pour into her. She no longer needed or wanted revenge. She no longer wanted to live with anger. She wanted what Thor had shown her the night before, had been showing her for weeks. She wasn't sure she could reach out for it, even if she knew quite what it was. But she did know she no longer wanted revenge. She wanted retribution. And she wanted Thor Clarke-Jarmon.

But her thoughts were broken by a shot, then two more. Her breath caught in her throat, then her heart speeded up. Horrified, she realized she had been daydreaming when Thor was out putting his life on the line. She slipped her rifle out of its sheath, then grabbed the bag with ammunition. She started to run back down the path, then stopped. No, she might run right into them.

Instead, she turned back toward the hills, moved quietly behind them, staying out of sight behind the trees, then ran quickly until she had a view of the lava where the trail ended. Thor lay on the black lava, like a broken doll. Turnbull and his two gunmen stood over him in triumph.

366

She almost cried out to Thor, but stopped herself. Had her selfishness killed him? Had Turnbull added one more person to his list of victims? Well, he would add no more. This time she had the advantage. As she took aim, she ignored the pain in her heart, the small voice inside herself that cried out at her loss. As she cocked the rifle, she realized with a blinding flow of emotion that she loved Thor. Rather, she *had* loved him.

The pain at her realization and her loss was so great she trembled all over, but love was abruptly replaced by hate. That emotion she knew well, only too well. She focused on the man who had caused her so much pain. "Turnbull, you're outgunned." Her voice carried across the lava flow. "You and your men throw down your weapons. Now!"

She wasn't even surprised when they didn't. She felt quite detached from herself, cool and calm. She was the outlaw leader again. When they turned to fire in the direction of her voice, she realized they had no idea how good a shot she had become, especially with a rifle and open targets. Several bullets hit the rock near her head as they tried to protect themselves while they looked for cover. But they were surrounded by black lava.

Taking careful aim on one of the gunmen, she knew she'd have to make her first shot good. Once they knew her exact location, she'd be prey instead of hunter. She gently squeezed the trigger and watched with satisfaction as one of the men clutched his chest and fell. She turned her rifle toward the other, expecting trouble. Instead she watched in amazement as Thor raised up on one elbow and shot the other just as the man turned to fire at him again.

It was all over that quickly after so many months of running, hiding, and finally hunting. She hesitated only a moment to see Thor turn his pistol on Turnbull who had raised his hands high in the air. She ran down the trail through the trees as fast as she could. She glanced up once to see the peaks towering over her. She whispered a quick word of thanks to the Kachinas. Thor lived. She would never take that fact for granted again.

Still carrying the rifle as well as wearing her .45, she reached Thor. She knelt by his side. "Are you all right?"

"They caught me by surprise and nicked my shoulder. I acted like it was worse than it was."

She felt incredible relief wash through her. And love. "Don't ever scare me like that again. I can't take it."

"Yes, ma'am." He grinned. "You got your man. Now what do you want to do with him?"

Harmony turned to Turnbull. She kept her rifle pointed at him as she walked slowly up to him and looked him over. He didn't appear so superior now. His face was beaded with sweat. His fine suit was covered with dust. His arms trembled as he tried to keep them in the air.

He wasn't a big man. Somehow over the months he had increased in size, looming larger than life. But at most he stood five inches taller than her five feet. He was thin except for a belly that pushed outward from his waistline. His hair had thinned and grayed many years before. And his gray eyes appeared faded and sunken in the sagging skin of his face. He would never be a powerful giant to her again.

Thor stood up, then checked each of the gunmen to make sure he was dead before walking over to Turnbull and making sure he was unarmed. He stepped back.

"You aren't going to kill me, are you?" Turnbull's voice ended on a whine.

"Isn't that what you wanted to do to me? And the girls?" Harmony frowned.

"No!" Turnbull shook his head back and forth. "You've misunderstood. We merely wanted to help you and the orphans. We tried to find you in Chicago and—"

"How stupid do you think I am?"

He blinked several times. "Smart. Of course, you're very smart." He glanced up at his hands. "Please, can I lower my arms? I'm not used—"

"Don't move a muscle. After so long on the trail I'm itching to pull the trigger." She caressed the rifle with her left hand.

Turnbull paled.

Thor picked up a handful of black lava rock and put it in one of Turnbull's coat pockets, then filled the other with more rock. "That's what your life is worth right now, Turnbull."

"I'm afraid I haven't had the pleasure of making your acquaintance, sir."

369

Thor leaned down closer to Turnbull's face. "I can see the whites of his eyes. You want me to shoot him now? We can bury all three bodies in the lava and sell their horses."

"Please, don't shoot me. I'm a wealthy man. I can give you gold, property, businesses, anything you want. All you have to do is name it."

Thor looked at him in disgust, then turned and walked back to stand beside Harmony.

"What I want is the lives of those hundred sweatshop workers you murdered in Chicago."

"I didn't do it. I swear it. I owned the shop, yes. But I didn't run it. I don't know how that door got locked."

"Then why did you tell the police I did it?"

He shook his head, his entire body quaking now. "I didn't. Why would you think such a thing of me? I'm a good man. I have a lovely wife and daughters."

"I pity them." Scorn roughened Harmony's voice.

"Please, let me lower my arms. The pain—"

"Keep your arms up." Harmony frowned.

"Let me kill him." Thor stroked the butt of his pistol. "He needs it."

Turnbull shook all the harder, sweat pouring down his face. "Please, don't hurt me. I'll do anything you want, give you everything I've got. You've misunderstood. I wouldn't hurt anybody. Think of my family. They need me."

"You lie." Harmony's brown eyes blazed. "I'm

thinking of all the sweatshop workers who needed you to make their lives a little easier."

Turnbull puffed out his chest. "I provide jobs. I do good works in the community. You don't understand what an important man I am."

Harmony took a step toward him, menace in every line of her body. "I know exactly what kind of man you are. And now you can keep your life in only one way."

Turnbull fell to his knees and bowed his head to the ground at her feet, hugging his arms around his chest. "Name it. Anything. Please don't kill me. I beg you."

Thor kicked him. "Get up."

"Anything!" Turnbull's words were muffled as he began to cry and wail. "I'll do anything."

"You will agree to go back to Chicago with me and turn yourself into the police and tell them that the girls and I had nothing to do with that fire. We were innocent victims who were lucky enough to escape. Then you will tell them that you ordered the door locked, that you are responsible for the fire in an overcrowded, dangerous shop that you owned and ran."

Turnbull stopped crying and looked up at her in horror.

"And if you have any more businesses, you will reform them to help workers."

Turnbull clasped his hands under his chin. "Please, I'll make you both rich. You'll never want for anything else in your lives. I'll even give money to those girls. As much as you want. I only ask that you take the money and disappear into the West."

"You're not in a position to ask anything." Thor prodded Turnbull with the toe of his boot.

"Think of it. Money!" He turned to Thor. "All the women, drink, and power you can possibly use for the rest of your life. Isn't that what you want?"

"No." Thor shook his head in disgust.

Turnbull turned back to Harmony. "Isn't that why you robbed stages and trains? Didn't you want the money? Isn't it what you want from me? Money is everything."

"No, it's not."

"How dare you disagree? Russell H. Conwell, noted Christian minister, has preached the gospel of wealth over six thousand times all over this country. *Six. Thousand.* He says, and he's not the only preacher saying it, that it is our duty to get rich. You can't question God!"

"Or you?" Harmony's voice dripped with sarcasm.

"You want money. I know you want it. I'll give you enough to make you a rich and powerful lady. You can dine with the elite of the world."

"When I worked in your shop, I could barely eat on what you paid me. Now you want me to dine with robber barons like you." She shook her head. "No thanks."

"Nobody turns down money." Turnbull stared at her in disbelief. "And nobody can't be bought."

"You may be for sale, Isham Turnbull, even

your very soul, but I'm not. And neither are my friends." She tightened her grip on the rifle. "Thor, do you still have that rawhide."

"Yes." He pulled a length out of his pocket.

"I think you'd better tie Turnbull's hands behind his back."

"Wait!" Turnbull jumped to his feet, raising his hands high again. "Don't you want the money?"

"I told you what I wanted." Harmony leaned forward. "Now do you want your final resting place to be in this lava or do you want to go back to Chicago and stand trial?"

Turnbull paled, took several deep breaths, glanced at the dead bodies of his gunmen, then looked from Thor to Harmony. "I can't deal with unreasonable people. Money is all that counts and anybody with any sense knows it."

Harmony growled.

Turnbull trembled. "Fine. Take me back to Chicago. I'll go to the police and tell them exactly what you want." He straightened his shoulders. "But, remember, I'm Isham Turnbull, scion of Chicago society. You, my dear, are nothing but a lowly shop worker and an outlaw with a price on her head." He looked at her with scorn. "In fact, you're worth less than nothing."

"Wrong!" Thor stepped forward and grabbed Turnbull's coat lapels with one fist. He lifted the man off his feet so they were face to face. "Isham Turnbull is a murderer. And Harmony Harper is an avenging angel."

Turnbull's eyes bulged in fear.

"The fact of the matter is your life is worth exactly what Miss Harmony Harper says it is."

"And I say it's worth the hangman's noose." She cocked her rifle. "No more, no less."

Part Four
Hammer of Sun and Moon

Twenty-two

Harmony sat on the grimy floor of a rear room in a tenement in Chicago's South Side. She'd drawn up her knees and rested her chin against them. There was no worse place in the city to live unless you were without a home, living on the street, sleeping in police or train stations if you could.

It was not cheap to live in the slums, but the immigrants who mainly filled its tenements didn't know that. They took what they could get and held on to it unless evicted. Many men had gotten rich and were getting richer on slum property. They knew the cost and price of everything, but the value of nothing.

Robber barons. Their stench filled her nostrils just as strongly as the smell of boiling cabbage filled the air, clung to the walls, permeated the building. From where she sat she could see out the prized single window in the one-room flat. Patched linen hung on pulley lines crisscrossing between the windows that overlooked the gap from dirty brickwalls called a yard. She remembered there was no Monday wash day in the tenements. The poor washed every day because they couldn't afford a change of clothes.

She looked upward, but couldn't tell the color of the sky because the air was filled with soot and pollution from the nearby factories. Slum dwellers had no choice but to live near the places of work or providers of work because they couldn't afford transportation. She could hear the sounds of babies and children whimpering, women and men talking, occasionally shouting, hitting, cursing, and the hum of sewing machines through the thin walls.

This was the Chicago she knew only too well. And hated. She looked to the right. And smiled, a grim twist of her lips. She'd brought Turnbull deep into the heart of the world he'd help create and fed on still. He lay on the floor, gagged and bound by hands and feet. She glanced away, unable to stand the sight of him alive and healthy.

Thor sat on one of the two chairs at a scarred, rickety wooden table, writing on a clean, white piece of paper. The sheets of paper on the table were in sharp contrast to everything else in the room. A single iron bed, with a sagging, stained mattress with no sheets, was pushed against one wall.

Outside, the sinks in the hallway were used by all tenants so that everyone was poisoned by summer stenches. She could hear the pump squeak at the hydrant where the thousands who lived in the block carried pails to get water. In summer, when so many were desperate for water, it dried up quickly. She thought of the long walk through dark, narrow, twisting stairs, up and down floor after floor to get water or find the hydrant empty.

She should be glad it wasn't summer or winter, the worst times of the year for the slums of Chicago. She always thought of it as the crying time, for it was then that the weakest of the tenants died. Week after week the small, undernourished, overworked bodies of children were carried from the tenements. Most hadn't yet reached the age of five, but over that age they weren't considered children anymore. So who cared?

Their families. Most did their best for their children, but they needed the small, nimble fingers to work, helping to make ends that never met come closer. In cramped, hot or freezing rooms whole families, many times with tenants of their own, lived and worked and died. And perhaps sometimes had the energy to love.

If a child died while working at sewing on button after button or making paper flowers or other endless types of work, only the number of family members needed to bury the child in an unmarked grave in potter's field stopped work. They could never afford for everybody to stop work at the same time.

Harmony clenched her fists, the smells, noises, sights, sounds opening up old wounds she'd thought healed. How she hated robber barons like Turnbull. A human life had meaning for him only in how much work he could get out of it for the least amount of money. Sixteen to eighteen hours of steady work a day was normal. In sweatshops that meant seven days a week. Factory and shop workers had been agitating for ten- and twelve-hour days. But the people in the slums couldn't even imagine that luxury.

She knew. She'd worked her way out. But she hadn't grown up in one. She'd known the difference from the first. When she was young her father had held a steady job in a factory. They'd lived just above the tenement level. But that had come to a halt after the great Chicago fire. They'd survived it, but lost everything they'd owned. Afterward her father had started drinking and no longer had worked steady.

Like so many women without husbands or families and with children to support, her mother had taken in sewing to make ends meet. The pay was so low that Harmony had helped from the first. It had made her father angry and he had insisted that their work made him feel less of a man. But it wasn't long before he had quit trying to find work and had spent his time in nearby saloons. From there, their lives had quickly gone downhill. And her mother had been grateful to get them work in a sweatshop.

Harmony turned to look at Turnbull again, knowing she couldn't even imagine his type of home compared to the tenements that had gone up so fast after the great fire. They housed the sweatshops.

She thought of the system. A wholesale manufacturer hired a contractor to sublet work to a "sweater." His shop was usually the larger of two rooms of a tenement flat. He employed six to twenty "sweating" men, women, and children who worked in that room. He used the other room as his living, sleeping, and cooking area. He boarded the workers who ate at their work and slept on the goods.

But it could and did get worse. A single family of "sweaters" who lived in one or two small rooms in a tenement subcontracted work to "homeworkers" who lived with them. Her father had tried his hand at subcontracting to "homeworkers," and her mother had made it work for as long as she could. But the money had never been enough to get them out of the tenement because the profit was "sweated" from the worker below till it reached the bottom. And they were much too near the bottom.

Sweatshops. She'd worked her way up to a factory, Turnbull's shop. But she knew he contracted out much of the work to "sweaters." She'd considered his factory a sweatshop because of its dark, cramped, crowded conditions. She'd been a silk worker and better paid than many women, but it hadn't been enough to support herself. Yet she knew the women and children who were paid by the task would have been grateful for her wages.

She gave Turnbull a dark look. After the fire that had destroyed Chicago, there was no greater fear for anyone who lived within the city. She'd thought never to experience such horror and desperation again. She'd been a child then and terrified, but being older hadn't helped the fear. Turnbull well knew that nothing could have been worse than to accuse her of starting a fire in Chicago.

Maybe she would never get over the nightmares, but she would see justice done if it was the last thing she did. And maybe in the process she could make a difference for other workers.

Unable to stand her thoughts any longer, she got up and paced the narrow confines of the room. She stopped in front of Turnbull. He looked up at her, fear in his eyes. Good. She wanted him to know fear and hunger and thirst. But most of all she wanted him to feel desperation. Could he? Was it even possible for a man like him?

"Leave him alone, Harmony." Thor set down his pen. "I don't want to take him in battered and bruised."

She wheeled on Thor and strode over to him. "I still don't like the plan."

"I know you don't." He frowned. "You'd like to waltz into your old police precinct and hand Turnbull over yourself. Then you'd like to hear his confession and watch them put him behind bars."

"Yes!"

Thor ran a hand through his hair and looked tiredly at her. "I'm not going to fight you on this anymore. If I have to tie you up like Turnbull, I will." He took a deep breath. "You aren't going anywhere near the police. I hate to think how fast they'd have you behind bars."

"But—"

"No! If they asked questions of you at all, they'd ask them too late."

"But what about Turnbull's confession? That frees me." She threw a hard look at Turnbull.

"Damn it!" Thor wiped his face with a handkerchief. "It's so hot and stifling in here I can hardly think. The noise from so many people packed in together is making my mind feel like mush." He pointed a finger at her. "And you want to argue this over and over."

"But Thor—"

"We discussed this every which way from Sunday on the train from Flagstaff. And I haven't changed my mind. Think, Harmony! You're a wanted woman. They'd like nothing better than to make you a scapegoat. If the police get their hands on you, I don't know if you'll ever see the light of day, no matter what Turnbull says. Remember, Chicago police *hang* labor agitators."

"Haymarket Square." She shivered. "Two years ago police broke up a labor meeting there, but it caused a riot. Seventy people were injured." Her voice lowered. "Seven policemen were killed that day, but the police had earlier killed six men when they tried to break up a worker meeting along Black Road."

"Right. And they *hung* four Haymarket labor leaders."

"It frightened us all."

"And you've got more than the Chicago police to worry about. The army built Fort Sheridan on the lakefront after Haymarket to reassure Chicagoans that their property wouldn't be destroyed. And that doesn't count the Pinkertons who've been hired by many a robber baron to stop strikes in his factory. These rich men have every intention of continuing to pile up their millions no matter the cost in life. Harmony, I'm only going to say it one more time. They *kill* strikers and labor agitators around here."

"But I'm not either."

Thor hit the table with his fist and stood up. He paced to the window, looked out, then turned back. "I don't know how the hell anybody survives summer in this hellish hole."

"A lot of them don't."

"I'm sorry." He crossed the room and took her in his arms. "I can't stand to see you in a place like this and the idea of you living in a tenement for years makes my skin crawl. I want you out of here, out of this city as fast as I can get you." He set her back and looked deeply into her eyes. "And that's why I'm not letting you go anywhere near the police."

"But I don't know if your plan will work."

He walked back to the table and sat down. "I'm almost done." He picked up his pen and looked up at her. "You're safe here, Harmony. So is Turnbull. Nobody could find you here and that's why this is the best place to be till we get this matter settled with the police. But don't make us spend any longer here than necessary."

"I don't want to be here either. But I'm not sure—"

"As soon as I get these statements written, you'll sign yours and Turnbull will sign his. I'll get the hell out of here and go to a lawyer. That lawyer, without knowing where you are, will take Turnbull and the statements to the police."

"And you'll take the second set of signed statements to Monique O'Sullivan at the *Chicago Daily News?*"

"Yes. It's the biggest newspaper in town and we need their support to help keep you safe."

"That's not why I picked the *Daily News*. I want Monique O'Sullivan to break the story. She's written articles before about the plight of working women and children. We'd find them sometimes and share them at the shop. She's sympathetic."

"That'll help. And you need it." He went back to writing. "Now let me concentrate."

"Thor, I want Miss Sullivan to be there when you hand Turnbull over to the police."

He looked up. "I'm not going to hand him over. The lawyer I hire will take him to the police station. We aren't going to get directly involved in this."

"But Thor—"

"The police aren't going to see your face or mine. And if I have to, I'll get you out of this town so fast it'll make your head swim." He frowned. "I'm taking no chances. I don't trust anybody involved in this. And I don't know how the hell you're going to prove anything anyway."

"I don't want to bring the girls back to testify."

"That's what I mean." He tossed down the pen.

385

"The more I think about this whole mess, the more worried I get. Who the hell is going to believe shop workers over the owner? Harmony, I just don't know."

She started to respond, but heard a groan from Turnbull. She glanced in his direction. He'd sat up and was trying to speak. She strode over to him and kicked his leg. "Be quiet! You just want to offer us more money. You make me sick."

"I heard enough of his whining on the train to last me a lifetime." Thor gave them both a hard stare, then went back to writing.

Walking back to the table, Harmony watched him a moment, wishing she could write so beautifully. Maybe one day she and the girls would learn. She started to speak, then firmly closed her lips. She didn't want to disturb him. The sooner he was done, the sooner it'd be over. She walked back to the window and looked out at the depressing scene. Thor was right. About everything. She knew it, but she didn't want to accept it. For months she'd had this vision of walking into the police station and presenting Turnbull.

If she did that, she'd be more likely the one arrested. But it didn't seem honest to hide behind some faceless lawyer. It didn't seem fair to have Thor step in and do what she should have done. But she wasn't capable of writing the letters in just the right words. She couldn't hire a lawyer. She didn't have the money or credentials. And she didn't want to involve the girls.

What had happened to the leader of the Wild

Child Gang? Out West she'd felt so powerful, so in control. But back here in Chicago she once again felt helpless, outgunned at every turn. If Thor wasn't helping her, she didn't know what she'd do. She looked back at Turnbull. Yes, she did. She'd have followed her original plan and damned the consequences.

But now she had too much to live for. The girls. And Thor. Thoughts of Turnbull no longer ruled her life. She wanted retribution, not revenge. If she couldn't get him convicted, she could at least get his good name questioned in newspapers and she could call attention to the problems of workers in Chicago. Was it enough? She thought of the fire, of the screams, of her friends. No. Somehow, she must find a way to stop Turnbull.

Thor threw down his pen. "Okay. I've got two copies of both statements. In his, Turnbull admits his guilt. In yours, you tell about the locked door and your narrow escape. Your innocence."

"And you put in that I've never been a labor agitator or organizer?" She walked over to the table.

"Here, read it for yourself." He pushed a piece of paper toward her.

She hesitated, picked it up, nodded, then laid it back down.

"You didn't read it." He looked puzzled and pushed it at her again.

"Thor, please." She swallowed. "I can't."

"What do you mean, you can't? I thought I wrote it clearly."

387

"No. It's beautiful handwriting." She glanced at Turnbull, knowing he was listening. Well, what did she care? She raised her chin. "I can read printing, mostly, but my mother didn't get a chance to teach me more than that. We went to work in a sweatshop and—"

Thor stood up so fast his chair crashed to the floor. He rounded the table and took her in his arms, holding her close, patting her back. "I'm sorry. That was thoughtless of me." He hesitated. "What about the girls?"

"I'd been teaching them on the trail."

He set her back. "One of the most important things that must be done for all children, boys *and* girls, is to get them the right to an education."

She nodded, tears misting her eyes.

Turnbull groaned.

They looked at him.

Turnbull shook his head, trying to throw off his gag.

Harmony quickly crossed the room and pulled down the bandanna. "All right. Say what you want."

"You two do-gooders make me sick." Turnbull cleared his throat. "You think money doesn't matter. You think everybody should be equal. What are the principles on which this country was founded?"

"Equality." Thor spoke softly.

"Equality, yes." Turnbull turned his gray eyes from one to the other. "But equality for white men who've got the guts to make whatever they want

388

of themselves. Anybody who can't or won't do that deserves what they get."

"Sweatshop work?"

"Yes!" Turnbull leaned toward them. "It's all some people can do or want to do. And most children shouldn't waste their time on learning to read and write. They should be helping their parents earn a living. If they stopped working, who the hell would take their places? Their mothers?"

Harmony jerked his gag back into place. "You're wrong. Nobody wants to work in sweatshops or similar factories and shops. And it's not the work they mind. It's the slow starvation. Your greed gives them little choice now. But times change. Men like you die. And robber barons will one day be allowed no more."

Turnbull lay down and turned his face to the wall.

"I don't think you've got the right audience." Thor put an arm around her waist. "But your heart is in the right place."

"I want to get this over with as quickly as possible. I can't stand to be around Turnbull any longer." She walked back to the table and picked up a pen.

Thor slid two sheets of paper toward her.

She slowly, carefully wrote her name at the bottom of each page, then glanced up at him in triumph. "My mother taught me how to sign my name. She didn't want me to ever have to use an X."

"You did well."

"What about Turnbull?"

"I'll take care of him." Thor picked up the chair he'd overturned. He walked over to Turnbull, lifted him, then deposited him in the chair. He quickly untied the rawhide binding Turnbull's wrists. "Sign both sheets with your usual signature."

Turnbull jerked down the bandanna, then glared at them. "If I hadn't already been convinced of it, now I'd know for sure. Workers are stupid."

"You're the one who got caught. Not me." Harmony glared at him.

Turnbull cast a baleful stare on Thor. "You had his help."

"Sign the papers." Thor held out the pen with his left hand while putting his other on the butt of his pistol.

"You wouldn't shoot me here. The noise would bring the police."

Harmony laughed. "The police? You don't really think they'd dare or care to come in here? And who'd notice or care about the sound? We could kill you and dump your body in the yard. Tenants would walk over you till you were nothing but bones."

"The smell would bring the police." Turnbull glared.

"Your rotting corpse would be perfume compared to the other smells in this place." She shook her head. "You don't understand, do you?"

He simply stared at her.

"You sit in the middle of a tenement and still you think it has nothing to do with you. It's not even real. You don't comprehend it at all." She stepped back. "And you don't want to."

"I don't need to." He gestured around the room. "This has nothing to do with me."

"And the deaths of one hundred women and children in your shop had nothing to do with you either, did it?"

"No." His gray eyes never wavered.

"You're dead inside, aren't you?" She leaned forward and grabbed his lapels and shook him hard.

He raised his head. "I will not respond to your violence."

"Oh no?" She slapped him hard across one cheek, then the other.

He stood up, touching his face with a hand. "How dare you touch me?"

Harmony rounded the table, her fists raised.

Thor caught her around the waist and pulled her back. "You'd better sign those papers, Turnbull. If nothing else, I'd like to see her carve up your pretty face so your outside looked like your inside."

Turnbull hesitated, glanced from one to the other, then sat down. "I said it before and I'll say it again. There is no way to deal with irrational people. And you two are clearly insane." He quickly scrawled his signature at the bottom of each page, then thrust them away from him. "There. The sooner I get away from you two the better. I'm sure the police will treat me with the respect I'm due."

"Respect!" Harmony struggled against Thor. "Let me at him."

"No." Thor shook her and set her back. "We've got what we wanted." He retied Turnbull, replaced the gag, then picked up the man and dumped him back on the floor.

"I'd really like to hurt him, Thor."

"I know. So would I. But our lawyer won't want him bruised, trust me."

"Do you think the robber barons own the law?"

"A lot of it, but not all of it." He walked back to the table and stacked the papers together.

"How long will you take?"

"Not any longer than I have to take." He took off his gun belt, laid it on the table, then pulled out his pistol. He unbuttoned his shirt, slipped the .45 inside, then rebuttoned his shirt. "I'm going nowhere in this town unarmed." He looked at her. "I've got to go out and get a hotel room, buy a good suit, contact a lawyer, then get the process started."

"I want to go with you."

"Who'll guard Turnbull?"

"We can tie him up real good."

"Do you think it's wise to leave him alone?"

"No." She exhaled sharply. "Not here. If anybody found him, they'd need the money he offered so badly he'd be gone in no time."

"Okay. Wait here. I'll be back by sundown if I can." He rolled up the papers.

She walked over to the door and opened it.

Carrying the signed confessions in one hand, he

walked over to her. "Trust me." He placed a gentle kiss on her lips, then stepped from the room.

She shut and locked the door, unable to watch him walk into the darkness of the tenement, into the danger, and away from her.

About love and the future, she refused to think.

Twenty-three

Hour after hour passed as Harmony paced the room, looked out the window, and resisted her impulse to kick Turnbull. She had brought a bottle of water, plus some bread and cheese in a carpetbag. Although she didn't feel hungry, she forced herself to eat, then drink a little water. She refused Turnbull anything. As far as she was concerned, he was lucky to be alive. As time passed, she become more and more convinced she should have buried him in the lava rock of Arizona. But she wanted retribution, not revenge.

By late that afternoon, she feared Thor wouldn't be able to do everything that day. It was a lot, but she wanted it done now. She could hardly stand to be near Turnbull, even though for the most part he lay sluggishly on the floor. She'd like to see him sew on buttons for eighteen hours a day, week after week, month after month until he couldn't see anymore. But he'd never make it, not here, not anywhere. He'd never had the strength or courage. He'd simply curl up and die, like he had already started to do.

She gripped the butt of her pistol. She had carried it in the carpetbag all the way from Arizona. Once she'd entered this room, she'd strapped on her gun belt. As an outlaw she'd grown used to a .45's protection and she hated to be without it. She'd also refused to change out of her outlaw clothes. She hadn't trusted Turnbull not to try and escape during that long train ride from Arizona. A dress would have hampered her movements and she wasn't ready to give up any part of her safety until he was behind bars.

Her spurs jingled as she walked over to Turnbull. She prodded his back with the toe of her boot. She could still put a bullet in his head. It'd all be over and she could begin to live again. Maybe she couldn't live in Chicago, but there were plenty of other places around.

He groaned and turned his eyes toward her. She was surprised to see how fast he was failing. He'd only been in the tenement since late the day before. He hadn't been mistreated. He'd had food and water that morning. Now he lay in a pool of his own sweat, his eyes unfocused, his body limp. A man like him wasn't strong enough to survive the tenements. He had to pay people to pamper him, to do the work for him, and to bolster his courage.

She turned away from him in disgust. She walked back to the window. Each time she looked out, she hoped she would see a different, better view. But its bleakness never changed. She knew that only too well. Yet she was lucky to be able to afford a window with any type of view, any type of fresh air circulating in the room. It could be worse, much worse.

As she gazed out the window, a knock came at the door. She tensed, dropping her hand to her pistol. She walked quickly across the room and paused just inside the door. The knock came again.

"It's me, Thor."

She unlocked the door, not that the flimsy wood would have kept out anybody determined to enter, then opened it. After he stepped inside, she quickly shut and relocked the door. It was then she noticed his clothes. He reminded her of when she'd first kidnapped him off the train. She wasn't sure she liked the transformation.

"It's all done." He smiled at her, then tossed a package on top of the table.

She closed her eyes in relief.

"I didn't get the best, not lawyer or clothes, but I got the newspaperwoman you wanted."

"Oh, Thor!" She started to throw her arms around him, then realized she was dusty and dirty. She dropped her arms and shrugged. "I don't want to muss you."

He laughed and jerked her against him. He gave her a hard hug and a quick kiss that turned longer and longer till he left them both breathless and wanting more.

"We've got to hurry." He glanced at Turnbull. "How's the prisoner?"

"Like you left him."

"He looks half dead." Thor picked up his gunbelt off the table, strapped it on, then slipped his pistol in the holster. He buttoned his suit coat so it wouldn't show too much.

"I can't help it if he's a spineless, gutless robber baron."

Thor picked up the jar of water and hunkered down beside Turnbull. He turned the man over and splashed water over his face, letting him drink as he poured it. "That'll help."

"We should let him starve to death."

"No time now." Thor got up, then put the water, bread, and cheese in the carpetbag. "Open the package. It's for you."

"Really?" She walked to the table suspiciously. "I don't need anything."

"Yes, you do."

She pulled a black duster out of the package. "What am I supposed to do with this?"

"Wear it. I hope it fits. I bought a boy's size."

"Why?"

"Harmony, what you're wearing will call attention to you out there. You don't have any other clothes and I didn't have time to get you anything more complicated than that."

"I wouldn't have worn it anyway."

"I figured that, too. Go ahead, try it on."

She slipped the duster on one arm, then the other. The linen coat reached her ankles and had a split up the back to allow her to sit astride a saddle. It could be buttoned up the front, but she left it open.

"Good." Thor walked over to her and adjusted the collar. "It fits fine."

"And covers up my pistol."

"Exactly."

She smiled and put her hands around his neck to pull his face downward for a kiss. "Thanks, partner."

He pulled her hands slowly from around his neck. "Much more of that and I'm going to forget all about Turnbull."

Shaking her head, she stepped back. "Later. Now, tell me what's going to happen."

"Like I said, we've got to hurry. I've got a carriage waiting for us outside. The driver's not going to wait in the tenements long." He walked over to Turnbull and took the rawhide off the man's ankles and stuffed it in his pocket. Jerking Turnbull to his feet, he pulled down the bandanna.

"You're going to leave his hands tied, aren't you?"

"Yes." He led Turnbull toward the front door.

She picked up the carpetbag.

He glanced at it. "Leave it here. We don't need it anymore."

But she'd lived in poverty too long. "I don't want the tenement owner to get it."

Turnbull cleared his throat, then glared at each of them in turn. "I'm going to see you both dead and in hell for what you've done to me."

Harmony rounded on him. "Done to *you?*"

"No time now." Thor opened the door. "We've got to get out of here. The lawyer will be waiting near the precinct station."

"All right." She walked through the doorway and watched as Thor pushed Turnbull into the hall. She shut the door, then followed them through the darkness, down stairs, past badly smelling sinks until they finally emerged on the front steps of the tenement. She couldn't resist the shudder of relief that passed through her as she hurried toward the waiting carriage.

As Thor pushed Turnbull into the carriage, she glanced around and saw a young girl, maybe five years of age, standing still as she stared in amazement at the horse and carriage. She hurried to the girl. She opened the carpetbag, pulled out the book Deidre had given her and stuffed it in a front pocket of her duster. Smiling at the small girl, she set the carpetbag down in front of her.

"You can have it."

Frightened, the little girl stepped back.

"It's not too heavy and you can have it. I don't need it anymore. There's food in it. Take it home."

The little girl took a step forward.

Harmony stepped back, watching to make sure no bigger child tried to take it from the smaller one.

Grabbing the bag, the little girl hefted it up into both arms, then raced for the front steps and disappeared inside the tenement.

"Come on!" Thor motioned to Harmony.

Tears misted her eyes as she hurried to the carriage. She knew how much the small gift would mean to the girl's family. The child reminded her of the girls she'd left in Arizona. She missed them, but soon now they'd be reunited. As Thor grabbed her hand and helped her up to the carriage, she renewed her vow to help children.

Inside the closed carriage, she moved closer to Thor. He squeezed her hand. Turnbull glared at them from the opposite seat, but said nothing. As the carriage rolled down the street, she wondered how long it would take to get where they were going. The streets of Chicago were always crowded with people, carriages, trains, and now the fancy new cable cars. She'd never ridden in one, but she'd seen them.

With one hand in Thor's strong grasp and the other near her pistol, she endured the ride. She watched nothing but Turnbull, afraid he'd make a sudden dash for freedom. But she shouldn't have been surprised that he sat so still since he believed the law was on his side.

After a while, the carriage pulled up to the side of a street and stopped. Thor handed Harmony down, then turned back for Turnbull. When all three stood on the sidewalk, Thor walked over to the driver, talked to him, then gave him money. As the carriage moved away, Thor took Turnbull by the arm and turned to Harmony.

"If you'll do as I say, everything will be fine."

Thor's blue eyes blazed. "Across and down the street is the precinct station nearest Turnbull's shop that burned. In that cafe on the corner awaits the woman you want to meet. If you'll go directly there and talk with her, I'll deal with Turnbull."

"But—"

"Harmony, are you going to trust me or not?"

She nodded, realizing she had finally come to trust him completely. Otherwise, she could never have let him take over this last part of bringing Turnbull to justice.

"Go ahead. I'll join you soon."

She gave Turnbull one last look. He watched her with disinterested gray eyes. She wasn't even surprised. She turned from them and set off down the sidewalk. When she'd gotten close to the cafe, she glanced back. Two men had stepped out of the shadows of a building and approached Thor. One wore a fine dark suit. The other looked rougher, less well dressed. He took Turnbull's arm. Thor stepped back into the shadows while the three men quickly walked across the street and headed toward the station.

Relieved, she turned back and walked to the cafe. She pushed open the front door, stepped inside, then looked back. Turnbull and his two escorts entered the police station. She smiled. Justice, at last. She glanced back down the street, but didn't see Thor. He was probably waiting to make sure no one noticed him.

Now it was finally her turn. She took a deep

breath and walked into the cafe. A young woman in a stylish green dress with bright red hair under a green hat waved to her from a table near a front window. She walked to the table, sat down, and glanced across the street at the police station.

"I'm Monique O'Sullivan. Thanks so much for this opportunity to interview you. I have the statements. My boss has approved the article. We're all set."

Unprepared for the straightforward young lady, Harmony could only sit and stare. After so long and so much difficulty, could it all be so easy now?

"You are Harmony Harper, aren't you?"

She nodded.

"You must want coffee. And perhaps a treat of some kind. This place has wonderful pastries."

"Thank you." She finally found her voice, but her face felt frozen. This woman seemed so full of energy and self-confidence that she didn't know quite how to respond. She wasn't used to women like this, except for Deidre. Suddenly she felt too small and plain.

"Coffee and pastry then. The *Daily News* is picking up the tab."

"Miss O'Sullivan—"

"Do call me Monique."

"And call me Harmony, if you'd like."

"My pleasure, believe me. You're a heroine and no doubt about it. Imagine, catching Turnbull and getting him to sign a confession! Every young woman in this city is going to be green with envy." Monique looked up. "Oh, Thor Clarke-Jarmon, please join us."

Thor sat down so he could look across at the police station, then he nodded at Harmony.

"Will you have coffee and a pastry with us?" Monique motioned to a waitress.

"Coffee, thanks." Thor didn't spare a glance for the newspaperwoman as he watched the police station.

Harmony noticed Monique give the order, impressed with the young woman's ability to deal with a world she had seldom entered.

Monique turned back to Harmony. "Mister Clarke-Jarmon has given me your basic story, but I'd like to know more, whatever you're comfortable telling me. I've done articles before, but nothing so big as the fire. We tried to find out more at the time, but we only got Turnbull's viewpoint. Now, I'm anxious to set the record straight."

"You have only my word for it."

"We had only Turnbull's before." Monique leaned forward, her green eyes narrowed. "You will be safer with your story in the papers. Turnbull and men like him think they're above the law. Sometimes they are and it makes them dangerous."

"I know. Believe me." Harmony hesitated, knowing she would have to confide more than she wanted. "I don't trust the police, either. They've hounded me as well."

Monique nodded, then glanced up as the waitress set their order on the table. "I understand. They follow orders, many times passed down from the very men who are creating the problems." She took a sip of coffee. "But you can trust some policemen."

"I hope so." Harmony realized she was hungry. She bit into the creamy pastry and realized she'd never eaten anything like it before. It was delicious. And the coffee wonderful. If Thor hadn't been gazing out the window with such concern, she'd have felt more relaxed.

Monique leaned back in her chair, and smiled. "In fact, I'm engaged to a Chicago policeman. He's an Irishman named Johnny O'Banyon." Her green eyes widened. "He's full of the blarney, but a good man. I'd like to tell him about you and the girls if you'd agree."

Harmony glanced at Thor. "What do you think?"

Thor looked at her, then resumed his vigil. "It wouldn't be a bad idea to have somebody on the inside."

"Johnny's mother was an immigrant and worked in a sweatshop. Believe me, he understands." Monique looked from one to the other.

"All right." Harmony finished the pastry, then held the cup of coffee for warmth. She felt chilled at how fast everything was moving. She'd trusted so few for so long she only hoped it wasn't a mistake now.

"There are a lot of good people in Chicago." Monique leaned forward. "And a lot of lovely places to live that aren't palaces built on the backs of sweatshop, factory, and shop workers. If the wealth being made by robber barons is shared, then everyone will have a good home and job. Until that happens, workers will continue to form unions and strike. And reporters will continue to write about the problems."

"I hope you can make a difference." Harmony thought about the change a good home and job would have made for the girls and their families. She missed them so much. They were her family. And she wanted to be with them. She almost didn't care about Turnbull anymore. She just wanted to be back with her girls. But she couldn't forget the fire.

"We can only report the news, the truth." Monique shook her head. "It is for the people to change." She cocked her head to one side. "I understand you were *not* the leader of the Wild Child Gang, notorious stagecoach and train outlaws throughout the West."

"Oh!" Harmony looked shocked, then turned to Thor.

"He didn't mention it. I follow the news stories from around the country. The Wild Child Gang even made our paper. And I always watch for interesting and unusual stories about women and children. Besides, look at the way you're dressed. Are you really wearing a forty-five under that duster?"

Harmony felt her face flush. She hadn't expected this. And didn't know how to deal with it.

405

"Never mind! It's just that I'm so excited to meet you. You're a real live heroine. You're a living symbol for other women and girls. You give us all courage."

Harmony glanced away in embarrassment. "I don't think you need much."

"Believe me, I do. I'm a woman so I hang on to my job and everything else in my life by my fingernails. But things are changing, no matter how slowly." She paused. "Have you read Mary Wollstonecraft's *Vindication of the Rights of Women?*"

Harmony pulled her copy of the book out of her duster and held it up. "Thor's sister gave it to me."

Monique dragged an identical copy out of her handbag and held it up, too. She laughed.

Thor looked from one to the other. "I'm glad Deidre's not here. The three of you would talk through the night and tomorrow, too."

"That would be wonderful." Monique replaced her book. "If your sister is ever in Chicago, please tell her to look me up."

Thor smiled. "Her name's Deidre Clarke-Jarmon and if you're in New York City, look her up. She's going to college and getting involved in Clarke Shipping."

"I'm impressed." Monique nodded. "Times' are changing."

"But not fast enough." Harmony put her copy of the book back in her pocket.

"I know." Monique shrugged. "But we do all we can do. Now, if we're to get this article in the paper tomorrow, we must get on with it. First, I want to check a few facts. Is it true that rent in the slums is from ten to fifteen dollars a month?"

"Yes."

"And weekly earnings are usually eight to ten dollars?"

"For a man yes, but for a woman or child less. A woman might earn four to six dollars and a child two or so." She held up a hand. "But even less if they work in a sweatshop or do home-work."

"Isn't that a huge sum for a tenement dwelling to be taken out of such small earnings?"

"Yes. And it seems even less when you try to live on it."

Monique nodded. "Isn't it also true employers believe working women are defenseless so many don't hesitate to cheat them? I've heard some don't even bother to pay them or they deduct a large part of the pay for supposedly imperfect piece-work."

"Yes. I'm afraid that's all true."

"I believe women are still getting only six cents for each shirt they make at home."

"I don't know that fact for sure, but it sounds about right." Harmony glanced at the police station. Turnbull was still inside. Good.

"That's okay. I've done some research already, although there's not too much available."

Harmony nodded again, beginning to think that even if Turnbull was put in jail it would hardly touch the problem. How much good could a few newspaper articles do? She felt terribly tired as she watched the police station. Thoughts of the girls returned. Maybe Thor had been right. Maybe she did need to help workers.

"Harmony?" Monique touched Harmony's hand. "Please, I know this is hard for you to discuss, but think of inspiring others, think of justice. And I wondered if you had thought of joining one of the labor unions and working for the rights of women and children workers?"

"No, I hadn't. This is so far from being settled."

Monique squeezed her hand, then picked up her cup of coffee. "Please, think about it. Mary Stirling, Mary Hanafin, Leonora Barry, Mary O'Reilly, and others have made such a difference. Mrs. Barry actually collected figures on what women are paid. Imagine, a seal-plush coat that sells for forty to seventy-five dollars is made by cloak-makers who are paid eighty cents or a dollar a piece!"

"Women can't live on it." Harmony shook her head. "It's why some of them turn to prostitution. They can earn fifty to two hundred dollars in one week."

"You can't blame them. This is exactly why women need someone like you to stand up and lead them."

Thor set down his cup of coffee. "Miss O'Sullivan, I'm trying to convince her of the same thing."

Monique smiled. "Good. But we can talk about that later. Right now, we should get on with the interview." She leaned forward. "Trust me. The *Daily News* is supportive of the need for worker reform. Now, I want to hear about your work and especially about the fire."

Harmony closed her eyes and began to tell about her friends, the working conditions, the locked door, the smoke, the heat, the screams . . . and the deaths. When she was through, she glanced up. Tears ran down Monique's cheeks as she shook her head in horror.

"Please, would it be asking too much if you would meet me at the burned building tomorrow?" Monique hesitated, glancing at Thor, then back to Harmony. "We can't do this in only one article. I'd like to do a drawing of you in front of the ruins."

"I don't know." Harmony shook her head.

"I wouldn't make it a good likeness of you. I don't draw all that well anyway. But it would give the readers a better idea of what happened. Could you do it?"

"You don't have to go." Thor looked at Harmony.

"I will." She inhaled sharply. "If you think it would help."

"It would." Monique smiled. "Could you meet

me there at, say, four in the afternoon? I want to do more research on this during the day."

Harmony nodded. "Maybe we'll know more about Turnbull then anyway."

"Sooner than that." Thor turned to Monique as he pointed out the window. "That's the lawyer who's handling our side of the case. If you want to talk with him, now is the time."

"Thanks!" She slapped some money down on the table, then stepped away. As she headed for the door, she glanced back. "See you tomorrow."

Harmony watched her confront the lawyer outside. The man with him slipped quietly away. The lawyer spoke quickly, then left. Monique followed.

"I hired a gunman along with the lawyer. I didn't trust Turnbull not to try and get away at the last moment." Thor watched through the window.

"Smart idea."

"Miss O'Sullivan's good." His voice held admiration.

"And beautiful, smart, talented." She couldn't keep the envy from her voice.

"And she's in awe of you. What does that tell you?"

"I don't know." She held her breath.

"That you're the most wonderful woman in the world."

She shook her head, pleased despite knowing it wasn't true. She looked back at the police station. "Turnbull didn't come out."

"It's only the first step." Thor stood up. "Let's get out of here. I want to be alone with you."

"Yes, we've much to discuss."

"I didn't have talking in mind."

Twenty-four

Thor hung up the telephone in the best suite of the Lakeside Hotel in Chicago. From where he stood he could see the huge lake rolling in to shore like an ocean. The breeze through the open windows was humid and cool. The hotel was infinitely better than the tenement, but he still wanted to be back in Louisiana.

He well knew the tenements and sweatshops were only a part of Chicago. The city was also beautiful, vigorous, and cultured. Every place had its dark side. New Orleans did. New York City, too. But he'd never been caught up in the underbelly of a city so deeply before. And he wouldn't be now if not for Harmony.

He listened for her in their private bathroom. He heard a splash in the bath. She needed the time alone and she needed to wash the stench of the tenements from her, if she ever could. After spending one night in the slums, he'd never be able to forget it.

Pacing the room, he walked to another window and looked out. From there he could see the city spread out in all directions along the lakefront. Trains connected Chicago's heart to all the suburbs. It was a mercantile center, from the elegant Marshall Field to Montgomery Ward to Sears and Roebuck. Its center fed on manufacturers and suppliers like McCormick Harvester Works and sent merchandise outward to the rest of the country.

Chicago was impressive in other ways, too. It had a professional baseball team with its own ball park. It supported the arts, music, entertainment, colleges, and seven newspapers. Only a few years before the Tacoma Building had been constructed of a completely wrought-iron skeleton to support its thirteen stories. The city boasted some of the most luxurious and innovative architecture in hotels, business buildings, and homes in the world.

He knew all that as fact. He'd seen a great deal of it while taking care of business earlier that day. But all he could focus on were the pale, pinched faces of the children in the tenements, of Harmony's girls working in terrible conditions, and of Harmony growing up amidst squalor while a few miles away robber barons lived and dined in opulent luxury.

Before meeting Harmony and the girls, he'd had a very different view of the world, *his* world. While his family wasn't as rich as the robber barons, they owned a sizable ranch in Texas, a plantation in Louisiana, and a shipping company in New York City, with a fine house in each place. It was a comfortable life. They employed many people, but none lived or worked in conditions such as he'd seen in the tenements. If others did, he hadn't noticed or cared.

Now his life was changed. He realized from the moment Harmony had kidnapped him on the train, he'd been destined to be a different man. And, surprising himself, he liked the change. For the first time his life had meaning, purpose, just as Deidre's did. He understood better what drove his sister. He now felt driven, too.

Strangely enough, just as he realized how much less rich and powerful he was than he'd thought he was, he also felt much richer and more powerful because he was so important to one woman and seven girls. They *needed* him in a way no one ever had before. To them, he was rich and powerful, but in ways he'd never imagined.

Their strength and determination in the face of so much adversity and their need made him determined to continue to help them. But they also made him think of others in need. When the girls' lives were secure, then he could think about expanding his goals to helping other children and needy workers.

He glanced at the bathroom door. Would Harmony let him continue to help? Would she return with him to Louisiana and send for the girls? Would she make her stand in life by his side and on his plantation? Would she want to aid labor reform in Louisiana first or would she want to stay in Chicago and help there? One thing he knew for sure and that was that she would never turn her back on workers. But how did he get her to stay with him? He'd never known a more independent woman unless it was his sister.

Walking across the room, he stopped beside the bed. He reached down and touched the soft covers. If her body was the only way to bind her to him, he would. Later he could win her love. *Love.* He had to admit he'd come to love her, in many different ways. He surprised himself that he hadn't fought it. Before he'd met her, he would have fled from any woman he thought was capturing his emotions. But Harmony was different. He'd been fascinated with her and wanted her from the first. Now he understood how Deidre and Hunter felt about each other. And his parents, too.

He paced back across the room and looked at the lake again. Boats and ships of all shapes and sizes plied the water. It reminded him of New Orleans. He wanted to go home and he wanted to take Harmony Harper with him. Now. But how did he do it?

A frown creased his forehead. She wouldn't want to go anywhere till Turnbull had been brought before a judge and jury. He knew that well enough. He glanced at the telephone, a luxury of the suite. The lawyer had called earlier with bad news. Turnbull had walked from the police station several hours after he'd entered, if not a free man then well on his way to being there. One of the highest-priced lawyers in the city was now sitting on Turnbull's side of the issue. That didn't bode well for Harmony, the girls, or the dead workers.

And he didn't know a damn thing to do about it except fight, maybe a losing battle, or get Harmony out of town fast. He didn't know which one would be the harder to accomplish. Maybe the newspaper stories would turn public support in Harmony's favor. Maybe the police would decide neither Harmony nor Turnbull were guilty, and the fire was simply an unfortunate accident. That was really the best he could hope for and what he'd get the lawyer to fight for. But would it satisfy Harmony? Did it satisfy him?

Of course not. But life wasn't fair. He knew it. He'd always known it. Yet he wanted Harmony and the girls and the dead workers to have justice. Maybe there wasn't such a thing. He'd been twenty-one going into this. Now he felt forty-one. If he wasn't careful, he'd become cynical and give up. He couldn't do that. Besides, it wasn't really his battle. Harmony would make the final decision. And he hoped like hell he wouldn't have to kidnap her and take her to Louisiana.

He smiled. Maybe that wasn't such a bad idea. She'd kidnapped him and held him hostage. He could do the same. Damn it all to hell, he would if the danger got any worse. One thing for sure, he wasn't going to lose her. He sure as hell wasn't going to let Turnbull get her. And he was going to bind her to him for all time, even if he had to keep her in bed for a week.

With that idea in mind, he walked to the bathroom and opened the door. She sat in a bathtub full of fragrant bubbles reaching to her chin. Her long, dark hair had been piled high on top of her head. Her eyes had closed, long lashes sooty against her fair skin. From the heat and moisture, her lips had darkened to a rosy hue.

He felt the familiar ache and stifled a groan.

"Isn't our bargain complete yet?" She opened dark brown eyes and looked at him.

"I don't think it's ever going to be."

She raised a brow, then slowly rose from her bath, letting the water cascade down her body. The bubbles moved more slowly, sliding down the slopes of her breasts, caressing the curves of her hips, disappearing down her inner thighs to reappear on her calves, then merge with the water once more.

Thor had never wanted to be a soap bubble more.

"You make me feel beautiful. And smart. And capable. And desirable." She stepped from the bath onto the thick white mat on the floor. Her body gleamed in the pale light of the room.

"You are."

"Nobody ever looked at me like you do."

He swallowed hard, trying to make his brain work but all his feelings had solidified in his groin.

"Nobody. Ever." She stepped closer, leaving wet footprints on the tile floor.

"I thought Turnbull—"

"No! I was an object. Something he thought he owned because I worked for him. I was something to use like a knife or bowl or glass." Her brown eyes glowed hot like heated amber.

"You can't be owned." He felt so hard he wondered if he'd gone pale all over except for one vital area.

"I want our bargain at an end."

He closed his eyes, surprised at the intensity of the pain . . . in his heart. Now that she thought Turnbull was in jail, she wanted to end it. She didn't need him anymore. She wanted to go her own, independent way.

"Tonight I'll pay the last of my debt to you."

He could feel the warmth of her breath, the heat of her body as she neared him. But he didn't open his eyes. He was afraid of what he'd see in them. He should tell her the truth. He should tell her that Turnbull walked the streets a free man. He should, but he couldn't. He wanted her to have at least one night of rest, of believing she had accomplished her goal. And he wanted that one, good, free night to be spent with him.

"Afterward we will decide what is between us." She reached out and stroked him, feeling the erection inside his trousers.

He groaned and looked at her.

Raising her arms, she pulled the pins from her hair and let it fall free, thick and dark and luxuriant, to her hips. She licked her lower lip. "You've bought me for the night, Thor. Only you can make me feel beautiful and sensual enough to be a kept woman." She stepped closer still. "Do what you will. I'm yours."

He was already inflamed by the sight of her, by the enforced separation from her. Now her words pushed him over the edge. He growled and lifted her into his arms. He crushed her against his chest, then carried her to the bed. He laid her gently down, much too aware of the feel of her soft skin against his hands, of her natural fragrance, of the silkiness of her hair. His body was rebelling against any control at all.

"Let me take off your clothes." Her words were like a purr.

Glancing down, he was surprised to find he was still dressed. He frowned, suddenly furious at the intrusion. He looked at her, then back to himself, growling in frustration. When she laughed, a soft, tinkling sound, it vibrated up and down his spine and settled heavily in his groin. If he got any harder, any bigger, he would explode.

She stood up on the bed. "This is better any way. We're almost the same height now."

He couldn't speak. He could only feel her hands taking away his tie, then slowly, tantalizingly unbuttoning his shirt, then pulling it away. When she put her hands to the buckle of his belt he couldn't stop the shudder that shook him. "Maybe I better—"

She stopped his words with a fingertip to his lips, then went back to work.

When the belt lay on the floor with his other clothes, he felt her hands on the buttons of his trousers and he thought he might go mad with need. But finally she had them down and his un-

419

derclothes with them. He stood ready before her. It took all the willpower he had to calmly sit down on the bed and strip the trousers from his ankles, then pull off his socks and boots. Sweat beaded his forehead by the time he turned to her.

She had pulled the bed covers down and lay naked against white sheets. She was so big in spirit, he sometimes forgot how tiny and perfect her body was formed. Her small breasts were tipped with amber nipples. He reached out to touch one, then the other. They hardened, making him feel powerful. He touched the dark triangle of hair between her thighs, then slipped a finger lower. He was surprised at the moist heat. Could she be ready for him already?

Glancing up at her face, he saw passion there and what he hoped was love, but he couldn't be sure. He had to bind her to him now with his body. He had to make her realize they belonged together forever, despite their ages, their backgrounds, their differences. Love. That's what he wanted to see in her dark eyes.

"I don't think I can wait." He spread her legs.

"I'm yours, remember." She smiled. "Why should you wait?"

"Damn it!" He turned away. "I don't want it to be this way. I don't want you to owe me." He took several shuddering breaths, then felt her small hand on his back, gently massaging.

"But the bargain?"

"To hell with it!" He couldn't stand her touch. He stood up and crossed the room to stand in front of a window. He hoped the cool air would help his inflamed senses.

"Thor?"

He heard her get out of bed and move toward him. When she reached out and put her arms around him, snuggling her body against his back and buttocks, he lost all control. Twisting around, he grabbed her and lifted her into the air, swinging her around to the front of him. To regain her balance she grabbed his shoulders and as she did so, he pushed in between her thighs. As she wrapped her legs around him for support, he pushed her against the nearest wall, then thrust his erection into her softness in one fierce drive.

She moaned. But he didn't care, couldn't care about anything except the excitement, the hunger, the pleasure of moving in and out of her, faster and faster, plunging ever nearer the center of the vortex she had created for them both.

When he felt her moving with him, felt her wetness and her heat, and felt the hard tips of her breasts against his chest, he succumbed to her lure. He exploded deep inside her, losing himself completely in her, merging as he'd longed to do from the first moment she'd fascinated him. When he heard her small cries of pleasure and pain and felt the shudders running through her body, he entered the vortex, not alone, never again, but with her . . . his wild outlaw woman . . . and spun into infinity with her.

A long moment later, he caught his breath. Sweat gleamed on both their bodies. He still had her trapped between his body and the wall. She lay quietly against him, like a small bird caught, its wings folded for the moment. His love stole over him in softness, nothing like the raging passion of the moment before. Now he wanted only to comfort her, to protect her, to soothe the wounds he might have inflicted on her. How could he have been such a beast to her? But she had driven him to it with her beauty and her words and her need.

"Thor?"

"I'm sorry." He quickly carried her to the bed and gently laid her down against the softness. "Are you all right?" He searched her body for signs of his depravity. He'd left hand marks here and there. "Damn!" He stood up and turned his back to her.

"What's wrong?"

He whirled around. "You hate me, don't you?"

She sat up, a smile turning her rosy lips upward at the corners. "Why would I do that?"

"I was too rough, a beast." He truly felt ashamed. She was so small, so delicate. He knew better.

She patted the edge of the bed beside her. "Come here."

He walked warily over to her and sat down. "There's nothing you can say to change what I did."

"I don't want to change what you did." She reached up and pushed back his sweat-dampened hair. She smiled, then tugged on his hair, hard.

"Ouch!"

"I've punished the bad beast. Now, will he come to bed and make more apologies?"

Thor sat very still. "You aren't mad at me?"

She smiled once more, then twined her fingers in the gold chain around his neck. She tugged and he moved lower until his face was over hers. She placed a light kiss on his lips, then teased the corners of his mouth with her tongue. "Tell me about the pendant." She let go of the chain and traced the shape of gold.

He moved back. "You're trying to distract me. Are you playing a game?" He looked around the room, as if to get his bearings, then focused on her again. "You aren't mad?"

She plumped up two pillows against the headboard, then leaned against one and patted the other. "I'll only be mad if I never see the beast again."

Thor felt relief wash through him. She was wonderful, more perfect than he could have imagined. He leaned back against the pillow, put an arm around her shoulders, and pulled her to his side. If she wasn't mad at him after that, then she had to love him.

"Please tell me. I've been wondering about it for a long time. I've never seen anything like it."

He watched as she stroked the gold medallion, teasing the hair on his chest at the same time. He'd begun to believe that not only had he gotten kidnapped by an outlaw but by a wanton as well. He couldn't have been more pleased.

"Are you going to tell me?"

"It's from Norway. It belonged to my great-grandfather, Olaf Thorssen. He brought it from the old country and gave it to my grandmother, Eleanor Thorssen Jarmon. Olaf lived in New York City and raised my mother, Alexandra Clarke, and ran the Clarke Shipping Company until he died. He sent her to see his daughter and grandson, Jake Jarmon."

"So that's how your parents met."

"It's a longer story than that. You'll have to get them to tell you the details sometime."

She gave him a questioning look, then went back to gazing at the medallion. "Is it an anchor?"

"It does look a little like one, but it represents the magic hammer of the Norse God Thor. The old stories say he makes thunder and lightning when he throws his Hammer against his enemies. Vikings used to wear Hammers to bring them luck. Someday I'd like to go back to my great-grandfather's fishing village in Norway and learn more about him and my heritage."

"I think that'd be wonderful."

"Would you like to go with me?"

She moved away from him. "Thor, please. This night ends the bargain. You know it. I know it. We don't know what the future will bring."

"I know." Thor stood up and walked across the room. He'd been mistaken. It was all part of the damned, stupid bargain. He'd used it to keep her with him and now it was turning to dust in his hands. He paced the room, then noticed her boots and spurs and gunbelt. Her other clothes had been sent out to be cleaned. Spurs. He smiled. He wasn't done by any means. She'd yet go to Norway with him.

He unstrapped a spur from one of her boots and walked back to the bed. He pulled the pillows loose and threw them on the floor.

"Thor?"

"Lie down."

"Thor?"

"If the bargain's not over till dawn, then I'm going to enjoy it all night long."

"All right." Her voice sounded unsure as she slipped down in the bed and lay flat.

He sat down beside her, already growing hard again. "I believe we have that matter of the spurs to decide."

She chuckled. "Silken or silver?"

"That's right." He ran the rowel from her chin to her navel, then back again. He felt satisfaction at the shiver that ran through her body. "What do you think?" He teased her again.

"I can't think when you're doing that."

He leaned closer and tickled her ear with the tip of his tongue all the while plying her body with the spur's rowel.

"Oh!" She shivered again and reached for the spur.

He lifted it out of reach. "No fair. I'm in control. You're mine till dawn. Right?"

She moaned with pleasure. "Yes."

He used the spur again, moving it lower and lower, feeling her body heat and tense under his hands even as his own body followed the building passion of her own. "Do you like this?"

"Oh, yes."

"Is the spur silken or silver?"

"I can't think."

"Tell me."

"It's both. No silken."

He used the spur harder.

"No silver."

He lightened the touch.

"Silken. Oh!" She sat up in bed, grabbed the spur, and threw it across the room. "I don't care!" She held out her arms. "Come here you great beast of a man before I take the spurs to you again."

Chuckling, he pulled her against his chest and placed soft kisses in her hair. "Obviously, I'll do anything if you threaten me with your spurs."

Twenty-five

Harmony jerked awake at the sound of the telephone. Disoriented at the unusual sound, she felt a warm hand on her shoulder, then a kiss on her forehead. She glanced into Thor's blue eyes and relaxed.

"I'll get it."

As he slipped from the bed and crossed the room, she smiled in appreciation at his muscular body, one she now knew better than she had ever imagined she would. As he picked up the telephone, she noticed the bright light coming in through the lace drapes over the windows. She realized it must be late in the day. Shocked, she got out of bed and headed for the bathroom.

She started water in the bathtub, then enjoyed the wonderful convenience of the room. She stepped into the doorway, watched Thor talk on the telephone, then glanced around the open suite. It was decorated in shades of rose and pink and gray. At one end was a sitting-room area, with a settee, a desk, and two chairs. The bedroom was dominated by a canopy bed, a dresser, and a clothespress. The furniture was of gleaming oak. The suite was comfortable, but not fancy. Thor had chosen well.

As the conversation continued, she turned back and stepped into the bath. As she sank down into the warm water, it soothed her body. She remembered the night that had lasted well into the morning, and blushed. Thor was a wonderful lover and she'd proven herself an eager pupil. She didn't know when she'd slept so deeply or so well. But she knew why. She'd felt safe and happy in Thor's arms and with Turnbull behind bars she finally had been able to relax.

As she bathed, she realized she felt more hungry than she had in a long while, too. In fact, she couldn't remember a time before now when she hadn't been worried or tired or scared. She'd worked so hard all her life, run so long and hard with the girls, then struggled to bring Turnbull back for justice that she'd never had the chance to relax. Not until the night before. It was such a luxury she'd never even imagined it existed. Now that she'd tasted its pleasure she never wanted to let it go.

But she had to go back out into the world soon. She couldn't relax any longer. She finished bathing, then let the water drain. She had a meeting at four o'clock with Monique. And she was anxious to see their article in the *Daily News*.

As she dried off with a fluffy towel, she wished she could push away the outside world for some more private time with Thor. Yet it wasn't possible.

She must get finished in Chicago as quickly as possible so she could be with the girls. She missed them and she knew they worried about her.

"Harmony." Thor stopped in the doorway, a worried frown between his eyes.

"What's wrong?" Her heart beat fast as she wrapped the towel around her middle.

He looked at her for a long moment, then smiled. "Nothing. I had to get a few things straightened out with the hotel. I ordered breakfast. They said it was time for lunch."

"What time is it?"

"Two.

"What!"

He nodded, then leaned forward and placed a warm kiss on her lips. "Good morning, sleepyhead."

"How could we have slept so late?"

He grinned. "You can ask?"

Chuckling, she turned back to the bath. "Do you want me to run water for you?"

"Yes, but no bubbles."

She started his bath, yet kept her attention on him.

"They're sending up food, along with our clothes. Early this morning I set out our boots and my suit to be cleaned."

She turned back to him. "And I never heard a thing."

"You were exhausted, for more reasons than one. You needed a lot of good sleep."

"I know." She leaned against him, then traced a finger from his throat downward.

When she reached his navel, he grabbed her hand and held it away from him. "You'd better get out of here before we miss your appointment."

She pouted, then flounced from the bathroom, blowing him a kiss as she went. When she heard him splash into the tub, she turned back. "Are you sure you don't want some help?"

"Me or Monique?"

"Wash yourself!"

She had no intention of missing her appointment and if she and Thor got distracted one more time she knew what would happen. She started to straighten the bed, then stopped herself. She knew she shouldn't do that in a hotel, but she still felt guilty for letting someone else do it for her.

Walking across the room, she looked out the window over the lake. She'd never had such a good view before or realized how cool and fresh the breeze coming off the water could be. She was beginning to see a very different side of Chicago and it was one she liked. But she could never forget the tenements. Nor Turnbull.

A short time later, Thor joined her at the window. He wore a towel wrapped around his waist and his hair was clean and damp. When he put his arms around her, she leaned back against his strong chest.

"How do you feel?" He hugged her against him.

"Good. Wonderful. I can even see beauty in Chicago. Amazing, isn't it?"

"No. It's what most people see."

"But not the tenement dwellers."

"Someday it'll change for them, too."

"I hope so." She turned to look up into his eyes. "I want to thank you for your help. I don't know what I'd have done without you."

"You don't have to thank me. I'm glad to have helped. I want to make a difference, too."

"Oh, Thor!" She raised up to put her hands around his neck, pulling his face toward hers. But she was disturbed by a knock at the door. "The food?"

He nodded. "Hold the kiss."

She stepped back and watched him walk to the door. There was a discussion before he returned, wheeling in a tray of covered dishes, boots tucked under one arm, and clothes hanging from the other. She hurried over to him and took the clothes from his hands. As she set them on the bed, she heard him kick the door shut.

"They were determined to come inside and help." Thor frowned. "No way in hell am I letting strangers in here."

She smiled and took the boots from him, then set them at the foot of the bed. "I'm glad you're around to protect us."

"If they knew you were a notorious outlaw, they'd have stepped more carefully around this suite." Thor chuckled.

"You're right, of course."

He wheeled the cart near the window overlooking the lake, then set two chairs at each end of it. As he took a cover off plate after plate, delicious aromas filled the room.

More hungry than ever, she hurried over and sat down. "Feed me!"

Laughing, he sat down across from her. "What do you think?"

"I can't believe all this food. Steak. Potatoes. Biscuits. Honey and butter."

"Milk and coffee." Thor grinned. "I needed a thick, juicy steak after you used me so mercilessly."

"I used you?" She gave him a mock frown. "I believe it was the other way around."

He laughed as he cut into the steak, then grew silent as he tasted everything on his plate.

Following his example, she knew she'd never eaten such delicious food before or so much of it, either. In fact, she didn't think she'd ever seen so much on one plate except at the institute. When she'd eaten her fill, she leaned back in the chair and held her cup of coffee. Full and content, she once more didn't want to leave her warm and safe haven with Thor. He'd given her so - much, done so much for her that she didn't know how she could ever repay him. They'd made the bargain and she'd kept it, but it had been so much pleasure for her that she didn't see how it could be enough.

"Harmony, now that you've eaten and slept well I've got a few things to tell you."

She looked up at him in concern. He sounded terribly serious. Her stomach tightened. Maybe she shouldn't have eaten so much. "The girls?"

"No. As far as we know, they're fine."

She sighed in relief.

"It's Turnbull."

Setting down her coffee, she took a deep breath. "What?"

"They didn't put him in jail."

She felt depression settle over her. "That's what the call was about?"

"Yes. I ordered breakfast afterward." He reached across the table and squeezed her hand. "But he's been out since yesterday."

"No!" She stood up and paced the room. "When did you find out?"

"Yesterday when we got back."

"Thor!" She hurried over to him and put both hands on her hips. "Why didn't you tell me?"

"I wanted you to get a good night's rest just like I wanted you to eat a good meal today. You'd have worried all night and you know it."

She sat back down and slumped in the chair. "You're right." She bit her lower lip. "You mean they're not going to do anything?"

"I don't know. Turnbull's lawyer called our lawyer. They saw the article in the *Daily News*. Turnbull wants to make a deal with you and the police. He will now say he realizes you weren't responsible and he will settle a certain amount of money on the girls for their education. He will do this if you will say the door wasn't locked and the fire spread so quickly everyone was overwhelmed except you and the seven girls. Also, this has to be printed in all the newspapers."

She felt sick. "What about the police?"

"I imagine they'll be glad to have it crossed off their list as a tragic accident."

"But that means it will have all been in vain."

"No. It means you win. You and the girls have your names cleared. The girls will have education money set aside for them. And Turnbull will have to be more careful in the future."

"But the hundred women and children—"

"Are dead. You can't do any more to help them."

"The signed statements?"

"Turnbull swears they're forgeries. He says you can't even read or write."

She bowed her head, feeling lost. She stood up and walked across the room. She looked down at her .45 nestled in its holster. She stroked the butt of the pistol. She'd gone so far, endured so much to return to where she'd started. But the girls were safe. She was alive. And Turnbull was willing to give something. Still, it wasn't enough.

Thor followed her and put his arms around her, pulling her against his warmth. "You don't have to make a decision right now. I told our lawyer to tell Turnbull he couldn't reach us."

"Good." She turned to look up at him. "I'm not going to let Turnbull off that easy, even if you think it's the best thing to do."

"It's your decision."

"I want to get dressed and meet Monique at the shop or what's left of it. I want her to do another article. It'll put more pressure on Turn-bull."

"All right." He tucked a strand of dark hair back behind her ear. "But you shouldn't drag it out. He's got a lot of power behind him and he can hire as many gunmen as he wants."

"I know." She turned back to touch her pistol. "But I want to do what's best for everyone."

"Come on, let's get dressed." Thor grinned. "By the time Monique's done with him, he may never be able to hold his head up in this town again."

She chuckled. "I'd like that a lot. And I want to see the article." She walked over to the bed and began pulling on her outlaw clothes. Until Turnbull was behind bars or dead, she didn't feel safe without her weapons.

"I'm sure she'll bring a copy of the newspaper with her." Thor started dressing, too.

A short time later, they locked the door to their suite behind them, walked downstairs, and stepped outside. They quickly hired a carriage, then rode away from the Lakeside Hotel.

Harmony watched the people hurrying here and there, the women clothed in corsets and dresses. They didn't know what they were missing. It would be hard to get her out of trousers again, or the pistol off her hip. Thor's idea for the duster in town was perfect. She glanced at him. He'd had to stick his .45 in the back of his trousers. It wouldn't be as easy to reach as the one she wore on her hip, but at least he had it.

She grew more tense as they rode toward the

435

place she'd last seen in flames, the screams of the dying ringing in her ears. She leaned closer to Thor, wishing now she hadn't agreed to return. But maybe it was best to confront her fear.

When the carriage drove into the district, she recognized the shops and factories in the area. She had walked past them day after day. As they neared the burned shop, she clung to Thor's hand. When the carriage pulled up in front of it, she was shocked at the charred debris. Rain and wind had scattered the ashes, but the black hulk of several of the corners still rose into the air. Maybe Turnbull now wanted to put it all behind him so he could rebuild.

But she was simply delaying having to confront her past. She couldn't rely on Thor forever. She must gather her courage, think of the girls, remember the dead workers. She must go alone to face her past. She looked up at Thor and tried to smile.

"I'm with you." He squeezed her hands.

"I want to go up there alone."

He frowned.

"I need to do this if I'm ever going to build a new life." She turned and started to step out of the carriage.

"Wait." He got down, then paid the driver before helping her out. "He'll be back in an hour to pick us up. Is that long enough?"

"Yes. Thanks." She held on to his arm as they walked up the sidewalk toward what had once been the front of the building. "Monique will be here soon. I want to walk in there. I need to see it alone."

"Are you sure?"

"Yes." She patted his arm. "Why don't you wait near that tree and send Monique to me when she arrives."

"I'll be right over there. Call if you need me."

She gave him what she hoped was a reassuring smile, then turned to walk up the sidewalk. As she neared what had been the front of the building, she could smell the charred remains. Memories assaulted her. Tears stung her eyes. So many dead. So needlessly.

She paused, looking into the blackened ruins. How could so little be left? To her right a corner remained, forming a nook she couldn't see around. She would look behind it in a moment. She didn't want to leave any part of the ruins unseen. She had to know there was truly nothing left, nothing else she could have done.

"Harmony."

For a moment she didn't place somebody calling her with the present. She had moved back in time to the fire, to so many voices screaming and crying and calling. If only she could have reached more before the flames overwhelmed them. If only she had thought of the window sooner. If only the door hadn't been locked.

"Harmony!"

The voice broke through her thoughts. It sounded familiar. She turned, a puzzled expression

437

on her face. Turnbull! She felt so shocked she could only stare as he walked to her and stopped.

She gazed in stunned amazement as he pulled out a derringer and pointed it at her. Then she glanced past him and saw Thor caught between two of Turnbull's gunmen. How could she have been so lax? How could she have thought a newspaper article would make her safe? Or had she simply wanted to believe in the fantasy she and Thor had created the night before?

"You thought you had me, didn't you?" Turnbull smirked. "You thought you could insult me, kill my men, drag me all over the country, then send me to the police and I'd do nothing."

She tried to make her brain work, but it seemed to have died along with the women in the shop.

"I should have used your fine little body while I had the chance. Now you're no good to me. You let that big Southerner paw you, didn't you? You're nothing but the whore I always thought you were, like all you little worker girls."

Anger slowly crept into her. She blinked, glanced back at Thor, and felt chilled. They would *kill* him after Turnbull killed her. And nobody would see anything and nobody would do anything. No! She shook her head to clear it. She had to do something.

He leaned closer. "You're not half bad cleaned up. If you hadn't made so much trouble, I'd still toss your skirts and tumble you in some corner."

"Turnbull, you make me sick."

He held the gun steady. "I'd make you real sick if I had the time and you'd like it or pretend you did because you had no choice."

"How many women did you corner and force?"

His face glistened with sweat. "More than I can count. That's the way the game is played, only you were too dumb to understand. If women want to work, they've got to pay."

"No! An employer pays them."

He shook his head. "Women are lucky to get anything a man wants to give them. That's the way it is. Now, you're going to step back into those ruins and I'm going to see your body goes under the new cornerstone. You're so damned concerned about workers I'll let you watch them toil forever." He laughed and leered and sweat trickled down his face.

"What about Thor?"

"He's a dead man. He'll go in potter's field and nobody'll be the wiser."

"There are people in the shops around here. Somebody will see you."

"No windows. No eyes." He motioned with his derringer. "Now walk back in there."

"Tell me something first. You ordered the door locked on this shop before it burned, didn't you?"

"Sure. You women and girls were taking too many breaks."

"We hardly ever left our work. We couldn't afford the loss of pay and you know it. You wanted

439

to make sure you got that extra hour or two out of us. That's why you locked the doors. Admit it!"

"It doesn't matter why. It never did. I'm the boss. I do what I want. If somebody wants to work for me, I own them. I do what I want and I pay what I want." He narrowed his eyes. "Now turn around and walk in there."

"No."

"Do what I say and I'll let your Southern gentleman die easy. Otherwise, he can live a long time in pain."

Unable to look at him any longer, she shut her eyes. She felt helpless, as if everything she'd struggled for had been taken from her. As she stood there, the smell of smoke came to her. She could see the fire again, hear the screams. She imagined Thor dead in potter's field and Turnbull locking more doors, year after year after year. Fury washed over her and she snapped open her eyes.

"Ready to go, little sweatshop girl?"

She nodded, moving her left arm slowly behind her as she stepped backward to cover her movement. When she grasped the fabric at her side with her left hand, she looked Turnbull hard in the eyes.

"Move!" He wiped the sweat from his face with the back of one hand, but held the derringer steady on her. "I haven't got all day."

"You don't need it. You won't ever hurt anybody again. You're bad and you're dead." She jerked the duster back from her pistol with her left hand and drew with her right. She had the satisfaction of seeing his shock and his reaction as she twisted to the side and fired into his chest, aiming for his heart even as she felt the slug from his derringer hit her.

As she fell she knew she didn't mind dying. The girls were safe. The workers had been avenged and they'd gotten retribution, too. And she'd been loved by Thor. It had been worth it all to stop Turnbull. She only wished she could have stopped all the robber barons.

"Harmony!"

She recognized Thor's voice and his touch as he pulled her to his chest. He was safe. Nothing else mattered. Then she noticed other voices. Monique O'Sullivan and a man in a Chicago police uniform. Well, it was too late for the police. She'd done their job for them.

"Harmony, you're all right." Thor stroked her face. "Can you hear me?"

She tried to nod. What did he mean? She'd done her best, but surely Turnbull had hit her.

"That was a damn fancy piece of footwork and shooting." Thor held her tightly against him. "But don't you ever do anything like that again."

"You're the bravest woman I've ever met." Monique leaned close, awe in her voice.

Harmony realized the ringing had stopped in her ears. She wasn't going to die?

"You're shot in the side." Thor stroked her face. "But you're so tough you'll pull through."

"Turnbull?" She finally realized her mouth still worked, but she felt weak and woozy.

"He's dead. You got him."

"Miss Harper, don't worry about a thing."

"This is Johnny O'Banyon, my fiancé." Monique gripped Harmony's hand. "We got here early and were in that area out of your view. We heard everything."

"That's right, Miss Harper. The Chicago police heard Turnbull's confession. You and those girls don't have to worry about anything now. And I got a look at those gunmen he hired before they ran off."

"I've got the biggest story of the year." Monique patted Harmony's hand, then stepped back. "Don't worry. We'll have you to a hospital in no time."

"I'm going to live?"

"Yes!" Thor kissed her softly, then placed his lips near her ear. "You're free now. And as soon as you're able, we're going to have a long talk."

She smiled. "What do you think now? Are my spurs silken or silver?" Her voice was husky, barely above a whisper.

"Neither. They're pure gold. Just like you."

Harmony and Thor stood on a windy hill, the autumn sun warming them as they looked out across Jarmon Plantation in southern Louisiana.

"I thought I'd never get you here." Thor gazed down at her. "Are you sure?"

She reached up and stroked his face.

"You gave up a lot in Chicago. Monique made you a celebrity. Everybody wanted you to speak, to head their organization or their institution or their committee on women and children workers. And you weren't even out of the hospital. You'd never have wanted for money or position or anything."

"But I'd have wanted for you."

He glanced up at the antebellum mansion, its columns gleaming white in the sunlight. Seven whirls of color appeared on the veranda, then danced down the wide staircase. "You didn't come here just for the girls, did you?"

"I couldn't take them back to Chicago, not till the bad memories faded."

"I know. That's why—"

She put a fingertip to his lips, then put her hands around his neck to draw his head downward. She placed a soft kiss on his lips, then leaned back to smile.

"You're going to marry me if you stay. And we're going to adopt the girls."

She nodded.

"You know I love you."

She nodded again.

"But is it enough to keep you here?"

"Yes." She looked out across the vibrant green land, gray moss hanging from the ancient trees, and felt a deep sense of belonging. "But you offered me a job back in Tucson. I'm taking you up on it. Together we can look into worker reform at the cotton mills of the South. I'm planning to stay in touch with Monique and my other new friends. There is a lot of work to do for workers everywhere."

"I agree. And I want to help."

"But there will always be time for us." She twined their fingers together. "I love you."

"That's all I ever wanted to hear." He started to kiss her, but stopped as he noticed the seven whirls of color float down the path and came to a stop, separating into seven girls in brightly colored dresses.

"Are you going to be our new mommy and daddy?" Blaze asked.

"Can we live here forever?" Star whirled around.

"I love the land." Tara smiled shyly.

"The house is beautiful." Jasmine beamed.

"And don't forget . . ." Faith said.

"We'll always be . . ." Hope continued.

"The Wild Child Gang." Charity finished.

Thor chuckled. "Then it's settled. The Wild Child Gang becomes the Harper-Clarke-Jarmon Gang."

"Why don't we have the wedding in the spring?" Harmony glanced around the group.

"Maybe we can even get Deidre and Hunter to make it a double wedding."

"Good idea. Alexandra and Jake will come. Alberto, too. The whole family will be here."

Harmony held out her arms and drew the girls against her. With them snuggled close, she reached out for Thor. When he enfolded them all in his embrace, she felt completely happy. "We have our own family now."

"And it's only the beginning. By the time we're done, I want to fill every room in the house!"

Harmony laughed. "And who is going to be filling all those rooms?"

"You and me." He grinned. "And we'd better get started on it right away."

"No need." She touched her stomach. "You've already earned your spurs."

AUTHOR'S AFTERWORD

In 1993 as in 1888 in the United States of America, sweatshop workers, homeworkers, and migrant workers still toil long hours for a marginal existence and many are still immigrants. Despite unions, laws, and humanitarian concerns, many workers are still subject to unsafe working conditions and harassment. In most states a woman earns 69¢ (up from 50¢ in 1988) to a man's $1.00, women still do not receive equal pay for equal work, and equal education is not available to all children.

Worker suffrage continues.

ABOUT THE AUTHOR

JANE ARCHER is proud to say she is a Texan and part Comanche. She is the best-selling author of a number of historical romances including *Wild Wind!* and *Silken Spurs* the sequels to her romance classic *Tender Torment,* all available through Pinnacle Books.

"My mother promised me her spurs . . . when she gets through with them," says Jane, adding that she doesn't count on getting them any time soon. For now Jane writes novels because she can't get storytelling out of her blood. "My cousins tell me I've done it since I was a child, only now I get paid."

She has also worked as an advertising artist (she has a degree in graphic design) and has worked as a model, and in fashion sales. "But," Jane says, "writing is my heart and soul because, as my editor Alice Alfonsi so aptly puts it, 'romance is women talking to women.' And that's what I like to do, with or without the spurs."